AMONG THE WICKLOW HILLS

~

NICHOLAS BYRNE

Copyright © 2007 Nicholas Byrne

All rights reserved.
No part of this publication may be reproduced in any form or by any means—graphic, electronic or mechanical, including photocopying, recording, taping or information storage and retrieval systems—without the prior written permission of the author.

Cover artwork by Trudi Doyle

ISBN: 978-1475158144

Book layout by Robert Phair,
Computers of South Dublin (cosd.com)

Table of Contents

Preface	v
Acknowledgements	ix
The Doctor's Dilemma	1
The Curse of Black Hazel	16
The Skull	48
The Good Samaritan	71
The Jaycloth	79
The Square Box	100
The Dream	165
The Counsellor	191
The Undertaker	206
The Fugitive of Avoca	216
The Rising	227
The Mission	229
The Spalpeen	250
The Village School	275
Terry, the Village Urchin	278
Waiting for the Call	297
The Road Overseer	312
Ned's Romance	337
A Fall from Grace	351
Pete the Farmer	376
A Reprieve for Old Dan	379
The Culchies	391
Glossary	404

Preface

This book is a collection of original short stories about ordinary people in West Wicklow, Ireland almost a century ago. I have recorded what I can remember about them before it all becomes a confused mist in the recesses of my mind and lost forever.

These stories were collected by journeymen who travelled around our locality, plying their trade when and wherever their services were required. They knew every house in their area, the people and their quirks and foibles, and they had collected a myriad of fine stories on their sojourns among these simple people.

I remember as a young lad these journeymen rambling to my Uncle Martin's house next door. He was also a journeyman in his day. In the warm glow of the turf fire in his modest kitchen they would while away the nights, reminiscing in their own inimitable way about the exploits of these simple people. They were a joy to listen to by one and all. To all those faithful departed may they rest in peace.

These journeymen, just like Martin, were more than eighty years my senior. They were a link with the way of life that I might have missed but for him. That was long before electricity, the telephone, the television or even the radio invaded our homes. It's the story of the spade and shovel, the scythe, the sickle, and the horse and cart that were in daily use. It is also the story of Wakes and funerals, the Mission and fairs, the card playing for the goose or turkey or a brace of chickens at Christmas time, also the matchmaking, the story telling around the open fire at night.

These men, as well as being skilled tradesmen in their own right, were also renown storytellers in the best tradition. They spoke with a genuineness that appealed and aroused the spirits and curiosity of their listeners. They embellished these narratives with animation to make listening a pleasure, playing on a flute or violin, dancing a jig, or whatever was handy. All these stories were told with a mixture of wit and true feeling as they were brought on stage by the journeymen. You found yourself loving these people long since gone even while the tellers mimicked them. That was their gift of telling.

Since these journeymen have gone to their eternal rest I have found other people with their own tales of happiness, sadness, joy and sorrow in their lives. I have listened to them and written about them much in the same fashion as those journeymen did in their stories. The lessons I learned from all I have observed of these people through the years is timeless, of an age known to all mankind. It is lessons I have learned about life.

I'm sure anyone of rural background would recognise in these stories from the Wicklow Hills the happenings and events he or she lived through in their youth. They could have happened in any part of Ireland in those times.

In conclusion I hope all you readers will get as much pleasure out of reading these stories as I have had in writing them. It has been a journey back in time for me.

As I set forth to record these stories I have taken great care to conceal the true identity of all these people of whom I write, also of the townlands of this enchanting part of the Garden of Ireland. Resemblance to any person or place in these stories is just coincidental. These peasant though proud people are long since dead and are entitled to their anonymity. It would be insensitive of me to do otherwise.

Nicholas Byrne
Co. Wicklow, Ireland
September 2007

Acknowledgements

I would like to thank, most sincerely, my nieces Ethne, and Mairead and her daughter Richael, for all their hard work in proofreading and encoding my script for me.

I would also like to thank Nancy Davis for editing and proofreading my script.

The Doctor's Dilemma

It had snowed all day in and around the village of Shinrone, a small hamlet in the Croughan Valley in South County Wicklow. Towards evening a gale rose up, whirling the loose snow into blinding drifts and blocking the countryside.

Closing the big hall door after seeing the last of his patients off his premises, Doctor Dan McCay shuddered with the cold. Turning, he gave a plangent sigh as he made his way to the warmth and comfort of the sitting room where he joined his elderly mother and the maid for their evening meal.

Entering the sitting room he made straight for the armchair and flopped into it. Again he sighed, even louder this time.

To himself he uttered a little prayer, 'Please Lord, let there be no more calls tonight.' He nodded in agreement but didn't speak for a few minutes.

"I think," says he, "I'm coming down with another attack of malaria."

Doctor McCay had been a doctor with the British army during the Boer War. He contracted malaria while out there. After a period of convalescing at the base camp he was discharged and advised to return to Ireland. He applied and got a post as doctor in Shinrone so he brought his mother and the maid to live with him.

After tea and a quiet nap he felt much better.

He jumped in the chair with a start and murmured an unholy expletive which startled the mother. She looked up suddenly from her knitting.

"I forgot to feed and water the horses," says he, "they're in the house all day and not one to even talk to them."

Little Babe as he called his bay saddle horse, loved to be talked to and patted and combed down.

Putting on his boots and the coat with the fur collar on it, he trudged through drifts of snow in the courtyard on the way to the stable. Little Babe and Doll gave him a great welcoming whinny. After feeding and watering and combing them down he bade them good night, leaving Little Babe til last. He gave him a parting pat on his shiny rump. This was the horse he used most to make house calls.

"You can rest in comfort tonight old boy," says he, "there won't be any call out tonight."

The Doctor settled himself into his armchair and stretched out his long legs in front of the glowing turf fire. He was going to savour one free night with his elderly mother, a rare treat indeed. He took down the novel and began reading where he had left off the night before.

"What's the night like, Dan?" the mother asked looking up from her knitting.

"The wind has quieted a little, mother. Just intermittent light snow falling, but," says he, "I'm afraid the storm is not yet over."

The mother gave a nod of approval and continued with her knitting. He glanced at the maid who appeared to be keenly engrossed in her embroidery at the big mahogany table in the centre of the room, but really in reality was keenly observant of her master's every nuance and glance. Looking up, she acknowledged his silent command, left her needlework and went into the kitchen to prepare his hot drink of Bovril. He returned to his reading to finish the chapter before putting it away for the night.

He was interrupted by the resonance of the heavy door knocker as it went bap-bappy-bap-bap. 'Who can that be on such an atrocious night?' he sighed to himself, at the same time hoping it wouldn't be a house call.

"Dan, you won't go out tonight, you know you have …", but he was already out in the hall to open the door.

When it was opened a flurry of snow enveloped him. It was like a mini blizzard. It almost took his breath away. He shuddered with the cold. He peered at the snowy figure in front of him in the doorway, his face and beard were so encrusted with frost and snow as to be unrecognisable, standing knee deep in a drift of snow.

"Doctor," the man said in a voice barely audible, "my neighbour Paddy Williams of Boholla is dying, come have a look at him, sir."

He beckoned him into the hall and closed the door. He peered at the man again, trying to recognise him from the faint glow of the kerosene lamp with the polished reflector that was hanging in the vestibule.

"Who are you?" says the Doctor curtly, "or who sent you?" Half thinking it might be a prankster, "What ails this man?" All the words and expressions came in one hurried breath.

"I'm Peter Dooley of Lackeen. Mrs. Williams sent me to implore you to come and attend to her son. He's locked himself into his room and refuses to come out. He has a big bread knife with him and he says he'll use it if anyone attempts to go near him. All the entreaties from the poor mother and ourselves to no avail, he would not be coaxed into coming out or even open the door."

Peter rubbed the melting snow from around his face and beard before continuing. "The moans and groans and the involuntary cries of terror from the room. It's as if he is in great agony. They were piteous."

The man drew a deep laboured breath.

"The neighbours and myself," says he, "have been keeping watch day and night for the last week and looking after the stock for the old woman as well. A few hours ago we decided to smash down the bedroom door for we couldn't tolerate it any longer. The neighbours are keeping watch over him lest he do himself an injury til you come."

"What did you find?" the Doctor asked urgently.

"He had drawn himself up into a ball in the bed and was tearing at the bedclothes with his teeth. There was froth coming from the corners of his mouth and sparks from his eyes like the sparks from a blacksmith's anvil. It was frenzied looking. It really frightened me and I'm not easily frightened."

The Doctor nodded his head in agreement for he knew Peter's ability as a horse trainer. Even the most stubborn of them were subdued and trained.

"It's a strange disease he has for sure."

The Doctor turned his back to the man and began shuffling papers on his desk. To himself, 'A strange disease indeed,' shaking his head.

"Will you come Doctor and give him something to ease the pain? We can't be held responsible if something should befall him. The poor mother is out of her mind with torment, the poor creature, and she almost ninety."

The Doctor was in the horns of a dilemma. After rubbing his chin and cogitating for a few moments, 'If I don't go,' says he to himself, 'and anything should happen to him, especially after Peter putting his life at risk just to be a good Samaritan, I might be held responsible.'

He turned and glanced at the man in front of him whose encrusted beard and clothes were beginning to thaw out.

He nodded his head.

"Will you saddle up the horse," says he to Peter,

"while I'm getting ready, the little bay in the first stall."

The Doctor hurried to the sitting room to fetch his gloves, coat and hat.

"Dan," says his mother, "do you think you'll make it to the Williams' house? You know," says she, looking at his tired face, " the roads and fields are one solid blanket of snow and it's starting again so the man says."

The Doctor considered this a long moment then turned to Peter.

"Are you going back to the Williams' house now?" he enquired.

"No," the man says, "since you are going there, there'll be no need for me. The old woman will understand, but I'll be going as far as the Pluckers Cross. It's not very far from there."

Mounting his bay saddle horse, they set up the street at a lively clip but were soon slowed down by the deep drifts on the country road. The Doctor leaned forward in his saddle as he travelled at the lee side of Peter's horse to avail of whatever shelter there might be, but the snow was coming at such an angle that his hat gave little protection against it.

Parting company at Pluckers Cross, Peter wished him good luck and safe journey as he gave him directions. It wasn't that the Doctor didn't know where the Williams lived for he had been there on numerous occasions with the old man before he died. It was the blanket of snow that had turned roads and fields into one solid white carpet. At every gateway there was a mighty drift. He urged on Little Babe who negotiated every drift with the surefootedness of a mountain goat.

He could feel himself getting stiffer and stiffer by the minute with the cold. The drifting snow had forced its way inside his shirt collar, making him even colder.

The further he went, the deeper the snow became and

his sense of direction became impaired. It was the first time in his life that he feared for his safety. Not since the battlefield in Africa did he experience such fear.

Then, without portent or warning, his horse almost disappeared into a deep hollow save for his head which was resting on the bank of snow. He himself was flung up and out of the saddle when the stirrups bounced off a solid bank of snow on either side of the horse. He found himself standing on the bank with the reins still in his hands. Momentarily he was dumbstruck at the awful situation he was in. He shuddered on the bank more in fear than with the cold, for he knew if his horse wasn't to be lost forever he would have to act fast.

The biting cold wind didn't seem to affect him anymore. He held steadfast onto the reins. Then he leaned forward, allowing his eyes to adjust to the gloom of the moon.

There he could see his horse struggling furiously to get to his feet. He was peddling hard with his hind legs to get purchase on the soft snow. When he got to a standing position, the horse seemed to the doctor to be sinking deeper into the hollow. He prayed with all his might that the good Lord would save him and his faithful friend the agony of being buried alive. For, at that very moment, he could see nothing but his obituary in the paper:

> *Doctor and his horse disappears without trace. Dr. McKay, an able and keen horseman disappears while making a house call to Patrick Williams of Boholla on Wednesday night and no trace of either horse or man has been found to date.*

He tensed as the chill of foreboding swept over him.

'If I could get him turned around,' he says to himself, 'he would no doubt be capable of exiting the hole.'

He talked to his horse kindly to calm him down.

"Ho-boy, hee-boy, that's my boy. Come around. That's me boy."

Coaxing and cajoling him for a short while, at the same time pulling gently but firmly on the reins, the horse got his rump against what seemed like a rock. He reared up on his hind legs and, with his master's gentle but firm pull, the horse gave one mighty heave and jumped out of the hole and stood on the bank. He slacked the snow off his back like a dog slacing rain off his coat.

The Doctor gave a great sigh of relief. His knees shook so much that they nearly crumpled under him on thinking of the acute danger he had found himself in. He went with a waddling gate to the horse and put his arms around his neck and hugged him.

Having regained his composure, he looked around to see if he could see any light in any house he could go to, even if it was only to enquire the way. He could see nothing but banks of snow all around him.

Peering at the huge mound of snow in front of him, he thought, 'If I could climb up there, maybe, just maybe, I might be able to see the Williams house.'

At this very minute to see any light would be a godsend. At his master's command, Little Babe stood still but turned her rump to the drifting snow. The Doctor climbed up the mighty drift. Eventually he reached the top and, seeing what he thought was a pillar or a wall, he grabbed it. Holding steadfast to balance himself he glanced around the white country. Sure enough there in the distance he saw a light.

'That has to be the Williams house,' he says to himself, 'Peter told me they would leave the light in the window as a landmark for me.' His heart missed a beat when he saw it.

Then, for no known reason his hand felt warm. He

pondered a long second at this strange phenomenon because at this very moment he felt as cold as the man that came to his surgery door earlier that night. Save for his hands.

Gingerly he dragged himself to the apex of this object. To his dismay a great gust of warm air eddied around his face.

"Be cripes," says he, jerking back like a frightened cat, "Am I at the gates of Hell or what?"

But at this very moment he didn't care where he was or what had befallen him. He leaned forward again and allowed his eyes to adjust to the blackness. Well, to his amazement he found himself looking down the chimney shaft of Jimmy Crow's thatched cottage!

He was both elated and apprehensive at the same time but he held on steadfast lest he should fall through the thatch into Jimmy's kitchen.

'How in the name of God did I end up here?' he says to himself. Then it came to him.

Jimmy's cottage nestled at the lee side of a large cliff just off the road leading up to the Williams. There was only a narrow passage between the back of the house and the cliff rock, so that the snow piled up to form a wedge between house and rock, and the landscape looked, from ground to ridge, as one continuous acclivity. This is where the Doctor's horse disappeared.

"Anyone in there?" yelled the Doctor into the maw of the chimney.

When the resonance of his voice died away, he could hear shuffling at the hearthstone. Then, as luck would have it, the fire yielded a sudden blink of flame and in that brief moment it allowed the doctor to discern a disembodied head of a man with a dirt embedded wrinkled face, his lips puckered and swelled one minute then sucked in rosy the next on account of having no teeth. He was poised at a precarious angle peering up the chimney shaft like a frightened gnome.

"O, holy Lord God above," he moaned, "Please, please, don't call me yet, I haven't gone to Confession in the last five years," the little gnome said, falling on his knees on the hearthstone, the flat of his hands tight together raised above his face in a prayerful pose.

"Please, Lord," says he, "give me a chance, I'll go to Confession when the snow clears."

"I'm not the Man above," cried the voice down the chimney. "Well, I am the man above now, but I'm not the Man above if you know what I mean." The Doctor was beginning to get confused himself.

'If I don't get down from here very soon,' he says to himself, 'I'll certainly be with the Man above and that's for sure.'

"I'm not the Man above," yelled the Doctor again. "I'm Doctor McKay, I'm on an urgent call to the William's house, I'm on horseback. Can I come in and heat myself?"

"Well, praises be," says Jimmy, pursing his lips, "I thought it was … come in, come in and bring your horse as well."

With relief, with the effort to get to his feet, Jimmy lost his balance and nearly topped into the dying embers of the turf fire. He was still mumbling to himself when he opened the door.

Sitting on the sugan chair beside the now replenished fire in Jimmy's modest kitchen, the Doctor thanked him profusely. The old man tendered him a whiskey which he accepted with alacrity. They drank their drinks in silence as the wind howled in the chimney. The horse relaxed on three legs in the nave of the kitchen, nonchalant to his strange surroundings.

Jimmy was the first to break the reverie. He rubbed

his pursed lips with the back of his hand.

"So, it's up to the Williams you're going?"

The Doctor nodded but didn't speak right away. "This Paddy lad is gravely ill, or so Peter Dooley says. He came by earlier tonight begging me to come and attend him."

"HAA," says Jimmy, chucking spits like bait into the ashes at the side of the fire. The drop on his nose danced in a frenzy of contempt as his piggy eyes bored into the Doctor's face.

"That rapscallion of the devil is no more sick than I am."

He clasped the glass in a vice-like grip between his two hands, his elbows on his knees, staring into the blazing fire. His lips puckered and turned in on themselves as if in a fight to the finish. Everyone knew that the two families were at each other's throat for sixty years or more. Veiled insults, taunts and jibes had taken deep root.

"Do you know," says he, "this whole shenanigans started many years ago, before you came here. Ould Tom and his wife wouldn't let Paddy marry Katie Daly from the Millbank Cottages in Shinrone. My own cousin's daughter at that. They said if he did he would have to clear out of the house and out of the country, never to darken their door again. No way were they going to share their hearthstone with that interloper. 'Look for a farmer's daughter,' they said, 'one with a pedigree. That's what we want here'. "

"I'll tell you something for nothing, Doctor. Them crowd up there," he flicked his eyes in the direction of the Williams house, "always thought they were a step above buttermilk." He had raised his voice an octave, "I know they haven't got two halfpenny's to jingle on a tombstone."

He continued: "Confronted with this choice, Paddy

yielded to his parent's bidding and in shame Katie went to America. In revenge, Paddy would take to the bed when he was most needed on the farm. He'd refuse food and water, but faith I knew that gent filled his gut unbeknownst to his parents. He would lie in his bed moaning and groaning and thrashing his arms in frenzy, and the old Doctor Brown coming every other day administering bottle after bottle to relieve the trauma, and, says he, he's going to kill the poor ould mother before he leaves that bed."

Having pondered a long moment, over what the old man had said, the Doctor came to the conclusion that this rascal was just playing the goat. He had duped his mother and his kind neighbours and Doctor Brown, and now he is trying it on him. The more he thought about it the more irate he became.

'I could,' says he to himself, 'be tucked up in my bed. Instead I am stuck up here in this God forsaken place, frozen to death.'

He glanced from his drink to this kindly old man opposite.

"I could be dead by now only for you, and that rapscallion of Hell," he flicked his eyes in the direction of the William's house, "tucked up in his warm bed and now at everyone in the neighbourhood's beck and call. And all for what?"

He tossed the last dollop of whiskey into his mouth and then jumped up with such a start that the veins of his neck stood out like stretched cords. 'I'll give you your comeuppance very shortly,' he says to himself.

Mounting his horse he set out the short distance to the Williams. The journey was slow and hazardous, through the incessant blinding snow. He dismounted his horse in the yard just outside the kitchen window where the glass bowl kerosene lamp with its two wick double burner was lit. He gave a great sigh of relief. He was so glad to be at his destination. How he was going to get back he didn't know.

As he tossed snow from his boots and coat, he could hear muffled conversation in the kitchen. It resembled the resonant humming of bees, and when it became animated it sounded like the distant gaggling of turkeys. Then there would be a pause and in that pause there would be piteous moaning and groaning coming from the bedroom. The Doctor knocked severely on the kitchen door and pushed it open.

Immediately a great silence pervaded the house. Giving a cursory glance around the sparsely furnished kitchen, his eyes came to rest on the old woman at the ingleside who was, with the rest of the neighbour's, on her bended knees saying the Rosary. They sprang to their feet.

"O Doctor," says she, "I'm so glad to see you could make it," and thanked him profusely for venturing out on such an atrocious night. At this minute he was in no humour for exchanging pleasantries.

"Where is he?" says he.

There was menace in his face as he followed the old woman, shuffling before him, into the bedroom with a lighted candle in her hand while the cohort of neighbours huddled in a phalanx at the back wall of the kitchen, giving furtive glances at each other and at the doctor's austere manner as he strutted into the bedroom after her.

"There he is, the poor creature, Doctor," says she. "Please help him if you can."

Taking the candle from the old woman he ordered her out before going to the corner of the big room to look down at the recumbent figure in a foetal position on a straw sick. He was facing away from him towards the wall, the nether portion of his body was naked.

The Doctor stooped down and put his hand on the

naked form.

Too warm, he thought, for a person to be stripped for very long in such a cold room, on such a cold night.

"Are you asleep?" the Doctor says curtly.

"No, Doctor," the sick man answered, his voice strong though mournful.

"Haaa," says the Doctor angrily, "you don't look like a sick man to me. Sit up there," the Doctor barked at him.

With great effort the sick man sat up and looked at the Doctor holding the flickering candle near the sick man's face. It stood out pale and frenzied.

The Doctor's large frame loomed soft in the pale candlelight. He checked his forehead and his jugular. There was no temperature, that he was sure of. Taking a pace back, he placed the candle in the receptacle, which was a gouged out hole in a turnip that sat on the rickety sugar chair beside the dilapidated looking bed. He tucked up his sleeves, and gnashed his teeth. He was thinking of all that Jimmy Crow had related to him and every word was very true. He also thought of the ride through the drifting snow up this mountain, and almost losing his life in that hole.

'All for what?' he scowled to himself. 'This scoundrel, and he just playing the goat.' His rage burst forth at the thought.

The sick man was sitting waiting for the good Doctor to issue his findings and administer him with some special medicine for his bodily ailments, just as old Doctor Brown did after every visit. He certainly wasn't more knowledgeable than Doctor Brown. How could a man no matter how well he was medically trained understand the working of the brain?

Paddy had badly underestimated the new Doctor's vast knowledge, gained while working with the depressed and traumatised of the war. He could in an instant recognise a genuine case from a fraudster any time and this gent was certainly one of them.

Then, without portent or warning, the Doctor landed an almighty sock on the sick man's jaw. The thud was so loud you'd think something horrendous had exploded in the room but it was only the bed collapsing under the sick man from the impact.

He was ejected about two feet into the air with the suddenness of the blow. He roared and screeched as he flew through the air. The writhing and wriggling and wailing was piteous.

"OOO, me jaw is broken!" he yelped, "O, me jaw!"

Turning like a cat, he landed on all fours on the ground between the wall and the bed. A gust of wind blew out the candle. The Doctor groped around in the dark searching for his quarry, but his quarry had escaped under the broken bed, lying as meek as a mouse.

""Come out here, you scoundrel" says he. "If I lay me hand on you, I'll, I'll kill you," he yelled into the maw of the black room.

When the resonance of the breaking bed and the screeching and wailing of the supposed sick man reached the kitchen, the neighbours glanced from one to the other, then at the old woman, and then cowered in their seats.

"Glory be to God," exclaimed the old woman, "what ails him at all?" as tears began rolling down her work worn wrinkled face. "It must be something awful that has happened to him, the poor creature."

Unable to locate his quarry in the dark the Doctor stormed out of the bedroom and stood momentarily in the nave of the kitchen, his face deadly pale and serious. He looked at the old woman, crouched in the corner of the ingleside. She had turned her head and glanced at the Doctor with her eyecorner, fearful of what his diagnosis might be.

"Send these people home, Mrs. Williams," says the Doctor, "I think they are needed worse at home than here, to look after their own families and sick."

"And what about …?"

The old woman's eyes went to the room where her son was.

"He's a new man already," says he, "all his maladies have disappeared."

To himself, 'If I have to call on him again he'll regret the day he was ever born.'

The neighbours gazed in anxious silence as the Doctor disappeared out the door. Satisfied that everything was going to be all right they put on their coats preparatory to leaving.

The Doctor put his foot in the stirrup. He looked back at Paddy's room window and gnashed his teeth. He mounted his horse and, with a touch of savagery, urged him forward. Trudging through the snowdrifts, the doctor shuddered from the biting cold and rage. He took a deep breath and half closed eyes and with an angry scowl on his face, he turned his wrath on Paddy's parents who were the cause of all this wholly sorry affair.

He cursed and threatened the mountain of snow with his clenched fist and roared out loud, "This innate sinfulness of man, this depraved passion that is called love."

The Curse of Black Hazel

From the recesses of my mind's eye I can still see Uncle Martin as he entered our kitchen with a startled look about him. Mother had sent him to the village for a bag of groceries which he put on the table.

"What's the matter with you," says Mother, "has poor ould Billy-Joe snuffed it?"

Billy-Joe was one of Martin's oldest card playing buddies. "No, thank God," says he, "but you won't believe what I'm going to tell you.

Mother stalled in her bread making, anxiously waiting for him to continue.

"Black Hazel," says he, "she's back in the village. I was on my way to see Billy-Joe when I spotted her caravan at Nestors Corner there at the end of the village. Mark you my word," says he, "that woman, being of a vindictive nature, has returned after all these years, or it must be her daughter, for it's the exact same caravan."

"She can't be back," says mother, "she was banished from this area many years ago by Major Ralph Alexander. I heard my mother talk about it many's a time when I was young."

"Listen," continues Mother, "don't you be worrying your head about her. Come over here to this armchair and I'll give you a nice cup of tea and a dollop of whiskey added." This was always mother's antidote for all ills.

With the aid of a cup of tea and whiskey, Martin

calmed down.

In the comfort of the armchair he lit his pipe and, having prodded it into easy operation, he began to relate the narrative of Hazel Blackmore and the Alexanders of Rathmullen Estate.

I replenished the fire with sods of turf from the ancient scuttle close by before making myself comfortable on the sugan chair opposite in the ingle:

"I was just a nipper like you," says Martin to me. "I was on my way to school. It was a bright, crisp morning. It was the cusp between winter and spring, the sort of morning voices carried in the clear air.

"There at Nestors Corner, just before entering the village, I spotted Hazel's caravan parked on waste ground. Her old piebald horse was tied to a tree bough, nibbling hay, nonchalant to the outburst within.

"I felt a surge of anxiety tear through my brain. The hairs on the nape of my neck began to rise.

"Momentarily I stopped and yanked the schoolbag up more comfortable on my back. Nervously I tiptoed up to the caravan door and peered in. I could hear her boisterous snarling, screeching voice coming from the nave of the wagon. I was petrified of what might happen if she caught me and petrified too if Mother was to find out. But my curiosity was far greater than Mother's rebuke or the witch's reprimand.

"She was oblivious to my presence as I peered in over the half door. She was sitting at a small wicker table, staring into a huge crystal ball in front of her. This cadaverous looking old lady was dressed all in black, her long Grecian nose seemed to sail down over carious peg teeth that were as crooked and jagged as the Cliffs of Moher. A protruding chin was sharp as a razor. She had a wicked snarling look about her. Unkempt hair fell in plenitude around her shoulders Long nails on skeleton thin hands were tearing at the surface of the crystal ball.

"A shaft of light entering the room through an aperture in the curtains was shining on the crystal ball, emitting a kaleidoscope of colour on to her face, and gave the impression – to young minds not used to ghost stories – that sparks were coming from her eyes like sparks from a blacksmith's anvil. Her tongue was vile.

"When she had finished her orgy she got up from the table and did an Indian warlike dance around her broomstick in the nave of the room as if her mission had been accomplished.

"The argot that had reached a crescendo had now abated. A great calm descended the caravan."

Mother offered Martin another dollop of whiskey which he accepted with alacrity. When the dollop of this rich beverage reached it's destination he smacked his lips, gave a benign smile and turned to stoke his pipe. He turned it upside down and drew gently, then leaned back in the chair and crossed his legs one over the other.

" Where was I?" says he. "Oh yes."

"Hazel and her husband came that spring, from where nobody knows. They parked their caravan on waste ground at Nestors Corner there at the edge of the village. The wagon was red and green with great ornate lettering on the side. It read:

HAZEL AND MALUPSY ROAD SHOW
ALL ARE WELCOME – NO COVER CHARGE

"We ran all the way home from school that day to tell Mother the exciting news, and begged her to let us go to the show.

"She looked at us severely, but we knew it was a benign look behind that serious face that she always put on.

" 'That's if ye are good,' she warned.

"It was like Christmas all over again! We made sure to be on our best behaviour leading up to the opening night.

"A great crowd of us kids had gathered long before the show was due to begin. It opened with Hazel regalin us with some fine dancing like jigs and reels while Malupsy played the fiddle. They also sang duets together like, *The Moon Behind the Hill* and *The Old Bog Road*, after which tickets were sold and a small prize given to the winner.

"After the show the men moved on to play at the billiard table, watched by a great audience including us who had never seen such a game in our lives.

"Hazel invited willing participants in to her caravan to have their fortune told if they crossed her hand with silver.

"In order to supplement her meagre living Hazel travelled around the country selling haberdashery, while Malupsy stayed at home minding the children and making buckets and cans and an assortment of mugs and jugs for sale.

"Then tragedy struck. One autumn, Malupsy died suddenly, so Hazel was left to bring up the two children on her own. She had to close the show, and rely on the sales of her haberdashery and generosity of the local people.

"Then, just before Christmas, Hazel herself became very ill and was confined to bed. With no income coming into the house and two young children to provide for she soon fell into dire straits. She was almost on the point of starvation. She dragged herself out of bed and, with the children, knelt down on the cold floor and prayed with all their might that the good Lord would send someone to her aid and relieve her of her abject affliction.

"Well, her prayers must have been heard for no sooner had she got up off her knees when a knock came to the door. It was Mrs. Roche, the charwoman up at the Major's house, enquiring after her health because she hadn't seen her out lately and asked if she could be of any assistance.

"When she saw the emaciated condition of the trio she was moved with great pity. To add to the calamity, there wasn't a spark of fire in the grate.

" 'Come up to the big house,' says she, 'and I'll give you plenty of leftovers. There has been nothing but feasting and drinking in that house for the last week and it will continue until the New Year.'

"She warned the children to enter through the orchard.

" 'That way,' says she, 'nobody will see yous. Knock on the side door and I'll have a parcel ready for you.'

"Hazel thanked her profusely.

" 'Think nothin of it,' says she. 'He wouldn't be so hard-hearted as to refuse a sick woman in need, especially at Christmas time.'

"Both Mrs. Roche and Hazel had badly underestimated the Major's vehement reaction when he discovered the two children scampering through the orchard with parcels under their arms.

(May I add at this point that mendicancy was strictly forbidden in the Bailiwick of Rathmullen at the time)

"The Major immediately had the two children captured and put into care. Hazel herself was summoned to appear at the next court sitting in the Village Square to answer all charges laid against her. On the whole the Magistrate was known to be a fair man, but this case before him he viewed with abhorrence.

"It was a cold December morning, the morning of the court. A razor sharp wind was blowing from the east. Flurries of snow were eddying around the Square.

"Hazel found herself standing between two law officers in front of the canopied rostrum, awaiting instructions from the Magistrate. From his vantage point on the rostrum he observed the inanimate pale faced assembly, some of whom were conversing in whispers.

"He removed his pince-nez with due ceremony. Then taking a large handkerchief from his pocket, he began to clean his glasses, at the same time keeping an eagle eye on this emaciated old lady. He gave a bronchial cough as he checked himself for addressing her as such. 'A lady indeed,' he chortled.

"He was of the opinion that she was practising fortune telling and witchcraft in the caravan since she arrived in the village, but he couldn't prove anything.

"However, like all English nobility and their descendents before him, they abhorred such depraved practices. They were superstitious of these antichrists and their ilk in their midst, for fear they might lay a spell on them, their families and their estates. He could recall many of his friends whose families were cursed by these witches, all because they were obliged to administer the law as laid down. At last the opportunity had presented itself, for which he had been waiting for so long. He would impose the maximum sentence on this old bedlam and then banish her from the Bailiwick of Rathmullen for good.

"He checked himself for being so hasty. 'I'll have to take into consideration the villager petition on her behalf, since they are here to voice their objection if compassion wasn't shown ... it being the season of good will to all men.'

"He leered at her.

" 'Bring the culprit forward,' he advised.

"The two officers manhandled their charge onto the rostrum. She rebelled at first. Her body was writhing and wriggling from the vice-like grip she was caught in. The law officers released their hold on her and pointed to where she was to take her place on the rostrum.

"She turned and stuck out her tongue at the two as

she moved forward in obsequiousness to take her stand.

" 'You are hereby,' says he, 'charged with the heinous crime of mendicancy and encouraging your two children to do the same. How do you plead?'

" 'Guilty my Lord.'

"The Magistrate gave a great sigh of relief. 'At lease she's honest,' he says to himself.

"The assembled audience that were lethargically huddled in small groups in the Square, on hearing this, suddenly became animated.

" 'She must be dying,' they were heard to say, 'when she has admitted to the crime. It was only last week that her children were horsewhipped for non-attendance at Sunday School.'

"Maggy Mooney, the local wench, said she heard her as she was returning home from her own tryst late one night. She heard her calling down the wrath of God on the Major and on his family and on his Estate, and now she was pleading guilty. She must be dying. That was their only conclusion.

"But Hazel thought differently.

"It was the only logical course of action open to her. To do otherwise was inviting the ultimate sentence which was a public flogging in the Square. She knew she was too weak for such punishment. She had her children to think about although they were already placed in care at His Majesty's request up in Kildare. She gnashed her teeth in vehemence at the Magistrate but she daren't show any animosity towards the chief law officer of the state. She knew she and her ilk were an anathema to all Cromwellian settlers.

" 'Having considered all the facts,' says he, 'your present circumstances and the local people's concern for your well being at this time of the year … '

" 'Haah,' she sniggered under her breath, 'you're

worried about my well being …'

" 'Pay attention,' he cautioned her out loud.

" 'Yes, your Honour.'

" 'I hereby waiver the right to impose the maximum sentence, but this does not, ' he stared at her severely, 'diminish in any way the gravity of the crime. I now pronounce the following sentence.'

"The rabble class were jostling with each other to procure a vantage point near the rostrum. They had become more vocal.

"The Magistrate banged the gavel on his desk.

" 'Silence,' he ordered, 'or I'll clear the court.'

"He proceeded.

" 'On this day you will leave the jurisdiction of Rathmullen, never to return. To do otherwise would leave me with no option but to impose the maximum sentence set out. Do you understand?'

"Hazel nodded.

"It was in this vengeful state, when she was back in the caravan, that I heard her calling down the wrath of God on all the Alexander's and the offspring and the future of Rathmullen Estate. When she was leaving she let it be known that if she herself wasn't back her people would be and that they would have as much authority in the Rathmullen Estate as the Alexanders."

The years passed and Hazel, just like her curse, faded into oblivion. The village returned to its lethargic way of life.

Ever since the Rathmullen Estate was given to the Alexanders by Cromwell back in the 1600s, the Estate was handed down from father to son in an unbroken line. They were born and died on it. That was their only boast.

Now, two hundred years and more on, its newest and youngest owner was Philbin Victor Alexander, Major Ralph's son. He was the most progressive and canny of all the heirs to take the reins of power. But his reign was short lived. One night while returning from Dublin, his horse bolted in a violent storm outside Bray. He was thrown down a ravine and broke his neck, an omen the old people thought. It was the Curse of Black Hazel coming back to haunt them.

Lucy, their only daughter, inherited the Estate from her dead brother, Philbin. It was the first time in its history that a female became its sole owner. She did not have the same financial acumen as her dead brother or her father in running the Estate, and it soon fell into financial difficulty. Misfortune followed mishap without any apparent explanation. Speculation was further heightened when the process server was seen handing Lucy a letter in the hall. The whispering began among the staff, "Were their worst fears about to be realised?"

Old Ralph, now in his eighties, became alarmed at this turn of events. "The likes of this," says he, "has never happened before in the Alexander household." He was livid.

The shame of the process server at the house, the possibility of the banks closing in, the breaking up and selling off of the Estate to pay the huge debt and he himself ending up in the Poor House were all shameful. A man that had lived in luxury all his life since he left the army and had a title to boot now found himself almost homeless and penniless. It was a harrowing prospect for a man that had been held in such high esteem in the local community. He was so distraught at the prospect that he took to the bed and wasn't seen out again for a month.

Lucy, not realising the seriousness of the situation, continued regaling her friends with expensive soirees.

The old man was most unhappy. He knew that if something wasn't done and soon the Estate would be beyond redemption. He summoned Lucy to his study.

"You, you," he began in a raucous voice, "you have ignored all the agreements of accession to this Estate. I'm not going to stand idly by and watch you fritter away every last cent on your outlandish parties. I am now issuing you with an ultimatum. Find yourself a husband, a man that can redeem this place. Otherwise you must relinquish the Estate and the title you inherited with it."

She never saw him so decisive in his demeanour. She became very melancholy. Tears welled up in her eyes.

"Oh but Daddy," she protested, "I've tried but I can't find a suitable man."

"I'll find one for you," he cut across.

"But what, Daddy," says she, "if I don't love him?"

He twitched his walrus moustache, "Love, love," he snarled at her, "what has love got to do with anything, especially when you are on the brink of financial ruin. If action isn't taken and soon, we'll all be looking in through those bars of that gate and not out," he fumed.

Rathmullen, like all big estates at the time, employed all their own tradesmen. There was a groomsman, a carpenter, a blacksmith, a saddler and a thatcher. They all lived in lodges around the farm. The big house was equally well served with female staff. There was the cook, the parlour maid, the chambermaid, the nanny, the charwoman as well as all those staff who lived downstairs in the big house.

It was Michael McGovern, the Thatcher, that Ralph turned to for help.

'A most learned man,' Ralph thought, 'from the many books he kept in his small library, and a very travelled man also from the many conversations I have had with him.'

But, behind that pleasant and polite exterior, lay a most secretive person, one that Ralph could never fathom. That didn't worry him too much, as long as he did his work efficiently and reliably, and he was all of that.

Michael listened to his proposition. He would only be too glad to be of assistance to his master. "But Sir, I need time off to go to England to contact some of me old friends from the equine world."

That was freely granted.

"I don't have to emphasise enough," Ralph croaked, rasping hard in his throat, "time is of the essence, off with you now, me good man."

Well, Michael was as good as his word, for he returned two weeks later with great tidings. His contacts had borne fruit. He had located a most suitable man, he thought, a well-to-do man by the name of Henry Tyford. "But I must add," says he, "this man is none too young."

They were both standing in the middle of the Major's Library. The Major lifted an eyebrow and frowned.

"What do you mean, he's none too young?"

"Well, Sir," says Michael, "he's fifty five years old if he's a day."

"Huh," says the Major, "he's only a chappy. I was more than that when I got married."

It was the custom at the time when the match was made the bride and groom met only for the first time at the alter rails where they exchanged their marriage vows. To do otherwise was believed to be unlucky.

The wedding took place in Rathmullen Church three weeks later, with all the pomp and ceremony of the nobility. The breakfast was held in a specially erected marquee on the front lawn as had all the weddings of the Alexanders down through the years. The frolicking and dancing went on for two days. Food was in abundance and drink flowed freely.

In the sobriety of the days following, Lucy learned from her new husband that it was Michael the Thatcher who was the instigator of them coming together.

"How so?" she enquired, staring at him severely.

"Your Father," says the new bridegroom, "hired Michael to procure a suitable husband for you. I hope you're not disappointed in me?"

"Oh no, my love," says she as she went to him. Then that endearing smile twitched at the corners of her mouth as an assurance of her love for him. "It's just ..."

Lucy was well aware that for generations past all the Alexanders, male and female, were betrothed through the matchmaker, but to engage the services of an employee was more than she could tolerate. She refused to recognise Michael as a member of her staff, even though he was ensconced in the Lodge by her Father as a gift for services rendered. To renege on this solemn promise made to him in good faith by her Father would begat dire consequences.

Lucy became the sole owner of the manor on the death of her Father. When the funeral was over, she immediately went to Michael's Lodge and ordered him out. He was livid but not surprised at the Madam's attitude towards the proletarian class and toward him in particular.

"Madam," says he, "I must remind you that your father made a solemn promise to me on his deathbed regarding this cottage."

"I'm boss here now," she gave a toss of her head, "and what I say is final. Now move yourself from these premises immediately, you, you slibhin and never let me see you around these parts again." Her voice was harsh and boisterous.

"Madam," he addressed her calmly and courteously, "you may be the Lady of the Manor but your status and authority will be short-lived. The Lord's wheels grind slowly but surely."

"How dare you, you waif, implicating this family and this Estate in your wanton and scurrilous innuendo," she fulminated.

He leered at her. His eviction would not call down any supreme manifestation of revenge at this time. It could wait for another day.

Michael travelled to Galway where he plied his trade among the peasant's of Kileenbeg and the surrounding districts. He was always so animated and good humoured and willing to please that they christened him 'Smiley the Jovial'. He suppressed his palmistry and matchmaking talents while he worked on the Rathmullen Estate, but now they came to be known. and his services were in great demand.

He bought a cottage in the village and retired from his thatching to begin his new career even though he was at the sunset years of life.

Rathmullen Estate prospered once again under the astute management of Henry Tyford. Debts were paid off. New and more progressive farming methods were adopted. Two sons were born, Luke and Victor. When they finished their private schooling at home they were sent to England to learn the rudiments of farm management but, just like their Mother, they were more interested in having a good time. They regaled their friends with wild parties, all at the expense of the Rathmullen Estate but unbeknownst to the Father who was now old and feeble.

When Henry died the two lads returned home to help in the running of the Estate. But both men lacked the drive and management skills of the Father, so once again the Estate fell into serious financial debt.

Lucy herself was getting old and feeble and the strain of keeping the Estate afloat was taking its toll with no sign of her son and heir Luke getting married.

One night as she lay in a reverie in her bed the spectre of Black Hazel mirrored before her eyes, making wakefulness a terror and sleep a nightmare. Lucy cowered in her bed at the thought of Black Hazel and what she had said, her ire was so vivid and threatening:

"One day, in the not too distant future, I'll be back and if not, my people will, and they will have as much authority on the Estate as the Alexanders."

As the nightmare could not be shaken off for some time after waking, so the image of this cadaverous old woman Hazel held for Lucy an ambience of dread. Next morning in the Study, while awaiting the arrival of her sons, a cauldron of strange thoughts flooded her brain.

All the heirs to this Estate for generations back were all betrothed by the services of the matchmaker and now history was repeating itself once again, she mused. She was convinced more than ever that the curse of Black Hazel had returned with a vengeance. She made up her mind to hand over the reins of power to her son Luke as soon as a suitable girl was found, and relieve herself of this awful burden she had carried for so long.

Next day a missive was dropped into the post box inviting her Uncle Victor to dinner and seeking his advice on matters of great importance. The parley went on for many hours and drink flowed freely.

"My dear Lucy," says he, "if it's at all possible to locate a suitable match for Luke, I'll be honoured to be of assistance."

Lucy clapped herself on the back for her foresight. To herself she said, 'No, the spell of Black Hazel will be waylaid forever and the anathema of the matchmaker on the Rathmullen household will be laid to rest.'

True to his word Victor did procure a girl of substantial means for Luke. Unbeknownst to Lucy, he availed of the services of a matchmaker.

In the warm glow of the turf fire in Smiley's modest kitchen they chatted about many things of mutual interest, exchanged many well-worn items of news, before Victor approached the subject for which he had come in the first place. Victor was taken aback by this man's great knowledge of world affairs and his conversational abilities. He came to the conclusion that he was a man he could trust.

Victor related the story of the Rathmullen Estate for generations past, and their inability to find suitable partners for their offspring. Now they were once again in the grip of terror lest they should lose the Estate.

Alone in the kitchen Smiley leaned back in his chair and closed his eyes. He could see in his mind's eye the past of Rathmullen Estate: him procuring a wealthy husband for Lucy, then she had unceremoniously evicted him from the cottage, the cottage her Father had promised him as a token of services rendered.

He repeated Lucy's name several times in ire.

'I have the right girl for Luke,' he thought, gnashing his teeth as he rammed his closed fist into the other open hand. 'Yes, and the right girl to fulfil Hazel's long time wish.'

He smiled to himself at the turn of events as he sat in the warm glow of the turf fire. 'The Lord's wheels grind slowly but surely', says he to himself.

Luke and his prospective wife met for the first time in the Shannonside Hotel in Athlone. They were going to break the mould of a time honoured tradition whereby the bride and groom only meet for the first time at the altar where they would exchange their marriage vows. Luke was dressed in his red hunting jacket, a polo neck jumper, jodhpurs riding breeches and leather boots. 'A most handsome man,' Violet thought.

Violet herself was dressed in a special lime green knee length dress that emphasised her comely figure. Her rich brown hair fell in plentitude around her shoulders. A pearl necklace sat warmly at her throat, showing off her pink and fair complexion.

The rendezvous was a great success. Although Victor and Smiley joined the couple at dinner so as the acquaintance would go smoothly there was no need. The conversation between them was like a river that had been hindered by many weeds and undergrowth but was suddenly freed from captivity. It was love at first sight for the young couple. They spent the next week touring around Galway, getting to know each other, satisfied that their love was mutual. Luke invited Violet to Rathmullen to meet his Mother and brother.

On this first visit Lucy was hugely impressed by the well-groomed and comely young lady and extended a courteous welcome to her. But she was more interested in her financial status than in her other qualities at this time and she wasted no time in pursuing this course of action.

"I have a thousand Pounds in the bank," says Violet, "and I have my own house in the City. I do hairdressing for the wealthy people in Galway City and the surrounding areas."

Lucy rubbed her hands with glee, her eyes wide with anticipation at the thought. She made such an impression on Lucy that tea was ordered on the lawn, a ceremony Lucy reserved for special guests.

Away from the entertaining, in her bedroom, Lucy rejoiced. 'The Estate would be redeemed and be even more prosperous than ever before. How convenient things should happen this way,' she thought to herself.

She had only heard lately from a friend in America who had started a hairdressing and beauty room out there, and said it was the latest fad in lady's beauty care to hit America. Yes, Lucy would insist that the new premises be called *Violet's Hairdressing and Beauty Parlour*. She could imagine all the rich and famous women of Leinster coming to this new establishment and she would be acting as hostess. She suddenly became animated at the thought.

Back in the cottage in Galway, Smiley and Violet had a celebratory drink together. Smiley raised his glass and expressed his great delight and happiness and good wishes to her and her prospective husband. But his happiness had a more sinister aspect to it. At this time, however, Violet was not to know.

He took down his Pandora box and fetched from it a gold locket.

"This is for you, my dear," says he.

Violet gapsed in awe at its great beauty. "I will treasure it forever Uncle Smiley," says she as she hung it around her neck and looked at herself in the mirror. She was overcome with elation.

"How can I ever repay you for all your kindness?"

Smiley gave her a wry smile.

"My dear Violet, there's only one request I ask of you."

"Anything, Uncle," says she as she ran to his side and put her arms around his neck. "Just name it, your wish is my command."

On Violet's next visit to Rathmullen, she let it be known about the gold locket and the great secret hidden therein:

"It is not to be opened or its contents revealed until the wedding day. Many generations ago, on my mother's side, Lady Boscawn of Heather Glenn in Avoca was the proud owner of the locket. It was held in trust by my uncle, to be bestowed on the first female of the clan of Smiley's choosing to get married, and on condition that the secret written therein be fulfilled. If I marry Master Luke," says she, "and I see no good reason to the contrary, these wishes for which I have given a solemn promise must be fulfilled."

Lucy was in a quandary of monumental proportions as to what to do. She summoned her two sons to the Library to discuss the matter. She stood by the bay window, clenching and unclenching her fists as she looked out over the lawn that was verdant green. The rhododendrons fulminated and fronted all over the southern slopes of the garden. The leaves from the maple and elm trees were wafting to and fro in a light breeze.

Looking down the valley to Kilglossery Wood, her mind wandered back in time to when she and her late brother used to play hide and seek among the oak trees and rhododendrons, and then gathered a basket full of wild flowers to fill the vases in the Drawing Room. Those were the days, she thought.

Looking further down the valley she could see the Herity brothers sawing up some of the finest oak trees, 'her trees', and carting them away to their own sawmill and not as much as a bye your leave. She gnashed her teeth in ire at the thought of these brazen rapscallions purloining all this fine timber to feather their own nest at her expense. When she quizzed her Father about it he cautioned her against interfering in matters of the Estate until she knew all the facts.

"These matters and more," said he, "are in writing in the bank and I do not wish to have them revealed until after my death."

Her mind flashed back to that secret letter in the bank, 'and now,' thought she, 'this same sordid mess has raised its ugly head again with my own son.'

Lucy's argot was rapid and raucous as she turned to face the boys. She was rasping hard in her throat just like her father when a dilemma of monumental proportions confronted him.

She stared hard at her son Luke who was standing beside the ornate fireplace. The green in her eye that had not been noticed for manys a year now for the first time was fierce amid the muddy pallor of skin and flossed hair.

"This is the most outrageous agreement this family or estate has ever encountered," she upbraided her son. "It's like buying a pig in a poke."

Luke leered at her. To himself he thought, 'You bought a pig in a poke and it turned out satisfactory,' but he kept his silence.

"How you could have allowed yourself to be talked into such a ridiculous agreement is beyond me," she bellowed at him in vexation. "I see no good reason why this secret cannot be made known at least to the family before the wedding day."

"Yes, there is, Mother," Luke spoke at last. "Protocol must be observed."

"Nonsense," she remonstrated.

Young Victor cut across her caterwauling. "If this locket," says he, "is purported to be that old then its significance cannot be all that important. It could be to our advantage."

"If that be so," Lucy countered, "why can't its contents be revealed?"

She staggered over to the armchair and flopped down into it. She gave a long, deep sigh of anxiety and closed her eyes. For a moment the spectre that had held her in that grip of pain some nights previously came flooding back to haunt her and with it a premonition of all that was going to happen.

She opened her eyes and sat up straight.

"That woman," says she, "is going to wreak a terrible revenge on this Estate, mark you my words, I have that feeling of foreboding. This wedding," says she, "must be called off at once."

She looked at Luke with stern eyes. "We will summon your great Uncle Victor and seek his advice."

Luke stepped into the nave of the room and fulminated at his mother's domineering attitude.

"Mother," he boomed, "I'm going to marry this girl no matter what stipulation is placed on this locket. Now, I don't have to remind you that this Estate is about to go under and the only way I can redeem it is by marrying a moneyed person as you did all those years ago. I have little choice, notwithstanding that I love the girl."

The wedding was a mighty extravaganza, attended by only the aristocrats and nobility from the manor houses of the county. They danced and frolicked on the front lawn to the music of Maurice Mulally and his orchestra. It was a fitting climax to a week of feasting and drinking.

'An occasion to be remembered and savoured with pride,' Lucy thought.

She took a seat on the veranda beside her Uncle Victor who had made the journey from Athlone especially for the occasion. She relaxed, drink in hand, secure in the knowledge that she had done the right thing. She closed her eyes and let thoughts carry her back, back to her own wedding day more than twenty years ago on the very same lawn. A tear of sadness oozed from the corner of her eye and down her rouge cheeks for her husband who had passed away. How proud he would have been, she thought to see his favourite son settle down and take on the mantle of power.

If there was any regret in her life, it was the eviction of Michael McGovern, the Thatcher from the gate Lodge. She upbraided herself for being too hasty in that respect and the character assassination she meted out to him without proof. After all it was him who procured a husband for her and saved the Estate from bankruptcy. Without him this day would not have been possible. She wondered, would she ever see him again or was he even alive. She knew he had travelled to Galway to take up employment there. She wondered in her own mind how she could repair the injustice she had inflicted on him. She knew that forgiveness wasn't one of her strong points, but if he came back maybe she could offer him his old job and the gate Lodge as well. Maybe that would repair the damage between them. She was pondering over these things in her own mind when she was shook back to the present by Luke's voice booming over the sound of the orchestral music.

"Friends, noblemen and country cousins, lend me your ear for just a few moments."

Lucy sat bolt upright in her chair, a pang of anxiety reverberated through her frail body. The moment of truth had arrived, the truth she viewed with trepidation. She hoped she would be proved wrong, but she firmly believed that the secret in the locket was a cover-up for a more sinister motive. But she had agreed to the conditions laid down in the locket, now she was party to it.

Violet joined her husband on the rostrum. She looked radiant in her long white satin dress. Her sparkling brown hair fell around her shoulders. The gold locket sat snugly at her throat.

"This locket," Luke continued, " was owned by Lady Boscawn of Heather Glen in Avoca. It dates back many generations. It was last held by Violet's Uncle Smiley in trust for the first female of the clan he thought fit to be worthy of this precious gem, and on condition that the secret therein be fulfilled by whomever she should marry. This we have pledged to wholeheartedly."

Luke gave his wife a loving hug of affection. A rapturous applause boomed out from the crowd present and could be heard in the village a mile away. He was happy to have won the love and affection of Violet and he was sure they would be happy together.

Lucy craned her neck to get a better view at the young couple as they set about to open the locket. The cronies gathered round the rostrum and gazed at its splendour and beauty. They turned to one another and began to converse in whispers. 'It's magnificent, it's charming ...this lady must have the four leaf shamrock to be favoured with such a precious gem,' they were heard to say.

Luke took the locket from around Violet's neck and kissed it before opening it. He extracted a neatly folded note.

Lucy stood up to have more of an advantageous view of the proceedings. 'Can't be much written on that,' she thought to herself. Then she tugged at Victor's coat sleeve.

"Who is that old man at the back of the crowd or who invited him?"

"That's Smiley," says Victor, "that's Violet's uncle from Galway."

"Beckon him over til I get a better view of him. I seem for some strange reason to know that face from somewhere."

Smiley came forward with alacrity and stood in front of Lucy and Victor on the veranda. He took off his hat and greeted Lucy amiably, "We meet again, old girl," he uttered.

Lucy peered at him severely, then at Victor. The rouge on her cheeks, that Violet had spent many hours perfecting that morning, had vanished. Her face had turned slate gray. She had a sudden weakness and collapsed on the veranda. Victor, not too robust of late, came to her aid and, between himself and Smiley, they succeeded in getting her over to the armchair without undue alarm where she fell into a deep trance.

In her reverie she could see the whole past laid out before her: her Father hiring Michael, the Thatcher, now known as Smiley, who produced a wealthy husband for her in England so as to redeem the Estate; her eviction of him from the gate Lodge that her Father had promised him as a gift for his good deed. She vowed that she wasn't going to be held ransom to this curmudgeon of the Devil, and now everything he promised and everything he predicted was coming true. She gave a long deep sigh.

When she opened her eyes, there in front of her was the vision of a man she hoped she would never see again.

Victor offered her a copious dollop of spirits, hoping it would restore her equilibrium. When the rich beverage reached its destination, she came to life and sat up straight. It provided her with the strength and courage to confront this rapscallion of the Devil.

"Who … who …," she croaked, "invited him here?"

She was staring at Victor with eyes that were now severe and searching. "Get him off this Estate," says she, "before I send for the police."

Victor was taken aback by her sudden outburst. He raised his hand in quiet assurance.

"We don't want this day," says he, "to be spoiled by any unpleasantness." He went to Lucy and put his arm around her shoulder to unction her. "My dear Lucy," says he, "I can explain everything." He took Lucy's hand and spoke slowly and deliberately.

"Do you remember not so long ago you sought my assistance in providing a suitable girl for Luke, a girl with the right credentials?"

Lucy nodded knowingly.

"Well," says he, "I travelled the highways and byways of the Midlands and the west of Ireland in quest of such a girl without success. On my departure that day you emphasised on more than one occasion, may I add, that time was of the essence. So as not to disappoint you, I took it on myself to seek the assistance of this man, Smiley, a man who is held in the highest esteem by all the people of Connaught and from all social rankings."

"Until today," continues Victor, "I knew nothing of this locket or its contents"

'But I knew the minute I clapped my eyes on him,' thought Lucy, 'that an ill omen would befall us all.'

Out loud Lucy said, "So you have changed your name so as to deceive an old dowager like me in front of all my family?"

Smiley just chortled at her.

Attention was called for again from the bandstand as Violet, the more erudite of the two, gave the note a cursory glance up and down before she read it's contents in more detail to get the gist of it before she made it known to the receptive committee.

She was gravely agitated as well as elated at its revelations. She was agitated at her uncle for not informing her of her relations being still alive. Here she believed all these years she was a loner in the world except for her uncle. Here she had felt all this time sadness in her heartstrings for those relations who could not be present on this special day to see her marry the young squire of Rathmullen Estate. Now ...

She read the last paragraph slowly. She couldn't believe her eyes. She read:

"Your relations will be joining you on this Estate as soon as this note is read out."

She suddenly became animated at the thought. She read on hurriedly. "The receiver of this locket shall be bound of its contents."

She looked at her husband for reassurance. His smile and his embrace said it all. To do otherwise would bring a greater disaster than the Great Flood.

Lucy peered sullenly at Smiley, who was now sitting near the veranda smoking his pipe. He let out a mouthful of smoke and smiled back wryly at her. Her wan face was flushed in the light.

Violet read out the last few lines:

"My people and their descendants shall have refuge on

this land without interference or harassment for the rest of their lives."

Lucy drew in a deep laboured breath and cranked up her vocal cords.

"What's the meaning of this, young lady? You told us you were an orphan."

"That's the God honest truth, ma'am, I know of no one except my uncle."

Lucy's argot became rapid and extremely bitter. She leered at Smiley.

"Well, Mickey or Smiley, you are a proper fly-by-night. What have you got to say about all this?"

"Only what it says in the locket ma'am," he retorted.

"And where might these friends of yours be?" she enquired.

"They're on their way here, ma'am."

With that Smiley stood up and beckoned to the man at the avenue gate. He then cupped his two hands around his mouth so that his voice would carry loud and clear:

"OPEN UP THE GATE, GEORGE," shouted he, "AND START THE WAGONS ROLLING."

Immediately when the word was given as many as fifty wagons began to thunder through the gate and up the avenue to take up residence near the big house.

Lucy, seeing how they had all been fooled, gulped down a large mouthful of air that went with her breath. She conked out and had to be carried upstairs to her bed and the Doctor sent for. A vigil was kept at her bedside day and night.

Out on the lawn the entertainment came to an abrupt end. The cronies were flabbergasted at the turn of events. They all began to converse in whispers.

'A day,' they said, 'that was to be preserved for the aristocracy and nobility of Leinster, on the most famous estate in Co. Wicklow is now being turned into a den for the gypsies and the rabble classes.'

The men folk, so disgusted at seeing what was taking place, began tacking their horses under their gigs and hansoms, and, with their wives and loved ones, drove from the Estate at high speed, vowing never to return again.

When the diaspora was complete, the rabble class descended onto the lawn to take part in the celebrations, but the only one left there was Smiley. With a large smile on his face, he raised a bottle of whiskey.

"Come friends," says he, "and let's celebrate. Lady Boscawn and Hazel's wish have been fulfilled."

Back in the bedroom Lucy was propped up on pillows in the big double bed, her voice just audible. The Doctor heard her last words quite plainly but didn't understand their meaning.

Lucy turned her head slowly and gazed at Luke and Violet with half closed eyes. She wagged her finger at them but no real audible sound came out. They knew the end was nigh. The Doctor looked at them perplexed.

"She keeps on repeating the same words over and over again," he said.

Luke looked at the Doctor quite concerned lest it should be something important they should know. "What is it, Doctor, what is she saying?"

The Doctor knitted his eyebrows and scratched his chin.

"She keeps on repeating these strange words, 'The Lord's wheels grind slowly but surely'," he said.

As soon as the funeral was over Luke went to the bank and demanded the letter. Now that the Alexander name was extinct and the bank manager was also dead, he saw no good reason to delay the publishing of this letter to at least his wife and brother.

Luke sat at the drawing room window, scanned the two page official letter, then checked the signature at the bottom before he started.

"To Whom It Concerns, I, Cornelius Melrose, owner and manager to the Shinrone Bank, along with my cousins the Herity brothers, also Michael McGovern, the Thatcher, another cousin, (who knew about the blackmailing but took no active part in it, he had his own agenda), have defrauded the Alexanders of Rathmullen Estate of a great sum of money by harvesting and selling over many years a great number of oak trees from the Estate."

The letter continued as such, Luke read on:

"An Agreement was negotiated by Major Ralph Alexander and his new wife Delilia that an overdraft with the bank was to be cleared from the sale of this timber and thereafter a nominal amount was to be sold each year to keep the estate solvent and have ready cash flow so that the Major could live in a manner befitting with his status. The bank manager was to be handsomely rewarded for his time. This arrangement was to cease when the first son would become heir to the Estate."

Luke rapidly read on, all the sordid details:

The bank manager had ceased honouring the enormous amount of cash flow cheques which came in from the Estate. To ward off threatening letters from the bank the bank manager deliberately inveigled Delilia into his private office where she was forced to offer him favours for his leniency in this matter. This she did on an ongoing basis in order to keep the Estate afloat.

When the first baby was born it was a girl. To say they were disappointed was an understatement. They christened her Lucy. Delila was strongly advised by her Doctor, on account of her age and her previously difficult pregnancy, to have no more children. But they ignored his advice. The solvency of the Estate for their heir was more important than her survival. She was willing to forfeit her own life for this cause.

The Doctor was so concerned for Delilia's welfare that he took her into his private nursing home for the confinement.

At the very same time Dolly Herity, wife of Theodore Herity, one of the Heritiy brothers, was also admitted to the home for her confinement. Delilia's baby was born first, another girl. They were so broken hearted that they couldn't bring themselves to put a name on her.

Within an hour or so Dolly's baby was born, a bouncing baby boy. She wasn't overly excited with the new addition for she had already six boys as it was.

The Alexanders, faced with this stark dilemma of having no heir, cooked up a plan in the strictest secrecy to swap their babies.

The Heritys would be handsomely rewarded with timber from any of their woods until their baby son Philbin became heir and head of the Estate.

But Philbin's reign was short-lived for he was killed coming home from Dublin in a thunderstorm. The Estate reverted back to old Ralph who installed Lucy as proprietor, the first woman ever to own the Estate in its long history.

Then Lucy almost bankrupt the Estate with her expensive soirees. Only for her Father's foresight the place would have went under for Lucy hadn't the same business acumen as her late brother.

Old Ralph hired Michael McGovern, the Thatcher on the Estate, to secure a husband for Lucy, a man of means which he did. 'It was my Father, Henry Tyford, and only for him we wouldn't be here today', thought Luke to himself.

Luke flung the letter into the window. He was physically disturbed at what he read and walked out of the house to stroll in the garden to clear his head.

'This place,' muttered he, shaking his head, 'was rife with schemes and scams on all sides. To think,' as he smacked his fist into the palm of the other open hand, 'that we, the Alexanders, were held in such high esteem and respect by the general public and our moral behaviour purported to be above reproach, and "we",' clenching and unclenching his fists, 'were no better than the rabble class that we barred from this Estate for thieving.'

'Just think,' says he waggling his finger at nobody in particular, 'that my grandmother Delilia was no better than a whore, my Uncle Philbin, he wasn't even an Alexander, he was a Herity. No wonder,' says he, 'they had free access to all the woods. And then Lucy, my Mother, who was her Father was anyone's guess.'

Then he thought of Violet, his wife. He gave a martyred sigh. 'To think,' says he, 'my Mother castigated her for being related to gypsies and a sorcerer. If she only knew the contents of that letter. What would she think? I suppose,' he thought, 'she'd be so high and mighty to think anything wrong other than what she was.'

Luke turned in the garden and, with a determined stride he set out to fetch his brother and discuss the matter with him.

Setting out for Shinrone village that day to buy the weekly groceries which was my wont every Saturday since Martin's death, I decided, on account of it being such a beautiful day, I would take the long mile road. This scenic road ran through Rathmullen Estate, dissecting it in two. It also passed quite near the big house, a spacious edifice of Gothic Architecture, built from the finest Wicklow granite.

It never crossed my mind as I set out that there was to be a wedding that day in the big house. I sauntered along at a leisurely pace, stopping occasionally to view the magnificent oak, elm and beeches in the nearby woods and to savour the rich aroma of the varied and many shrubs and flowers that grew in profusion along the road side.

I stopped to light my pipe, and while I was teasing the tobacco between my hands, a gentle breeze wafted the sound of music to my ears. I looked around, startled at such sounds in the middle of the day. 'It couldn't possibly be the fairies', I said to myself, as I tried to peer in over the ditch to see if there was a fairy fort in there. Satisfied there was nothing there, I lit my pipe and, after prodding it into easy operation, I set out in the direction from which the music was coming. I came to one of the lodges on the farm and peered in through the bars of the gate. Sure enough, there in the distance I could hear the orchestra playing and all the young people dancing and frolicking on the lawn.

I stayed a moment to look at the neatly thatched Lodge. I remember long ago Uncle Martin telling me that Michael McGovern, the Thatcher, lived there while in Ralph Alexander's employment. I reminisced in me own mind as I stood there looking at the Lodge, all that Martin had related to me, all those events years ago.

I remember Martin told me that Lady Boscawn was evicted from this Estate during the Cromwellian settlement in the 1600s. They were banished to Connaught because they were gypsies, but Lady Boscawn and her family and friends did not go, they hid out in the hills in Heather Glen in Avoca. She was elected Chief Sorcerer of the group and was a woman to be feared by all accounts.

At this time she set in motion a plan to take back the Estate. She found a broach in the fairy fort at Avoca and this was her trump card to achieve her goal.

Smiley and the ten other children of his family were all aunts and uncles of Violet. Black Hazel was Violet's great grandmother (through one of Smiley's sisters). Now Black Hazel was also a Sorcerer and was the last one to predict the fate of this Estate. She did this in her caravan in the village, down there just before she was banished from this Bailiwick by the Alexanders. This curse and prediction by Hazel in her caravan is what Martin heard when a small lad, peeking a look through her caravan door before she left.

So the broach passed down throughout the generations until it came to Smiley, grandson of Black Hazel. One night he had this dream and in his reverie he could see Lady Boscawn urging him to put her plan into effect, the time was now right. And sure enough everything she predicted has come true.

I pondered over these things in my own mind as I sauntered along the road to the village. 'I'll stop at the main gates,' I said to myself, 'I'll get a better view from there.'

When I approached the gates, I couldn't believe my eyes. There, lined up along the road outside the gates, were about fifty horse-drawn caravans. All the cabal of gypsies were huddled outside the gate looking in on the lawn.

'Well," says I to myself, 'what a day to be parked outside the Rathmullen Estate gate, especially when there's a wedding on ... or else what could be the meaning of this?'

My curiosity got the better of me, so I approached one of the gypsy women who was steadfast gazing up at the dancing and frolicking on the lawn.

"We're coming here to live," says she, "the secret is hidden in the broach Violet is wearing. She got it as a present from Smiley McGovern, her uncle, who in turn got it from Lady Boscawn of Heather Glen in Avoca, as it was passed on down through the years.. The contents is to be revealed any minute now. "

I could see a great air of expectancy in her demeanour. Then a loud holler was heard from the lawn to the gatekeeper to open the gate and let the wagons through.

I watched in awe as the caravans, one after the other, went in through the gates and up the avenue to take up residence near the lawn.

It was only then that I understood what Uncle Martin had told me all those years ago, that nobody should ever dismiss the wrath of Black Hazel. Her Curse was worse than the Plague.

THE SKULL

Owney McWilliams and Henry Coe were assigned to open the tomb for the burial of Major Philbin Alexander of Rathmullen Estate. His untimely death, by misadventure, occurred some days earlier as he was returning from Dublin.

The two men weren't prepared for the shock that was in store for them, and neither were the card players that had assembled at Widow Casey's house that same night. They were there to raise funds to send young Jimmy Barner to Lourdes. It was at this time that Tom - the Gomb as he was known, as he was a bit simple minded - threw his bombshell.

This tragic episode began one October night in 1910. The Major was returning from Dublin where he had been transacting important banking business on behalf of the Estate, as was his wont every month.

The morning of his departure was crisp and dry, an alpenglow sun was rising over Sugarloaf Mountain. There was a slight hoarfrost which was melting fast from the faint heat of the rising sun, but under the trees the unmelted frost still lingered.

Fine day for travelling, he assured himself. He had set off early as to be back before dark, in order to have a quiet, relaxing evening beside the open fire in the drawing room with his ladyfriend, Lady Jane Alcock.

Lady Jane had arrived only the evening before from

England for the occasion. On the morrow the opening meeting of the Beagle Season would take place, followed by the Hunt Ball that night in the specially erected marquee on the lawn. It would be there that he would officially announce his engagement to Miss Alcock.

He was in great spirits as his two bay hunters trot-jogged down the beech lined avenue, their brasses tingling softly and winking brilliantly in the morning sunlight. Midway down the avenue there was a large, late flowering shrub of broom, like a fanning mountain of pale yellow flowers leaning over the avenue and carpeting the ground under the horse's hooves with fallen petals. The birds that seemed to be rejoicing in the tree bough overhead as he passed gave no portend that his happiness would be short-lived.

He arrived in Harcourt Street after three solid hours driving that took him through Bray, Kingstown and Donnybrook. He stabled his horses in Lacy's yard where they were housed, watered and fed and looked after by Tom McNabb, Lacy's employee until the Major returned.

He walked the half-mile to the Shannon Hotel on St. Stephens Green where he was to have a working lunch with Peter Green, the manager of the Midlands Bank. His lunch meeting was a very relaxed and cordial one and time slipped by easily.

He hadn't anticipated the long delay, but wasn't unduly worried about setting out for home in the dark. It often happened in all kinds of weather. He always put his faith in his two bays who were surefooted in all weather conditions. When he came out of the hotel and parted company with his friend, daylight was rapidly fading, but the rising moon temporarily arrested the descent of darkness. He looked up at the sky and there, to the west, he could see dirty storm clouds gathering

Swinging into Harcourt Street from the Green, a gust

of wind vicious in its intensity almost took his breath away. He had to lower his head and swing around to catch his breath. A cold shudder ran up and down his spine. He felt the chill after being in the warmth of the hotel. He shook his shoulders against the cold as he set off up Harcourt Street at a lively clip.

'I was often out in colder evenings than this,' he says to himself. 'The whiskey inside will insulate me against any adverse weather conditions.' And he had a couple of Baby Powers in his pocket as a back up.

All the way up Harcourt Street the wind blew firmly in the naked trees and seemed to be getting stronger. By the time he reached the yard he could see more dirty clouds bubbling up over Dublin Bay. He stood momentarily to study them. They were heading northwards up the coast. 'I'm sure I'll miss the worst of the storm.' He was confident of that. Well, he always was a pretty good judge of the weather.

When the attendant harnessed the horses and took them out from their stalls to put them under the cart, they showed great signs of agitation. They began snorting and prancing. They'd dart forward, then backwards on their hind legs as if they were about to rear up. But Tommy, the experienced horseman that he was, calmed them down with his kind talk, "Whoo, boy … that's me, boy," says he as he patted them on the neck.

Not in all his years attending the Major's horses did he see them so agitated. Little did he know that in some strange way they were trying to warn him of impending calamity, but the Major didn't seem to be too perturbed by their antics. He put it down to the wind and the rattling iron on the buildings around the yard.

"They'll be alright once they get out onto the main road. Just you wait and see."

'Who am I to argue,' says Tommy to himself. He was

only the stable hand, but he still begged the Major to postpone his journey til morning and let the storm pass but he wouldn't listen.

"Tommy," says he, "I thank you for your concern. I appreciate it, but as you know, tomorrow is a special day for the Rathmullen Estate. It's the first Beagle Meeting of the season, and followed by the Hunt Ball that night. It's imperative that I be present."

Reluctantly Tommy opened the double doors onto the street to allow the Major to exit. As soon as he did, an impetuous flurry of the entering gust almost lifted him off his feet. He had to hold on to the door for support.

"Don't go," he again pleaded when he had regained his footing, "It's not worth it."

"Hold their heads," said the Major with determination as he caught hold of the reins. Then, putting his foot on the iron step attached to the side of the cart, he tossed the reins over the vertical board that blanks off the horses' rumps from the body of the cart. He sprang into the well of the cart. Tommy held steadfast to the horses until the Major tied his scarf tightly around his neck, flattened the two ends across his chest and buttoned the coat tightly over it.

He settled himself in the seat under the hood, his two feet against the front board to gain purchase so as he could control his horses. "Now," says the Major, "stand back and let me out."

The Major kept a tight rein on his animals as they pranced out through the door on to the empty street, guiding them on to the Donnybrook Road. It began pelting down in real earnest. The gale force wind drove the rain at such an angle against his face that the top of the hood did little good in sheltering him from the sleety rain. He gave the horses a light flick of the reins just to show that he was in control.

By the time he reached Jones' Pass outside Bray the wind had blown up to a banshee wailing. The Vartry River had overflowed its banks and was thundering down the gorge to the right of the Pass. It became a reckless torrent. He always preferred to go this route from Dublin during a storm rather than to go through Bray where slates could be ripped off houses and land on his horses. That would set them mad, but now he wasn't so sure. When he entered the dense wood the wind was making the trees whip their branches into a frenzy. Sheets of lightning tore the black sky open. The horses reared up in fright. Then all of a sudden, a gigantic gust of wind blew the horse and cart off the road and down the ravine, killing both horses and man.

The Major lay in state for three days to allow people time to pay their last respects to their good and kindly employer. It also afforded them the time to make all the necessary funeral arrangements. Alphie Smyth, the graveyard attendant and also a close friend of the Alexander family for generations passed, was assigned to supervise the digging of the grave and the lining of the sides and floor with moss as was the customary practice at the time for all nobility burials. He pointed out the Alexander tomb to Owney and Henry and the exact place therein the Major wished to be buried.

The old graveyard was at the end of a narrow byroad off the main road, in the townsland of Mullinaskes. It nestled at the lee side of a small grove of sycca spruce with the edifice of St. Mogue lying in gentle decay in the background. It was the first time in over fifty years that a burial had taken place in this old and overgrown cemetery. Only the families that had claimed their graves before its official closing after the Famine were allowed to be buried here.

All day the old gravediggers slaved at preparing a

pathway through the gorse and shrubbery to the tomb. This was to allow access for the pallbearers and bereaving family members and friends and those who wished to be present at the graveside for the internment.

It was late evening when Alphie returned to inspect the grave. It was dark save for the light from the full moon. He was disappointed at the little progress made by the gravediggers and the funeral was on the next day. They assured him that everything would be ready in good time.

"We have often dug graves by moonlight before," they said.

Happy with the assurance, Alphie turned to walk away. It was then that Owney told him about the three skulls they had dug up.

Well Alphie was flabbergasted. He sucked in a huge mouthful of air and gave a great sigh. A shiver ran up and down his spine at the thought. He blessed himself and said a short prayer as if to ward off some evil spirit.

"It's fifty years since anyone was buried in that grave. How come there's three skulls there now, bates me," says Henry, examining the skulls. "They don't seem to have the bone structure of the Alexanders."

"What will we do with them?" enquired Henry.

After due consideration, Alphie advised them to leave them to one side on the mound of clay til morning.

The card game was in full swing when Alphie arrived at the Widow Casey's house, situated on the main road beside the byroad that led down to the old graveyard where the gravediggers were working.

He was in a pensive mood when he entered the kitchen. Although an avid card player, he ignored the game in progress and made his way for the fireside where he sat with his head held low, staring into the embers of the turf fire. The card players didn't mind him. They put it down to having lost a bosom friend, but the Widow, a sensitive woman, could easily see that something was wrong.

"What's the matter, Alphie?" says she as she went over and put her hand on his shoulder to comfort him, "you look as if you've see a ghost."

Alphie sat up straight on his sugan chair and stared her in the eye for an embarrassingly long time before he spoke.

"The gravediggers," says he, "have unearthed three skulls from the grave. Nobody to my knowledge has been buried in that tomb in over fifty years, only the old Major that I can remember." He then turned back to the open fire and cupped his face in his hands to solace his grieving heart.

A great hush descended on the card players. Everyone sat bolt upright at this extraordinary revelation. They waited for Alphie to elaborate but he refused to be drawn any further, not even by the Widow's prompting.

"Maybe," says Sammy Eager, "he grew three heads!" giving a great guffaw and cackling with laughter at his own wit.

Sammy was the owner of the local emporium. He was enthusiastic to the point of impetuousness and a bit of a big mouth. The scamp never got on with his widowed mother so off with him to England after his father died and him only eighteen. There was nobody left behind to help the mother. He never wrote or even made contact with her in all this time away. But when the mother died suddenly, the bold Sammy hurried home post haste to take over the emporium. He was now sole owner of Eager's Establishment, but his demeanour had never changed.

From his vantage point at the head of the table Sammy leered at Alphie in the inglenook. His strong voice boomed out as was his wont when he wanted to attract attention, for his imperious manner was a facet of his quirky sense of humour.

"You should have brought one over while you were coming," says he, "and let us identify it for you."

Alphie turned sharply on his chair to face this 'upstart' as he called him. He stared for some little time before spoke.

"It is irreverent to interfere with the bones of the dead!" he uttered sharply, "no matter what creed they might be."

But the bold Sammy wouldn't let go.

"Tom the Gomb will go over and get one," says he, "that's if he's not afraid."

Tom Caulfield was known locally as Tom the Gomb. He was a bit mentally and physically slow, but given his head and a little time, Tom was more than capable of holding his own even against more astute operators. He had left school early in order to earn money to help the mother with the housekeeping after his father died. He could be seen early and late, winter or summer delivering errands, especially for old people who couldn't venture out themselves. Over a short period of time, Tom had built up a nice little delivery business on his own initiative.

'If only I could get myself a proper delivery bike,' he thought to himself, 'I would be a real delivery man and I could earn some real money.'

He began to dream in his own mind, him cycling up to a customer's door, ringing his bike bell to alert the householder of his presence. When the occupier would open the door, Tom would raise his cap in salutation, and in his best cultured voice he'd announce, 'Tom Caulfield at your service, ma'am.'

But his dream was short lived. How was he going to raise the Six Pounds necessary to buy a proper bike like the one that was on display in Harrington's window.

Day after day he religiously stopped to admire his

dream bike on display in the window; its sturdy black frame, its silvery hubs and spokes, its lovely bell on the handlebars. He imagined himself outside Mrs. Moor's house, where he was about to go now, ringing the bell to summon her to the door for her groceries. He examined the plaque hanging from the crossbar. He closed his eyes and imagined he could see his own name in large block letters on the plaque – *Thomas Caulfield, Delivery Service*. He felt so proud of himself at that moment. But the price tag hanging from the handlebars disheartened him. He gave a dispirited sigh. He was shook back to the present by the clanging sound of the cathedral bell ringing in the midday hour.

'I must hurry or Mrs. Moor will be out looking for me.'

He picked up his basket and was about to move off when his eyes caught another plaque hanging from the saddle. It was eddying about in the light breeze. He rubbed his breath off the window pane to get a better view. Yes, he could see it plainly now. He couldn't believe his eyes;

Two Pounds Deposit and Two Shillings a Week for Two Years.

He was so elated that he dropped the basket of groceries on the footpath and dashed home to tell the mother the exciting news.

He stormed into the kitchen, both breathless and speechless. The excitement had left him gasping for air. The mother jumped up from her sewing in a great pucker.

"What's the matter, Son?" says she, "what's all the rush for?"

Tommy's speech came in spasms.

"Mammy, Mammy, did you see that bike for sale in Harrington's window for Six Pounds?" says he, breathless. "Well, it's only Two Pounds now."

"Don't be silly," she cautioned, "that couldn't be. Why would Mr. Harrington reduce the price by Four Pounds? There must be a mistake."

"No, Mammy," says he getting agitated at the mother's refusal to believe. "It's Two Pounds deposit and Two Shillings a week for two years." He looked at the mother excitedly. "I can easily earn that Shilling a week extra to pay for it."

He had already worked out in his own mind what he intended doing. He was going into business on his own, delivering goods at a nominal fee per basket around the village and beyond if requested.

She looked at him with a heavy heart. "Where are you going to get Two Pounds deposit?" says she, "and you only earning Two Shillings and Six Pence a week, and I a little more."

Tommy strolled out of the house, his head held low. He clenched his fists. 'Some day and soon I will have that deposit. I have almost a Pound already. Maybe Mr. Harrington would extend the payments for another year if I ask him. That's what I'll do,' he murmured to himself as he skipped in and out through the crowd of shoppers up the street to collect his basket and be on his way.

He was pondering over all these things in his own mind as he sat at the Widow Casey's fire opposite Alphie. He sat erect on his sugan chair to get a better view of the card playing. He was overwhelmed by the large amount of money being placed on just one hand of poker.

'If only I could play,' he mused to himself, 'I could have that deposit before going home tonight.'

He was shook out of his reverie by a familiar voice he knew and loathed ever since his schooldays because it was forever mocking and jeering at him. It was now challenging him to what he had anticipated. He was prepared to meet the challenge with the stoicism of a Red

Indian. He needed that deposit badly for his delivery bike and he wasn't going to let this opportunity slip even if the trip to the graveyard was highly dangerous and hazardous.

He wasn't a vindictive lad, but he had put up with more than his fair share of ridicule and derision from this emporium upstart. He had a score to settle with him and now the opportunity had presented itself. He was going to show Mr. Samuel Eager and all and sundry that Tom was no lummox. He sat bolt upright on his chair and leered at Sammy who was grinning at his own facetious remark as he dealt the cards for the next game.

"I'll go near no graveyard," says Tommy in that determined voice of his. The cronies, or at least that was what Sammy thought they were, egged on their man at the table.

"You're afraid," says Sammy in that imperious voice of his.

"I'm not," retorted the Gomb, eyeballing him from the ingle side. "Go yourself," says he, "that's if you're not afraid!" he scalded.

"Me, afraid?" Sammy commented sardonically to the receptive committee, giving a great guffaw, all the while searching the faces of the other players at the table for support. But there was none coming, only a cacophony of sniggering at the way this so called cretin had embarrassed him.

At this point the Widow interjected to calm down the situation. "Take no notice of them, Tommy," says she, "they are only joking." There was another wave of mule laughter and sniggering from the table.

Sammy knew he was being isolated in favour of the Gomb. If he was to save face he'd have to claw back the ascendancy obviously so important to him. He'd have to do something spectacular. So he jumped from his seat and flung Two Half Crowns on the table. "I'll bet you that," says he, "you won't go to the graveyard and bring back a skull."

The other players at the table were dumbfounded at the enormous bet Sammy had placed. "Well," they said to themselves, "he was the emporium owner and could do as he wished with his money."

But Sammy didn't carry his wealth very well. He regularly boasted about it, especially when the Gomb was listening. He'd rattle the silver in his pocket for all to hear and then he'd toss a bundle of Pound notes onto the table before the game started, for all to see. He owned vast stretches of land at the Kilmeath side of the village. It was said that he was wealthier than the Alexander's of Rathmullen Estate, but this did not enhance his popularity.

Some of the players were tempted to take up the challenge, but on reflection they shied away from such a hazardous venture. The thought of travelling down the long, lonely boreen to the graveyard gate, then traipsing around the graveyard in the dead of night in search of Alexander's tomb, and the banshee having been heard wailing only a couple of nights before in the derelict monastery close by. Hoping to locate a skull by the light of the moon and bring it back in their bare hands to the Widow Casey's house sent shivers up and down their spines.

Nobody, they thought, would be brave enough for such a venture, not the Gomb anyway, they thought.

Sammy smiled to himself at his cunningness. He had saved face and was now in command. The ball was firmly in the Gomb's court. Would he be brave enough to rise to the challenge? He doubted it. He had listened to his own father many's a time telling the story about Alphie Smyth's father seeing a pitchfork battle between the Major's father and the fighting McGreggors of Old Bawn the night the

Major's father was buried. Seems the Major's father had evicted the McGreggors from their homes and they died on the side of the road from starvation. They promised one day they would give him his just deserts. The women of the clan were screeching and wailing and calling down the Curse of Black Hazel, that one day there wouldn't be the name of Alexander in Rathmullen Estate.

Monks came out of their graves fully robed to intervene among the warring factions, pleading with them not to disturb the other poor souls that were resting in peace. Who was victorious that night nobody knows, for Alphie's father was found dead the next morning outside the graveyard with a rope mark around his neck.

Sammy relaxed in his chair, pipe in hand, a grin of satisfaction beaming all over his face as he leered at the Gomb from over the pale flame of the lighted match. He was sure his bet was safe. There was nobody in the house that night, especially not the Gomb, that would be brave enough to venture into that graveyard tonight.

But Sammy had badly underestimated the Gomb's determination and will to succeed. If going into the graveyard at the dead of night would secure the deposit for his bike, he was more than willing to rise to the challenge.

He jumped up from the fire and stood stiffly in the nave of the kitchen like a bantam cock, ready for fight.

He leered at Sammy severely. "Double it, then I'll go."

Sammy glanced at him askance. He was dumbfounded at the way the Gomb had manipulated him into covering his own bet, and him supposedly mentally and physically slow. Sammy cursed himself under his breath for opening his big mouth. He clenched and unclenched his fists several times at the thought, but he wasn't going to back down and be embarrassed by this simpleton, to be a laughing stock of the village. No, the Eagers never backed down from any betting challenge.

Tom cut across his thoughts, "Is it on or off?" he demanded to know.

Reluctantly Sammy nodded his head in abject agreement. Then to add further to Sammy's embarrassment the Gomb demanded that the money be held in trust for him by Mrs. Casey until his return.

Tommy left the house that night nonchalant as if he was off to a picnic. He made his way down the narrow byroad towards the graveyard. Rags of clouds had moved in from the east. The pale moon slipped in and out of these strands of clouds so that Tommy walked in darkness one minute and light the next.

The midnight bell rang in Kilquale, a mile away, as he entered the graveyard through the lych-gate, not knowing the whereabouts of the tomb. He had to negotiate his way through the thick gorse and shrubbery, tripping and falling every few yards over coping stones and glass wreaths.

Owney and Henry were taking a well earned rest from the digging when out of the rhododendrons appeared a wraith.

Owney nudged Henry. "Looks like we're having visitors," says he.

Whether it was from this world or the next he couldn't tell. They withdrew to the shade of the nearby yew tree to await developments. They clutched one another's arm in fear and apprehension. It helped solace their anxiety. 'One false move,' they thought to themselves, 'and we could be waylaid like poor Alphie's father the night he went to the graveyard.'

As they anxiously watched, the figure of a small man approached gingerly, almost reverently in the pale moonlight and circled the mound of clay until he came to a stop beside the three skulls. The wraith moved closer and picked up one in his bare hands and looked at it as if he was checking to make sure it was the right person he was taking.

Owney whispered to his friend, "What will Alphie say when we tell him that the old Major's father came back for his head last night and we were supposed to be in charge?" They were on the horns of a dilemma.

"Don't stir a minute," Henry whispered to Oweny, who was the braver of the two, "til I climb up this tree so as I can get a better view."

Standing on a tree bough, he leaned forward and peered through the rents in the branches. To the observant eye Henry looked more like an owl looking out than a person. His eyes firmly focused on the wraith, he could see him about to move away with one skull, sweat was pouring out of his forehead and running down his face with fear.

He was wondering at that minute if this wraith made his way over to where Owney was standing what would he do. He was a little safer up in the tree. To deter this wraith from desecrating the bones of the old Major it was imperative that he act quickly and decisively to prevent this sacrilegious act, even at the expense of losing his and Owney's life.

He drew a deep breath and in a slow, raucous voice he uttered, "Leave that there. That's mine."

The wraith turned slowly and without comment returned the skull to the clay. He picked up another one and was about to move off again when the voice spoke again, an octave louder, "Leave that there. That's mine."

The wraith turned slowly and without comment or at least none they could hear. He picked up the third skull with a little more determination and urgency.

When Henry, who was getting a little braver, boomed out, "Leave that there, that's mine." The wraith turned sharply and looked in the direction from where the voice was coming from.

"Surely to God," says the wraith, "you can't own them

all!" Then without further comment he put the skull under his coat and disappeared in the direction of the lych-gate.

As the hours passed and no sign of the Gomb returning, the card players agreed that he must have gone home. Sammy, sensing that his four Half Crowns were safe, became more vocal. He looked at the Widow seated at the fire.

"I think," says he, "you can return the money now. I knew he wouldn't have the courage to go near that place."

"I think," says the Widow, "you boys underestimate the courage and determination of that lad. He was always true to his word, and I have no reason to believe otherwise on this occasion either."

No sooner were the words out of her mouth when in walks the Gomb with a box under his arm and a broad smile on his face. He was none the worse for his exploits. He stepped forward and left the box gingerly, almost reverently, on the table in front of Sammy. Sammy's face flushed in the wan light as the other players demanded the box to be opened.

"It's your pleasure, Sammy. You sent for it."

Reluctantly Sammy lifted the box. 'There's nothing much in that,' he breathed the words to himself, convinced that this was so.

Sammy stood up from his chair and, with a great air of confidence, he seized the box in both hands. He leered at the Gomb standing with his back to the fire, looking at him.

To himself, 'If you think that you are going to make a fool out of me by putting a few stones in the box, pretending it to be a skull, you're mistaken.'

With that, he gave the box a quick turn of the wrists and dexterously flicked the contents out onto the table. The skull whirled around several times before it came to a sudden stop, resting its lower mandible in the centre of the table, grinning up at them.

A shocked silence pervaded the room. Instantly you could hear the loud clattering and clanging of chairs around the kitchen as the players rushed to get back from the offending object on the table. They gulped down large mouthfuls of angst, as they did so. Standing a safe distance away in a huddle, mouths open, they looked in awe at the skull as it sat on the table, grinning up at them.

An unholy silence came over the kitchen.

All eyes were glued on the object on the table. They were all watching it like a cat, watching its prey lest it should attempt to move.

Loe Hanberry was the first to break the silence, "Which of the Alexander's is that, Alphie?"

After a short silence, Alphie, without turning his head to look at Loe or the offending object on the table, spoke gravely and vehemently, "I don't know," says he curtly, "but one thing I do know is that the skull should not be here. It's unlucky. It's even sacrilegious to tamper with the remains of the dead."

When the uneasy banter had died away, an eerie feeling of apprehension pervaded the kitchen. Soon there was a muddy pallor on every visage. The card players refused to return to their card playing or even sit at the table until this sickly creature was removed from the house.

The Widow got up and stood in the nave of the kitchen. She looked sternly at everyone present, not just Alphie or the Gomb.

"Whoever," says she, "is responsible for bringing that creature into this house, remove it or I'll throw the lot of ye out, skull and all."

"Sammy is responsible." You could hear them chorus in unison in a low voice. Sammy leered around the kitchen at his so-called cronies, pale faced and rejected, but they all kept their heads low. He knew he was more isolated than ever before. There was nobody on his side. He had to act quickly and effectively lest the Widow throw him out into the exterior darkness, the skull flying after him. Then he would have no choice but to return the skull to the graveyard himself. He shuddered at the thought. He kept his composure lest he be sneered and laughed at. He could almost see the wry grin on their faces.

He looked at the Gomb rather somber.

He was hoping that Tom would relieve him of his predicaments if he asked him courteously. He says to himself, 'He'll never let me down. After all, I gave him some delivery work in the shop.'

"Tom," says he, "you can return that skull to the graveyard. Then Mrs. Casey will give you your money."

The Gomb looked at him wild eyed and severely. "I have no intention of returning that skull. Leave it back yourself," says he raising his voice an octave to emphasise the fact.

The emporium owner's heart missed a beat and jaw dropped. A nauseating feeling began churning his stomach at the thought of going to the graveyard in the dead of night, and maybe meet the same fate as Alphie's father did. He turned a pure pallor of marble at the thought.

The card players were taken aback at the Gomb's determination. It was out of character they thought for the young, jolly lad they encountered everyday walking the streets delivering goods in his basket, but they didn't know Tom's intentions and he wasn't going to enlighten them until he was good and ready.

The Widow knew that Tommy was a malleable chap with a little coaxing, but she also knew he had a stubborn streak in him too, and if he refused to go, all the entreaties in the world wouldn't shift him. The Widow stood up from the fire where she was having a quiet chat with Alphie and pointed to the skull on the table, at the same time eyeballing Sammy.

"I can assure you," says she, "someone is going to return that skull this night. That chappy is not going to stay here over night."

Suddenly the big hall door knocker went bap-ady, bap-bap that seemed to shake the house.

"Holy Mother of God!" exclaimed the Widow, putting her hand to her throat, "who can that be at this hour of the night?"

All the card players were present, so who could it be? She shook in her shoes in anger. All the card players looked from one to the other in a stony silence, then at the skull on the table. The silence that pervaded the house was broken only by the shuffling of feet on the floor. Nobody was prepared to answer the door. Was their worst fears about to be realised? They didn't know and nobody was willing to find out.

The brave men among them, who thought that Hades and his ilk were only a canard told to children to cause as much fear as possible to young minds not used to ghost stories, were having second thoughts.

A louder and more urgent knock reverberated in the now silent kitchen. The Widow took down the Sacred Heart lamp that was illuminating the picture of the Sacred Heart over the sideboard.

"Holy Mother of God, guard and protect us all this night," she said in a whisper. The hair on the back of her neck stood up in trepidation. She was stony faced and shaking like an aspen leaf.

She searched the faces of the assembled audience for some solace, but they all kept their heads held low lest she might ask one of them to answer the door. 'I'm sure,' says she to herself, 'if I asked Tommy to go he would willingly oblige, but I couldn't do that.'

The Widow blessed herself several times. Then taking the lamp in one hand she moved gingerly and with great trepidation towards the door. She stopped every few steps, her mind full of foreboding, the light shimmering in her shaking hand. If this poltergeist insists on demanding his skull and the culprit that was the real cause of removing it from the graveyard, she would have no qualms about naming Sammy as the offender.

She opened the door slowly and cautiously a sliver. She held her foot against the back of the door lest the ghoul should prance on her. A flurry of light from the Sacred Heart lamp rested on the man's face.

"Thank God," says she, breathing a sigh of relief at knowing it wasn't a ghoul or a shade. Satisfied that this was so, she opened the door fully and stood stiffly in the opening. A well-dressed man stood in the full glow of the Sacred Heart light.

"Good night, Mrs. Casey, ma'am," says he, raising his hat as he did so. "I'm John Ellis, the farm manager above at the Alexander place. Could I have a word with Mr. Smyth a minute, if you don't mind?"

When Alphie heard the voice, he froze in his seat, his face turned chalk white. He was hesitant about moving. He looked at the skull on the table, then at all the players present. His mind was in turmoil. Was it the missing skull he was in search of, or was it about the grave not been completed? He didn't know. If he insisted on coming in for a game of cards as he had often done before and finding his old friend's head sitting on the table grinning up at him, it would be unforgivable. He shuddered in his boots at the thought, and he above all people being party to such a sacrilegious act, he being the Major's most trusted friend. He had to act fast lest he be caught in this compromising position. He motioned to Sammy to get rid of the offending object before he left his seat.

A short time later, Alphie returned, a much more relaxed and happy man. "It was about the funeral arrangements for tomorrow he wanted to see me about," says he as he made his way to the seat at the inglenook.

Mrs. Casey was livid at the turn of events. She gnashed her teeth in the nave of the kitchen. Never did I see her so irritated. She was determined to have this skull removed from the house before another unwelcome guest should arrive.

She turned on Sammy with a vengeance. Her voice was loud and shrill.

"You started this unseemly affair," says she, "now you finish it and quick. I was worse to have allowed that thing in here in the first place."

She was eyeballing Sammy severely. You could see the anger simmering in her brain. Sammy looked around the house for some solace but none was forthcoming. He could really see he was being treated as a pariah. Never before in his life was he in such a dilemma. You could see he was too scared to even touch the skull, let alone go near the graveyard, lest some bad luck might befall him.

He looked at the Gomb pleadingly, "I'll give you another Shilling if you return it, Tommy." He was almost polite and courteous.

"I'm going home," says the Gomb, making his way slowly for the door. "Me mother will be worried about me being out so late." Tommy knew he was in the driving seat as it were, and he intended pressing home his advantage. Since he was soon to be a businessman he deserved respect, and the emporium owner was the first to be taught that lesson.

"If you double your first bet, I'll go," says he putting his hand on the latch of the door as if in the process of opening it. He gave the latch a click and pulled at the door as if he didn't care whether he went to the graveyard or not. In his own mind he was confident he was going to bleed the emporium owner good and proper.

"Is it on or off?" he challenged as he opened the door a sliver and looked out into the dull moonlight night, bidding everyone a very good night all the while looking back at Sammy.

"I can't afford that sort of money," he protested, "that's four weeks wages for a man."

"I don't care," says the Gomb, "take it or leave it." Again he bade all the household a very good night and was half way through the door when Sammy called him back. Humiliated, he reluctantly yielded to his demands.

Night had turned much colder as Tommy made his way down the winding byroad to the graveyard. Rags of clouds that were there earlier on had spread out to join hands. Dull hazy light made his negotiating much more difficult, but he had given his word and as an up and coming businessman he couldn't go back on it. The only thing he was thankful for, since he had no storm lantern, was the moon, although it was hidden behind a blanket of thin clouds. A rabbit in distress, having been attacked by a stoat, startled him out of his skin. He jumped with fright, the skull almost slipping out of his grasp.

Coming near the tomb he stopped suddenly. He was sure he could hear voices. It's probably only the frosty grass under his feet, he thought to himself. He edged his way cautiously and with a little trepidation.

'I should never have agreed to this journey,' he upbraided himself, but his self-reproach was assuaged somewhat by the fact that he now had the deposit for his bike.

Again he heard voices. This time he was sure they were coming from the open grave. He froze stiff. It was the first time in his life that such fear had gripped him, but he wasn't going to be deflected, come what may. He had given his word. 'Business men,' he thought proudly, 'don't renege on their promise,' and he had a reputation to uphold now.

He crept gingerly up to the graveside. He could discern the figures of two people in the hallow, padding the sides of the grave with moss. He watched and listened in the faint glow of the moon. The voices spoke again. This time he could hear them quite plainly.

"Be cripes," says one of the men, "if I don't get out of here soon I'll die with the cold."

Then as brave as you like the Gomb spoke, "I wouldn't wonder," says he, "haven't you kicked all the clay off yourselves."

Looking down at the two forms in the grave, he says, "If it's your head you're looking for, well there it is," dropping the skull into the grave beside them.

Then without further comment he turned on his heels and sallied out of the graveyard, sure in the knowledge that tomorrow Thomas Caulfield would be starting his own business.

The Good Samaritan

"Do you know what a Good Samaritan is?" says Martin to me one night as the two of us sat around the open fire in his modest home. He was mending a horse collar for Matt Carey of Cooladine as he spoke.

I looked at him blankly, not knowing how to spell it, let alone its meaning.

He looked at me without ridicule. "Well," says he, "I'll tell you." He took the pipe from his mouth and clucked a spit into the greesach at the side of the fire where it sizzled and died out.

"A good Samaritan or do-gooder," says he, "is a lad who thinks he has a moral duty incumbent on him towards the maintenance of law and order. He would even risk a good thrashing in order to keep the warring factions apart, especially if they were his friends. If he succeeds in quelling a rumpus or mayhem or what have you, he is despised by the on-lookers for depriving them of their normal expectations, like a bare-knuckle fight or brawl, for free-gratis and at no expense to any bystander who would wish to take delight in such a set-to. I can assure you," says he, "that, if he is foolish enough to intervene in such a full blown row he would be set upon by the antagonists for depriving the normal drive of rowdy men, men that were hell-bent on fighting til one or the other surrenders or drops dead."

"One such lad was Fred McMurry from the village

down here," says he, pointing over his shoulder with the stem of his pipe to the village of Kilquale.

I sat back and made myself comfortable in the warm glow of the turf, listening to Martin relate another interesting story in his own inimitable way.

"Many years ago," says he, "Fred and the Mother arrived from Arklow and took up residence in Bart Dooley's cottage there beside the blacksmith's forge in the village. Bart was the last of the family to pass away so the house remained vacant, that is until Fred and the mother took up residence there.

"Fred was a big brawny lad for his age. The way he used to lift and throw things around, the boy didn't realise his own strength. This was often demonstrated if an altercation took place in the schoolyard or the ball alley, and it was sure to happen among a crowd of young lads showing off their strength and ability to fight. Fred was a peace loving lad and averse to brawls. He would jump into the fray and separate the warring factions, sometimes at the expense of a black eye or bloody nose, which was often executed deliberately, but Fred would never retaliate.

"The Mother for some strange reason known only to herself, liked to be called 'Mrs. McMurry' by us young lads. She even threatened to tell our parents and the schoolmaster if we didn't respect her wishes. The older people knew that she had never been married, but this information wasn't for our innocent ears.

"Many's a time we hid behind the graveyard wall opposite her house and hollered, 'Mary, Mary, quite contrary.'

"It drove her to a frenzy. She would storm out of the house with a broom in her hand, screeching, shouting, 'You rapscallions of the Devil, I'll report yis to the Master in the morning.' "

I was puzzled beyond comprehension as to why a

woman should be called 'Mrs.' when she wasn't married. To lay this mystery to rest and to satisfy my curiosity, I probed Martin further as to Fred's existence in the world and the Mother not married.

Martin looked into the fire, drew on his pipe, then looked up the chimney shaft as if searching for the right words to satisfy my inquisitive mind. He then turned towards me, his face was stern but amiable.

"His Mother," says he, raising his cap, "committed an unforgivable sin by giving herself in love to a sailor on a ship in Arklow port without holy words being spoken over them by either priest, minister or parson."

I looked at him still more puzzled than ever.

"I'll put it plain," says he, "she had a baby out of wedlock, and since she lost her amour propre, she was treated as a pariah in the town and eventually was forced to leave the area."

Fred grew up to be a strong, muscular man but never aggressive. He tried hard to please in order to be one of the gang and not suffer the same fate as the Mother. Whether it was his size or his Mother's influence, Fred felt he had a duty towards the maintenance of law and order, while ignoring other people's right to savour a little uninterrupted fracas or tuggery or what have you. They promised that sooner rather than later Fred would receive his just deserts for his annoying, interfering behaviour, for interrupting men whose brimful of ire should be let loose and not stifled even if damage is inflicted and blood spilt.

"There is no better way," says Martin, "to drive a man wholesale mad than to block him from executing his vengeance. The consequences for his wife and loved ones could be disastrous, even life threatening. I knew of a man," says he, "who was so violent after being thwarted in his quest for revenge that he had to be tied to a gate pillar and left overnight to cool off, and another man had to be lowered into a barrel of ice cold water to unlock his fists."

"And of course," continued Martin, "there was this incident between Robert Joyce, Val's father and Pat Redgrave, Jim's father that began long before Val or Jim were born. It arose out of some half-forgotten incident that should have been buried in the past, but wasn't allowed to die by two stubborn old men who should have had more sense. So it grew and grew through the years into a bitter and fierce family feud.

Then, on a fateful day in July, Pat Redgrave determined to put an end to this damnable feuding once and for all. He stormed into Robert Joyce's turnip field with fire in his eyes. Fred was hired by Robert Joyce that day to thin turnips and was on his knees thinning beside Robert when Pat approached, ready to do battle.

One cutting remark and stinging reply and verbal abuse borrowed another and soon the antagonists were squared off against each other in the middle of the turnip field. Coats came off, sleeves turned up above the elbows, fists up in a sparring position. Each eyed the other as they jigged around the turnip drills preparatory to land the killer punch.

The loser, if still conscious, would make the ultimate sacrifice and apologise to his opponent for the years of hurt and character assassination and from henceforth an amicable relationship would ensue, between each other as well as between their respective families and assorted loved ones.

Being a man of peace Fred was loath to see his two friends, and both also his employers from time to time, hell-bent on killing one another. He sat back on his haunches in the turnip drills and pleaded with them not to carry out their threat.

Refusing to heed his advice, Fred had to leap up and step into the fray to separate the two antagonists from killing each other. He advised Jim to go home and not make a spectacle of himself. With the result, the row was never settled, the hatred and bickering continued, and Fred got the blame for prolonging the agony.

Val and Jim were always bosom friends, having grown up and went to school together. Seeing what the years of hatred and feuding had caused between their respective families, extended families, and friends over the years the two men were loath to carry on their fathers' feud. So they set about to teach Fred a lesson, one he'd never forget: to mind his own business and let grown men settle their own disputes in their own time and in their own way without interference from any do-gooder.

Every summer a great travelling show came to the village in Shinrone, about five miles away. Their tents were set up on the Miley Estate and a great evening's entertainment was had by all and for just a few pence.

When the Sunday evening's handball game was over a gang of us, Fred included, were going to set out for Shinrone on our bikes to attend the show.

As it so happened, on this particular Sunday evening Val Joyce and Jim Redgrave said they would join the party. Most of us knew they were hell-bent on giving Fred his just deserts. They were going to teach him a lesson, once and for all, to mind his own business and let it be a warning to others to do likewise, to let grown men settle their own affairs in their own way without interference from any damnable do-gooder.

"What's the use," says Val, "of grown men losing energy, getting worked up into a paroxysm of madness and then be deprived of a little bit of blood letting, all because of some do-gooder."

At Rathwood, on the way home from Shinrone, Val and Jim threw their bikes into the ditch and jumped back onto the road. They tossed their coats off and turned their sleeves up above the elbows. The two antagonists had their fists clenched, in a sparring position. The altercation had reached a crescendo, unholy expletives were being hurled at one another when the main pack arrived.

Cronies divided into separate camps and began cheering on their man,

"Give him a left hook," advised Jim's supporters.

"Give him an upper cut and finish him off, the ould bollocks," was the response from Val's corner.

The resonance of jeers and shouts trailed down the valley to the sister hill beyond, bringing a response from every dog in the countryside.

Fred was at the horns of a dilemma as to what to do. How could he take sides as they were both his friends and he worked for both their fathers from time to time and hoped to do so again soon. His instincts took precedence over other considerations and he jumped into the fray.

He caught each warring opponent by their shirt fronts to separate them. A great cheer went up for Fred.

Val, having waited a long time for this moment, didn't waste any time. He lunged forward, pretending to land a mighty sock on Jim's chin but instead connected with Fred's nose, sending a river of blood down his face and on to his white shirt.

Val, to himself, 'I'll teach you to mind your own business in future. If you hadn't intervened into my father and Jim's father's feud they would be bosom friends today.'

Out loud, Val says, "I'm sorry, Fred, I didn't mean it, it was intended for that other canat, so sorry."

"That's alright," said Fred, "I know you didn't mean it."

On the other side, Jim was in a frenzy struggling to free himself from Fred's vice-like grip. "Let me at him, Fred, and I'll kill the bollocks." Lunging forward, Jim landed an unmerciful sock onto Fred's chin. Fred staggered from the impact but still held on.

"I'm so sorry, Fred, it's that cur of a Joyce that was intended for, I'm very sorry."

"That's all right, that's all right," was Fred's only reply.

From both sides, heavy blows were landed on Fred's face. It was just pure physical strength and determination that kept him in the perpendicular as he struggled to keep the two warring factions apart. They pulled him, pushed him, wrestled with him, kicked him in the legs in an effort to break free. At least that's the impression Fred got as he held them in his vice-like grip, all the while advising them to leave it so and shake hands.

Fred was by now a sorry sight. He had two black eyes, a bloody nose, a cut lip and the white shirt his mother felt so proud of seeing him in was now as red as beetroot, and in tatters.

Val and Jim, satisfied that their mission was accomplished, called a truce and shook hands. A rousing applause went up for Fred that vibrated through the valley in the cool morning air.

Next morning Fred was sitting at the kitchen table when the Mother came in from the shop. He had his hands cupped around his swollen face, the blood-splattered shirt was still on, or what was left of it.

The Mother stood in the nave of the kitchen for a long minute, not able to believe her eyes, what she was witnessing.

"Hoooly Mother of God," says she, blessing herself several times. "You look as if you were trashed with a slashhook." The Mother became very distressed, sobbing tears trickled down her wrinkled face. "You're getting much too old for being a good Samaritan, you could get seriously hurt one day."

When she had regained her composure, she railed out at him.

"You promised me, son, that you'd never again get involved in other people's rows. They are sure to turn on you and vent their anger on you for thwarting their wreak on one another, will you ever learn?" she chided him.

This same conclusion came to Fred as he lay awake in agony and pain in his own bed that night.

'How come,' he thought to himself, 'that there were no marks on these two so called antagonists, no black eyes, no bloody noses.'

He peered up at the Mother through bloodshot eyes, feeling sorry for himself, but more than that it was the way he was tricked.

"There's one thing, Mother, I can assure you. From now on I will never act as the Good Samaritan, even if it was Henry the Eighth himself marching into combat against the Pope for not granting him a Catholic divorce, will I intervene."

The Jaycloth

As Jim Brolly was freewheeling down Knocknagran Hill to home on his Raleigh bike darkness was descending over Sugarloaf Mountain that cold October evening. Crows were returning in one's and two's to their rookery at Carrighill, a drove of starlings rushed by as if trying to get to the next county before dark. There was an icy nip in the air indicating that another frosty night was in store.

Jim didn't seem to notice the cold. He was acclimatized to it after all those years of outdoor life working for the Council. He was singing a song to his heart's content that was almost fitting for the occasion. Although he was no Bing Crosby he was crooning:

The longest mile is the last mile home when you've been away, the sweetest dream is the dream of home.

He was pre-occupied with his thoughts as he freewheeled down towards the house, thinking on the things he would do that weren't possible before, like putting a new roof on the turf shed, or putting the garden into better shape. The house was in need of painting inside and out, and he would decorate the spare room that now looked shabby against the newly refurbished sitting room. Oh yes, and Fr O'Brien could do with a handy man around the chapel and presbytery.

'Bridie always liked me to get involved in parish

work,' he remembered her saying. "Give a lead, others will follow," she would say.

'I felt proud,' says he to himself 'of the year I trained the parish school football team and celebrated the satisfaction of beating the county champions in the Final. Yes, my talents were recognized as a footballer and a trainer in my day ... but that was yesteryear.'

He was musing these things to himself when all of a sudden he was shook out of his reverie by a thunderous shriek that almost knocked him off his bike.

"Come back out of that," the voice screeched, "there's no need to do a lap of honour for the Council. They won't give you any medals for it."

It was only then that Jim realized he had passed his own gate!

"Oh my God," says he, half falling off the bike as he dismounted, "am I going senile already and am not an hour retired yet?"

He turned his bike on the road and returned to the gate a little embarrassed. There Bridie was excitedly waiting for him.

"Happy retirement, Love," says she, giving him a big hug.

She didn't realize until then that he was so tall, or was it that herself had grown smaller over the years. Whichever it was she wasn't going to be put off expressing her endearment in public or anywhere else for that matter. This was a special occasion and she was going to savour every minute of it.

Jim was a big, well-built man of over six feet tall with a mop of black curly hair going gray. His bushy eyebrows seemed to cover his eyes that were set deep in their boned sockets. He had a long, lean face and an equally long nose that ended in his nicotine stained walrus moustache. His peg teeth were prominent and discoloured from pipe smoke. To people who didn't know him, he looked a fierce brute one minute and everybody's favourite uncle the next. He was called 'the gentle giant'. For all that, Jim carried his own private hell that taunts him to this day.

Bridie linked him in along the driveway. He was embarrassed with his wife's show of affection in public, but there was nobody looking at them.

"Put your bike in the turf shed, Love," says she, "You won't be needing it so early in the mornings any more."

Jim had always kept his bicycle in the scullery at night for safekeeping. He arrived in the scullery to wash his hands and hang up his lunch bag. It had become a habit of his over the years.

He heard a great hum of merriment coming from the kitchen.

'Be gob,' says he to himself, 'what's going on in there? It's certainly not Bridie. She can't sing.'

"Come on," says Bridie, "I have someone here to see you." As he entered the kitchen Mary and Lizzie, his two daughters, ran to him and put their arms around his neck.

"Happy Retirement, Daddy!"

"Thanks, girls," says he, "this is a surprise. I wasn't expecting you lassies until Christmas."

"Oh Daddy," they said in unison. "We couldn't let this day pass without a celebration," added Lizzie.

"Isn't that very thoughtful of them, Mammy."

"It is indeed," says Bridie trying to look surprised.

They all sat down to a splendid meal specially prepared by the girls. "That was a gorgeous meal, girls," said Jim when he had finished. "You can thank your mother for the good training she gave yis."

Lizzie proposed a toast while Jim blew out the candle on the iced cake.

"To the best Father and Mother in the worldl. We thank you most sincerely for everything."

"Here, here," says Mary.

They retired to the new sitting room that was once Mary's bedroom. There was no need for it as a bedroom anymore since the girls long ago went to Dublin and Mary had got married.

Jim sat into his favourite armchair in front of the glowing turf fire, a glass of whiskey in his hand. The girls were seated either sides of him, the mother seated in the inglenook beside the coalscuttle.

"Must keep the home fire burning," she says glancing down at the full scuttle of turf.

Jim felt himself getting drowsy from the heat of the fire and the strong drink. He wasn't a drinking man as such, but he liked a drink on a special occasion. He listened to Mary and Lizzie in his half drowsy state, reminiscing about their youth and the mischief they used to get up to.

"Daddy would caution us very wickedly, 'I'll kill the two of yis before this day is out. Yis have me heart scalded', but he never raised a hand to us."

"Sure hadn't I to try something to keep the peace somehow? says Jim. "Still and all," says he, "yis were good girls, weren't they Mammy?"

"A, they were," says Bridie.

"Have another drink, Daddy," says Lizzie, filling up his glass.

"I won't get over this for the next week," says Jim.

"Sure haven't you all the time in the world now?" says Mary.

Jim relaxed, closed his eyes and slipped into a light sleep as the girls continued rehearsing all the funny incidents of their youth.

"Do you remember," says Mary in an excited voice, "one evening Mammy sent us to the shop after school for messages? She warned us not to leave the village until

Daddy came and collected us. 'It's too dangerous,' says she, 'for young girls to be out after dark on their own.' We protested but she wouldn't listen. She said if we were naughty the cloud shadows would run away with us which of course they never did.

"Daddy would arrive on his big Raleigh bike. The carbide lamplight was so bright that you could lamp rabbits with it. I remember one evening coming home and the carbide lamp went out. It was near Christmas I think. Daddy caught hold of my hand and insisted that I hold on tight to Lizzie's. I could feel his shivering pass through to me from him.

"I asked him, 'Are you afraid, Daddy?' I didn't think that he could be afraid, not Daddy anyway, for he was so big and strong, but we never got a real fright. 'Shut your mouth,' says he, 'someone might hear yeh.' When we came to Cragies Cross which was only a hundred yards from our house I thought it was safe to talk as we could see the light of our kitchen window. Mammy always put it there when Daddy was out after dark. 'Are you afraid now, Daddy?' says I. Daddy raised his voice and hollered a reprimand, 'If you don't shut your mouth, I'll run me fist down your neck.'"

They both burst out laughing.

Then, not to be outdone, Lizzie chimed in with great excitement.

"Do you remember one evening we were coming at Cragies Cross? Darkness was beginning to fall, but there was sufficient light for us to see. A full moon was shining through rags of clouds. One minute it gave plenty of light, the next it was semi-dark. In this dullness the moon silhouetted our outlines and cast shadows on the road as wispy clouds drifted by. To me it gave the image of cops and robbers in full flight. The tops of the bushes took on demonic shapes that left an eerie feeling in me, but we knew we were safe when Daddy was with us.

"Then suddenly Daddy went all silent. We couldn't make it out for we hadn't said or done anything to upset him. We could tell he was agitated and looked very worried. When we came to our gate outside there we asked Daddy if there was something wrong. But he never spoke until he got us and himself inside the gate and had closed it.

" 'I know,' says he, 'I shouldn't be telling yis this, but you'll have to be told someday soon.'

"We became very apprehensive and worried. 'What is it, Daddy, tell us?'

"Daddy took a deep laboured breath, hung his head and let the air out of his lungs like a man with all the world's troubles on his shoulders.

" 'Did yis see that old man with the long beard lying up against the ditch smoking his pipe as we passed Cragies Cross?'

"We girls nearly got weak with the laughing.

" 'It's no laughing matter,' says he, looking sternly, 'That road,' says he, 'is highly dangerous at night. There has been reports of strange sightings on that road lately.'

"Between the tears and the laughter Mary got to answer Daddy.

" 'That was only Mollo Gahan's goat lying up against the ditch chewing the cud. We pet her every day going and coming from school. She's a real pet.' "

The laughter woke Jim up.

"I suppose," says he, "yis are talking about me."

"Oh no," says Lizzie, "we are only having a giggle."

Mary offered her father another glass of whiskey which he took with alacrity.

"I'll leave the bottle on the little table beside you so you can top up whenever you feel like it."

After taking a few copious dollops of this alcoholic

beverage, Jim became very drowsy. He settled back into the comfort of the armchair and dozed off again. Bridie and the girls took the opportunity to tidy up the kitchen and indulge in their own girlish talk with the mother, while Jim was sleeping off the effects of the drink, or what Bridie maintained was 'dreaming it off'.

Jim stretched out his long legs to make himself more comfortable. He was going to savour every moment of his newfound freedom. After awhile his slumbering became erratic. Every thought, word and deed of the last fifty years seemed to come back to him and become magnified a thousand fold in his subconscious.

The images came to the surface. He let them come.

His mind slipped back to earlier times when he first met Bridie at a dance in Carlow, her lovely black hair tied back in a bun at the nape of her neck, her sparkling blue eyes, her friendly smile, and yes that lovely green dress that showed off her comely figure. He tried to capture the image of a young woman whose lighthearted garrulity had first attracted him. He knew she was the girl for him, and sure hasn't it turned out very well? Indeed, after thirty years of marriage and two fine, healthy girls, reared and out working.

Jim's mind was drawn to the tragedies that had befallen him over the years. Their consequences still haunt him.

He remembered the Slattery's Stile episode only too vividly. He cowered in his chair at the thought of it.

It happened one night in late November. He was coming home from visiting Tom and Nellie Corcoran of Kilcarr who were an elderly couple living on their own. Jim went to visit them almost every evening. He brought them their groceries and local gossip if any.

The entrance to the farm was at the top of Knocknagran Hill. To reach it you had to go down a long, steep, winding lane with high ditches on both sides that were laced with firs and hawthorn. The lane was a dirt road cut up with flood waters over the years. It would surely never be repaired for Tom and Nellie had no family or relations and the Land Commission would probably take it over when they died, and divide it up among the local farmers.

When visiting them Jim always took the short route. He crossed the road from his own house into Davie Doran's boreen opposite, through Davie's yard and into the field at the back of the house and over to the boundary ditch. There were two stiles, four steps up on to the crest of the ditch at Davie Doran's side, then down six steps into Corcoran's lane, then down the short distance to Tom and Nellie's house. It was only half a mile as the crow flies that way.

It was at this stile that many's a chilling story was told of sightings of strange objects of a spectral nature. Jim recalled one December evening Mrs. Corcoran was on an urgent errand to the parish priest. The evening was cold and very blustery. The sun was already low and yellowing over Carrig Hill. Black clouds trailed their shadows across Carrig Bog. She gave a furtive glance over to Sugarloaf Mountain. A full-blown storm was approaching she thought. There was no time to waste. She trudged on. She picked her steps over loose stones and muddy pools of water along the unkempt lane with the certainty of seventy years of living in the valley. When she climbed the stile and on to the crest of the ditch, to her horror, there it was, a spectre of a prodigious size peering out at her through the firs. It was grotesque looking. In panic to get away from this monster she forgot about the steps that led down to Doran's field. Instead she jumped down off the ditch, landing on rocks and spraining her ankle. She hobbled on to Doran's house as best she could, occasionally glancing over her shoulder for fear this monster was following her.

When she reached Doran's house, she was in great distress. She tried to keep her composure so as not to alarm the Doran family but when she entered the kitchen she collapsed on the floor.

Mrs. Doran put her hand to her throat and gave an almighty wail, "Oh my God," says she, "she's dead! What are we going to do at all, at all?" She screeched for Davie to go for the Doctor and get the priest, guick, hurry.

A great commotion took place in trying to revive her.

"She'll be all right in a minute," said Davie Doran calmly. "Lift her into the chair."

They were hoping the movement would knock her out of her torpor. When she came out of a trance, she was temporarily dazed and confused.

"Where am I," she kept saying, "Is he after me?"

"Have this cup of tea, Mrs. Corcoran," says Mrs. Doran, "then you can tell us all about it."

When Nellie was fully conscious and relaxed after the tea, she related her story. She cowered in the chair at the thought of it, tears running down her cheeks.

"You wouldn't believe it," says she, "it had a frenzied look about it. It reminded me of some terrible gargoyle. I'm not going over that stile ever again until that monster is apprehended," she swore.

The old woman was cringing with pain as Mrs. Doran bandaged her ankle. She then requested her husband Davie to take Nellie home.

" Don't delay," says she, "Tom will be anxious about her."

They were back on the boundary ditch. Nellie was holding steadfast on to Davie's arm for protection for fear the monster might jump out of the bushes at her. She pointed out the place to Davie where she saw the ghostly figure.

"Hold a minute," says Davie, "and I'll check."

He put his arm into a furze bush and pulled out a long piece of a smudged, torn garment.

"I think," says he, "this could be your ghost."

They examined the offending article only to discover it was Mrs. Doran's long johns that must have blown off the line earlier in the day with the storm. It finally came to rest in the furze bushes on top of the ditch.

Jim didn't believe in such a spectre. He laughed at other people getting all nervous when there was talk about such things.

One frosty winters night Jim was coming home from delivering messages to the Corcorans. The moon was shining through a blanket of thin clouds, and the long grass rose in footprints behind him. He felt happy in himself. He had a good and loving wife and two healthy daughters. The world had been kind to him, he thought. He was only too glad to be of assistance to his neighbour, especially Tom and Nellie Corcoran who weren't too robust these last few years. He felt like singing a little ditty but decided against it until he crossed over the boundary ditch.

Jim found great difficulty climbing the slippery steps and when he eventually got on to the crown of the ditch he stood up to balance himself. When he did, he lost his footing and tumbled backwards, in over the firs and into what was locally known as Slattery's Hell Hole, a most dangerous swamp beside the boundary ditch in big Matt Slattery's bog. Manys an animal was known to have got stuck in it while some says that other animals disappeared altogether.

Jim was waist deep in mire and choking on green scum before he realized what was happening to him. He struggled to hold on to the whins of grass everywhere around him.

He remembered shouting, "Pull me out! Pull me out!" as the icy waters were penetrating his bones.

It was a cry in the wilderness, he thought. Who would hear him anyway at that hour of the night and he not within half a mile from any house.

He started to pray. "Lord," says he, "if you never done anything for me before, I implore you to help me now if only for Bridie and the girls' sake."

He could see his obituary in the paper:

A man disappears without trace while out visiting a friend. Jim Brolly, being of sound mind and body, disappeared while returning from visiting his neighbour Tom and Nellie Corcoran of Kilcarr at approximately ten o'clock on the night of the thirteenth of November. No trace of him has come to light as yet. We are appealing to people to come forward in the strictest confidence with any information as to his whereabouts.

Jim was imploring the good Lord to save him, when out of the furze bushes scrambled a monk in his white robe and hood. He took off his cincture and flung one end to Jim.

"Catch that rope, my son," says the monk, "and I'll have you out in a jiffy."

Jim scrambled on to the bank, all slimy and soaking wet, but before he could get to thank the monk he had disappeared into the furze and up the double ditch and away. He didn't know what was more terrifying, seeing the monk or drowning. Jim took to the bed and all entreaties couldn't coax him out again after his ordeal.

It was only for Patsy Doran, Davie's son's quick thinking that helped to allay Jim's fears about the ghostly figure. But the big problem Patsy had was keeping a serious face when relating his story.

Patsy, a lovely, kindhearted lad just like his mother, was always willing to help a neighbour. This was unlike his brother Christy who was 'a proper scamp' as Fr O'Brien called him. He was always ready to laugh at other people's misfortune. "Your day will come my boy," the priest often admonished, "you'll get your comeuppance."

When Jim related the adventure from his bed he was in a very agitated state, both mentally and physically. Patsy tried to console him and give him the true story, or rather one that would at least convince Jim and calm and satisfy both him and his wife. Bridie had become very concerned about Jim's sanity and thought that if something wasn't done and soon to allay his fears, he could end up in the mad house.

"Do you remember," says Patsy, "me telling you that there was a Mission over in Rahanna parish?"

Jim and Bridie nodded knowingly.

"Well, the Missioner was staying with Fr O'Brien for the week. He was out making sick calls and lost his way."

"Well, that explains it," says Bridie, "your fears are now over. I knew there was a simple explanation."

The next morning there was a great commotion at Dorans. Christy had announced that he was going to England.

"You're what?" exclaimed his Father dumbfounded. "You can't go anywhere with a face like that, or what dog fight were you in last night? Don't you know there's a civil war on and if the authorities see you in that condition they could take you in for questioning and they might even shoot you. Put that nonsense out of your head and wait until the troubles are over."

But Christy knew he had to get away. How could he face Jim Brolly after what he had done?

Patsy joined Christy in the bedroom where he was

packing his suitcase. Christy went to the window, opened it and looked out onto the farmyard to where the fowl had gathered, anxiously awaiting their food, and the geese and goslings were wading their way to the stream at the bottom of the orchard. He stood for a few minutes, basking in the watery benevolence of the morning sun. There was a cloud formation trailing its shadow across Kilcarr Plain. Patsy addressed Christy who was still looking out the window.

"Did the ghost episode," says Patsy, "not turn out to your satisfaction last night?"

Christy turned and looked at Patsy for an embarrassing long time. He shook his head and with a cracked voice spoke slowly and deliberately.

"It's unlucky to frighten a man the way I did last night. He'll never forgive me if he knows it was me. So I'm going off to England for awhile until everything settles down."

You see, what really happened was that Christy had told Patsy that he was going to play a trick on Jim Brolly. He had seen him going to Corcorans earlier in the evening and knew the exact time he would be coming home and would be at the boundary stile. He figured he would pose as a monk to frighten him, just for a laugh.

Patsy advised him against such foolishness. He thought the repercussions could be detrimental, for everyone knew Jim Brolly was rather a nervous man in the dark. He often declared that he saw strange things. They were only moonlight shadows but he believed them to be real. However Christy wouldn't listen.

Patsy was so angry at Christy's weird idea of a joke that he decided he would teach Christy a lesson he would never forget. 'Then he'll know what it's like to be frightened,' he thought to himself.

After Christy left the house dressed up as a monk, Patsy himself also dressed up as a monk and went out to the boundary stile by a different route. He went up Knocknagran Hill from the house to Concorans' official entrance and down their lane, making as little noise as possible. When Patsy was a short distance from the stile, he pulled the robe – which was a white bedsheet -securely around him, and began to make noises of feet dragging on the frosty ground and a rasping cough, just like Jim Brolly.

When Christy heard the dragging footsteps coming up the stile and the rasping noise he was sure it was Jim. "Now is me chance," says Christy, as he stood up on the crest of the ditch, about to give his friend a rare surprise.

But instead of seeing Jim Brolly, he was confronted by another monk dressed in the same garb as himself. With fright, he lost his balance and his footing and tumbled backwards into the furze bushes and hawthorn that were at the edge of the ditch just over Slattery's Hell Hole. As well as getting enmeshed in the bushes and hawthorn, he also banged his head off a rock. He lay there in a torpor, half concussed for what seemed like an eternity, his hands and face badly scratched and torn.

When Patsy heard Christy thrashing around in the bushes, he quickly turned and fled the scene for home.

Christy was shook out of his swoon by the pleading of a man that said,

"Pull me out, pull me out. I'm drowning!"

Christy recognized the voice. "Oh my God," says he, "what's going on at all, at all, or where am I?"

With much grunting and exertion he finally extricated himself from the hawthorn and bushes, only to find himself standing beside the swamp. He could just about discern Jim Brolly's head and shoulders bobbing up and down in the swamp. His moans were pitiful. Christy was in one hell of a dilemma as to what to do.

'I can't let him know who I am,' thought he to himself, 'for there will be murder if they found out at home'.

And neither could he let his neighbour drown. He could be brought up for murder if it was discovered. He was in a real quandary as to the best approach to his predicament. As unholy as he was, he prayed to the good Lord for guidance.

Then a thought struck Christy. Why not act out the part of a monk, now that he had the cloak on? Jim would never suspect it was him.

He took off the rope from around his waist and flung one end over to Jim. "Take that end my son and I'll have you out in a jiffy".

Jim shuddered in his chair so much that he aroused the women in the kitchen.

"Have a peep in," says the mother, "and see is your father OK."

"I'll make some coffee," says Lizzie, "and we'll have it in the sitting room with Daddy and the special iced cake he likes."

In the meantime Jim had settled back into the chair. His mind was drawn to the years he had worked for the Council and the time he was appointed Foreman by the County Engineer, Mr. Partland.

He also remembered the instructions he was given for that day.

"In the morning," says Mr. Partland, "take four of your best men and go to Harrods Cross. The road has caved in." Then he whispered in his ear, "Now don't be late, Jim," says he, "it gives a bad example to see the Foreman late."

At dinner that evening Jim announced that he was made Foreman and that tomorrow morning he had to go to Harrods Cross because the road had caved in.

"Oh my God," says Bridie, "is that where they race the dogs in Dublin?"

""Oh no, no," says Jim, "it's near Gorey. It's about ten miles away."

He drew himself up to his full height and tapped the table with the heel of his knife.

"Pay attention a minute," says he. "I have to be up very early in the morning, much earlier than usual, about five thirty at least. Now girls, I want yous to finish up your lessons. We are all going to bed early tonight."

Sleep didn't come to Jim for hours. The pressure and apprehension of his new appointment was getting to him. He was most uneasy.

"If you don't relax," says Bridie, "we won't get any sleep tonight." Eventually they did slip into a deep though erratic sleep.

Next morning Jim woke with a start and immediately felt apprehensive that he had slept too late. He groped around in the dark with his hand on the bedside table to find the box of matches. Having found it, he extracted one hurriedly only to find it was a dead one. He extracted several more before he came on a good one. He cursed Bridie under his breath for putting those used matches back into the box instead of putting them in the fire. He put the lighted match up to the face of the clock to check it and true enough his worst fear was realized, it was six o'clock.

He panicked. "Bridie," he bellowed, "get up, the blasted clock didn't alarm, look at the time!"

With swift, impulsive movement Jim sprang from the bed and in the process the bed collapsed under them. The two landed on the floor, the broken bed enmeshed around them.

"Get up out of that, you crack pot of Hell," Bridie screeched, "or do you want to kill me, or have you no patience?"

Eventually Bridie extricated herself from the broken

bed and hobbled to the kitchen, cringing in pain where a board had struck her on the foot. With her personal skills as a cook in the Seven Seas Hotel in Carlow, she had Jim's breakfast ready in a jiffy.

"Sit down," says she, "and don't be fussing about. You make me nervous."

Jim was eating and talking at the same time. "Is my lunch ready, is the carbide lamp lit? Check the wheels of the bike and see if they are hard enough."

In his anxiety to have everything checked and right, he turned over his mug of tea on himself. It swam around the table making a terrible mess. He jumped up from the table, giving a few unholy expletives. "I'm scalded," he moaned.

"Leave it," says Bridie as he jerked away from the table. She raised her eyes to Heaven at him in vehemence. "You crack pot of the Devil," says she, "what's going to become of you at all, at all? Get yourself more tea while I mop up that mess."

Brigid went to the scullery and fetched a large jaycloth. With Jim's newfound status in life, the name went from dishcloth to the euphonious 'jaycloth'. She mopped up the mess hurriedly and, in the commotion of the moment, she flung the jaycloth from where she was in the kitchen into the scullery, not heeding as to where it landed. "I'll wash it out later," says she, "when there's a bit of peace in the house."

Jim hung his lunch bag across his back and fixed the carbide lamp on his bike so quick that he was out the gate before Bridie could say goodbye or wish him luck.

He had to climb Knocknagran Hill, that long hill up from the house before he would mount his bike. This morning it seemed to be longer than ever. Midway up the hill the carbide lamp went out. He put a few unholy expletives out as he struck a match, hoping the lamp would come to life. It failed to respond. An omen, he thought. 'Well, that's all I need,' he swore to himself.

The darkest morning of the year and the most important as far as Jim was concerned. He strode on, his mind in turmoil. He mounted his bike at the top of the hill and settled himself on the saddle. He began pressing fiercely on the peddles, and grinding his teeth in the process. There was no time to lose. He knew he was already late but with Jim's skill as a bicycle rider he knew he could just about make it in time. He was just getting into his stride, passing Corcoran's lane, when a strange hissing, purring sound took place at the general direction of the back wheel of his bike. He thought he could see with his eyecorner the face of a wizened old woman. Its appearance was grotesque. She seemed to be moving at the same pace as himself.

He cycled faster and faster as an unearthly fear gripped him. He thundered on down through Knocknagran and onto Shinrone. The faster he went the noisier this wraith became. He was convinced it must have four legs. He was certain that no human being could keep up with him. After all, he was a champion bicycle rider in his day. 'It will have to tire sometime,' he said to himself as he leaned hard on the pedals.

The four men that Jim had selected to undertake this important job at Harrods Cross were walking up Carrigduff Hill to the village of Carrigduff, pushing their bikes, when they heard someone coming in the distance.

"This could be Jim," says Pat Swale.

"We'll have company for the rest of the way," says Jack Ryan.

"But he has no light on his bike," says Tom Friel, "that's not like him," for they knew Jim was a very nervous man in the dark.

Instead of dismounting to join his friends as they

thought he would, Jim thundered on at an enormous speed.

"He's in a great hurry," says Joe Gogarty, joining in the conversation. "He doesn't intend losing his stripes," was their general remark.

Jim was puffing and blowing and rasping hard in his throat as he left the village behind him and was once again on the level road. He pressed on and so did this poltergeist. He would remind you of a cyclist in sight of the finishing line in the Tour de France and nothing was going to deflect him.

As he approached Ballindine Wood, about a mile from his destination, a great weakness came over him. His clothes were saturated with sweat and clinging to his body. There were beads of sweat standing out on his ruddy forehead and running down his face. He prayed with all his might that something would befall this spectre before he reached his destination. He knew that if he was to get any peace of mind this demon would have to be confronted. Darkness was beginning to give way to light. The eastern sky was beginning to outline the distant hills.

He pulled hard on the brakes and brought the bike to a sudden standstill in the centre of the road and jumped off it. He released his grip on the handlebars, abandoned it where it was and frantically leaped away about ten paces from it, hoping it wasn't after him. He gave a furtive glance in the direction of the bike. At the same time he was ready to make a run for it least this poltergeist attacked him.

"Well, that baits all," says he out loud, "there's nothing there that I can see."

He was surprised and in a way disappointed now that he had made up his mind to confront this demon. He returned to his bike lying in the middle of the road and stood it up. He wheeled it over to the ditch and leaned against it to examine it further.

Well, to his abject embarrassment, what should he find only the jaycloth!

Bridie, in the rush earlier that morning, thinking she had thrown it safely onto the scullery table, had instead landed it on the carrier of Jim's bike. There it sat snugly, one corner hanging over the side of the carrier of his bike, where it came into contact with the spokes of the bike, causing a continuous hissing, purring sound.

Jim was beside himself with rage when he discovered the offending article and not the polergeist he had convinced himself it to be. With one fell swoop he grabbed the dishcloth off the carrier of his bike, lest he become a laughing stock to his subordinates who were travelling behind him and would soon catch up on him.

With the cloth rolled up in his hand he stood with his arm outstretched behind his back, like a javelin player, to exert maximum delivery power. He tossed it over the ditch and into the wood, forever out of sight and gone.

In his reverie, thinking of this grand toss, Jim instead caught up the bottle of whiskey on the little side table and smashed it against the fire grate. The whiskey caught fire and in an instant the room was engulfed in flames.

On hearing the breaking glass, the women rushed into the room and, to their horror, flames and smoke came belching and bellowing into their faces. Bridie was aghast when she saw her newly decorated room going up in flames.

She let out an almighty screech that would wake the dead ... but not Jim. He slept on!

"Oh my God," says she, "the house will be burned down and that crackpot of the Devil fast asleep in the middle of it. Get up!" she bellowed, her wail was at a crescendo, "or do you want to be burned to a cinder?"

Jim leaped from his chair in a panic. He couldn't

believe his eyes when he saw the flames all around.

"Oh Bridie, the house is on fire," says he, half dazed.

"Oh great," says she, "you have noticed it at last. Get water and do something, you imbecile. This is not the first time this has happened, but I can assure it will be the last for tomorrow you are going straight down to Fr O'Brien and take the Pledge!"

The Square Box

The old man gave a great sigh of relief as he pottered lazily around the kitchen. His eighty years of hard work were taking its toll and it wasn't helped by the fact that his arthritis had left him more debilitated of late. The spryness and spring in his step were gone. He was glad of the peace and quiet that pervaded the house. He could do the myriad of chores in his own time without any perpetual nagging from his wife.

For many years now his wife Mary was blind save for a modicum of vision in one eye. Every morning Jim would help her dress and bring her down to the kitchen where she would sit in her high chair, giving orders. Her lack of vision was more than compensated for by her acute intuition and mental perception of all transactions undertaken inside the house and out. Even though Jim would do his utmost to hide many things from her, being sensitive as she was she could easily perceive his eagerness to avoid confrontation by pretending to forget.

From day one of their marriage, and many believe even long before that, Mary was boss and she also held the purse strings. Pragmatic, Jim was only too happy with this arrangement, as he often said he wasn't blessed with the same financial acumen as his wife. But as Swank Carbery, the local wag, concluded one night in the pub, Jim had little choice.

Often times he would withhold a Pound from the sale

of a batch of pigs or a few sheep, hoping Mary wouldn't detect it. For he was partial to a little alcoholic beverage, and the gregarious atmosphere of the public house was the only diversion he had. But he couldn't deceive his wife, no matter how hard he tried.

She could discern in an instant the difference between a Pound note and a tenner, between a tenner and a fiver, and as for the coins she could trace them with her thumbnail and be certain of the value from whether it was a bird, an animal or a fish on it. People that saw her flick through the paper money with such ease were flabbergasted at her astuteness.

When she'd discover a deception she would fly into a paroxysm of rage. She would bang her walking stick violently on the floor.

"I never thought," says she, "I'd see the day you'd stoop so low as to deceive a poor blind woman. You should be ashamed of yourself,"

She would berate him for days, then order him down to Confession lest he would die and his soul be dammed in Hell forever.

To himself Jim would breathe a silent whisper, 'Am I not in Hell as it is?'

Jim sat in the warm glow of the turf fire and lit his pipe. He stretched out his long legs and relaxed, luxuriating in the warmth and peace of the kitchen to snatch a well-earned rest after his morning chores. He drew reflectively on his pipe and directed the aromatic smoke up towards the ceiling. His eyes followed the thick cloud as it coiled up into the exposed joists.

'My Individual,' as he called her, 'is up there in bed.' He took the pipe from his mouth and sent a large spit careering into the hot greesach at the side of the fire where it sizzled and died out. 'If only she'd stay up there more often,' he said to himself, 'I'd get a little more peace.' He gave a martyred sigh.

He closed his eyes and imagined he could hear her voice booming down at him. When she'd start she was more like a regiment than a woman. You'd think everyone should fall into step behind her. He could repeat her every word and syllable, "clear the grate! light the fire!, cut the bread and make the tea and bring it up to me!, did you feed the pigs?, are the cows milked and the calves fed?, did you let out the hens and collect the eggs?". The litany went on and on.

"What time is it?" she demanded to know.

"It's eleven o'clock," came back the instant reply.

"Oh holy Mother of God," she ranted, "if I don't keep yelling nothing will be done in this house. Come up here immediately and help me dress and bring me down them stairs in case I break me neck."

'It might stop you from bladdering for awhile,' says he to himself.

Jim was shook back to the present by a loud knocking on the front door. He raised his six foot skeleton-thin frame laboriously from his seat, grunting with exertion as he did so and shuffled to the hall door. He made a dry cackling noise, the sound rising from deep within his throat.

Pat the Post thought he heard a laugh. 'That's most unusual,' says he to himself, 'what's he to laugh about?'

"Answer the door," the voice boomed from upstairs.

'If you're blind you are certainly not deaf,' was Jim's silent retort.

"Yes, yes," he croaked, "there's no rush."

"With you," she retorted, "there's never any rush. The house would want to be falling down on you first before yis would move." Jim ignored her bladdering as he called it.

"Good morning," came the cheery salute from the

Postman when the big oak hall door creaked open. "A letter and a parcel for your wife, sir. This parcel must be signed for by your wife. It's her name is on the parcel," says he archly.

Pat knew that Jim's mental agility was as slow as his physical energy and to spring a surprise like that would leave him tongue-tied, especially when he'd have to consult his wife when someone was present and waiting for a reply. These foibles Pat the Post exploited to the maximum for his own amusement and that of his cronies when at night he would regale them in the pub.

Jim was at a loss for words as he pranced around fitfully in the hallway, trying to think of his wife's name. No matter what he did it wouldn't come to him and Pat wasn't going to enlighten him even though her name was on the parcel.

Jim never addressed his wife other than as "My Individual". He looked at Pat blankly, the parcel and letter still in his hand.

"You'd better ask her to sign it," says Pat, anticipating an almighty furor would ensue and he was going to savour every minute of it.

Jim hobbled through the kitchen to the stairs, leaned his elbow on the newel post, cleared his bronchial throat and drew a deep laboured breath as if the effort to speak was going to be too much for him. After much cackling and stammering and ah-humming he finally hiccupped into gear.

"Is your name Mary?" says he, his voice slow and long drawn out.

"Haa!" says she, she couldn't believe her ears.

Jim raised his voice an octave. He wasn't a man to overstrain his vocal cords. "Is your name Mary? The Postman wants to know."

"Holy Mother of God," she screeched, "you've been

married to me for thirty years and more and you don't know me name yet! Of course it is, why does the Postman want to know that for?" says she curtly..

"He has a letter and a parcel for you," came the reply.

"God almighty," says she blessing herself several times. "What have you been up to at all, at all, or is there someone trying to play tricks on me behind me back?"

Pat watched Jim for his reaction but said nothing.

"Did you tell anyone in the pub it was our wedding anniversary? Knowing you, you could say anything when you have drink taken, the world and his mother knows that." Mary sat up in the bed as was her usual wont when she wanted to give her lungs greater expanse.

The furor was in full swing and Pat was enjoying every minute of it immensely. As he often said, it was better than any circus. But for all their haranguing and petty quarrelling, mostly on Mary's part, they were a most united and harmonious couple as ever lived.

Jim spluttered and coughed several times before he could crank up his vocal cords again. He leaned his elbow more heavily on the newel post for support.

"I forgot the anniversary, love," says he, the last word trailing away as if it was too much of embarrassment for him to say it.

"Forget!" she boomed, "Sure you forgot. Haven't you forgotten it for over thirty years?"

Jim listened to her outburst with silent impatience. He was getting irritated at her unwarranted attack on him in front of the Postman. He cut across her caterwauling, "You have to sign for this parcel."

"Don't you know well enough that I can't see to sign anything? Sign it yourself."

Pat the Post was sitting beside the open fire after lighting his pipe, there was no hurry on him, not this morning anyway. He was hoping that the parcel would be opened and its contents revealed before he'd leave.

Its arrival in the post office earlier that morning had created an enormous curiosity. Its every detail was scrutinized by Mags Lyons and her cronies, who had arrived there as soon as the postal delivery arrived, with the pretense of buying some item or other but their intentions were well known. On the morning in question the brazen hussies took the parcel to the door where they could get a better view, each in turn examining it up and down. They studied its size, approximate weight and most importantly the postmark. I could hear their chattering streets away. It was like a flock of starlings in late autumn in a field of stubbles.

"Austraaalia," they cooed in unison through pursed lips, "Austraaalia."

Mary was well aware of these craw-thumping newsmongers and their snide remarks, for she was often at the receiving end of their vile tongues. She also knew that Pat would skulk around the house until its contents were revealed if he was allowed, but Mary was determined that he wouldn't.

"Sign that slip," says she, "and don't be keeping the Postman waiting."

When the Postman had left Jim returned to the foot of the stairs, "Will I bring them yokes up?"

"Of course you'll bring them up," says she curtly. She was still vexed. with Jim for allowing the Postman to loiter around the kitchen looking for information. "You're hardly going to give them to the pigs," says she.

'Oh she's in her tantrums again this morning,' he breathed deeply and raised his eyes to heaven, pleading with the good Lord to grant him patience.

Jim climbed the stairs in slow, labourious steps, leaning heavily on the balustrade for support. His arthritis was much worse this morning but she wouldn't understand. He nodded to her bedroom door in front of him as he climbed. He wanted to sleep downstairs but she wouldn't hear of it.

He handed her the letter.

"Where's the parcel" she snapped at him.

"Oh, I forgot it," says Jim.

She gnashed her teeth at him in vehemence as he made for the door. Struggling back up again he put the parcel in her hand.

"That's not a parcel!" says she, "that's a square box."

She traced the outline of the box before she shook it vigorously, at the same time listening for any sign of movement inside. "I can hear nothing," says she. Then she hoisted it up and down in order to determine its weight. "I wonder what's in it," says she.

"Maybe it's a bomb," says Jim with a roguish smile on him.

"Holy Mother of God," says she, "so you want to frighten the living daylights out of me?" as she dropped the box on the floor, "and me nearly at death's door as it is."

"Will I open the box first?" says Jim.

"You certainly will not," says Mary. "Read that letter first while we are still alive."

Jim sat over by the window that looked out onto the front yard. The sun was high in an azure blue sky and streaming in through the curtained window. The house cock was standing on the midden singing his song of salutation to a beautiful morning. On hearing Jim's cough the dogs barked and rushed around the yard barking frantically as if to ward off some intruder in the process. This scattered hens and chickens that were picking food in the vicinity of the kitchen door of their thatched house where Jim fed them every morning. Ducks and geese were waddling their way to the pond at the end of the garden, the cat with her kittens was already settled down on the windowsill to dream the day away. The cattle and sheep grazed on the lush late summer grass on the hillside field beyond the yard.

Jim took a gulp of fresh clean air and relaxed in his chair. He took off his glasses and began to clean them with due ceremony, using the tail of his shirt as a handkerchief. Then, as if making a dramatic gesture with the fluttering cloth to dislodge any chaff from it, blew his nose with a loud report like a foghorn.

Mary jumped in the bed. "Oh my God," says she, "is that the box exploding?"

Jim coughed and ahummed: "To Mary Fox-Dooley, Coolbeg, County Wicklow. It's written in block capital letters." Jim knew from bitter experience that it was always better to relate every word and syllable, otherwise she would scald him for not giving her all the details.

"Where was it posted?" she inquired.

"How should I know?" says he.

"Look at the postmark," says she curtly.

"Australia."

"Australia?" She furrowed her brow, then whipped off her wool cap that sat on her head like a tea cosy, as if to give her more room to think. After some thoughtful moments she clicked her fingers: "It's me Uncle Mick," says she, "that's who it is for sure."

She suddenly became animated. "He went out foreign about fifty years ago. I remember well the day he left," says she. "Isn't it great news altogether, love?"

Jim glanced at her askance but stayed his thoughts for he knew only too well, but didn't want to get into an argument with his wife, especially at this time.

"He must be coming home for good," says she. "That's probably his life's savings he has sent on for us to keep safe until he arrives himself."

"I remember," she continues, "Pat McGuire of the

Red Dales did the same thing when he was coming home from America." She got physically excited at the great news. She swung her legs out of the bed, sat on the edge and patted her hair. She imagined him coming into the room and finding her still in bed and it almost midday.

"Oh Jim," says she, tenderly. "Wouldn't it be great to have him home here with us? He'll be great company for us."

"Humm," was Jim's only reply.

"He must be a very rich man by now," says she. "He was always so clever. I remember him telling us once that he worked for a big financial company in Dublin. Do you know," she rambled on, "those fellows were known as high fliers?"

'Well be gob,' says Jim to himself, 'he must have been, for he scampered off very quick when he robbed the bank in Ballinaglass. He mustn't have stopped til he landed in Australia and me only wish is that he stays there. That man is trouble!'

Jim turned and looked at her in the bed and smiled wryly. "Maybe," says he, "it's himself that's in the box."

"Don't be daft," she scolded. "How could they get a man his size into a small box like that?"

"Oh God, I feel faint," says she, sighing out loud. "Get me a glass of whiskey to steady me nerves. I'll say a decade of the Rosary while I'm drinking it."

She returned to the bed, leaned her back against the headboard, closed her eyes after taking a few dollops of the whiskey and fell into a reverie. She was no longer aware of Jim in the room. She was back, back more than fifty years to the days of her youth and the exciting future, full of promise that stretched out before her.

Telepathy seemed to pervade the room for Jim's mind also lapsed back to earlier times as he reminisced.

He remembered when he was a young man. It was a

mental picture that portrayed happiness and a carefree life. He would grow up to inherit his father's farm. He could have fathered a daughter or two as pretty as their mother and a son as robust as himself in his day. He would die a respected father and maybe a grandfather as well. That's how it should have been. But then he didn't meet the right girl and when he did it was too late. For all her petty chiding and haranguing he loved Mary dearly.

Jim and Mary Fox lived in a two-storied thatched house that nestled at the foot of the Coolbeg Mountain, a short distance from the main road that led to the village of Glenmore in County Wicklow. He farmed fifty acres of prime land and hill grazing rights left to him by his father. Being an only child he never wanted for anything. He was well off by local standards. He had five cows and their followers, and two sows and their young and some sheep on the mountain. He sowed corn and potatoes and killed a fat pig every autumn for winter meat. Mary churned and sold butter and eggs. She also carried on her dressmaking business until her eyesight failed her.

Jim was a big man about six foot tall. He had a heavy mop of brown hair, a strong muscular face, deep-set blue eyes under bushy eyebrows, a rufous walrus moustache, a full set of peg teeth that were discoloured from pipe smoke. He was the most placid and easygoing man in the parish. His admirable virtues and traits of character were the hallmark of a perfect gentleman and his talents as a musician brought untold enjoyment to a great many people. He possessed an amazing repertoire that spanned back to the turn of the century. He was very fond of company and a bit of craic. So it came as no surprise that he kept an open house for his card playing friends or anyone that wished to drop in for a chat and a little banter. When the card game passed midnight, which was a common occurrence, Mary would call for the rubber to be played. The rubber was known as the last game of the night. Jim would never dream of making such a gesture to his cronies. His retort to her would be, "Sure there's no hurry, tomorrow is another day."

"Yes," says Mary, "whenever we get up."

Mary herself was a beautiful girl in her day. Her natural blond hair cascaded down to her shoulders and, with her rosy complexion and comely figure, she was the envy of all the young girls in the village and beyond. She was forever in demand at parties and house dances where she would regale her audience with some of her fine displays of jigs and reels and would warm the cockles of your heart with some of her beautiful airs. Mary always cut a dash with the assurance that comes from being the daughter of a wealthy businessman, but for all that she was a very down to earth kind of girl with a happy disposition. Then, just a few years before the great turn of the century into 1900 ...

"I remember it," says she, "and I still in my teen years, not yet twenty. My whole life was shattered when the sergeant came to our house and informed us that my father had died suddenly at his place of work."

She could still remember him giving her a big hug and kiss before going out to work that morning. Being an only child there was a great outpouring of grief for her loving father. She gave a great sigh at the sadness and upheaval it caused at the time.

No sooner was that calamity over when they were landed into an even more serious catastrophe. Unbeknownst to them their father had plunged the business into irretrievable financial debt. The banks closed in on all his assets. They were not only forced to sell the business but also their home. After the disposal of all the property which was a huge embarrassment, especially to her mother, they went to Dublin where her mother got a job as charwoman in a hotel on St. Stephen's Green, and Mary trained as a seamstress. The mother, apart from her work, became a recluse. The shock from being the wife of the local squire to having to take on menial work in a hotel was so unbearable that she never returned to Glenmore again. Mary was very much attached to her father, which in later years seemed to draw her to older men for company. She even found it difficult to settle into the anonymity of a big city, so she made up her mind that one day she would return to Glenmore and set up her own business there for she had no real attachment to the city.

Mary was over thirty years old and in Dublin when her mother died. Now free to pursue her own goals she began to think of her options. Being away from her native village for so long, she had lost contact with everyone she had once known. Who would know her anyway after all those years? All the old people she once knew were mostly dead, and as for the young people, well, they had probably moved away to foreign lands in search of a new life.

Mary sat in the armchair in her two room apartment in Carrigmines, staring into the dying embers of the coal fire She furrowed her brow and pondered over these questions while her finger nails tapped on the leather covering of the chair. Then, as if by magic, it came to her. "Jim Fox" she uttered, and nodded her head as if she was conversing with another person although there was no one there.

She sprang from the armchair and pirouetted in the nave of the kitchen like when she was young. She stopped suddenly and checked herself for getting so animated. If his wife knew she was writing to him looking for favours and he a happily married man, she might not like it. There again, she consoled herself, it's worth a try. She thought, 'From what I can remember of him he was a most generous and obliging man. I don't think he'll refuse.'

She pointed her finger at the open fire, hoping it would verify the fact, but the only response she got was a burst of sparks emitting from the log of wood she had just put on which she took as a "yes".

Without further ado, she jumped up from her seat, gave a toss of her head and went to get the writing paper.

11 Carrigmines Heights, Dublin

Dear Mr. Fox,

My apologies for intruding on your privacy. Now that my mother is deceased, I feel that I have no further reason or interest to remain on and live here in Dublin. I am anxious to return to Glenmore and start a little business there as a seamstress. I would appreciate if you would kindly let me know if there is a small cottage for sale in the village that I could buy. I would also be most grateful if you would keep this matter between us for now. Wishing you and your wife a happy and holy Christmas. Looking forward to hearing from you.

Yours Respectfully,

Mary Dooley

When the envelope with a handwritten address to Mr. James Fox of Coolbeg arrived at the post office, it created an enormous interest and curiosity and speculation for the news-hungry gossipers of the village. At that time it was a rarity for anyone to receive a letter. Only parents whose families had emigrated to America or Australia could expect a letter and that was only at Christmas time.

(My dear readers: may I interject at this juncture to point out at that time the Postman was also the bearer of news throughout the district which he served for good or bad, births, marriages or deaths. News-hungry housewives would loiter around their grates and ambush Pat the Post as he passed, for the latest bit of news that surfaced that morning. Pat was as eager, if not more so, than any of them for fresh news. He felt it was a duty incumbent on him, as if it was part of his everyday work. He would stand in the centre of the road, his bike lying against his hip, from where he would pompously air his knowledge. It would pass from mouth to eager mouth and relish in the eye. It would certainly lose nothing in the telling.)

"Dan Conway's horse was found this morning in Slatteries Hellhole, that swamp you pass on your way down to Concorans of Kilcarr. He was as dead as a doornail when they found him."

"Ohooo," the women would say with their pursed lips, from behind cupped hands, at this latest bit of fodder.

"The wife was telling me last night that Nancy Sheridan, that waif up in Coolishal, is in the family way."

By the time these snippets of news had done their rounds and reached the pub that night they had magnified a hundredfold and, as already said, they would lose nothing in the telling.

Jim did not yield to Pat's search for news, certainly not this particular morning anyway. He just dumped the letter on the kitchen window saying to no body in particular, "I'll read it later, when I have all me chores done," and headed for the back door, leaving Pat in the nave of the kitchen with little option but to exit the house and be on his way.

Out in the haggard, beyond the barn, Jim attended to the myriad of chores he had to do before he went out to work in the fields, and he was late already.

The cows and calves needed their hay before he let them out, horses were whinnying for their oats, the pigs were kicking up an almighty racket once they heard Jim rattle the galvanized bucket, looking for their feed. But Jim's mind was distracted by the letter. He couldn't concentrate on the work in hand, so much so that he flung the bucket on the ground and headed for the house.

'Yis can wait awhile,' says he to himself, 'Yis won't die for one morning.'

He sat at the table and scrutinized the letter front and back.

'Beautiful hand writing,' he thought to himself, 'a lady's hand writing that's for sure. Who could possibly be writing to me?' he mused. 'I never got a letter from anyone in me life, only the rate demand and it came in a brown envelope.'

He held the letter delicately almost reverently in his hands as if it was too precious to open, but his curiosity outweighed its splendour. He extracted the letter from it's wrapper and gave a cursory glance at the beautiful hand writing all the way down the page until his eyes came to the signature.

"Mary Dooley," he repeated several times. His eyes were almost bulging out of his head, like a crushed rabbit in amazement.

"The Squire's daughter writing to me." Momentarily he was dumbstruck.

He closed his eyes and tried to get a mental picture of her as a young girl when she had lived in the village with her parents. He also remembered her as a young girl dancing all those jigs and reels at the house dances and parties. And a lovely singer she was too. He nodded his head at the old dog lying at his feet, as if to confirm that fact.

He would love to help this young girl. He still thought of her as such. But he was in a terrible dilemma. He wasn't a very literate man and his letter writing left a lot to be desired. Who to discuss this private and delicate matter with he didn't know. It had created a problem of monumental proportions for him. She asked that he not divulge the contents of the letter and he intended to respect her request. This was the dilemma.

To seek the Postman's advice was like putting it in the local paper. It would be all over the parish before night.

'There has to be another way,' he thought to himself, as he cupped his face in his hands, his elbows on the table to ponder what to do. He thought on, then out of the blue it came to him. He banged his fist on the table.

"Tom Quale of Kylebrack in Avoca! That's the man I'll contact! It almost slipped my mind."

Tom was known far and wide as Tom the Master, although he didn't follow his father's footsteps into the teaching profession. But to distinguish him from other families of the same surname, he was known as Tom the Master.

Tom had extensive knowledge of letter writing and advising people in matters of the heart. He was known throughout the whole seven parishes around Avoca.

One cold January evening Jim tackled his pony under his trap and set out for Avoca. His visit would have to be a short one as he must be back before night to feed the stock. He regretted now making that promise to Mary, but being a man of his word how could he back out now.

He arrived at Tom's house which was high on the windswept mountain that overlooked Avoca village. Snow was falling steadily and was being whipped along by a cold, bitter wind into small drifts. Jim had only to knock once when he heard Tom's voice, "Come in and welcome," was the instant reply. "You must be frozen or what made you stir out on such an atrocious evening?"

Jim entered the modest kitchen where Tom was crouched over the open fire with his overcoat on.

"God save you kindly and welcome," says Tom, at the same time beckoning Jim to take a seat opposite in the ingle.

He looked at Tom awhile before he spoke.

"You must be very cold," says Jim, "that you would wear your overcoat at the fire."

Tom gave a sneer of a laugh. "You wouldn't say that if you lived here for awhile. Look at the cut of me. I'm no better than a black man. The soot and smog has pervaded every nook and cranny in the house and every pore in me skin, it's outrageous, that's what it is."

Tom looked around the house to emphasize the fact. "The Council," says he, "built this house for me a few years ago. They forced me out of me old cottage up at Bracken Cross. They wanted to make a new road up to the new dump and my house was in the way. So here I am, looking out over half of county Wicklow through that monster of a chimney." He gazed up the chimney to emphasize the fact. "It'll draw more tears than smoke."

Jim and Tom exchanged many well-worn items of news before Jim could pick up the courage to approach the subject for which he came in the first place. It was as if protocol had to be observed. The two sat in the warm glow of the replenished turf fire, smoking their pipes as the wind howled in the chimney. Eventually Jim took the letter out of his pocket and passed it to his friend.

"You know, Tom, I'm not very good at that sort of thing. You'll have to write a letter for me."

Tom read the letter once and again.

"But sure," says Jim, "I'm not married."

"No, but she thinks you are. After all, she left the village almost twenty years ago and has lost touch with everyone. She says she wants to start a little business as a seamstress."

"What's that?" says Jim.

"That's a woman that makes and mends clothes."

"Oh, be dad," says Jim, "she would come in handy around here," as he looked down at his own shabby clothes.

Tom promised he would write the letter on Jim's behalf and give her all the details of a lovely cottage for sale at the edge of the village. Mrs. Toughy owned it and Jim would be only too glad to secure it for her if she so wished. "You know, Jim," said Tom, "she's like yourself, she's not married."

Tom peered over his horn-rim glasses at Jim for his reaction but Jim just kept on staring into the fire, not comprehending what Tom had said.

He tried again. "You know, Jim," says Tom innocently, "this could be the start of something big."

He shook the letter at Jim to get his attention. He looked at Tom rather concerned. For Jim, women and marriage was the last thing on his mind. He was resigned to the life of a bachelor and he was happy with his lot. He looked at this favour as just another kindly act, one that he would do for anyone in similar circumstances.

Jim tossed the last of the whiskey into his mouth, then, holding the glass between his two hands, his elbows on his knees, he stared into the whiskey glass as if searching for courage and inspiration to express his true feelings. He knew that his upbringing had left him a stranger to female artifice and the art of courtship. So it was no wonder he was apprehensive about expressing his true feelings in public, but he need not have worried for he was talking to a true and understanding friend.

"When I was a young lad," says Jim, "I was anxious enough to get married but I was too shy to ask a girl out, and now," says he pondering awhile, "now I am too old to be thinking of the like. Who would have me anyway."

"A man is never too old to get married," says Tom,

cutting across his thoughts. "You with a fine farm of land, nonsense me good man. I have a feeling that this could be the beginning of something exciting."

Jim glanced at him askance. "I can see nothing exciting about it. I wish now that I had just thrown that letter in the fire and forgot all about it."

Tom wrote the letter to Mary and at the end he added his own tidbit but didn't tell Jim. He wrote …

> *Looking forward to your presence in the village once more. You always were a breath of fresh air. Looking forward to hearing from you and do call when you come to the village.*

Over the coming weeks letters began arriving at the post office for Jim. The influx of mail set tongues wagging and heads nodding. They were all gaggling at once among themselves as they stood on the street corner which was a good position of vantage. A man that never got a letter in his life was now the recipient of an almost daily delivery. They all pursed their lips. "And it comes from a woman at that!"

It was in the kitchen of Mags Lyons' house that these superannuated shiulers and their cronies gathered every morning to chew on the latest bit of fodder, cups of tea in hand, their lips sucked in rosy because they had no teeth, their mandibles flapping like the hammers of Hell as they tried to out do each other with the latest stories

"He's taken to travelling down the country a lot lately," says Sall Neary. "Nobody seems to know where."

"Maybe he's courting," says May Phelan.

"Who would have him anyway?" interjected Nan Scott rather vinegary. "A confirmed bachelor out and out, that's what he is." Everyone knew that Nan's daughter had tried with all her womanly wiles to win Jim but all to no avail. So she left and went to America, her pride badly dented.

"I don't know," says Mags Lyons, "strange things have happened." She was now standing in the nave of the kitchen pompously airing her knowledge. She was pouring out three cups of tea as she did so. "Remember George Jones of Hillbrook," says she, "sure he went and married a young wan of twenty and him nearly sixty a the time."

They all nodded their heads knowingly. Not even Pat the Post, with his uncanny knack of finding out everyone else's business before they knew it themselves, was able to extract even a sliver of information from him. "He's getting very cute," says they, "in his ould age." Their voices were whinny and sardonic.

Then, to their surprise, one morning in March, on the cusp between spring and summer, the sort of morning that voices carried in the clear air, they heard, without portent or warning, a rickety old lorry packed with furniture come thundering into the village. It coughed and spluttered and backfired before coming to a stop outside Toughy's vacant cottage. Dogs barked frantically and ran to repel this inanimate monster in the process, scattering hens and chickens that were picking in the vicinity of Mrs. Healy's white-washed thatched cottage.

The village was unceremoniously shook out of its reverie by this alien intrusion into what was otherwise a lethargic place. Anyone who didn't run out onto the street to investigate was behind curtained windows, their bright piggy eyes searching on the proceedings. It would remind you of the valley of the squinting windows. Two burley fair-haired men got out of the lorry and began to unload its contents. Curtains twitched and necks craned and eyes narrowed as they focused steadfastly on the proceedings.

After awhile a smartly dressed woman alighted from the lorry and crossed the road to the priest's house. Almost immediately she returned and unlocked the cottage door.

'I wonder,' says they, 'had she bought the cottage? ... how did she know it was for sale? ... I wonder, will she be staying long?'

All these thoughts were going through their minds as they peered out through their latticed windows. Like all small communities these answers would be public knowledge before the day was out, and if not it wouldn't be Mags Lyons or Pat the Post's fault if it wasn't.

As soon as the furniture was unloaded the Postmistress left her shop and sauntered over to welcome the newcomer to the village.

She extended her hand to welcome Mary to Glenmore.

"I'm Mrs. Bates from the Post Office," says she. "If there is anything you want, anything at all don't hesitate, just come over and ask."

"Oh thanks," says Mary. "It's so nice to know I have still got some friends left here."

Mrs. Bates peered at her for a long minute, pretending not to know her, or at least that's the impression she tried to give.

"You don't know me, Mrs. Bates, I'm Mary Dooley."

Searching Mrs. Bates' face she said to herself, 'You must have changed since I was last here for it was a well known fact that you opened every letter that came into the Post Office, what has changed?'

Out loud she said, "You must know me, I'm Captain Dooley's daughter."

"Oh Mary," says she, looking ever so surprised, "You are a sight for sore eyes. It must be all of twenty years since I saw you last."

"It is indeed," says Mary.

"We didn't know it was you that bought the cottage."

Mary leered at her but stayed her tongue.

"I never liked Dublin," says she, "and since my Mother died some months ago I just had to get away from the place. So I thought, where better to live than in my own village. So here I am."

"How did you know the cottage was for sale?"

'Here we go,' thought Mary to herself, 'nothing has ever changed.'

"Mr. Fox," says she. "He was the only one I could think of. It's such a long time ago. I remember he used to play the accordion at the dances when I lived here, so with his help and the help of the parish priest, I secured this little gem."

She looked around the newly refurbished kitchen to emphasize the fact.

Mrs. Bates was now in full cry and she was going to take full advantage of it before Mags Lyons and her cronies put their construction on things.

"Are you going to retire or what?" says Mrs. Bates. She always liked to have her information straight from the fountainhead and not some half-baked version of events from those with an altogether different agenda.

"Oh goodness gracious no," says Mary with a deprecating little laugh. "I'm a seamstress. I'm going to open a little business here in the village making and mending clothes."

It was now Mary's turn to take advantage of the situation. "Maybe," says she, "you'd be kind enough to spread the word around." Mary knew quiet well that once Pat the Post got hold of the information it was better than putting it in the local paper. Every house would hear about it. "Maybe," continues Mary, "someone might avail of my services."

"I must dash now," says Mrs. Bates, "and let you unpack. You must be tired after the long journey, and once again a heartfelt welcome to Glenmore."

"Oh thank you," says Mary, "you are so kind," and not believing a word of it. "I must go up soon and thank Mr. Fox," says she, "for all his kindness and help."

"He will be delighted," says Mrs. Bates, giving her a furtive glance as she turned to leave.

"I hope so," says Mary archly.

Following several visits to Coolbeg and long friendly chats with Jim around the open fire, Mary began to daydream about Jim and his farm. She knew she could make a nice home for herself and Jim if given a chance. They were both financially independent so there was no problem in that field. The problem was Jim, so she set about snaring him in her own devious way.

She cooked some of her finest stews and some of her special homemade bread and cakes for him. Jim was overwhelmed by her culinary skills and her attention to detail when making the homemade bread and cakes for which he was forever singing her praises. Ever since his Mother died he had to cook his own 'mixum-gatherum' of victuals. When the meal was over Jim would sit back in his armchair rubbing his middle and looking at Mary with a broad smile.

"Do you know, alana," says he, "these meals are a life saver. May God bless your hands."

Mary looked at him then looked away. 'You are taking the bait,' says she in her own mind.

Jim was fascinated with all the attention being lavished on him. He looked forward to her regular visits and her company. He wasn't a great man for the talk, especially where women were concerned, but he was happy to sit with her in the warm glow of the turf fire and listen to her light hearted rambling as she chatted easily with him. His emaciated frame soon filled out and his haggard looks soon disappeared.

Her regular visits didn't go unnoticed by the shiulers

of the village, but when they heard about the bread baking and the pot stews, tongues really began to wag."

"She's getting her claws into him slowly," says they. "She won't stop until she has him hooked. No ordinary fellow like Gerry Turbidy or Tim Wager," they continued, "would be good enough for her. It would have to be someone big."

"The poor fellow, God help him, he doesn't know what he's getting himself into," says Mags Lyons.

"Sure hasn't he got one foot in the grave as it is?" says Nan Scott.

"She has given him the kiss of life," says Mrs. Bates. "He looks ten years younger since that woman came to the village. It'll be nice to have young blood in the village again."

"Well," says Kit Moran, "it won't spoil his growth, he must be all of sixty if he's a day. Wait til she gets him, that will put an end to his open house and leisurely life style. She'll put the skids under him, that's for sure."

"I wonder, did she put a dollop of philtre in his tea?" asked May Fagan.

"She'd want to put several dollops, if you ask me," says Nan Scott, "to get him going. Do you know that at that age men often go quare in the head, especially if a young girl gives him the glad eye."

That was the kind of banter that went on every morning in the Post Office.

After a year visiting Coolbeg and having tried with all her womanly guile to prod Jim into talking about matters of the heart had proved futile, she became apprehensive about her own ability to enamour and lure the opposite sex. But she didn't intend giving up, not yet anyway and neither did she intend spending the rest of her days as an unpaid skivvy. She knew that his upbringing had left him shy and reserved, especially where women were concerned, but in time she hoped to change all that.

Rising from her chair in Jim's kitchen she exhaled loudly and gave a quick, penetrating glance over her shoulder at him. He was sitting like a contented child, impervious to Mary's frustration.

She joined her hands as she sauntered around the room, looking at family photographs hanging on the wall, but in reality was imploring the Good Lord for guidance. 'Yes, a different tack was necessary,' she told herself.

She came to the back of Jim's chair and put her hand on his shoulder. "It's never too late for a man …" says she. Her last words trailed away.

Mary left that day with the firm intention of not returning to Coolbeg until her strategy bore fruit. 'I'll take a holiday in Dublin,' she thought, 'and let him do his own washing and cooking for awhile. Then he might appreciate all I have done for him. Absence makes the heart grow fonder Daddy used to say when he'd arrive home after a long business trip.' She smiled a wry smile as she poured herself a nightcap.

Jim sat in his kitchen, an expression of comic woe on his face. He couldn't understand it. Ever since Mary came to the village she had never missed her daily visit to Coolbeg. He became very perturbed. Had he done or said something to offend her? He couldn't remember. To soothe his thoughts Jim began the ritual of lighting his pipe. Cleaning the bowl, he stopped, suddenly deep in thought.

'Maybe she's sick or confined to bed,' he nodded to the empty bowl. 'That's the most likely explanation.'

He upbraided himself for his lack of concern.

'But there again,' thought he, 'I didn't hear of anyone being sick in the village. And I was there only last night. Maybe she has taken up with another lad.'

But he had his doubts. He knew she was very pretty

and was any man's fancy. He rammed his fist into the palm of the other hand with concern.

'If I've lost her I'll have nobody to blame but myself,' he cursed himself for his shyness.

Whether it was by accident or design they met the following day in the Village Square. Jim was going to the forge to have his horse shod and Mary was going to deliver a dress she had made for Alice O'Gorman. Jim's face beamed with delight when he saw her.

"Good morning Mary," says he jovially. They had been on first name terms for a long time now and he saw no good reason why he should address her any other way just because they were standing in the middle of the street.

"Good day Mr. Fox," says Mary, her voice was low and earnest.

Jim was taken aback by her cool response. He knew they had become good friends, and to be calling him 'Mr. Fox' was out of character with the girl he had come to know and love. He pondered a long minute at her odd behaviour. 'I wonder,' says he to himself, 'is it all over or is it just an old man's infatuation?' He wasn't sure, but one thing he was sure of was that her absence had left a huge void in his life. He repeated those very words he had heard Mary say the last time she was up with him, 'Absence makes the heart grow fonder.'

"I ... I thought," says he, "you were sick or something. I haven't seen you this long time."

'You noticed,' breathed Mary to herself.

"Did I say something to offend you?" he looked at her searchingly.

"Good heavens no, Mr. Fox, nothing like that at all."

Jim was getting quite agitated. Out of the corner of her eye Mary could see by all the curtains twitching that all the eyes of the gossip housed in the village were on them. She could almost hear their tongues wag.

"There has been talk," says she, lowering her head like a guilty child.

"What kind of talk?" says Jim looking at her gravely, his eyebrows furrowed and his eyelids reduced his eyes to slits staring at her.

"Stories are going around about us, I overheard them in the Post Office the other day. Anyway," says she, giving a toss of her head, "we can't talk here, there are too many looking."

Mary turned as if to walk away.

Jim was in an almighty fix. He began to prance from foot to foot like someone that had been made to stand on a hot griddle in his bare feet. If he let her go now he might never get a chance to talk to her again. Going to her house was out of the question, anyway he would be too shy to knock on any woman's door, especially a single woman. It would certainly cause tongues to wag.

"Come up to the house later on this evening, alana, and we can talk about it."

Mary turned and gave an archy smile as she sallied forth to make her delivery.

Her intuition told her that Jim was a malleable man but to get him to pop the question was a different matter altogether. She was determined to use all her womanly wiles to achieve her goal, otherwise the rendezvouses would have to cease. She was still pondering over these things as she knocked on Jim's door later that evening.

When Jim opened the door his face beamed with delight when he saw Mary's cheerful face and sparkling blue eyes looking back at him. His heart missed a beat.

He stood to one side and beckoned her to enter.

"Come in and welcome, alana," says he. He tendered her a drink and an invitation to sit at the fire at the same time. They exchanged well-worn items of news as they sat in the warm glow of the turf fire, sipping their drinks.

Jim knew the onus was on him to initiate this heart to heart chat for which he had invited her. He took a copious dollop of the precious stimulant in the hope it would provide him with the courage he so badly needed. He became agitated as his toes did a shuffling gyration on the hearthstone and he implored the Good Lord to loosen his tongue. After much humming and hawing and throaty cackling he finally got his vocal cords into gear. Mary gave him an encouraging smile.

"What's all this talk you heard in the Post Office about us?"

He was now staring at her hard, but Mary didn't return his stare. She kept her head low as she fiddled with her hands awhile before she spoke.

"It's about you and me, a single man and a single woman in the same house day in and day out and us not married. The more bitter among them are saying, 'God knows what they're up to'."

"I don't know," says Jim, "why they want to be talking about us, sure we're not doing anything."

'That's the problem,' says Mary under her breath.

She looked at him earnestly and spoke, "Word has got back to the parish priest that I've been coming up here every day cooking your meals and baking bread for you. It's reported that there's going to be a Mission in the parish soon. Then we could have the Missioner coming up here giving us a lecture on our moral behaviour. You know the parish priest would only be too delighted to let the Missioner make an example of us off the altar. I'll never be able to raise me head in the village again. I have my reputation to think about," says she, staring at him earnestly. She took a deep laboured breath and exhaled loudly. "If you have nothing further to discuss I'll be taking my leave for fear we give anymore fodder to the scandal loving tongues of the village gossip."

Mary reached down and picked up her handbag off the floor as if to leave.

Jim cupped his face in his hands, his elbows on his knees, staring into the dying embers of the turf fire. His face had turned slate gray and there was mist in his eyes. His mind was in turmoil, his heart racing. A myriad of strange things were eddying around in his brain. The homemade bread and cakes and the cooked dinners that he had come to enjoy so much would be lost forever, all because of these bladdering shiulers.

He knew that in a few years time he would be old and feeble. His friends of similar vintage would stop coming to his house for a game of cards and a chat. He would be left alone on this windswept mountain. He'd be put into a home when he'd get too feeble. The place would be sold by the government to defray expenses. The thought frightened him, filled him with dread. He shuddered in his chair. We Foxes were the founding stock of moral decency from time immemorial and to let the name be tarnished at this time of my life would be unforgivable. He was shook back to the present when Mary, who had been eyeing him owlishly and could easily presage his dilemma, put her hand on his shoulder.

"Are you all right there love?" says she, her voice soft and amiable.

On hearing her calling him love, Jim tried to reciprocate but he found such endearments hard to express, even in the confines of his own kitchen.

He sat bolt upright in his chair as if his brain was suddenly activated by the precious dollop of spirits. He looked at Mary gravely,

"You're right me girl, love," he found himself saying, "I never thought of it that way before. Those scandal loving shiulers would be only too happy to see our characters tarnished."

With the corner of his eye Jim saw Mary open her handbag and take out her gloves. She closed it with a loud click, then proceeded to put them on. She shifted in her chair as a gesture of impatience.

Jim too shifted his position sharply and began shuffling his feet on the hearthstone, beads of sweat began oozing from his brow and trickle down his face.

"It's now or never," says he, jumping up and out of the chair as if stung by a bee and prancing around the kitchen, his head bobbing up and down as he banged his closed fist into the other cupped hand in agitation. He implored the Good Lord to help him find the right words to ask Mary to marry him. If she left the house now that would be the end of their relationship. How could he follow her down the hill and propose to her in the middle of the road. What a laughingstock he would be if it was found out.

Mary looked at this worried specimen of a man standing in the nave of the kitchen. A handsome man, she thought. Any woman would be proud of him as a husband.

"Can I be of any help?" says Mary. "You look awful worried."

Jim looked up to Mary, his shoulders drooped as if the whole world's troubles were on them. A long sigh broke from him.

He knelt down on one knee and took her hand in his. She yielded willingly. He began his usual stuttering and stammering but nothing audible would come out. Mary moved her face closer to his and looked into his stressed eyes.

"What is it love?" says she, "what are you trying to say?"

Eventually, throaty, he blurted out the words Mary had been waiting for so long to hear.

"Will you, will you be, be my individual?" says he.

"I'm taking it," says she, "that you are proposing to me?"

"Yis, yis, that's the word I've been searching for."

"I'm taking it then that you are asking me to marry you?" Mary wanted there to be no misunderstanding.

Jim nodded his head.

"I'll be honoured to be your wife," says she, giving him a kiss on the cheek.

Jim flopped into the armchair, exhausted. He never envisioned that making a proposal of marriage would be so nerve-racking. He was relieved it was all over.

"What you need," says she, "is a large whiskey to calm your nerves."

"I would appreciate one," says he, "and that's for sure."

The Parish Priest read out the banns on the first Sunday of the Mission, to the general bemusement of the villagers who had long since dismissed Jim Fox as a confirmed bachelor. The wedding was to be held soon afterwards and was to be a very private affair.

Before the wedding Mary hired Mick the Mason, as he was called, to refurbish the house and install a lavatory in the little room off the kitchen. She was used to the modern conveniences and she didn't intend starting married life without these basic necessities. Jim couldn't understand why all this extravagance was necessary just because they were getting married. It conflicted with his own frugal comforts.

"What's the use hoarding all this money in the bank if you don't have comfort?" was Mary's war cry.

The refurbishment completed, Mary and Jim set out for Carlow to buy Jim his wedding outfit. Jim complained vehemently at spending such a large amount of money on such grandeur. "We won't have a penny left to our name by the time this wedding is over."

"Don't be silly," she reproached him demurely as she tucked her arm into his and led him out of the shop. "Don't you know we'll have to look our best on our wedding day? The whole village will have us under scrutiny. You know how they are going to talk."

Mary suggested that they go for a meal to celebrate their first outing together, but Jim wouldn't hear of it. "Enough spent for one day," says he, "I have to get back to look after the stock."

When they hit the high road the pony began to trot in real earnest but not half quick enough for Jim. He kept urging him on aggressively. "Gee up, Neddy, gee up Neddy," says he, all the while tapping the animal with his whip.

Mary couldn't understand his sudden urgency to get home or why he was so agitated and restless in his seat. She tried talking to him about their day in Carlow, the things they saw and the people they met and the bargaining that went on with the draper over the price of the suit. She hoped it would break the melancholy, but Jim evinced little interest. The only sound to break the despondency that evening was the noise from the iron shod hooves of the pony and the steel bands of the trap wheels on the granite hard road.

When they entered the yard Jim brought the pony to an abrupt stop and jumped out of the trap, garnered all the parcels under his arm and made a beeline for the house with Mary in hot pursuit. She still could not understand the urgency.

"What's the matter, love?" says she, entering the kitchen breathless after him.

She could see him in the nave of the kitchen disrobing himself. He threw his clothes on the floor and turned to leave so fast that he collided with Mary in the doorway.

Jim's dilemma suddenly dawned on Mary and his reason for rushing home. She raised her arms to halt his exit from the house.

"Go into the back room," says she, "Don't you know Mick the Mason has the lavatory working?"

Jim didn't argue with her. Not being every well versed with the workings of the flush toilet, he would have preferred the shelter of the privet hedge that he had used all his life, but he had little choice and even less time to make up his mind. He turned and dashed for the toilet, his pants at half- mast. All shame had deserted him.

"I haven't got any toilet paper at the moment," says she. "You can use the newspaper on the floor if you like."

"What do I want newspaper for? Sure I can't read very well."

"Pull that chain," says Mary, "when you are finished and it will flush the bowl itself."

Slowly and hesitatingly Jim pulled the chain as instructed. Not having seen a toilet flush before, he wasn't prepared for the avalanche of water that entered the bowl. He stood dumbfounded as he heard the water thunder down the long pipe from the cistern high up on the wall and fill the bowl to almost overflowing. Would it stop of it's own accord or would it flood the house? He didn't know and was not prepared to wait to find out. He stormed out of the room in great panic.

"Get out quickly," he pleaded, "the house is going to be swept away. There's a deluge of water pouring into the room. I'll go for Mick the Mason," and at the same time reaching for his coat.

"Calm down, you crackpot of the Devil, it's supposed to do that. That's how it works."

"Oh these new fangled ideas," says he rubbing his head, "I'll never get used to them."

Mary raised her head in silent prayer, 'Lord grant me

patience,' she pleaded.

When Mags Lyons and her cronies heard about Jim and the lavatory she smiled slyly. "It's almost impossible," says she, "to house train a man. They have a wild streak about them. They like the open country."

The wedding was held in Glenmore Church, attended only by their closest friends and relations. The reception was held in their own house in Coolbeg. There they frolicked and danced til the early hours of the next morning. Mary thanked them all for coming and assured them that they were all welcome to call at any time. Just because she was the new mistress of the house didn't change anything. She looked at Jim for confirmation which he gave willingly.

Jim and Mary settled down to married life on the farm and to Jim's amazement Mary was more than a willing partner. She quickly learned how to milk cows and make butter. She also looked after the pigs and fowl and continued her dressmaking business whenever she had a spare hour.

At night, friends and neighbours would call to congratulate the newlyweds and wish them luck and happiness for the future. The women folk would be ushered into the parlour where they would present Mary with their wedding presents. She in turn would fill their glasses with her finest sherry. Glasses would be raised and a toast would be proposed for the newlyweds, wishing them a long life and happiness. The men would repair to the kitchen for a game of cards and some light-hearted banter. Farming activities as well as current prices of stock were given an airing. The party would break up about midnight with a cup of tea in the parlour for all.

"After a year of married life and nothing doing," as the old people used to put it, Mary got very anxious. She was now in her forties and if something didn't happen soon it would be too late. She prayed to every saint in the heavens. Novenas were repeated time and time again. The First Fridays were undertaken hail, rain or snow. The Rosary was said nightly and trimmings added, but nothing happened. She began to have doubts about her faith. Nobody above was listening. She tried to talk to her husband about her concerns but him, in his naivete, made light of her troubles.

"You worry too much," says he, giving her a reassuring smile. "The man that made time made lots of it."

"Jim Fox," says she, "You don't seem to understand that I'm running out of time. If I don't get help soon the chances of me giving you an heir is remote."

Jim suddenly became animated at the mention of an heir. He sat bolt upright in his chair. In his mind's eye he could see a small boy trotting around the kitchen, then dashing back to him with outstretched arms for Jim to take him up.

'How could this happen?' he paused in thought. Ever since he was a child he believed he was found under a head of cabbage. That is what his Mother told him and he was still of the opinion. Mary berated him for his imbecilic notions.

"What are we going to do?" says she one day to her husband. "Since poor Mrs. Mannering, the midwife and confidant passed away there's nobody in the locality to turn to. She was better than any doctor when it came to making a philtre for love sick couples that couldn't conceive and she was there at the end to bring that infant into the world." Mary looked at her husband, the tears began trickling down her face like lonely drops of rain.

Jim put his arm around her shoulder. "Love," says he consolingly, "don't be crying, I'll think of something, just you wait and see. You know God is good." Mary glanced at him askance and let the matter rest.

Next morning at cockcrow Jim brought Mary her breakfast in bed. She looked at him wild eyed and surprised. "What's the matter with you this morning? You haven't done this in ages."

Jim gave her a great smile of satisfaction. "I have a solution to your ... our problem," he corrected himself.

Mary sat bolt upright in the bed, raised her eyes to heaven and sighed deeply. "If you have, it's the first time in your life you have," says she, pushing the tray away, temporarily losing her appetite. "What's this brainwave you have suddenly come up with?"

"Tom Quale of Kylebrack," said he, quite pleased with himself for thinking about him. "You know Tom, he's a great friend of mine. It was him that helped me write them letters to you before we got married. His parents were schoolteachers from Kerry. Tom's father was also a renowned matchmaker, a great letter writer and confidant of the highest order. Tom is the only one left out of a family of five. They all succumbed to the dreaded disease of tuberculosis, the curse of the age. I'll go this evening and have a chat with him. There could be snow out before morning, then we mightn't be able to get out for a month."

(At that time, gentle readers, may I add, married women seldom if ever left their homes after they got married, except to go to Mass on a Sunday, maybe a visit to a sick neighbour or to attend a Wake. The Christmas market was a special occasion for a woman. There she would sell her fat turkeys and geese. This was called pin money and with this money safe in her purse she would buy clothes for the family, toys for the children, loose material for mending clothes and wool to knit socks. She would make sure to treat herself and her close friends to a sherry in Monaghan's snug to solidify their friendship. It was unbecoming for a woman to be seen going to a doctor or a midwife and certainly not be seen going to seek advice from a quack. It was a long held tradition that the man of the house undertook these important missions.)

Mary was well aware of Jim's incompetence when it came to discussing matters of the heart. To avoid any misunderstanding she wrote a short letter outlining their dilemma and Jim's lack of adventure in that field.

Around the fire in Tom's cottage in Kylebrack they smoked their pipes and chatted desultorily about nothing consequential. Tom could easily presage by Jim's body language that he had come, or was sent, on a special errand and he also knew, from past experience, that protocol would have to be observed.

After a couple of hours of light-hearted banter and all the well worn items of news exhausted and numerous halves of whiskey lowered, they were silent for awhile with their thoughts as they half dozed with outstretched legs crossed at the ankles at the side of the fire, whiskey glasses clasped between their hands across their stomachs.

The lethargy that pervaded the house quickly vanished when an almighty clap of thunder rattled the glass panes in the kitchen window. They jerked in their seats with the shock.

"What was that?" declared Jim as he swung his long legs away from the fire and wrapped his overcoat around him more tightly with concern.

Tom rushed to the window and peered out over the gray, rugged landscape that cascaded down to the sea. There was a menacing blanket of gray clouds enveloping the seashore and crows were hovering around the yard in bursts of flight. They would swoop down and back up again without catching anything. A mighty gust of wind sent leaves dancing and swirling frantically into a whirlpool before coming to rest at the lee side of the midden, 'a sure sign of a severe storm', thought Tom.

He glanced at Jim with his eyecorner, saying to himself, 'If he doesn't soon make a move it will be too late, then Mary will blame me for keeping him out.'

Tom looked at his watch. It was three full hours since Jim arrived in Kylebrack and not a solitary hint as to the reason for his visit. He knew that if he didn't put the question to Jim soon and get his vocal cords going he could be snowed in.

Tom turned to face him. "Jim, me ould friend," says he, putting his hand on his shoulder, "what business brought you down here this wretched evening?"

This question was Jim's cue for which he had been waiting for all evening to broach this very personal subject. "It's me Individual," says he. Jim had taken to calling her that lately.

Tom winked at the old dog lying prostrate on the hearthstone. "I told you this was the big one." The old dog sensed that Tom was telling him something important, raised his head and blinked his eyes as if in acknowledgment of the fact that the wait was worthwhile.

"What about her?" says Tom. "Is she sick or something?"

"Oh no, no, oh Lord no, but she's very worried."

"About what?" says Tom, pretending not to know.

Jim stared at him for an embarrassingly long time before he spoke. "She's worried that she won't be able to give me an heir."

"Ahum," says Tom leaning back in his chair, covering his mouth with his hand to obscure his wry smile. His good sense told him that it was not the time or the place for levity. His old friend had come a long way on this special mission and to be discourteous would be unforgivable.

Jim swallowed the last of the whiskey and took a deep laboured breath before launching into his customary habit of stuttering and stammering before getting his throaty voice going. He outlined in his own inimitable way their dilemma.

Tom had already read the letter Mary had sent. For the last two years of constant endeavour, as Swank the local wag would put it, there was no sign of an addition to the family, no family at all. Jim leaned toward Tom lest anyone might hear him.

"As man to man," says Jim, "Maybe you could make up some of your special philtre you were telling me about. It might give her the boost she's looking for."

Tom's lips flexed their corners into the beginning of a smile. To himself he said, 'It's you that needs the philtre and not Mary, she's passed childbearing this many's a day.' But Tom would not be so bold as to inform him so. A bit of romance is good for the soul.

Out loud he says, "Certainly," going to the dresser and removing a large bottle and wrapping it in brown paper. He passed the bottle to Jim who was getting up from the fire. "All the instructions are on the bottle," says he, "read it carefully when you go home."

He offered Jim his hand. "I wish you and Mary the best of luck, I hope yis won't be disappointed."

Back in the house that night when the card players had left, Jim put the proposal to Mary as outlined on the bottle. She stared at him severely.

"Do you want to burn me alive in the bed?"

"No, no, no, it's not like that at all," says he. "We quench the fire first, then we erect the bed in the ingle under the arch there. It's too cold in the bedroom for any intimate relationship," says he, "we must be warm and cozy."

Mary looked at him blankly. "I suppose it's worth a try," says she evenly.

Jim hauled the big bed down from the bedroom and

erected it in the ingle as directed. The storm that had threatened earlier that evening had arrived with a vengeance. Great gusts of wind were pelting hail and snow against the windowpane. They repaired to bed with two large measures of Tom's special concoction.

"That would make your blood boil," says Mary, giving Jim the glad eye before snuggling up close to him. Jim reciprocated with a broad smile and put his arms around Mary's shoulders and gave her an amorous hug. Then they leaned back against the bed head and sipped their drinks. The flame from the votive oil lamp was flickering gently inside its glove where it sat in a recessed ledge at the ingle.

The storm was raging and the wind was howling with all its wrath in the chimney stack.

"I remember," says Jim, "not long ago that chimney opening was so large that when it rained the drops used to fall on me head, but Mick the Mason repaired it. He said he hung a bucket in it and not a drop has ever come down since."

"I hope," says Mary as she snuggled up closer to him, "that it doesn't come in tonight."

They were silent for a while, chewing on their thoughts as they sipped their drinks companionably. It was Mary who broke the reverie.

"I'm so glad to be here in the warmth of the kitchen tonight and not above in that cold room. It's so warm and cozy here." She shuffled her shoulders to make herself more comfortable beside her husband. "We must do this more often," says she.

They were now lying quietly in an amorous embrace, having finished their drinks. Jim's blood began to boil. The magic potion was taking its effect.

'At last,' says she to herself, 'he's coming to life.'

The old boards under the straw mattress moaned and groaned under the combined assault of the two activated bodies.

"Am I getting you excited, love?" says Jim, drawing her closer to him. He was beginning to find it much easier to express himself in a more romantic way.

"O love," says she, "I didn't think you were so romantic, you are a real charmer when you get going."

A surge of tide rose within her so high that she cried out her desire. They were about to reach the summit of erotic sensation when a gigantic thunderbolt struck the house with such force that the glass rattled in the windows, pictures fell off the walls, pots and pans danced on their rack, mugs and jugs rattled on the dresser, then high in the chimney above their heads a terrifying rumbling sound began.

They could hear the clattering noise of the iron bucket as it pummelled from one boulder to another in the chimney breast as it made it's descent. It smacked straight on Mary's head, and a deluge of sooty water enveloped them as they lay prostrate in bed. Whether it was the shock of the thunderbolt or Jim's impetuousness or what but they crashed to the floor, the bed smashed under them and they were swimming in murky water.

"Oh, oh my God!" she wailed. "I'm killed!"

"Get up," she screeched. "You latchko and light the light, move yourself for once in your life," she wailed at him.

After numerous attempts to extricate himself from the mangled bed and the sopping clothes he eventually scrambled out. He was like a drowned rat. His nightshirt was dripping like a mini waterfall. When he got to the perpendicular he was standing ankle deep in sooty water. He groped around in the dark until he found the matches in the window. He struck match after match with no answering flame before he came to a good one. He was uttering unholy expletives under his breath at his wife for putting the dead matches back into the box instead of discarding them into the fire.

He lit the oil lamp hanging on the wall but, before returning to assist his wife, he stood momentarily and looked into the mirror beside the light at himself. He was shocked at the image looking back at him. He jumped away a pace like a frightened cat. Just two shiny blue eyes peering out of a coal black face was all he could see.

When Mary regained her equilibrium and saw the state of herself and the bedclothes swimming in sooty water, she was frenzied. She was so distraught that momentarily she forgot about the head wound and began bellowing at her husband.

"Get this bed or what's left of it back up them stairs immediately. You dimwit with your harum-scarum ideas, I was worse to listen to you."

She jumped around the kitchen ankle deep in murky water in a paroxysm of rage, clasping her head in her hands to ease the pain. The moaning and groaning reached a crescendo. It was so loud it woke the pigs in their stys, the house cock was shook out of his reverie and began crowing, the dogs ran around the yard barking frantically as if repelling intruders. There was mayhem and bedlam in the house and of course it was all Jim's fault.

"I would rather," says she between the groans and the moans, "to stay childless than to go through that ordeal again." Her eyes were piercing into Jim's face.

Jim knew his best course of action was to play dumb.

For many weeks afterwards Mary was confined to bed. Every day of her convalescence Jim came ingratiatingly to where she lay with her head heavily bandaged and whispered, "I've brought your dinner love and I haven't forgot your favourite apple pie and custard."

Mary's return to full health got a further setback. When she would get out of bed she felt light headed and nauseous. At first she put it down to the severe dousing she got the night in the ingle and all the sooty water she drank. It was causing her great discomfort and no sign of it abating.

Alone in her bed Mary's mind wandered back to the night she spent in the ingle. It was their first real lovemaking experience, something she would savour for a long time to come. She was pondering over these things quietly. 'And now,' thought she, 'for no reason this nausea has hit me.' She stopped abruptly as an idea came to her. If it was what she thought it was she would gladly suffer the nausea and discomfort for the whole nine months. She had convinced herself that this was the only possible reason for this nausea.

She got out of bed and pirouetted around the floor in ecstasy, a pillow clasped against her ample bosom. She raised her eyes to heaven in silent prayer, imploring the Good Lord to grant her this one special wish.

The sudden pummelling on the floorboards overhead brought Jim hurriedly to her bedroom. When he opened the door Mary flung her arms around his neck and danced him around the floor.

"I'm pregnant, I'm pregnant," she exclaimed excitingly, giving Jim an affectionate kiss on the cheek.

When the ecstasy and delight had abated, Mary's thoughts turned to the forthcoming event although a long way off.

She checked herself severely. She would first have to get her pregnancy confirmed officially before making it public. But since Mrs. Mannering the midwife and confidant had passed away and nobody appointed in her place Mary was in a dilemma. Being pregnant for the first time and she in her forties, it was imperative that she have it confirmed officially and as soon as possible. Her absence didn't go unnoticed by the card-players who frequented their abode every night, or at Sunday Mass where the front seat in the church that Mary and Jim always occupied was now vacant. Heads began to nod and tongues began to wag.

In the harvest field some days later, Jim and his four hired hands were cutting the last of the corn and garnering it into a rick before the impending storm.

Mary stormed into the field, stood on the midden inside the gate and emitted such an ear splitting screech that it echoed down the valley and would have awoke the dead in Kilranlagh graveyard five miles away. The crows that were gorging themselves on the loose grain were sent cawing and squawking in panic to the safety of the next field. The rabbits that were frolicking and dancing among the sheaves scurried to their burrows in fright.

The two horses that pulled the mowing machine with Jim on board stopped so abruptly on hearing Mary's voice that Jim almost toppled out of the moving machine seat and into the path of the cutting knife bar in the swarth. Jim was dumbfounded as to why his two faithful animals should act in this way. Having regained his balance and his composure he glanced anxiously around in all directions to find a reason for the horses' sudden stop but could see none. He sat momentarily in a sort of reverie, gazing at the serrated knife in the cutting bar and the narrow escape he had made. 'Me leg could have been cut off,' says he to himself.

He was shook back to the present when Larry O'Gorman, one of his hired hands, came racing up to his side and informed, "The missus, the missus," says he as he kept pointing toward the gate. Being a little deaf and with the noise of the mowing machine Jim didn't realize that it was Mary's voice that had stopped the horses.

He hopped down off the machine and threw the driving reins to Larry. "You take over," says he. "I'll be back in a few minutes." His face had turned the colour of marble as he went running to his wife at the gate, his mind full of foreboding.

Before he could inquire the reason for her calling him or even draw his breath she railed out at him. "You promised me last night," says she, "that you'd go to see Dr. McKay this evening for me."

"But the harvest," Jim kept pointing to all the loose sheaves waiting to be garnered into the rick. "We could loose the harvest," says he looking at her pleadingly.

"Harvest of no harvest," says she, wagging her finger at him furiously, "you are going to the doctor now. I have the pony tackled and under the trap."

Reluctantly Jim set out for the doctor in Shinrone, well aware of the nodding heads and wagging tongues of the village gossipers were he to be seen going through the village, and on a fine harvest day especially, without his wife accompanying him. He could almost hear their tongues wag from behind the curtained windows.

"Did you see Jim Fox pass by and he all dressed up, heading in the direction of Shinrone?" says they. "It must be very important," says another, "leaving the men in the field on such a fine day to go gallivanting around the country." And says the third with pursed lips, "There's more to it." They gave one another knowing glances. "I must get my Jack to ramble up there tonight," says Mags Lyon, "and find out what's going on." ... " And I'll tell Christy," says Julia Doyle.

So, as to avoid any such gossip, Jim went by an altogether different ingress that bypassed the village. Daylight was giving away to darkness, the evening had turned cool and crisp. He alighted from the trap at the doctor's house and reconnoitred the spacious edifice of brick before tying his pony in the forecourt. As he made his way gingerly towards the surgery door, at the side of the house, he kicked at the loose pebbles in a desultory fashion. He was much more nervous now than when first setting out and had nearly forgotten the myriad of questions Mary had warned him to ask. Jim groped around in the dark and came to a door. Emboldened by the light under it and the boisterous chatter from within he rang the bell.

Then, without portent or warning the door burst open and a young woman burst out of the surgery, a handkerchief held against her mouth. She stood momentarily in the yard and erupted blasphemous barrages in the direction of the surgery.

"You, you butcher, you animal, you rapscallion of the Devil, you shouldn't be let near anyone let alone pull their teeth." A stream of invectives continued to pour from her. Her tongue was vile.

With the fright at hearing this stream Jim teetered on his heels and staggered backwards a step and cowered against the wall. He was flabbergasted to think that a woman could mouth such unholy expletives to anyone, especially a doctor. Through all the wailing she spotted Jim in the half-light, cowering against the wall.

She removed the handkerchief a minute and exclaimed, through the pain and agony caused by the extracted tooth, "Don't go in near him," she implored. "He nearly slit me gullet." She then dashed away down the avenue, still holding the bloodied handkerchief to her mouth.

A dilemma of monumental proportions enveloped Jim as he stood perplexed and shuddering against the wall. Should he take the woman's advice and flee the scene before this alleged monster would seize him, or stay and see his mission through? To desert and run, he knew, would draw down the greatest manifestation of Mary's anger and wrath on his head and here he only recently had been restored in her good graces after the bed in the ingle incident.

He was cogitating over these things when a great bulk of a man appeared and stood on the doorstep, clutching his arm. He stared at Jim in the half-light.

"Do you want to see me?" he inquired.

Being suddenly confronted by this thunderous voice, Jim began stuttering. "Yeh, yeh, yis doctor. Just for a minute doctor."

Following the doctor into the surgery Jim stood just inside the door, holding the trilby hat to his chest. Under the doctor's scrutiny Jim shifted his weight from foot to foot nervously as he looked from side to side as though seeking a way out of the room. He was staring at the doctor as he set about bandaging the deep gash in his arm.

"These bloody women," says he to nobody in particular. "They think I can extract rotten teeth without hurting them. Look at that arm," he invited, "she nearly bit it off."

Turning to take his seat at his desk he invited Jim to do likewise which he did nervously, still clutching his hat to his chest. "Now mister emm ... what can I do for you?"

"Fox is the name," Jim spluttered out.

"Well, Mr. Fox, what seems to be the problem?"

"Aba, aba, it's not me," says Jim, "it's my Individual."

"Who?" says the doctor, his eyebrows furrowing.

"The missus."

"What's wrong with your wife?" says he curtly.

"She, she thinks she's pregnant."

With the votive oil lamp hanging on the wall, the doctor peered at the visage of this old gray haired man sitting opposite. 'He must be all of sixty years,' he thought to himself, 'how could they be so naïve as to believe that it could be possible at her years?' Then a pang of pain shot through his arm as if checking his unkind thoughts. He couldn't resist a jaw-dropping smile at the foolishness of their thoughts as he jotted down in a terse fashion, all that Jim had related and all the personal details Mary had enclosed in the letter.

Without hesitation the doctor deducted from the file that she was well and truly passed her childbearing years. Whatever was causing her sickness, it definitely was not a result of being pregnant, but he could not be so bold as to inform him bluntly and dampen their conjugal pleasures.

'No, there has to be another way,' he thought to himself, awhile sucking on his pen as he pondered his stratagem. With his eyecorner he glanced at Jim sitting straight in the chair opposite, eyeballing him back. He was anxiously waiting the doctor's opinion, and had convinced himself that at any minute the good doctor would confirm his dearest wish to be true. But the doctor's professional opinion told him that if such a thing was to happen it would be a miracle.

He stopped abruptly in his thoughts. 'A miracle,' he repeated to himself. 'That's the noun,' he breathed to himself. 'It seems as fitting as any explanation, for this imbecile won't understand its meaning anyway. He was sure of that, but his wife, … well, Mr. Fox can explain as best he can.'

The doctor leaned back in his chair and drew on his pipe.

"Now, Mr. Fox, having scrutinized your wife's chart and taking everything into consideration," the doctor sucked on his pipe, "I have come to a conclusion."

Jim was so distraught that the perspiration was rolling down his brow. The wait was almost too much for him to bear. He implored the Good Lord and the doctor to deliver his verdict and not to be keeping him in suspense.

Leaning forward in his chair the doctor spoke slowly and earnestly. "I've got to be frank with you, Mr. Fox, do you understand?"

Jim's head was in such a whirl of excitement that all he could do was nod his head.

"If your wife is going to have a baby," he left out 'at her age', "it will be a miracle."

Without waiting for the doctor to elaborate Jim leaped up in such a spasm of jubilation that he overturned the chair he was sitting on in the process.

The doctor put up his hand to urge Jim to sit and he would explain matters, but Jim, in his excitement, thought that the doctor was offering him his hand as a congratulatory gesture. He seized the doctor's hand and shook it vigorously before storming out of the surgery.

The doctor sat in a daze, staring at the open door where Jim had exited. He was dumbstruck at Jim's impetuousness. 'What has he to be jubilant about?' he asked himself. Failing to find a rational answer he shook his head as he got up to close the surgery door for the night.

So elated was Jim on his way home he began chanting this new found word to the rhythm of the click clack of the iron shod hooves of the pony on the granite hard road.

'It's a miracle,' he'd exclaim, 'Mary is going to have a little miracle.'

He stood in the nave of the trap and boxed the night air with his fist. 'My Individual is going to have a little miracle.' His chanting was so vocal that it brought a response from every dog along the roadside houses as he passed. 'My Individual will be so happy when I tell her. That's if I don't forget what the doctor said.' He scratched his head thinking what might happen if he did. The tongue bashing he'd get.

Jim's homecoming was eagerly awaited by the card players who had arrived earlier than their usual hour in Coolbeg in order to thwart Mary's plan for a private chat with her husband. They were also looking forward to the mirth and laughter that would ensue when Jim would relate, through stuttering and throaty cackling in his own inimitable way, the finds of his intercourse with the doctor.

Mary was in great spirits when Jim arrived home. The illness that had bedevilled her for some weeks past had vanished and there was a spring in her step as she set to work on the myriad of chores neglected during her stay in bed. It was further heightened on seeing her husband's smiling visage entering the kitchen.

Her heart missed a beat. 'It's good news,' she breathed to herself as she could read his face.

Around the card table knowing glances were exchanged and heads began to nod. The women were right. 'This was the big one,' they were thinking to themselves, but Mary's astuteness read their minds. If at all possible she was going to be the first to savour the good news before it was made public.

The card players were equally determined in their own devious way that she would not.

"Come up to the parlour, love," says she, "and I'll give you your supper. There's a lovely fire in the grate."

Jim stood with his back to the open fire in the kitchen, chatting with his friends while he awaited Mary's call.

"We need one more for a quorum," says Jack Lyons, dealing out eight hands of cards in front of Jim's vacant chair at the head of the table as an inducement. "Join in and have an ould game," says Joe White, "while Mary is making the tea." Enticed by the vacant chair and the hand of cards already dealt out Jim needed little encouragement to join in, for he was an ardent devotee of the game of Forty-Five.

When Mary returned to the kitchen to call Jim the

card game was in full flow. She was horror-struck to see her husband in the game of cards before he had even related to her the good news she was so longing to hear. She looked at her husband wild-eyed and gnashed her teeth in ire, but would not be so bold as to revile him in front of his friends. She stomped around the kitchen, pummelling pots and pans on their shelves in frustration. 'How could he be so inconsiderate,' she thought to herself and this she was hoping to be the happiest day of her life.

It wasn't all his fault, she was certain of that, as she gnashed her teeth. It's these cunning rascals who had deliberately set out to thwart what would otherwise be a very special evening, but polite Jim fell into their trap.

'How could he refuse, especially in his own house, it would be impolite,' she thought. Mary stood in the nave of the kitchen and leered from one player to another around the table. They were pretending to be engrossed in the game but her intuition told her otherwise.

Whether it was by accident or design Jim and his partner were winning every game. As his winning began to burgeon, so too was his enthusiasm, so much so that he forgot all about his tea and his earlier visit to the doctor.

Every time Mary tried to intervene she was met with a barrage of shoos and a decretory wave of a hand. "No interruptions, please."

Unable to contain herself any longer, she gave a petulant toss of her head and pompously marched to the head of the table where Jim was seated and railed out at him.

"Jim Fox," says she, her voice strident with anger, "I have been waiting here all night to hear what the doctor told you, but you seem to be more interested in your ould game of cards than me."

Jim looked up at her momentarily in wonderment, then it dawned on him.

"Oh God, I forgot … the ould cards you know … ,"

"Who knows better," says she gnashing her teeth. She leered at the others around the table. Their piggy eyes were fastened searchingly on Jim's face with sniggering smiles behind their cards. "You might as well make it public now," says she, sure in her heart that the news was a positive one, "and take us all out of our suspense."

The sudden spasm of denunciation made Jim stutter and stammer. He was visibly upset. He gave a plangent sigh and glanced over his shoulder at his wife with searching eyes, thinking 'How could she do that in front of me friends, could she not wait til the card players were gone?'

She knew better than most that it would only give fodder to the scandal loving tongues of the village gossip. But Mary wouldn't let go. She was in full voice now and if the cauldron of fury which was at its zenith was not broached soon serious damage could be inflicted on her already frayed nerves, damage that might never be repaired between them.

She stood straight at the side of his chair, her hands on her hips, looking down her Grecian nose at him.

"Well … ," says she, "what did the doctor say?

This fulmination turned Jim's mind blank. It reminded him of the time when he was a young lad in school and the wicked school master, Mr. Dunne, stood over him with a cane ready to dash his brains out for failing to remember his catechism.

"Surely to God," says she, "you haven't forgotten already and it only two hours since you were with him, or is your head gone altogether?"

Eventually Jim cranked up his vocal cords and, through the spluttering and splattering of spittle all over the cards on the table, he eventually blurted out, "The doctor says if you are going to have anything it will, will, be, be a a a mackerel"

Mary looked at him dumbstruck and so embarrassed that the colour drained from her face. She teetered on her heels with the shock. She caught the back of Jim's chair before she over balanced into the fire. She opened her mouth to denounce him but no words would come out. She staggered backwards and flopped into the armchair. She cupped her face in her hands and lapsed into a reverie of abjectness.

When she woke some hours later the card players were gone. A deafening silence pervaded the house save for the chirping of the crickets under the hearthstone. Jim was still sitting at the table, his closed fists propping up his face, his elbows on the table, staring at the upturned cards. He was like a child that had got a severe reprimand.

Mary glanced at her husband and burst into tears.

"How could you humiliate me like that, especially in front of that cabal? I'll be the laughing stock of the parish. You …" and she stopped for more sobs, "a mackerel, what do you think I am, a fish or something?"

Realizing the awful clanger he had dropped, Jim came ingratiatingly to where Mary sat, half in a state of semi-collapse like a huge sack of flour, her full length black dress dipping into the valley of her sprawling thighs and gave her a kiss on the head.

"I'll never embarrass you again like that, love, no never again and that's the end of the card playing in this house, I promise you that."

Mary's shattered pride took a long time to heal but it eventually did. She was certain in her own mind that Jim would never deliberately set out to embarrass her the way he did. He wasn't that type of man. If there was to be any peace and harmony in the house she would have to accept these foibles in his character.

Jim and Mary settled down to the humdrum life on

the farm just like all their contemporaries in the parish. She resigned herself to the fact that she would never be able to give him an heir, but she hoped and prayed that their application to adopt a boy from the Orphanage in Ballinaglass would soon bear fruit.

As luck would have it, the Orphanage informed them soon thereafter that their application was successful and a ten year old boy by the name of Pete Maguire would be dispatched to them within days.

Mary was over the moon with her new ward. She was glad of the company during the long winter nights and more so lately since her eyesight was failing. She had to abandon her needlework that she was so fond of. And Jim could go to the pub with peace of mind, knowing that she had someone to call on if something should happen.

Peetie settled in quickly and soon learned the rudiments of farming. One day Peetie stormed into the kitchen, all excited and breathless, "Mammy, Mammy," says he, "Daddy says the sow is going to have a wheelbarrow."

Mary almost choked but kept the cough behind her hand so as not to embarrass the boy. "I think," says she when she had regained her composure. "I think what he did say love was that the sow was going to farrow. She's going to have a litter of piglets."

As soon as the sow farrowed it was celebrating time for Jim as was his wont after such occasions. He repaired himself to Malacky's pub and ensconced himself in the armchair in front of the open fire. Everyone who called for their groceries or any item of haberdashery was invited to join Jim in a celebratory drink. Some didn't know what he was celebrating and cared less as long as there was a free drink flowing in their direction.

It was late evening when Nanny Dolan came into the shop to collect her groceries. By this time Jim was well oiled. Even in his inebriated stupor he recognized his old friend and neighbour. He got up and half staggered, half groped towards the counter and insisted that she have a drink with him.

"I'm, I'm cel, celebrating me good luck," say he hiccupping.

'It doesn't have to be anything special for you to celebrate,' says she to herself, 'you celebrate every night.' But she would not be so bold as to accuse him. Out loud she says, "What are you celebrating this time?" as she took up the glass of spirits.

Jim clicked his glass with hers, then looked at her for a long second as he swallowed hard. He was unsteady even at the counter.

"Sh, sh, she's presented me with ten of the best last night."

"Who?" says Nanny, looking rather startled. "Mary?"

"Oh no, no." says he with half closed eyes and shaking his head. "The big black and white sow."

Nanny kept a wry smile behind her glass, staring at Jim with bulbous eyes.

"Come up," says he. "when they are ready for sale and you can have the pick of the litter."

"Well, do you know," says she, "Dan, me husband, was only saying last night that he was thinking of getting into a sow for the winter, and if he does I'm going to get into another."

Malacky who was washing glasses behind the counter as usual had his ear cocked listening to the conversation and smiled to himself.

It was past midnight when Jim set out for home. He was well oiled, unlike his old bike which creaked and rattled over rut and groove along the dirt road.

Because of Jim's inebriated condition and the squeaking of his bike he didn't notice the towering figure in blue until he was nose to nose with him.

"Where is your light?" bellowed the Guard, giving Jim one hell of a start with his sudden demand.

He soon recovered and began searching in his pockets. "If It's a light you want I have one here somewhere, that is if I can find it."

"I see," says the Guard, "that you have no light on your bike front or rear or a bell."

"Now, haven't you got great sight altogether," says Jim jovially.

"What's your name?" demanded the Guard, taking out his notebook.

"Oh, oh, Jim Fox of Coolbeg, and who are you may I ask?" says Jim swaying to and fro and trying to keep himself and his bike vertical.

"I'm Guard Flatley, the new Guard in Shinrone," he said curtly.

"Oh, oh Guard Flat-feet, it's nice to meet you."

'Is it now?' says the guard to himself, 'you won't be saying that the next court day in Shinrone.' The Guard stood toweringly in the middle of the road, preparing to give Jim a lecture before jotting down in a terse fashion all the details.

"What's the most important item on a bike when cycling on the public road of a dark night?"

Jim thought for a long minute. "Would it be the saddle guard?"

"Watch your step," says he, "or I'll have you arrested for the obstruction of the law. Where are you going to at this ungodly hour of the night," says he, "a respectable citizen like yourself?"

After some consideration Jim replied, "I'm going to a lecture, Guard."

"A lecture?" bellowed the Guard, the resonance of his voice reverberating down the valley in the cool morning air. "And who might be giving a lecture at this hour"

"My Individual," says Jim.

"Well, you better get going and not be keeping her up too late."

On arrival home, in order to delay a tongue bashing from his wife, Jim went to inspect the sow and her litter of piglets before retiring to bed. He sat down on the straw beside the sow to have a smoke, but sleep and the warmth of the pig house overcame him, so he stretched himself out on the straw beside the sow and bonhams and fell asleep. His head was towards the sow's rear end. Nothing unusual in that, gentle readers would surely say, a common practice to many farmers on such an occasion. May I also add at this juncture, sows are prone to purge themselves of foul air when lying down, especially after farrowing.

Sometime later Jim was unceremoniously shook out of his comfortable sleep by an explosion of wind from the sow into his face, wind so foul that it almost stilled him. He groaned and spluttered and snorted, trying to clear his throat.

In his slumber he thought he was in bed with his wife and gave her a dig in the belly with his elbow. "Lie over, Mary, your breath stinks."

It was mid October that Jim and Peetie set out for Ballinaglass fair with their litter of bonhams in the horse and crib cart. It was a cold, crisp morning. The sun rose with cardinal red over the eastern skies. 'Great hope of a fine day,' Jim thought.

"Wrap yourselves up well," came the voice from upstairs, "and don't get yourselves your death of cold. Wear that scarf," she barked at Jim, "the one you won in the raffle."

In the feeble pool of light from the candle Jim reached up and pulled down the scarf that was hanging on the clothes line over the fire place, knotted it around his throat, spread the ends over his chest and buttoned his coat over it tightly.

As they went along, the light got better and soon they were able to appreciate all the sights and sounds of the countryside. Jack Darcy's cockerel standing on the midden sang a song of salutation in the fine morning. On hearing the iron shot wheels of their cart on the granite hard road, dogs raced out of their road gates, frantically barking as if repelling their impending intrusion, in the process scattering hens and chickens that were picking in the vicinity of Jack's whitewashed thatched cottage door. Cattle and sheep grazed on the lush autumn grass. Every horse galloped to the roadside hedges and, if unencumbered by either harness or cart, stripped their teeth and whinnied, as if deriding and scathing them for compelling their compatriot to cart such an enormous load.

When they reached the outskirts of the town Jim's heart missed a beat for he loved the hustle and bustle of the fair, the wheeling and dealing that went on before a deal was clenched and the conviviality of the occasion.

But his spirits were soon dashed when a red haired woman alighted from a horse drawn caravan that was parked at the edge of the town.

"Good morning," says she jovially, "a lovely morning for the fair."

Jim sat bolt upright in the cart. An ill omen pervaded his mind. He gulped a mouthful of air so fast that it almost choked him. He wasn't a superstitious man by nature but at this moment a strange feeling came over him. He had often heard his father saying when he was a young lad that to meet a red headed woman when going to the fair was bad, even disastrous. 'But what can befall us,' he asked himself, 'we have arrived safe and well and the bonhams look comfortable and warm.'

Parking the cart in front of O'Malley's public house in the Square Jim unyoked his horse and put him in a stall in O'Malley's yard. He gave him oats and hay while he awaited the buyers to arrive. Jim was certain they would come in droves because they always regarded his pigs as the best quality in any fair. Women would be clambering to buy a sow bonham to keep as foundation stock.

Jim and Peetie sauntered up towards the town, examining and comparing other farmer's piglets and chatting with other farmers on their way. They came to the conclusion that, for their age, theirs were by far the better quality and size, but being the modest man that he was he dismissed it with a discreet wave of his hand.

As the morning wore on it became warm and sunny. Buyers milled about examining the many carloads of pigs before the real bargaining began.

"You'll have no bother selling them," says Peetie. "They look powerful."

But no buyer hung around Jim's cart. Having inquired the price they turned on their heels and sauntered away, grinning and sniggering behind their hands so as to stifle the sound less they give offence.

The heat of the day forced Jim to unbutton his coat and loosen his scarf. Disappointed at having no serious bid for his piglets, and the wry smiles of the passersby, Jim came to the conclusion in his own mind that it must be Peetie that was the focus of attention and driving the buyers away.

He called Peetie to one side and advised him to keep a low profile and not to be making a spectacle of himself.

"Don't you see," says Jim, "they're all laughing at you."

"It's not me they are laughing at," says Peetie, quite miffed, "it's you they're laughing at Daddy," says Peetie pointing at the scarf. Peetie had an inkling as to what the article was around Jim's neck but he would not be so bold as to contradict his father in the middle of the fair with all eyes cast upon him.

"What's wrong with the scarf?" says he, quite annoyed as he whipped it from around his neck and fluttered it up and down for all to see. He was about to say, 'have a good look at it, it's only a scarf'. He gave a cursory glance to confirm to himself that it was only a scarf. He could see in an instant that his scarf wasn't that colour. He gave it a quick but penetrating look. The colour drained from his face in abject humiliation. He gulped a mouth full of air. The impact almost choked him. He was mortified at the thought of everyone looking at him with Mary's long legged knickers around his neck and he thinking it was a scarf.

"Well, be the living sinner," says he, ramming the garment into his pocket. "Let's get out of here quickly before any other calamity should befall us."

Immediately the red headed woman crossed his mind.

Christmas time was the annual fund raising time for the Orphanage in Ballinaglass. Without exception everyone contributed in their own small way. Some gave donations, young people sold tickets, while the women folk knitted socks and slipovers and scarves. Since Mary wasn't able to contribute any of these on account of her eyesight, she held a card game in their home instead. A huge crowd gathered on the appointed night. There were three prizes, a turkey, a brace of chickens and a pair of hobnail boots.

(At this juncture in the narrative, gentle readers, I would like to state that at that time, it wasn't uncommon to see fowl roosting on the ledge at the back of the settle bed in the kitchen. It kept them safe from prowling foxes. The droppings that accumulated on the settle bed seat were cleaned out in the morning, the fowl turned out for the day, and the half door closed to deter them from re-entering during the daytime.)

The solid farmers and their wives were invited to play in the parlour where the glass bowl kerosene lamp, with it's corrugate crumpled chimney top opening proudly like petals of bulbs and stood in the centre of the large mahogany table. Mary, their hostess, was sitting in the armchair beside the fire, her eyesight preventing her from taking part in the game.

The regular card players gathered around the kitchen table where the standard lamp gave out a feeble pool of light. The turkey was roosting on top of the dresser for all to see. A dozen fowl were roosting on the back of the ledge of the settle bed, any two to be selected by the winner. The boots were hanging from a nail at the back of the kitchen door.

The game got under way in the kitchen. After each player played a card the next player, on account of the poor light, had to lean in over the table to discern the value of the card already played by the previous player before playing his own card. This was repeated by every card player with the result that the light at intervals was suddenly obscured, then quickly revealed. On and on it went, the kaleidoscope of light and darkness danced around the kitchen.

The turkey, not being used to the light and then the absence of light wafting around, got light in the head and toppled off the dresser, thrashing it's wings on the way down, sweeping mugs and cups off the dresser in the process. It landed, not on the floor, but into the churn of cream Mary was hoping to churn the next day.

On hearing the commotion in the kitchen, Mary and Mollo Gahan were soon on the scene and without undue commotion hauled the turkey out of the churn. Mollo, who was chief cook and bottle washer that night, held the turkey over the churn while swishing all the cream off it and back into the churn, in the interest of economy.

"You can't," says she, "be letting good cream like that go to waste."

The card playing over and the diaspora complete, Jim, Mary and Mollo sat in the warm glow of the turf fire sipping a well-earned drink while chatting about the great night that was had by all.

"We can have a well earned rest in the morning," says Mary.

It was only then that it dawned on Jim about the potato pickers coming the next day.

"You'll just have to cancel it then," says she. "There's not a scrap of bread in the house and I'm too tired to bake."

"I'll bake one," says Mollo, "it won't take that long."

"There is no room on the table with all the dirty delph," says Mary.

"I'll make it over there on the settle top," says Mollo

From the hoard of golden meal and white flour in the flour bin, Mollo extracted two large handfuls of white and wheaten meal and sieved it through her fingers onto the settle top. No bowl was used. She clapped her hands gently to slack the flour from them before going to the dresser and extracting a spoonful of bread soda from a brown paper bag. She locked it in the palm of her hand and returned to the settle again and crunched the soda over the flour. Then she added salt. Next she walked to the scullery and took a jug of sour milk, 'It's too thick,' she thought to herself. Taking an empty jug, she sent the sour milk sloshing like a waterfall from full jug to empty jug and back again. Satisfied that the viscid had reached the right consistency she returned to the settle and began mixing the ingredients carefully and lovingly, humming as she did so.

All the while the fowl were roosting on the settle ledge

board of the dresser, nonchalant to Mollo's activities below them.

Satisfied that the ingredients were fully mixed, she garnered in every last grain from the outer regions of the settle with the side of her hand into the hillock. Unbeknownst to her, on account of the feeble pool of light, she had also garnered in some fowl droppings in the process.

The cake made, Mollo placed the big mass of dough in the pot oven, flattened it out with the back of her hand and made the sign of the cross with the knife on it before stabbing each quarter in turn with the knife. She then lifted the lid by the tongues and covered the pot oven with it. She then put red hot coals on the lid. She gave it one hour to bake.

When it was ready she inserted the claws of the tongues into the loop of the lid and lifted it off. The cake had risen so high that it was pushing the lid off the pot oven.

Well, when Jim saw the size of the cake he couldn't believe his eyes.

"Well, be the living sinner," says he, "that's the biggest cake I ever saw. What did you put into it at all?" looking at Mollo. "May the Good Lord bless your hands, it'll be the lucky man that will get you."

Jim, still in his reverie with his reminiscing, reached out to give Mollo an affectionate pat on the shoulder. But instead he lost his balance and crashed to the floor from his chair.

Mary who had also been reminiscing in her reverie, almost fell out of the bed with fright.

"Mother of God," she yelled. "Is that the bomb going off?"

Jim, physically shaken, dragged himself laboriously off the floor, grunting with exertion as he did so. He rose joint by joint, not unlike a carpenter's rule, and slid himself back onto the chair.

"I must have fallen asleep," says he.

"Will you ever read that letter?" she barked, "and don't be keeping me in suspense all day."

Jim cleared his throat:

"*Dear Mary, I am penning you my last letter from this world. I have been struck down by a rare virus and my end is near.*"

Jim gave a great smile of satisfaction to himself, knowing that this troublemaker wouldn't be home again. 'I wonder did he ever pay back the money he stole from the bank in Ballinaglass,' thought Jim.

The letter continued:

"*I may not have been the perfect uncle but I hope you'll see it in your heart to forgive me, especially Jim.*"

"Haa," says Jim, "feeling sorry for himself now that he is off to meet his maker."

"Don't be so hard on him, love," says she, "he wasn't all that bad."

Jim didn't answer but only grunted.

"What's in the other letter?" says she.

"It's probably a bill," says Jim. "It's not the first time he stuck you to clear his debts."

Jim read on.

"*My last Will and Testament is enclosed, sent by Canton and Corcoran Solicitors, Sidney, Australia.*

"*To whom it concerns. My client, the late Michael Dooley, whose body was crem, crema, cremated last week, …*"

"What in the name of God," says Mary, "does that mean. Get the dictionary and see if you can break down that jawbreaker of a word. Oh God," says she, massaging her chin, "why can't they write simple English these … what does it say?" she urged.

"It says, 'to reduce a corpse to ashes by burning in the fire'."

"Oh the poor man," says she and began howling and wailing. "Jim, I always knew he'd go to Hell but now it seems the Devil doesn't want him."

When Mary regained her self-control she inquired as to his last request that he sought.

"... *asks that his ashes be taken to Bray Head and tossed into the Bay,*" said Jim.

Standing on the summit of Bray Head Jim wound up his arm for the throw like a bowler. He swung the box over and over his head until it hummed with power. Then he flung the box to his almighty best, aiming it out beyond the ravine.

"You were always a high flier," says he, "so off you go and good riddance."

The Dream

It was midmorning when Tom set out from his cottage in Kylebrack to the village in Kilmartin to replenish his larder. The sky was cloudless though hazed, so the blue looked faded and thin. The prospect of a fine, warm day Tom thought. He had his walking stick in one hand and shopping bag in the other. Trix, the black and white collie, greeted him with ecstatic barking as he danced and eddied around him, 'like a joint play top', in exuberant welcome before dashing to the road gate, frantically barking as if to repel some imaginary intruder.

Tom turned on the doorstep and tugged at the latch of the door, checking its security before setting off. He was in a pensive mood as he shuffled along, picking his steps over tussocks of hill grass and muddy pools of water that lay between the cart ruts along the dirt road. The ditches were laced with umbels of green and yellow blossom, on both sides down to the main road. Although an avid nature lover, this beauty did nothing to dispel the gloom that hung over him.

The thrush and the blackbird were in melodious voice, as were the finches. Crows in the oak tree overhead seemed to be very friendly and merry. Some of them came down from the tree bough, as if clapping their black hands when they landed on the road in front of him, squawking and cawing as if in a welcoming gesture. But Tom didn't seem to notice their jollification, for his mind was in turmoil as he trudged along.

He stopped at Rambo's Cross to rest and light his pipe. It might clear his head, he thought.

The view over Kilmartin was more beautiful than he had ever seen it before. 'Suppose,' says he to himself, ' absence makes the heart grow fonder.'

He remembered as a young lad, playing football on the beach with his friends, Saddler Harkins, Swank Hayden and the other lads of the same age.

Seeing young couples walking hand in hand along the beach while other couples were dancing and frolicking around the dunes brought back fond memories of his own courting days with Rose O'Brien.

That lissom Rose from Dublin, she was the heart throb of all the young eligible men in the village, and the envy of all the young nymphets in the area, but it was him who had won her heart and her affection. When she died suddenly of a rare fever he was devastated, so much so that he lost interest in girls after that and forever since.

For the first time Tom felt the cold penetrating his feeble frame. He knotted the scarf around his throat before moving on.

His recent stay in hospital had given him the warmth and comfort he now missed, but that wasn't his immediate concern. Why, he wondered aloud, was he getting all these strange dreams, dreams that he could neither comprehend or grasp their meaning. They weren't of a spectre nature, he was sure of that. Since his release from hospital, they had become an almost nightly occurrence. He nodded his head to nobody in particular, to confirm the fact. By the time he had regained his composure and was fully awake the dream, or at least that's what he thought it was, had vanished from his brain, but some sliver of his subconscious kept tugging at his heart strings, urging him to pursue these confounded dreams as a matter of urgency.

'Why a court case?' he kept asking himself as he stood on the middle of the road, considering the matter. He was never in a courthouse in his life, let alone being up in court.

'I know,' says he, 'we did a little moonlighting in our younger days, but we were never caught. I have no regrets for making that illicit brew. Didn't we keep manys a man, and woman for that matter, out of hospital with our brew, and manys an animal would have died but for us. My mind must be playing tricks on me,' he breathed to himself. 'Sure anything can happen to a feeble old man once he passes seventy'.

The midday bell chimed rustily from the steeple of St. Patrick's Church Tower in the village as Tom entered McDowels Public House. He liked this all-embracing establishment where he could get whatever his needs be, from groceries to his drapery, to haberdashery, oil for his lamp and he could also post a letter if he so wished. Most of all he liked Joey, the Proprietor. ' That amiable Joey was one who never forgets the sick or the needy,' he thought, 'Yes, he could always depend on Joey if he was housebound.'

A rousing chorus of welcomes boomed out for Tom from his cronies who had turned from their drinks at the bar. He acknowledged their welcoming gesture with a wave of his hand and a sad little smile before crossing the Bar to where the open fire was.

The cronies turned in on themselves and began to converse in whispers.

"The Master is not himself," they were heard to say.

Tom was known far and wide as Tom, the Master. His father, John Quale, was the local school teacher, and to distinguish him from other families of the same surname, he was known as Tom the Master, although he himself didn't teach school.

Joey, the proprietor brought over to Tom his usual order, hot whiskey with cloves.

"That's on the house, Tom, and welcome home."

Tom put his hand into his waistcoat pocket and extracted a piece of crumpled paper.

"There's me shopping list," says he, handing him the slip of paper.

"I'll be a little while," says Joey, "there's other customers to be served."

Tom looked at him blankly. "I'm in no hurry," came the instant reply.

Tom leaned back in the comfort of the old armchair, staring into the alpenglow of embers from the turf fire as he sipped his drink. With the heat of the fire and comfort of the armchair Tom's mind lapsed back to earlier times, when he was a young man with a mop of black hair. This mental picture portrayed happiness around Tom. He saw himself in a strong, active masculine role, who would grow up to inherit the farm, and, with his secure job with the County Council, in time maybe he would buy more land. He could have fathered a daughter or two as pretty as their mother and a son as robust as himself in his day. He would die a happy and respected father or maybe grandfather in the community.

He massaged his chin and nodded his head as he pondered these things to himself. That's how it should have been. He gave a plangent sigh. But when poor Rose, my lovely Rose, died suddenly, well …all those kind of plans fell through. He lost all interest in girls after that.

'Do you know …' says he to himself as he drew on his pipe gently, then nibbled the shank before oscillating it between his lips. He repeated this process several times as he sat in reverie in front of the open fire.

'I was in Dublin only once since Rose's death and that was at the wedding of my cousin, Sara. She married a nice young man by the name of Jamsie …' he rubbed his chin, 'something or other, I just can't think of it right now. Sure that was all of forty years ago.'

'I remember, they had a son, also called Jamsie after the father. Where he is now I couldn't tell.' Tom's eyes began to mist up with melancholy when he recalled the tragic death of Jamsie and Sara. They were at a dance at the Seabrook Hotel on the Quays on New Years Eve. A fire broke out in the basement of the hotel and, within minutes, the hotel was reduced to rubble. There were no survivors.

Young Jamsie was left orphaned and all alone in the world, except for myself. The child was made a ward of the court by Judge Joshua Charles Cordell. I'll never forget that name. He placed him in an Orphanage in Blackrock.

Tom gave another wearisome sigh, then took a dollop of the hot whiskey. 'If only I had been married,' says he. 'Jamsie could be with me right now. Instead, he is out there somewhere all alone, not knowing I exist,' and he leaned his head towards the lattice window, 'just like myself,' says he.

'It would be nice to have someone to keep me company in me old age, and to make me a cup of tea. He could have my ould shack for the rest of his life, such as it is. I remember,' says he as he slapped his closed fist into the cupped hand of the other to emphasise the fact, 'Fr. O'Brien went to great pains to trace his whereabouts without success. He said that all those boys in the Orphanage were boarded out to families around the country and the Orphanage closed down.' but somewhere in the recesses of Tom's mind something was urging him to try again.

He was shook back to the present when Joey tapped him on the shoulder.

"A penny for your thoughts, Tom," says Joey, as he

placed the bag of groceries on the floor beside his chair.

Tom looked up at him rather melancholy. "Well," says he, "if the thoughts would only come true they would be worth a lot more to me than that."

Lowering the last of the whiskey Tom sat erect in his chair. He adjusted the gray cap on his head, then reached for his shopping bag. The old dog was lying prostrate on the hearthstone, apparently asleep but in reality wide awake and listening, like all good and faithful dogs do, for their master's every nuance and glance.

"I'd better make tracks," says he, "before it gets too late." The old dog stood up lazily and stretched himself, then stood waiting for his master's next move.

Tom caught the shopping bag by its handles, one in each hand and looked into it. At first glance he noticed that the brown paper that Joey always wrapped his meat in was missing. To say it was a disappointment was an understatement. Tom used the brown paper across his chest, under his shirt, to act as a windbreak. It warded off the ravages of colds and flu. He firmly believed that it was better than any of those fancy scarfs, and now he must go home without any.

Joey noticed Tom's agitation. He became concerned for his old friend and called out, "Are you all right there, Tom?"

The old man, without taking his eyes from the maw of the bag, curtly enquired, "Have you got all me groceries in here?"

"O' no, Tom," says Joey, "there's no bacon this week. There's a strike on in the factory in Dublin."

"Well I bedamned," says Tom, mumbling through his whiskers into the maw of the bag, "this country is gone to hell and all the unemployment there is in it, surely to God," says he, "you could have parcelled up the bread for me," hoping this would embarrass Joey into parting with some of his precious wrapper paper.

But Joey didn't bite. "Don't you know there's a war on? I'm finding it almost impossible to get brown paper to wrap even the essentials."

"I'll tell you what," says Joey, taking up the newspaper off the counter, "Matty Walker, the Guinness's traveller, left this paper here after him. You can have it. He read out a few strange court cases just before you came in." Joey handed him the paper. "Being an erudite man like yourself you'll understand the ins and outs of those cases reported in it."

Tom took the paper rather sullenly. "It'll have to do I suppose," says he, "it's better than nothing."

Little did Tom know that Matty was a friend of Judge Joshua Charles Cordell, the presiding Judge over these cases reported in the paper and also the Judge that sent young Jamsie Peacock, his cousin, to the Orphanage in Blackrock all those years ago.

Having gathered all the goods into his shopping bag Tom grunted with exertion as he got up, steadied himself, then headed for the door, the old dog sauntering behind him. He thought of the long trek ahead of him up Quinberry Hill to his house. He gave a sigh of anguish at the thought. The sun was streaming down from a clear blue sky as he trudged along.

When he came to Rambo's Cross a great tiredness enveloped him, so he sat down on a granite boulder under the oak tree, a favourite resting place of his. He leaned back against the tree and stretched out his legs. It was a welcome respite after the heavy climb. Old Trix came back obediently when called to where Tom was sitting, and collapsed on the grass beside him, his tongue lolling out with the heat.

Tom relaxed in the shade of the old oak tree, lit his pipe and let his mind wander. He was in no hurry, there was nobody waiting for him. As he drew on the pipe, he raised his eyes and followed the narrow road opposite up the gradient slope, pass the graveyard on its right and up the boreen to Saddler Harkins' abode at the end of the cul-de-sac under the Quinberry Mountain.

A small group of people came to enquire the way to the graveyard, which Tom was only too happy to oblige. Americans he was sure by their accents. 'I suppose,' says he, 'searching for their ancestors' graves.'

It reminded him of his own parents, brothers and sisters lying up there, all having died of tuberculosis, the curse of the age. He gave a wearisome sigh and nibbled on the stem of his pipe. 'It won't be very long,' says he to himself, 'til I'll be joining them.' He looked around at all the changes that had taken place since he was a boy, all the families that had passed away to their eternal rest, while others had emigrated to England or America, never to return.

'Sure where would they be coming back to anyway,' says he to himself, 'a miserly plot of land and only the ribs of a house.' His eyes were drawn to the ruins of these once neatly thatched hamlets, of cottages that lay in gentle decay opposite the graveyard. He could name all the families that once lived there, Hanlons, the Gregans, the Whelans, the Roaches, the Conlons and of course the Slatterys. 'I remember,' says he to himself, 'rambling to all them houses in the time. There would be music, song or dance nightly in one or other of these houses. If not, there would be card playing. Our past times were never dull, but now … '

He tapped the bowl of the pipe against the palm of his other hand to loosen the dottle, then took a long draw before withdrawing the pipe from between his teeth, allowing the smoke to slid out slowly. And so he reminisced in his mind in the still of the afternoon of yesteryear.

Then, without portend or warning he was unceremoniously shook out of his reverie when a large white puck goat mounted the gable end wall of Slatterys' old ruins and stood on its apex. He reared up on his hind legs and pompously displayed his agility with a little war dance for his comrades. When he spotted Tom and Trix under the tree he widened his eyes and flared his nostrils before backing away, jumped down at the back of the old ruins and went back to grazing ... and Tom to his reminiscing.

Tom's lips flexed their corners into the beginning of a smile at the agility of the old puck when the episode of Slattery's wicked gander, called Rambo, came into his mind. He was better than any watch dog.

'I remember,' says he to himself, 'the day Mike Slattery's daughter Nancy was getting married to young Ned Doyle of Tombrien. I remember the wedding reception was held at O'Rahilies Hotel in Tombrien, a big affair it was.'

Tom took the pipe out of his mouth to ponder the occasion. He was thinking of his own wedding that was to take place the following week in Dublin. For a moment a pang of sadness pervaded him. 'I suppose,' says he to himself, 'it was God's Will.'

Well anyway, Andy Corcoran, a bit of a rapscallion, took advantage of the occasion and set out to rob Slattery's house, sure in the knowledge that no one would be there or would ever find out. He marched into the yard with brazen effrontery. "I'm afraid of no dog," says he, twitching his shoulders and clenching his fists. He stood momentarily, reconnoitring the house and surrounding yard for any signs of life before peering in through the kitchen window to scrutinise the inner sanctum. In an effort to get a better view, he stood up on a galvanised bucket. The bucket overturned, a thunderous noise ensued, but that didn't deter the bould Andy in the least.

The old gander with his cohort of females and goslings, lazing in the haggard behind the house after their morning fling in the nearby stream, as was their wont every day, were rudely awakened. Rambo with his great territorial instincts, detached himself from his ward and dashed from the haggard, squawking and hissing in excited feathered flight to the front yard to investigate the commotion.

Seeing a person dressed in red sent him into a frenzy. Red was one colour of clothing Rambo detested, so without breaking his stride he sailed through the air and landed on Andy's shoulder. To say he was taken aback by the viciousness of the bird was a vast understatement. With fright, Andy collapsed on the ground. Never in his life did he encounter such a vicious bird. It was the least of his thoughts when he entered the yard that he could be attacked by a wicked gander.

Rambo danced on his back and every peck he gave him on the head he extracted tufts of hair and flesh. Andy scrambled to his feet roaring and howling, only to collapse on the ground again from the vicious pummelling of Rambo's wings. He thrashed about with his hands in a bid to ward off this vicious bird but to no avail.

Then, in the midst of his agony, he spotted the rest of the gaggle sailing around the gable end of the house in half feathered flight. Certain that he was going to be devoured alive, he took an almighty plunge and rose to his feet, joint by joint as the carpenter's rule opens, under Rambo's enormous weight and dashed to the road. The gander was still on his shoulders pecking and pummelling him as he continued to move to the road. When he got to the cross roads, only a short distance away, he collapsed in agony and exhaustion. Then it was there that Rambo set about to finish him off.

As luck would have it, who should come along only Saddler Harkins in his pony and cart Andy thereafter claimed Harkins saved him from certain death, and ever since the spot was known as Rambo's Cross.

The old dog lazily got up and stretched himself, then looked up at his master as much as to say it was time we were getting home. Tom, grunting with exertion, raised his stiff frame from the boulder and sauntered up the hill and towards the house, tired and listless. He opened the gate that led into the front yard. All was silent save for the birds singing in the yard to welcome him home.

Then, just as he was about to enter the house, two magpies touched down on the midden in the middle of the yard. 'Two for joy,' he muttered and smiled briefly before turning to unlock the kitchen door.

He set about to replenish the fire with sticks and turf from the old tea chest to boil the kettle. He made himself a strong mug of tea with plenty of sugar and indulged himself in the fresh shop bread he had just brought home. As he drank his tea, he glanced at the paper and sighed gravely. 'I'd rather have one piece of brown paper than all that trash.'

Then, for no great reason, Tom's eyes were drawn to the heading on the paper: *The Leinster Leader*. He muttered the words to himself. 'I've never heard of that paper before,' says he, reaching for his glasses.

Above the fold it read, "*Super Horse Wins Again*. Judge Joshua Cordell of Curralawn Estate and stud farm near Portlaoise, a noted owner and trainer, won the Champions Hurdle with his horse *Charley's Pride* at the Curragh on Saturday, his fifth win in as many starts, and next Saturday he runs *Heathers Delight* in the Donnybrook Stakes."

He turned over the page and began to read, "Man kicked to death by a neighbour's mule."

He read another case, "Two men engaged in a brawl in Carlow town over the festival weekend, end up in the River Barrow, the fire brigade had to be called out to rescue them."

Another case, "A man is fined two shillings for allowing his donkey to wander on the public road after dark. 'John Tilsey,' says the Magistrate, 'you are hereby charged with unlawfully allowing of your donkey to stray on the public road and not for the first time may I add, how do you plead?' John, being a little deaf, cupped his hand around his ear, to aid his hearing. 'Haah,' says he, craning his neck. 'Sergeant Hendy summoned you here to answer charges relating to your donkey wandering on the public road after dark. Don't you know,' says the Magistrate, 'it's highly dangerous to other road users?' (John Tilsey thought to himself: if the Sergeant wasn't such a perpetual drunkard he'd see where he was going.) In answer to the Magistrate, he answered 'Not guilty your Honour.' 'How do you come to that conclusion?' the Magistrate asked curtly. John responded, 'Well your Honour with your permission sir, I would like to ask the sergeant that, on the night in question, what was my donkey wondering at, for I never saw him wondering at anything in me life' A great guffaw descended from the rabble class at the back of the courtroom. 'Order,' demanded the Magistrate as he pummelled the desk with the gavel, 'or I will clear the court.' "

"Begob," says Tom, "this is a great paper altogether." He turned over the page and settled down to an exciting evening's reading. Tom became so engrossed in the paper that his tea went cold. The old dog, lying nonchalant by the fire, became suddenly animated at his master's unusual interest in the paper and, not to be left out, came over to where Tom was sitting, leaned his head on his knee and flicked his eyes up at him as much as to say, 'read on, I'm listening.'

"Carlow and District Court for the Month of May, Nineteen Hundred and Ten: Above the fold in large letters, *Corpse Molested While Lying in State*.

"Jamsie Peacock of Grantstown, County Kildare, you are hereby charged with the heinous assault and battery of the corpse of the late Thomas Myler of Ardfoyle Lodge, on the tenth of October Nineteen Hundred and Nine, and you are also charged with the unlawful demolition of a double bed on which the deceased was lying in state on the same occasion."

"How do you plead?" the Judge said.

Judge Joshua Charles Cordell, the presiding Judge, winked one eye as he gave Jamsie a furtive glance. Jamsie stared him steadfast, said to himself, rubbing his chin, 'I recognise you from somewhere,' but he would not be so bold as to challenge a man of such standing.

Jamsie eyeballed the winking Judge severely and furrowed his brow as he tried to rack his brain. 'I've seen you somewhere before, that's for sure and that voice is very familiar. It couldn't be possible that the two men could have similar deformities.' His mind flashed back to the day he went to see the fortune teller in Portlaoise. He too had a winking eye and a missing finger.

'That rapscallion of hell charged me a small fortune for his service,' says Jamsie, 'two months wages in fact, but he assured me that I wouldn't be going to jail, but instead I'd be going on a long journey and would meet an old relative. But I have no relative, I'm certain of that. It couldn't be possible that this man on the bench is him.'

He upbraided himself for his unkind thoughts. This man is too refined and well dressed to indulge in such unethical practices.

'But wait a minute,' says he, his thin eyebrows furrowing, 'what's this that old man Pa Doyle said the day

I stopped to enquire the directions to Ralph Kettle, the fortune teller. I remember him looking at me with searching eyes and saying, "Fools and their money are easily parted. There's no such person," said Pa rather curtly.

So I took the letter out of my inside pocket of me overcoat and answered, 'I have an appointment with him this evening up at the mine shaft, and he said it was up a narrow lane beside Curralawn Estate and stud farm.'

'O, you will no doubt have a meeting,' says he, taking the pipe from his mouth, 'but let me tell you, it'll be one and the same Judge Joshua Charles Cordell, dressed up as a tramp. He can play that part very well,' says he, winking at me, 'he uses that pseudo and garb as a decoy in order to extract money from unfortunates like yourself, to feed his gambling habits and to regale his cronies to weekends of debauchery and depravity and the devil knows what, up there at the mansion.'

Jamsie, knowing the ways of old people, once you give them their head and a little incentive like a cigarette, they would tell you their life's story.

'My wife,' says Pa, 'may the good Lord have mercy on her,' says he, raising his cap, 'worked up there as a cook and charwoman.' He leaned his head up towards the big house, 'She was privy to all that weird and uncanny frolicking that went on. She was sworn to secrecy as part of her employment by the Judge. I wasn't surprised when I heard that he had met with an accident.'

'What happened,' says I, hoping he would relate to me all the uncanny practices without any further incentive, but I needn't have worried for Pa was in full flow and I don't think that even if the Judge himself was standing close by he could have stopped him.

'He was out one day,' says Pa, exercising one of his prize fillies when she bolted and, in the fall, his foot got caught in the stirrup and he was dragged through the fields and down the dale.' He pointed with the stem of his pipe, 'She was apprehended below by the lake. He damaged one of his eyes and severed a finger where the horse pranced on him.'

Jamsie was beginning to have grave doubts as to whether he should go any further when the old man spoke again. 'Don't let me put you off, good man,' says he, 'after coming all that way, go up that boreen,' and he pointed with his walking stick in the direction of the mine shaft. 'There is a hut which adjoins the stud farm and stables. There you will find your Mr. Ralph Kettle. Not wishing to know your business,' says he, 'but if it's anything to do with predicting the winner of a race or the outcome of a court case he won't let you down, that's if you have plenty of money.' Then turning his back and twiddling his walking stick as he was about to leave, he said, 'sure hasn't he got the inside tract on all his predictions.'

Jamsie was shook back to the present when the Judge this time spoke slowly and firmly.

"How do you plead to these charges as outlined?"

Jamsie drew himself up to his full height which was only five feet one inch. He was a slackly built man with a moon face that seemed to be perched on a spindle of a neck. His shoulder length brown hair hung loosely around his ears and helped camouflage his stem-like neck. A multicoloured moustache covered peg teeth.

He eyeballed the Judge confidently and after a short pause spoke,

"Not guilty your Honour," in a firm voice.

The Judge was taken aback by Jamsie's firm reply, or at least that's the impression he gave.

"How do you come to that conclusion?" the Judge enquired.

"Your Honour," says Jamsie, "with your permission I would like to lay the bones of my case before you and this court."

A great guffaw erupted among the rabble class at the back of the courtroom as word was passed from mouth to eager mouth and savoured in the telling concerning Jamsie's erudite vocabulary.

The Judge pummelled the desk, calling for order or he'd clear the courtroom. He then glanced at his watch from his eyecorner, and to himself, 'It's too late now to dash off to the Curragh to back my own horse, *Daisy Mist* in the bumper, even if I did guillotine these proceedings. Sure didn't I get Five Shillings off him last week for my predictions, that'll suffice. It would not be prudent to show undue haste, even though I have already heard the bones of the case if you'll pardon the pun.'

The Judge leaned back in his chair, his elbows on each arm, his muscular face broke out into what could only be construed as a grimace of a smile from behind his maimed hand at Jamsie's feeble effort to present the best case possible for his defence, but the Judge would have to bear with it.

"You can carry on, Mr. Peacock," he said.

The courthouse was full to overflowing that day. They had travelled from far and near in the gigs and jaunting cars, on bicycles and on foot, to hear the outcome of this strange case. Jamsie cleared his throat and drew a deep breath. The confident resonance of his voice belied the expression of concern on his face. Buying time, he took out his handkerchief and blew his nose in a loud rapport.

It made him feel good as he stood in the Witness Box. He said a silent prayer in the hope that the Good Lord would give him the courage and strength to present a convincing case. But little did he know that the outcome had already been decided by the Judge who was trying to rectify a terrible injustice he himself had created many years earlier by not allowing Jamsie to be placed with his cousin Tom Quale in Avoca. As luck would have it he was now able to right this unfortunate error with the help of his old friend, Matty Walker, the Guinness traveller by leaving *The Leinster Leader* in Joey's pub for Tom Quale.

Jamsie glanced down the courtroom and there, at the back of the courtroom among the large gathering, was Mrs. Carey of Grantstown, with a handkerchief to her weeping eyes. She was heart broken lest Jamsie be sent to jail. It was at Mrs. Carey's house at Grantstown that Jamsie found refuge after he ran away from his foster parents, Thomas Myler of Ardfoyle in County Carlow. She knew Jamsie was a good and honest lad and she could certainly vouch for him if called upon. She intended leaving him the farm after her death but all that would change if Jamsie was sent to jail. She would not live on her own on this isolated farm anymore without company, so she would sell the farm and go live with her cousin in Dublin.

Jamsie, best known only to himself, never divulged to Mrs. Carey the incident of molesting the corpse of Thomas Myler on the day he went to buy the cow.

They were both relaxing at the kitchen table after their dinner and having a casual conversation about nothing in particular, as was often the case, when Jamsie produced the letter. The Widow knew he had got a letter earlier that morning from the postman. She also knew he had no girlfriends or relations as far as she knew. Being an orphan, she wondered in her own mind who could be writing to him, but she would not be so bold as to pry into his private affairs. She knew he would talk about it in his own time.

When he related the story of molesting the corpse and the breaking of the bed the day he went to buy the cow in

Ardfoyle, and the Summons to appear in court the following week, she nearly had a heart attack. She groped towards the armchair in front of the fire and flopped down hard into it. She crossed her left arm under her amply bosom, then placed her right elbow in the palm of her left hand for support. She rested her face in the cusp between thumb and forefinger of her right hand and gave a long, deep sigh.

'Merciful Hour,' she barked, 'you'll go to jail as sure as God made little apples. I've never heard the bate of that in all my life and I have heard of some quare things.'

Jamsie remained still at the table. He wrapped his two hands around his face, his elbows on the table and sort of cuddled it with shame.

'I'm ruined,' says he, 'and I have ruined your good name as well and all you have done for me.' He looked at her with tear filled eyes, 'I'm sorry, Mam,' says he. He always called her Mam ever since he came to live with her for she was the only real mother he ever had.

'When I saw that roughen,' says he, 'lying in the bed, with all's I could describe as a wry grin on him, I really thought he was laughing at me. Well I couldn't control my anger.'

The Widow joined her hands in a prayerful expression, high in front of her face. Her eyes were cast heavenwards and she prayed with all her might to the Good Lord for directions. She was a very pious woman and she was confident that the Good Lord wouldn't let her down. Many years earlier when her husband died suddenly and she only married a few months in this rugged and isolated farm in Kildare she bombarded the heavens with prayers and supplications. Then out of the blue and without portend or warning who should she discover at her gate, only an emaciated and timid boy, sheltering under the beech from a thunderous downpour. Being the kindhearted woman that she was, she invited him in and sat him up to the fire so as he could dry his clothes and have something to eat in the warm glow of the turf fire. In order to gain his confidence they chatted desultorily as he wolfed down the thick slides of well buttered bread she had only just made.

The tea over, he relaxed a little and, with a bit of coaxing and cajoling, Mrs. Carey extracted the full story from him.

'I'm never going back there again,' says he, 'I'd rather go to jail first.'

'You won't have to,' says she, then in her own mind, "that's if I have any say on it."

Mrs. Carey sat bolt upright in her chair and smacked her two hands together. 'That's what we'll do,' says she, more to herself than to anyone else.

Jamsie gazed at her blankly, but he was too engrossed in his own turmoil to comment.

'Tomorrow,' says she, 'you'll go and see that fortune teller in Portlaoise. I believe he is very good and accurate with his predictions. I remember Kitty O'Neill going to him once when she was about to be evicted from her home, the poor creatuir, and she with five children to rear. The poor thing was nearly out of her mind with worry and torment. Well she handed the last shilling she had in the world to him. The way he snapped it she knew he was not too pleased with such a small offering. He was a trampish looking fellow with a missing finger and a winking eye. His hair looked as if it didn't see a comb for years."

He burst into the hut from what seemed an underground cave and sat at this rickety old table and gazed into the crystal ball and began mumbling incantations into it for some minutes. Then he stopped abruptly and peered at her with his good eye.

'You won't be evicted from your house,' says he, 'if

you do what I tell you.'

The poor creatuir gave a great sigh of relief, a great weight had been lifted off her shoulders.

'Wherever you might borrow the money,' says he, 'get it and back *Stormy Weather* in the three thirty on Saturday at the Curragh.'

'I know,' says Mrs. Carey, 'for I gave it to her, she won quite a sum of money, more than enough to clear off all her debts, with enough left to buy clothes for herself and the children.'

Back in the courtroom Jamsie began.

"Your Honour, a few months ago a milking cow was for sale over in Darcy's of Ardfoyle. Mrs. Carey asked me to go over there and buy it for her as all her own cows had gone dry for the winter.

"Mr. Darcy, who I well know from the time I worked at Mylers, informed me that the cow in question belonged to Tom Myler, and it was there I had to go if I wanted to buy the cow.

"Leaving Darcy's yard Pat put his hand on my shoulder. 'Jamsie,' says he, 'I know only too well the way that scoundrel treated you when you were only a garsun, but you need not worry anymore, the old codger was very low last night when I was leaving and the doctor said that he wouldn't pass the night.'

'I'm not afraid of him,' I said as I stood stiff beside my bike. 'As a matter of fact I'm looking forward to meeting him.'

"Lifting the heavy door knocker, its bappidy bap bap sound vibrated the inner sanctum and carried all the way to the kitchen where Mrs. Myler was resting. After a moment or two he heard feet shuffling inside the hall door. He shook his shoulders and braced himself for whatever the outcome of his encounter with the said Mr.

and Mrs. Myler might be.

"The big oak door creaked open a sliver and the wizen face of an old gray haired woman peered out through the narrow opening. On recognising Jamsie she jerked back and tethered on her heels. Her Adam's apple bumped up and down several times in its loose flesh, whether from guilt or surprise I do not know. Having regained her self-control she hastily tugged at the heavy oak door until its creaking hinges yielded and the door opened fully.

" 'Jamsie Peacock,' says she, 'you are a sight for sore eyes.' She looked at me up and down a few times before stepping aside to allow me to enter. 'Come in,' says she, 'and welcome, it's so nice to see you after all these years.'

"Jamsie, to himself, 'Well, I can't say the same about you,' and out loud, "No Ma'am," says he, "I won't go in, I've come to buy the cow."

"The old lady didn't answer, but turned on her heels, sauntered back to the kitchen and sat on her favourite armchair beside the open fire. Tears welled up in her eyes and slid down her sallow cheeks like lonely drops of rain.

"Ignoring the business for which he came, 'Jamsie,' says she through the tears and the sobs, 'poor Tom passed away last night.'

"Jamsie to himself, 'and good riddance to him,' and out loud, "Sorry to hear that, Ma'am."

"Seeing that you're here, it would be nice if you go up and pay your respects while I put on the kettle," she said.

"Jamsie climbed the familiar rickety old stairs. He noticed in the dim light where he had carved his initials with the penknife on the handrail all those years ago and he thought, oh the trouncing he received for it!

"By the time he reached the landing a great surge of anger had welled up in him. Stoutly, yet full of foreboding, he slowly opened the door to the Wake room a sliver and peered in through the aperture but could see nothing, only the end of the bed. Pushing the door slowly but cautiously, still holding on to the doorknob he stepped further into the room.

"There he was and no mistaking. The familiar iron jaw and dry grin, he was sort of propped up in the bed, a look of satisfaction on his leathery face from having inflicted a lifetime of misery and terror on all his wards. It seemed at any moment he was ready to start again. Jamsie's mind flashed back to the years of abuse, both physical and mental at the hands of this roughin. He vowed then that some day he would give him his just deserts.

"He remembered the time vaguely when his parents died in a fire in the Seabrook Hotel on the Quays in Dublin. Being only three at the time and no one to care for me I was placed in an Orphanage in Blackrock by the courts until a suitable home was found."

'I know,' says the Judge to himself, 'it was me that placed you there.'

"It wasn't until I was twelve years of age that Mr. and Mrs. Myler of Ardfoyle Lodge in County Carlow adopted me. They promised the Matron that they would look after me and treat me just like one of their own, but sorry to say that didn't happen. Every morning I was up at six o'clock to milk cows and carry out a myriad of chores before going to school, and then repeating the same chores in the evening before I got my dinner. If they weren't all complete he would beat me and call me names."

"What did he call you," the Judge enquired.

"The gosling, your Honour."

"Why such a name?" he asked with a dry grin behind his maimed hand.

"Well sir," he said, "I looked like one with my long neck."

There was an outburst of mule laughter from the back

of the court. The Judge banged his gavel on the desk severely. "Order," says he, "or I'll clear the court."

Jamsie continued. In a cauldron of fury and hellbent on fulfilling his promise, he forgot that his old adversary was already dead. His impetuousness fused with fury. He took an almighty leap and landed on the corpse's chest, tendering him with right and left hooks to the lower mandible with such vim and vigour that the ancient wooden bed collapsed under them.

From the kitchen the old woman heard the thunderous noise. She leaped in the chair with fright, then as if activated by some wire she sprung from the chair and raced up the stairs as quick as her old legs could carry her, her mind full of foreboding.

When she saw the two antagonists lying in a tangled mass of broken bed, the covers bought specially for the Wake badly soiled, she let out an almighty shriek.

"Hooooly Mother of God," she wailed, "look at the cut of the bed, you bloody clown, look at what you've done. The ould bed is smashed to smithereens." She looked at the recumbent form of her husband lying among the debris. "The poor man," says she, "you have him disfigured for life, what am I going to do at all, at all. The neighbours will be calling around any minute to pay their respects."

Thrashing his arms and legs, Jamsie extricated himself from the mangled bed. He looked at the corpse, then at the old woman. A smirk of satisfaction beamed all over his face as he made for the door. He glanced back over his shoulder as he left the room. 'Sure aren't they both rotten anyway.'

Jamsie turned to face the Judge. "Your Honour," says he, "those are the true facts of the case."

He waited nervously for the Judge to sum up the case and issue his findings. But the Judge never moved.

'He's in a trance,' says Jamsie to himself, 'probably hasn't recovered from late nights of wine, women and song and cavorting with his many mistresses.'

In his mind's eye Jamsie could see a definite resemblance between the two characters, a well-dressed Judge and a trampish fortune teller. He nodded his head in acknowledgement of the fact that this rapscallion of hell was in fact the pseudo fortune teller. 'I'll report him,' says he, clenching his fists, 'that's if I don't get a satisfactory hearing from him.' After all he had handed over, in Jamsie's world, a small fortune.

The Judge was shook back to the present by the great silence that pervaded the courtroom. He sat strutly in his chair and began to shuffle with some papers in front of him, not quite sure where he was until he looked over and saw Jamsie still in the witness box. Then he remembered. He gave a quick glance at his watch. He thought, 'I must have fallen asleep for most of this man's evidence, but didn't I hear it all before.'

"Mr. Peacock," says he, "I caution you to bring your evidence to a close."

Jamsie leered at him. 'If you'd go to bed early at night and not be frolicking til all hours, you'd know I have already finished my defence.'

After a short recess the Judge returned to the rostrum. The clerk of the court indicated to Jamsie to stand for the Judge's summing up and the issuing of his verdict.

"Having considered all the facts of this case," says he, "and your past record of good behaviour, I will show leniency, but I must warn you that in future watch your outbursts of temper."

Then he banged the gavel on the desk. "Case dismissed."

Tom read the case a second time. "This is unbelievable

what that poor man Jamsie Peacock, went through. Jamsie Peacock." Tom dragged out the name, then rubbed his chin and furrowed his brow in deep thought.

"If me mind serves me right," says he, "I'm sure that's the same man who's father married Sara O'Toole, my cousin, all those years ago. His name was Jamsie Peacock. Now I remember it well, the fire tragedy on the Quays and that same Judge Joshua Charles Cordell who committed him to the Orphanage in Blackrock."

Tom became suddenly animated. He looked down at the old dog who had remained steadfast by his knee all through the reading. He patted the dog on the head.

"Do you know?" says he, "that dream that has been haunting me for so long is going to come to fruition, I can feel it in me bones."

The old dog wagged his tail before withdrawing his head and going over to lie on the hearthstone. He looked back at his master before making several circular turns as dogs usually do before lying down, as much as to say, 'if you're happy, I'm happy.'

Tom tapped the paper with his knuckles where the court case was written, "I'll write to that man tomorrow," says he out loud, "nothing ventured, nothing gained."

Dear Mr. Peacock,

Please excuse me if I am intruding on your privacy, but since reading the court case in the Leinster Leader in which your name came up, I am of the belief that we might be related. I would be most grateful if you would confirm a few queries for me so as to satisfy my curiosity and to put to bed, as it were, once and for all this terrible dream that has been haunting me ever since my time in hospital. A Jamsie Peacock, an English man, married my cousin

Sara O'Toole in St. Johnbosco's Church in Ranelagh in eighteen hundred and seventy they had one son also called Jamsie, who I guess would be about forty years old now. His parents lost their lives in a fire in the Seabrook Hotel on the Quays, that son I do believe was placed in an orphanage in Blackrock. If the names and dates correspond we are definitely related and if that be so, I hereby formally invite you to my home in Avoca in County Wicklow.

Your long lost cousin

Thomas Quale

When Jamsie read the letter he sprang from the chair, the letter held high above his head as he pirouetted around the kitchen floor.

Flabbergasted, Mrs. Carey jerked in her chair, clasped her hand against her throat in angst and gulped down a large lung full of air. For a moment she thought he had got another summons.

"Heh heeee," said Jamsie, "I have got relatives in Avoca. I'm not a loner in the world after all!"

He took Mrs Carey up in a dancing hold and the two whirled around the kitchen until Mrs. Carey was breathless and dizzy in the head and gasping for air.

She stopped abruptly and drew in a deep breath. "Do you know," says she, "we both could go down to Avoca tomorrow."

The Counsellor

Anyone acquainted with the village of Kilquale during the early part of the last century must surely have encountered its most prominent and colourful character, the Hen Man. His real name was Tom Crouch but not a sinner would have known him by that appellation. The Hen Man was the nickname bestowed on him by the old women of the village on account of his selling and buying of fowl for a living.

My first encounter with Tom the Hen Man was one sunny summer afternoon. I was on my holidays at the time. I sauntered up the short driveway that he shared with his neighbour. The gable ends of their houses faced each other, also their kitchen doors. He was sitting outside his own kitchen door on an old rickety armchair with a newspaper in hand.

I made my acquaintance with him as I sat down on the granite doorstep beside him. He was crippled with arthritis in his hands and knees and hips. Two walking sticks resting against his leg bore out the fact. I was amazed at the high spirits he was in even though cringing in pain. What struck me most about him was the strange way he was holding the paper in his gnarled hands. But I would not be so bold as to criticise this old man outside his own front door, it would hurt his ego greatly.

I hadn't a need to introduce myself or the reason for my visit. My Uncle Martin had already told him about me and my interest in the local history of the area. I knew Tom, being such a travelled man, would have many a fine story to tell.

Tom let down the paper, took out a pipe from somewhere in a waistcoat pocket and clasped it between his gums. After many attempts a match was extracted from the matchbox. He didn't seem to mind the effort. He struck it against sandpaper on the side of the box and lit the pipe, drew savagely on it at first to get it going, then, satisfied that it was working, leaned back in the chair like a contented child. I thought he seemed glad of the company for a few hours, if only to take his mind off his pains.

We settled down in our seats. The usual topics and well-worn items of news were trotted out such as the weather, how well the countryside looked, the general health of my family. When two neighbours met, whether young or old, these topics were covered to get the conversation going.

"I was reading an article," says Tom, "in that paper about Daniel O'Connell, the Liberator, just before you came. Do you know?" says he, "he came from the same county as meself, Kerry."

You'd know by the way his leathery face yielded into a slight smile that he was proud of the fact.

""He was a great orator," says he. "Many's a fine speech he made in the House of Commons on behalf of the Irish people. Oh that was a long time ago now," says he.

Martin had often told me about Tom the Hen Man as an almost illiterate man, but no one dared refer to him as such in public. He had the gift of gab and spoke in his own inimitable way in the vernacular. He also had a great retentive memory. 'He must have had,' says I to myself, … ' thinking about the day I called on him and found him reading the paper upside down. This memory stood him in good stead when he let his name go forward for the local elections.

"I was evicted from my farm in Kerry," says Tom, "because I had joined the Land League. Our objective was to force the landlords to reduce the crippling rents that were being paid by tenant farmers. I must have been a thorn in the side of the landlords, for in order to silence me for good they evicted me from my lands and ordered me out of the county, never to return. And I was let to know that to refuse to leave would call forth swift retribution."

"My intention was to go to Dublin. My father's friend lived up there. But somewhere along the way I must have taken a wrong turn so I ended up here in this one horse village of Kilquale."

"Oh I was never sorry for staying. The people in general were kind and welcoming. Having made my acquaintance with the Parish Priest, Father. John Touhy, I outlined my plan over a hearty meal his housekeeper had laid on for me."

"Well," says Fr. Touhy when we were seated at the table, "the good Lord must have directed you this way," as he gave me a hearty welcome and his blessing. "It will be nice," says he, "to see some little industry coming to this village, no matter how small."

The Priest directed me to a vacant cottage at the far end of the street.

"I think," says he, "it will suit you down to the ground. It has a number of outhouses, such as they are, where you can keep your fowl and there's an acre of a plot at the back to keep your pony in."

"I thanked him profusely for his welcome and his kindness."

"We'll talk about the sale of it another day," says Fr. Touhy.

"Do you know," says Tom with a glance around at his thatched cottage and then at me, "this is the very same house I occupied when I first came here. Oh I had no reason ever to move."

After the meal, Tom and Fr. Touhy sat back in their chairs and relaxed, smoking their pipes. Only the casual word passed between as they enjoyed their smoke.

"But I couldn't help but notice the demeanour of the Parish Priest," says Tom, " the way he was shifting and shuffling in the chair. He seemed to be ill at ease with himself. He'd glance at me, then away immediately, thinking I didn't see him. He must have been sizing me up as to whether I was a man he could trust to keep his affairs about the villagers confidential. He didn't want to get caught up in any brawl or slagging match between parties where he might have to take sides."

"Again he gave me a quick glance as he drew on his pipe, then oscillated it between his lips as the smoke slid out slowly. He jerked his eyebrows up and down several times, then gave the slightest nod of his head as if he had made up his mind that I was a man in whom he could confide."

"Now that you're going to stay," says Fr. Touhy, "I would like to give you a little history of the village and the villagers and their quirks and foibles and ..."

He left the rest of the sentence hanging in mid-air, unsaid. "I don't have to tell you that this conversation must not be repeated outside these four walls."

Tom assured him with a nod of his head.

He stood up and sauntered over to the bay window that overlooked the wide street. It was deserted except for a batch of red hens sunbathing in the hot road.

He gazed out the window for some time in deep reflection as he drew on his pipe. He took it from his mouth and pointed the wavering stem at the street. He glanced over his shoulder at me as if inviting me to join him and savour in this new revelation he was about to impart.

Tom stood up and joined him at the window.

"It was said by learned clerics of old that these simple people all lived in harmony with one another until the Cromwellian settlement. At that time Cromwell's henchmen came and evicted those people that wouldn't give their allegiance to the Crown and replaced them with their own loyal friends. The more astute men did give their allegiance but reluctantly, in order to save their homes and families. These interlopers were despised by the locals and were treated as pariahs. Faction fighting broke out on an almost daily basis in the village with the result that the villagers had to be segregated. The Tooles and their cronies were placed at one end of the village, the Nails and their cronies at the other," says the Father.

"They haven't changed one iota in all these years. The faction fighting still goes on," he looked at me momentarily. He was thinking that I might just be the man to bring peace and harmony to the village.

"I'm sure you'll hear, on your daily travels around the locality, the old people repeating this ago old legend that this village was the last place God made because he left 'the nails at one end and the tools at the other'. And now you know the real reason why this is so."

"I'll tell you another phenomenon about this place Kilquale," says the Father. "It's called 'The Harbour' now. What do you think of that and we're not within twenty miles of the sea?"

Tom looked at him even more confused than ever but stayed his thoughts. He decided it was time to take his leave so as to digest these strange phenomenas in the peace and quiet of his new abode.

As he stood up to leave Father Touhy put his hand on

Tom's shoulder.

"Now, Mr. Crouch," says he, "you seem to be an honourable man and if I'm not mistaken, a man of peace."

Tom just smiled at the Father's ability to size up ones character so quickly. He flicked his eyebrows up and down and gave a slight nod of the head in acknowledgement of Father Touhy's keen observance. Now that Tom was going to be living in the village and be in daily contact with the Father he was pleased Father Touhy felt so highly of him.

"If you can save this village from damnation," says the Father, "I'll be forever in your debt, for they are the most contrary, cantankerous and belligerent people God put on this earth. No two families are on speaking terms and if they are, it won't be for long I can assure you that. The only time you'll see them all out together is when they are locked in battle."

"Jack Abraham and his wife haven't spoken to each other for fifty years. All communication was done through Jack's brother, Tom."

"The Kerr family, Peter and Jane, although they share the same driveway with the Dooley family and their kitchen doors, in the gable end of their houses, face each other and they could look into each others kitchen when their doors were open, were forever at each others throats. If an altercation or slagging match took place between them – and this was sure to happen – the verbal abuse and names they threw at each other weren't very nice, for the pedigree wasn't very clean on either side of the house."

"Dan Conway, the cobbler, wouldn't repair the Neary family's boots. The bitterness arose out of some half forgotten incident that should have been left buried in the past but wasn't allowed to die by two stubborn old men."

"Then there is 'the cracked Roach family' as they were called. There were two brothers and two sisters and they weren't on speaking terms, so much so that they insisted on using their own teapots."

"Burying the hatchet hasn't been easy for this hamlet of people, for veiled insults, taunts and jibes had taken deep root. But at the same time these same people have stood by one another against officialdom even though they were otherwise split into warring factions."

"They were also a superstitious lot. On one occasion they blocked the street and wouldn't let the Missioner in to attend Mrs. Grey and she at death's door. They said, 'She was a witch and was not worthy of the Sacrament of extreme unction, it's burned at the stake she should be.' The Missioner was so outraged by their unchristian behaviour that he put a curse on all the villagers and it would not be lifted until they saw the error of their ways, and only then by some Divine Intervention."

"I think you could be that Saviour I have being praying for all these years," says Father Touhy.

"Well be-gob Father," says Tom, "if I can be of any assistance in bringing harmony to this village I would be only too willing to help, just leave it to me."

"Maybe Father," added Tom, "you could give me a little mention off the altar on Sunday. It would help my business greatly, like."

The Parish Priest nodded his head, assuring Tom that he would.

"I think, me good man," says Tom to me in the telling, "I'll soon lie down the old bones. They are at me real bad lately. Martin or Swank or Twig, they were close friends of mine over the last forty years. They will fill you in on anything you want."

I thanked Tom for his kindness and for giving me so much of his time.

"I hope I haven't tired you out too much," says I.

"Oh no, no," says Tom.

"But before I go I'd like to ask this last question, Tom. I hope you don't mind."

He gave me a slight nod of his head, "Not at all," answered Tom.

"You seem," says I, " to be a very travelled man and very knowledgeable about world affairs and life in general," I didn't like to add, 'and you almost illiterate.'

"You must have got a very good schooling when you were young."

"I did indeed," says Tom, "but not in a school you are thinking of. I was educated in the best university in the world," says he.

I looked at him dumbfounded, 'what does he mean, the best university in the world,' I repeated to myself.

"The university of life," continues Tom, "it's the greatest educator of all, for when you learn something the hard way, you'll never forget it. I soon found that out, travelling around the locality, buying fowl. If I made a mistake in valuing a batch of fowl, I just had to suffer the loss and learn from my mistakes."

I returned home that evening in great spirits after my chat with Tom and I couldn't wait to arrange a get-together with Martin and Swank and Twig to hear at first hand their story about the exploits of Tom Crouch, the Hen Man.

On the evening of our get-together with Martin, Swank and Twig I brought along a few bottles of Porter my father had given me for the story tellers. As Martin always said, 'it's a great man for oiling the vocal cords'.

Martin set the scene.

"When Tom had the old thatched cottage trimmed up good enough to live in, he set out for Dublin to negotiate a deal with the Iver Brothers Wholesale Marchants for the purchase of his fowl and eggs. With no way of advertising his business he travelled the highways and byways on

Charley Daly's crock of a bike, promoting his business."

"No house was passed and left out, from the humble cottage dweller to the solid farmers. He got an enthusiastic reception wherever he went. The sellers, mostly the housewives, could now sell their produce toTom in their own home and not have to travel the six miles to the fowl market which, as often happened, some eggs would break on account of the rough, uneven dirt roads."

"Within a few short years Tom had built up a thriving business and, since the housewives knew they had a secure outlet for their produce at a competitive price, they increased their fowl population, some as much as a hundred percent."

"He could charm the birds off the trees with his gab," related Martin. "This was a gift Tom had and it stood him in good stead when dealing with the women folk. He could persuade any woman that she was getting 'over the odds' for her produce. This was only because it was her,' he said to her, 'for he wouldn't give that much to anyone else, and that's the God's honest truth, ma'am,' he'd say. And like all good businessmen he'd deliver that good news in a whisper into the woman's ear lest anyone would hear him."

"He assured every woman that the business transaction between them would be kept strictly confidential. This was a great assurance, for no woman would like to have her business broadcast around the locality, where the quality of her fowl and their agreed prices be compared and discussed publicly."

"Another trait he had was his willingness to help the poorer families and others in the locality with their problems. He'd help get school books for the poorer children, help families with their rent, often negotiate with a farmer for a few bundles of straw to thatch a villager's cottage. He would go over to the Council Office in

Caherbane and plead on behalf of the village men that were out of work to give them some employment, even if it was only repairing the roads."

"When Jack and his sister Nancy Roach's thatch roof caved in, Tom took them into his own home to stay free of charge. Nancy would do the housekeeping and Jack would dispose of the chicken feathers. They were 'black out' with each other but managed to keep their tongues quiet while under Tom's roof."

"When Tom had enough fowl and eggs purchased to fill an order he'd set a day aside to kill and pluck the chickens. This way he got more for his produce than selling them 'on the hoof', as it were. And in his own quiet way he was also setting the groundwork for what he had promised Fr. Toughy he'd do."

"He hired two of the men from the village that he knew were out and out antagonists. He also knew they would be only too glad to earn a few shillings in order to put food on their tables. Having work locally was a Godsend. The two workers would arrive at the plucking venue, neither one knowing the other was coming until they'd arrived there. They would eye each other with suspicion. One false word or derogatory remark from one or the other and they were ready for combat, but Tom was well aware of this impending situation and remained close by. If there was any inkling of bickering or snide remarks, he'd soon point out to them that no altercation or petty squabbling would be tolerated under his roof. If they wanted money they would have to work in harmony with one another. Otherwise he would sack them. This practice he repeated every week with other antagonists he'd employ. Within a very short period of time Tom had broken the stronghold on these warring factions and their animosity toward each other. They did not become bosom friends but at least they could live with one another without too much rancour."

"When Pat Carey, the local Counsellor, retired, soundings went out as to who might be the best person for the post. Several names were put forward from the higher echelons of society. We, meaning Swank and Twig and me," says Martin, " proposed Tom Crouch. In our estimation he was the best suited to the job."

"Sure wasn't he looking after the welfare of the people and their problems far better than Pat Carey ever did," says Swank. "If only we could get him to polish up on his parlance."

"A huge crowd had gathered in the school for the convention," says Martin. "The schoolmaster was elected to chair the proceedings and he and Joe Nusum were elected to count the votes. Nominations were received and seconded. Then each candidate was called upon to give an outline of his vision for the future of the village of Kilquale and its environs before the vote was taken."

"When Tom took the stand everyone listened attentively as he outlined in his own inimitable way, in the vernacular, all his achievements to date and his plans for the future if elected."

" 'I will shake up those boyo's over there in the Council offices in Caherbane,' says Tom, 'and make them give me money to help the poorer people of this village and God knows it's badly needed.' "

" And Tom continued: 'I know for a fact,' says he, 'the Council gave money to help the people of Shinrone and Tinahely with the thatching of their houses after the big wind two years ago. Pat Carey was too soft with those layabouts so we missed out on our share of the kitty but I won't let them get away with it,' says he, raising his voice several octaves. 'They are collecting enough money from rent and rates around this county and not a shilling is spent on this village. I had to plead with them to give four men here in the village a few weeks work repairing roads and trimming hedges. At least it helped them to get boots for themselves and their families for the winter.' "

" 'If I'm elected, I think I'm as qualified as anyone here for the job. I'll drive over immediately to the Council office and put in my claim for financial help and I can assure everyone here that I will use it wisely and all monies will be accounted for'."

"From his vantage point on the rostrum Tom could see by the glances of eyes and nodding of heads at one another that his plan for the village was receiving a warm welcome."

"With this encouragement he pressed on excitedly, 'but the first thing I'll do,' "said he, raising his voice an octave", 'I'll house the houseless of this village and beyond, I'll ignore no one that's in need of shelter, I'll clothe the naked and God knows there's enough of those poor, unfortunates around here in their rags.' "

"Then in his rush to impart his caulderon of ideas that were simmering around in his head he lost his train of thought and began stuttering and stammering, trying to regain his equilibrium. He wanted to say, 'he'd put shoes on the shoeless children', for he knew this would go down well with the parents of the village, but, in his haste to impart this good news about the shoeless children, he announced instead that 'he would put shoes on the footless children' "

"A chorus of mule laughter erupted among the assembled audience at this monumental clanger Tom had made. But, not one to be put off by this gaffe, Tom pressed on."

"With a wide sweep of his hand to allude to the flea-infested hovels around the village, 'I'll get rid of all those louse-banks and I'll make Kilquale as everyone knows it's always been called, 'The Harbour, a sae (sea) port town'."

"Be the living sinner," says Twig, "if that man could suck as well as he can blow, we could have Courtown Harbour up here in a few minutes."

"When he had finished, an ear splitting roar went up for Tom who, in their opinion, gave a rousing speech."

"When the votes were counted Tom Crouch was the clear winner. And that," says Martin, "is how Tom Crouch, the Hen Man, was elected local Counsellor."

No sooner had the village returned to its humdrum way of life when little Ann McCreely, daughter of Ann and Aiden McCreely, was struck down by what Dr. David Roach described as "a rare infectious disease". The whole village was in shock. The Doctor advised the parents, as a matter of urgency, that she be taken immediately to the seaside for a month to recuperate. But Dr. Roach didn't like to comment on the fact that it was the over-crowding and squalor she was living in that was the cause of her illness.

The only thing Aiden and Ann could do was to pray for a miracle, for such a financial undertaking was way beyond their means. On hearing this sad news Tom was moved with pity. He didn't hesitate about financing the child and her mother's stay in Courtown Harbour.

Everyone in the village was talking about his generosity and kindness. 'At least,' says Tom to himself, 'I have got them talking to each other, and what is money after all,' says he, 'it's for man's use and benefit.' He had a nice little nest egg stashed away in the bank and had equally as much due to him from the Ivor Brothers for the sale of his produce.

Little Ann McCreely took much longer to recuperate than was first envisaged, with the result Tom's reserves in the bank were soon all gone plus a loan he had had to borrow.

Then disaster struck at Tom's own door.

Tom was returning home one evening with his load of fowl and eggs. The road was covered with snow and ice. Coming down Barnaculla Hill the pony lost his footing and fell heavily on the hard road. With result, Tom, who was sitting on the fowl crates, also lost his balance and toppled out of the cart onto the road. The fowl crates came crashing down on him, breaking his leg. The pony damaged his spine and had to be put down.

Then misfortune followed mishap. The Ivor Brothers were declared bankrupt. Tom was left with an enormous debt and he depending for this money to clear his debt with the bank. When he defaulted on his repayments the bank threatened to close in on his assets, which was only his house, in order to recuperate their losses.

When the villagers became aware of Tom's plight, which had seeped out through the keen ears of Nancy Roach, they rallied round immediately. First to lend his services was Jack Crocoran. He brought Tom to John Molloy, the bone setter. When Tom returned home Jack and Nancy Roach took over and saw to his every need as a payment for his kindness when they were in trouble.

A meeting was held in the school to organise a fund-raising scheme for Tom and his pony. Their first plan was to hold card games and raffles in the school. Then residents went in pairs around the countryside making house to house collections. Everyone without exception donated generously. The Parish Priest Father Touhy was dumbfounded by the way everyone worked in harmony like they had lived together all their lives in friendly companionship with one another.

Before Tom went back to work a party was held in his honour in the school. The Parish Priest gave a moving speech. He was loud in his praise, "for the Mr. Crouch who single-handed brought this village from dead to life, from poverty to prosperity and such harmony that was unprecedented in my lifetime".

"Whatever charm he had over them," says Twig, "they all lived happy ever after."

The Undertaker

It was the end of an era in the village of Shinrone with the passing away of old Pascal Mooney, the Emporium owner and undertaker. The esteem in which he was held was borne out by the very large attendance at his Wake and funeral. Like his father and his father before him, he carried on his grocery business in the old-fashioned way.

Although the winds of change were coming, Pascal had refused to change with the times. It was said that he was too miserly to modernise this old, dank and dilapidated building. If anyone passed a remark about doing up the premises, his answer was always the same, "it'll do me my day."

Most of his trade was done through bartering. Farmers, mostly their wives, would bring in their baskets of eggs and firkins of butter to the shop on a Saturday morning. Pascal would take each customer into the storeroom at the back, where no one could hear what was being discussed between them, and there he would value the goods.

The woman was sure to refuse to sell at such a low price. She would threaten him with a little blackmail in order to extract the last farthing out of him.

"I've been coming here for the last twenty years," she would say, "and wouldn't it look very bad if other customers saw me leaving with me butter and eggs instead of me groceries, what would they say?"

Old Pascal knew the consequences of turning away such a loyal customer. They were dwindling fast as it was.

After much homming and hawing and rubbing his chin he'd up the price another few pence, then plead, "God is the truth Ma'am I couldn't give you another halfpenny."

After a little more haggling and coaxing they'd come to an amicable agreement. With the bartering slip in hand she could cross the shop floor to the grocery department where old Barney, the lank assistant and none too hygienic either with his weeping eyes and runny nose, would dole out the groceries.

Usually she would bring a daughter with her on these occasions, that's if she had one, in order to teach her the rudiments of buying and selling goods. The mother hoped this experience would stand her in good stead when she herself would become mistress of her own house.

Barney would shuffle around the shop weighing out the goods as the woman would call them out, "1/2 lb. of tea … 2 lb. of sugar," or whatever she deemed necessary for the week. There was flour, bread soda, salt, jam and above all a gallon of lamp oil. Any money that was left over, which the woman knew there would be from her long experience of running the home, this was given back to her in cash to spend as she so wished. Sometimes she could indulge herself or her daughter in a little luxury in the drapery department, but most times the money would be brought home to pay the rent or rates or for schoolbooks for the children. The rest was put aside for an emergency. There was no such thing as putting money in a bank. Only rich people had bank accounts in them times. These were thrifty experiences she was passing on to her daughter every week when she went shopping.

When Pascal's funeral was over speculation was rife around the village and beyond as to who might inherit the business. Since Pascal had never married, would it be Marta's son in Cork, or would it be Sara's boy from Dublin. Both had spent their summer holidays with him when they were young.

Then to their great surprise, Ellie's son Ned from England landed in Shinrone to take over the Emporium, lock, stock and barrel.

Once again the rumours were rife among the shiulers of the village that had nothing better to do than speculate. 'He'll never settle in this God forsaken place and he after being born and reared in England.' Little did they know that Ned was an astute businessman, having worked as a foreman at the grocery trade for many years in Manchester.

Ned saw great potential in the place. He'd refurbish the whole interior and repaint the outside. That would bring the place back to life. He would replace old Barney with a younger and more energetic assistant and, true to his word, within a short space of time he had won back all Pascal's old customers and had built up a thriving business.

He discontinued the bartering business that old Pascal had held on to so steadfast all his life. He paid cash on the spot for all the goods purchased. He could see the day coming when people liked to handle their own money and spend it as they wished.

He also knew that his customers wouldn't leave his premises without spending a fair amount of their cash on their weekly groceries once they were offered a competitive price for their own goods. He even opened on a Sunday morning for two hours to facilitate his customers who wished to buy some novelty for the Sunday dinner or to buy a paper. He knew he would be condemned by the Parish Priest off the altar, but Ned took no heed of him.

"Times are changing," says he, "and we must change

with the times," was Ned's cry.

The men folk were delighted with the new bar. It was now more comfortable and warm with plenty of seating and a cheery, good-looking woman behind the counter.

This was not like in Pascal's time when they had to stand at the counter all night long, and in winter they had to keep their overcoats on to shelter themselves against the biting wind whistling in under the door and down the stairs. They could now have a boisterous argument without fear of severe reprimand from the proprietor. Lorna was well able to parry off any exuberance diplomatically. At the same time she kept merry malice and craic in motion yet also kept in check the more high-spirited individuals. She had the knack of how to dampen down exuberance from the more unruly patron, especially when they'd get a little too intoxicated.

When the shop and pub were running smoothly Ned turned his attention to the undertaking side of the business. He sold the pair of black horses and the horse-drawn hearse and bought a mechanical propelled vehicle, the first of its kind in the locality.

As Swank Hayden said one evening in the pub, "I'll tell yis something for nothing," says he in that squeaky voice of his, "the first person that will be carried in that hearse will have the biggest funeral ever seen in the parish, for they'll come from the four corners of Ireland to see this new mode of transport."

And, as it so happened, what do you think, but it was no other than Swank himself! Well, Swank was sure to draw a huge crowd anyway even without a new hearse.

Ned was assigned to do the undertaking. Having no previous experience he begged old Barney to accompany him and give him the rudiments of the undertaking business, such as how he should act out the part, with dignity and decorum.

It was the duty of the undertaker to make all the arrangements, the buying of the coffin, get the habit in order, and the drinks and food for the Wake, along with the snuff, tobacco and clay pipes.

Although Swank was a bachelor, the esteem in which he was held by the whole parish was borne out by the huge attendance at his Wake, for two days, while his body lay in state in the kitchen of his modest house. Hilarious stores were told about Swank's exploits as they sat around the open fire and indulged themselves on the enormous supply of food and drink and tobacco and snuff by the woman that Ned had hired to lay on the occasion.

It was the way Swank would have wanted it. "Give them plenty and send them home merry," was always Swank's motto and now his wish was being fulfilled.

There was a huge gathering at the house for the removal of the remains. The kitchen was full to overflowing and there was a sizable crowd clustered outside the door. The Rosary said and the trimmings added, the mourners began filing past the corpse. Each one sprinkled the corpse with holy water from the stoup with the sprinkler, which was a sprig of boxwood.

The ceremony over, the people moved back to give Ned and Barney room to coffin the corpse. This was a very intricate undertaking, especially when all eyes from around the kitchen and those peering in through the open door were on you.

Old Barney took this part of the proceedings very serious and since Ned had scant knowledge of the business he was extra vigilant. From years of experience, Barney was confident that since the corpse had lain in state for two days, his neck was stiff enough to take the weight of the body.

Barney took hold of the legs under his oxter in a vice-like grip, making sure there was no mishap. Ned followed

Barney's example and put his two hands under the corpse's head. Barney moved out with his legs clear of the table. He again nodded to Ned that it was safe to do likewise. Everything was going fine in Barney's opinion, no mishaps. They'd have him in the coffin in a couple seconds. They were about halfway between the table and the coffin, only about three feet, when a most embarrassing calamity struck, the likes of which was never known in the locality and certainly not in Barney's time.

With the weight of the body, the neck folded up like a rag doll, with the result that Ned lost his grip on the corpse and it crashed to the floor with a plonking sound.

Barney, taken by surprise by the suddenness of the falling body, lost his balance and fell forward, landing on the corpse on the floor.

The crown jerked back mid a chorus of "uuus" and "aaas" and low sniggers as the corpse emitted a gurgling breath of foul air, air so foul that it almost stifled the whole kitchen.

All eyes were now on the recumbent figure lying prostrate on top of the corpse.

"Holy Mother of God," declared Mags Behan, putting her hand to her throat, "what has he done to him at all, has he kilt him altogether?"

After much puffing and grunting, with exertion Barney finally scrambled to his feel, raising his lank frame limb by limb as the carpenter's rule opens. His face was chalk white, with both shock and embarrassment.

Everyone had lost their sad and sorrowful looks and were sniggering behind their hands at the dilemma in which Barney had found himself … and he always so precise!

When Barney had regained his equilibrium he grabbed at the two legs like a man possessed. Ned took the shoulders of the corpse's habit and, with one mighty heave, they swept the corpse off the floor and landed it into the coffin.

Barney looked as pale as the corpse in the box. He took out his white handkerchief and wiped the sweat off his brow. He exhaled an almighty sigh of relief, at the same time giving Ned a severe look as much as to say, 'that's the last time I'll be caught doing this job.'

The walkers took off at a leisurely pace after the hearse to Shinrone chapel, about two miles away. Some had their pony and traps but most were walking.

The evening was mild and calm and the countryside was verdant green, which added to the pleasure of the walk, but there were billowing clouds gathering and coming in from the west, which indicated that rain wasn't far off.

To show respect to the dead everyone was conversing in low voices to the person beside him and to those within earshot about Swank's exploits over his long lifetime. They were having a jolly ould wag as they sauntered up towards Pluckers Cross where they used to hold the crossroads dances. Swank was the musician whenever there was a dance held there. Then, without portend or warning, the hearse began spluttering and belching and backfiring til eventually it conked out altogether.

"Begor," says Twig, "he must want to play for the last dance before he's laid to rest."

Barney sat bolt upright in his seat in the hearse. He was crimson in the face at the predicament he had again found himself in. 'If only we had the horses,' he says to himself, 'this whole unsavoury business could be avoided, these new fangled ideas … .'

Ned looked at Barney momentarily. "I think," says he, "the only solution is to get out and push."

"Well, if you are," says Barney, "you can do it without me. I'm not leaving this seat for anybody," he says curtly.

Ned had no trouble getting as many men as was necessary to push the hearse. They were willing to carry the coffin if needs be but that would show Ned up in a bad light and it just his first outing as an undertaker.

When the priest had blessed the coffin outside the chapel, four strong men stepped forward and solemnly shouldered the coffin into the chapel where they laid it on the beirer, in front of the high altar.

After the reception prayers were said. Ned slipped away from the church to find Jack Gallard, a handyman mechanic to fix the hearse. Sam Healy had told him that Pat Lydon, the garage owner was too dear altogether.

Next morning after Mass the coffin was placed in the hearse for Swank's last journey to Shinrone graveyard.

Well, to his abject surprise the hearse broke down again and it within sight of the graveyard gate. Ned cursed himself for hiring that fly-by-night Jack Guillard. He should never have listened to Sam Healy, the steam engine driver but it was too late now. Sam was caught out by Jack Gallard's shoddy workmanship, and now Ned had to return to Pat Lydon for help and repairs after castigating him for his exorbitant charges only a few weeks earlier.

Several men stepped forward and put their shoulder to the back of the hearse to push. They were under great strain on account of the steep rise up to the graveyard gate, and as well as that the night before had been an atrociously wet night. The dirt road was covered with loose sand and grit which left little purchase for the men to get a grip with their feet. Through the puffing and blowing and panting they still had time to have a little banter among themselves.

"I'll bet yis," says Twig, "that ould codger is in there laughing his head off at us, killing ourselves pushing this contraption. It's like buying a dog and barking yourself, isn't that right boys?" says he. They all nodded their heads in agreement.

At the graveyard gate the four men, including Ned, shouldered the coffin over to the open grave and left it on the two wooden skids until the priest had said the final prayers and blessed the coffin.

The four men took up their positions, two at each side of the grave, ropes in hand ready for the orders from Ned to lift.

Barney had a terrifying dream during the night that something even more calamitous would befall Ned before the grave was filled in, and he wasn't going to be there to witness it. He turned away from the grave and went home.

The four men strained on the rope, raised the coffin off the skids and moved it in over the grave, ready to lower it. Great care was taken as the ground around the grave was slippery and unsteady. Ned felt very proud at this minute for at last things were beginning to go right for him. He could see great potential in the undertaking business.

Well, he had no sooner said these things to himself when the greatest calamity of all occurred. Ned lost his grip on the rope and away goes the coffin, careening into the grave head first, landing in about four inches of water in the bottom of the grave. The other end was lying up against the side wall at a 45-degree angle.

Great gulps of air were inhaled by the onlookers as they glanced at one another, then at Ned as they anticipated his next move. Then they all began to grin at the predicament Ned found himself in, at the murky state of the grave and at Ned's good clothes that he specially had made for the occasion,

"Begob," says Twig in a loud whisper to his cronies, "he always liked to create a stir wherever he went."

'There's only one thing to do,' says Ned to himself, 'that is to get into the grave and place the coffin in its proper resting place.'

He slithered down the side of the open grave when, standing on the floor of the grave, he discovered he was standing ankle deep in water. After much pulling and tugging and whispering unholy expletives to himself, he eventually maneuvered the coffin to its proper resting place. He looked a sorry sight when he eventually scrambled out of the grave. He looked like a man that had been dragged through a quagmire.

In the pub that night he stood drinks to the whole house as an appreciation for all their help.

"Anytime," declared Twig, "you can always depend on us."

Ned nodded his thanks, raised his glass to the gathered crowd and declared,

"This is to celebrate the first and definitely my last undertaking job. Do you know," says he, looking out over the assembled crowd of customers in the bar, "anyone interested in buying a good hearse, I've one going cheap."

The Fugitive of Avoca

Like all my contemporaries before me I immigrated to London, hoping to make my fortune before returning home to start my own business. As advised, I made my way to Hyde Park Corner, also known as Speakers Corner, on my first Sunday over there. I was hoping to meet some of my old school friends who might be able to fix me up with work on the buildings and sure enough they were all there, hungry for news of home.

As luck would have it I spotted Pat McArdle, a large building contractor from home, strolling in the park with his wife Joan. Knowing my ability, he offered me a job as foreman carpenter on one of his building sites in Cricklewood.

Initially my lodgings were primitive and cold. They weren't what you might call home away from home, but when you are trying to garner all the money possible to take home, lodgings weren't a high priority. As long as you had a bed to sleep in you could always get your meals out in some café.

Most of my evenings were spent in the Irish pubs. That is if I wasn't working late. I enjoyed the craic and camaraderie with the other Paddies, listening to the ceili music and joining in a lively singsong to finish off the evening. At weekends we would frequent the Galtimore in Cricklewood. It was there that we danced and sang our loneliness away among our own kith and kin.

Word soon got around that I was a fair singer. One night in our local, the Red Lion, Tommy Boyle the proprietor collared me for a song. The Avoca ceili band were having a well-earned break. Shyly I climbed up on the stage and, in my best tenor voice, I sang Tom Moore's most famous melody, *The Meetings of the Waters*.

By the time I had reached the third verse, from my vantage point on the stage, I couldn't fail but notice that the plaintive words of the song were having a very emotional effect on my audience. The women were dabbing their eyes with their hankies and at that moment I too caught something of that nostalgia. When I had finished the song I was given a rapturous round of applause with requests for more.

As I was getting down I espied a frail, forlorn looking old man sitting at a corner table by himself, just inside the door. It really tugged at my heartstrings when I saw him. His forehead was resting on his scrawny hands, his elbows on the table, the tears were streaming down his sallow, wrinkled face.

When I joined my friends, he shuffled his way through the crowd and shook my hand warmly with his two hands, "You sang that with true feeling, sir," said he, "you are a gifted singer. Only a true vale man could sing that song the way you did."

"I am a vale man," says I, "but not from the village, as you must be."

"I'd know that rich Wicklow voice anywhere," and his smile widened so much that you could have slotted a slice of toast bread into it and his wan face flushed in the dim light.

"You must be a Byrne or an O'Toole," says I, "that's if you come from that neck of the wood."

"Jack Quale is me name," says he.

"That's not a Wicklow name," says I, "you must be a

blow-in."

He gave me a furtive glance, then his lips flexed their corners into the beginning of a smile. "The last lad that said that to me was when I was in school. O', what a fight we had over it. My father was from Kerry," says he, "I was only a baby when we moved to Avoca. He took up a teaching post there in the National School. We lived not far from the mine shaft."

"I know it well," says I. "I used to live near there with my cousin during the summer holidays."

He reminisced fondly of his childhood days around Avoca and the potholing in the mine shaft.

"Have you been back there lately?" I asked.

"No," says he, giving me a steely gaze from under his bushy eyebrows. Then after a short pause he spoke, "not since I set foot in this country, it's more than forty years ago."

"Now, I'm going home," says I, "at the weekend for a short holiday. You are welcome to come along with me, that's if you like, just to see the old place, like, and meet some of your old friends that are still around. I'm sure they would be only too glad to see you after all these years."

His eyes narrowed at the thought as he looked at me, then gave a sort of a laugh, then went all silent, just looking down at the floor. I knew by the way he was shuffling his feet that he wanted to ask me, or tell me something important, then on second thought he sang dumb.

I was in the Red Lion a few months later and I spotted him again. He was in his usual place, sipping a hot whiskey. He even looked more haggard and emaciated than before. The Mannion ceili band were playing there that night. Everyone was having a gay time, couples were dancing reels and gigs and half sets, others were tapping their feet and clapping their hands to the rhythm of the music.

"Cheer up, Jack," says I, wiping the sweat off me brow after a big swing, but he remained silent and withdrawn.

I brought him over a hot whiskey and sat down beside him. I put me arms around his shoulders to unction him. "Cheer up me ould friend," says I, "it might never happen."

He leaned back in his chair and looked at me with searching eyes for what I thought was an eternity but in fact it was only a few seconds, as much as to say, 'you must know something that I don't'. It was then he confided in me.

"I have been in hospital since I saw you last," says he. He took a deep laboured breath, "and I can tell you this, I know I won't get over it. The news ain't good, they are taking me in next week to have a lung removed." He became very melancholy as he said it. "I know in me heart I'll never be out again," said he.

"Never heed them doctors," says I, "they are not always right. I know several people that were given the dreaded news and they are still around to tell the tale, don't give up hope yet," says I.

"Death don't worry me in the least," says he, "it's where I'm going to be buried worries me more. I'm a loner in the world now," says he, "all my family have succumbed to the dreaded disease called TB, the curse of the age. My dearest wish has always been to be buried in Queensberry graveyard up over Avoca with me family and friends, and not in some God forsaken graveyard here in north London with all the other paupers where seldom or ever a visit is made or a prayer is said for the repose of their souls."

He took a dollop of whiskey before he spoke again. The noise from the band and the stomping of feet and the clapping of hands was deafening. The old man put his hand on me arm to draw me closer and, with great effort, he cranked up his vocal cogs so as I could hear him over the din of the music.

"I've written to the Parish Priest in Avoca," says he, "informing him of my wish and all the details of my family and where they are buried. I asked him to send a reply to the Irish Centre in London for me."

He then gazed into my face with tear-filled eyes. I knew the question he was going to put to me but I had to wait til he made the request first himself.

"I'd be eternally grateful if you could fulfil my wish for me. I won't see you out of pocket, I can assure you of that."

Happy in the knowledge that his wish would be fulfilled he relaxed in his chair and smiled wanly at me, then with a voice a little more than audible he joined in the chorus of *The Old Bog Road* while drumming his scrawny fingers on the table.

I visited him most nights in hospital after the operation and stayed as late as I was allowed.

"Would you ever be so kind as to call to the Irish Centre for me and see has that letter come yet?" he asked.

You could see the disappointment in his eyes when I informed him that no reply had come back yet.

Then one night it was well after visiting time when I called. The kindly night Sister allowed me in when I told her my story. You could see the relief on his sallow face when I read the letter from the Parish Priest. He looked happier than I had seen him in a long time because he would be buried among his own kith and kin in Avoca.

"I don't know what would have become of me, in this atheist country, only you came along," he sighed deeply, "you were a God-send." He gazed at the floor, then to nobody in particular he said, "probably cremated and me ashes dumped in the Thames."

Just as I was about to leave, he began searching in his

locker and eventually he pulled out a St. Bruno tin box and handed it to me.

I tried to protest but he just waved his skeleton thin hand at me, "Take it," says he, "you'll be needing it, that's my promise to you."

After a short pause he drew another laboured breath, "The last few months you have been a real friend to me, like a son I never had, may your kindness be well rewarded, you deserve it."

I pummelled the pillows for him before leaving. He leaned his head against them and closed his eyes. With a voice little more than a whisper he said, "There's not in this wide world a valley so sweet."

That night he died in his sleep.

It was an artic day the day we laid Jack Quale to rest.

Leaving the hustle and bustle of Dublin behind us I observed that not a soul was seen raising their hats or even blessing themselves to the passing corpse. We turned off at Kilmacanogue and took the scenic route through Roundwood and Glendalough and Rathdrum, reaching Avoca just before daylight faded. As promised, the Parish Priest was waiting for us outside the lych-gate of the graveyard, his breviary in one hand and the stoup in the other. Two grave diggers were present with their hats off against their chests, the beirer was at the ready inside the lych-gate.

The obsequies were a simple affair, because Mass could not be said at such a late hour. It was arranged for the next morning.

When I got out of the hearse the cold struck me like a knife. After lowering the coffin into the cold earth the Priest blessed the grave with the Holy Water from the stoup he had given me to carry. Then, after a short reading from his breviary, we said a decade of the rosary for the repose of his soul.

Later that evening I was having a quiet drink in Kati's Pub, sitting in front of the open fire trying to thaw meself out before going home to see my parents, when an angry looking man approached me.

When he spoke, his mean, snarling lips slid over a mouthful of discoloured teeth that were as jagged as the peaks of Lugnacuilla.

"Was that Jack Quale yis were burying up there this evening?" says he, eyeing me up and down intensely.

"It was," says I, "did you know him?"

"Huh," says he, "did I know him!" he spat out the words scornfully while a drop on the end of his nose danced in a frenzy of contempt. Again he repeated, "Did ... I ... know him?"

This was the opportunity I had been waiting for. I wanted to clear up the mystery behind Jack Quale's self-imposed exile in London all these years.

"I know," says I, "he wanted so much to return to Avoca. I even offered to accompany him once when I was returning for a short break, but somehow he seemed to be afraid, he became agitated and withdrawn when I mentioned it to him."

"It was more shame than fear," says he, "that's for sure," came the instant reply.

His angry outburst startled me so much that a mouthful of beer went with me breath and nearly choked me. Even the cabal, huddled at the bar counter, turned from their whispering to stare.

"I'll tell you," says he, "what he had to be ashamed of," he snarled. "That rapscallion of Hell promised to marry my only sister and then jilted her, left her standing at the chapel door in Avoca in her fineries for three hours, hoping against hope that he'd turn up. But there was no sign. It left her broken hearted, the shame and disgrace it caused her. She never got over it."

"But there must have been a plausible explanation for this sudden change of heart," says I, "to have upped his sticks and flee the country in the middle of the night."

"No reason that I can think of," says he.

"Well he seemed to me to be a real gentleman, that's why I promised to see to his funeral arrangements. He wasn't that type of a man as far as I knew him to purposely set out to disgrace or humiliate anyone or cause them grief. Had she a hold on him in anyway?" says I, trying to be as tactful as possible.

For a moment I thought by the way he glanced at me that he was going to strike me with his stick. There was an audible menace in this voice now.

"What are you insinuating," says he, quite wicked, "there was nothing like that with our Sara. She was a devout Catholic. Nobody was forcing him into marriage, certainly not Sara."

"Will you join me for a drink?" says I, hoping it would assuage his ire and make him a little more affable. He gazed at me uncertain as to what to do, then after a moment's thought he nodded and sat down beside me.

When his drink arrived he took a few sips, shuffled his shoulders and became more relaxed and friendly.

"I want to apologise to you," says he, "for being so aggressive to you, it wasn't your fault what happened."

"Apology accepted," says I.

"By the way," says he, "my name is Ned Mooney."

We sat in silence for a few moments with our thoughts as we sipped our drinks. So to break the monotony I made a venture.

"Do you remember them walking out together?" says I. It was an expression used at the time for couples courting.

"I did indeed," says he, "they was most friendly. Sara and him seemed to be the happiest couple in the Parish.

And no financial worries either. Everyone knew that his parents were schoolteachers here in the village. They were well off when they died. Old money in the bank. He could well afford to get married. I even gave him a hand at doing up the house. It was like a palace when they were finished."

"When did you last see him?" says I.

"The night before the wedding. I came by to pick up the wedding ring as Sara had asked me to do in case Jack would forget it in the rush the next morning. He was in high spirits. We laughed and talked into the early hours of the morning."

"When he didn't turn up for his wedding I became fuming mad. I got in my horse and gig and tore up to the house to investigate. I knew he hadn't slept it out for he was well-known to be an early riser. When I went over the brow of the hill I could see smoke in the distance coming from the direction of Jack's house. I thought maybe he was burning all his old furniture and bedding he had thrown out for he had his house refurbished only recently and new furniture and bedding installed. When I came around the turn of the road near the house, to my horror, the thatched cottage was burned to the ground. My anger turned to grief when I saw the last vestige of this once neat cottage gone up in smoke, man, savings and all, as I thought."

"A thorough search was made in the rubble but no body was ever found. His full furnished house was left to rot, the thatch roof collapsed in on itself. You can see the briers growing out through the windows and door. I believed he tried to sell it one time but nobody would buy it, not even the rookes would nest in the chimney as though there was a curse on it."

"Many years later a man was seen in north London answering to this description."

He took another dollop of whiskey. "O' we'll never know now," says he, "what really happened."

"Well," says I, "I often met him in the Red Lion. One night he was very drunk so he spilled out his heart to me."

"He told me he had joined the Irish Republican Brotherhood as a young lad, in his early twenties, unbeknownst to his parents or family. The avowed intention of the IRB, he said, was to overthrow the British rule in Ireland."

"On one of the secret missions Jack and his henchmen made to Dublin they were ambushed in a house in Thomas Street. Jack escaped by the simple expedient of nicking a Red Cross uniform he had found in the cellar. The others were rounded up and sent to the Curragh Camp in Kildare. They said Jack had informed on them. He swore to God that he never did. He said they threatened that one day they would give him just deserts. Then one night before the wedding they ordered him not only out of the house but out of the country, never to return. Otherwise they wouldn't be responsible for their actions. They set fire to his little house. Then one of the fellows said before they turned him out on the road that no informer will ever marry into his family."

Ned looked at me, startled. "I wonder who that might be," says he, rubbing his chin.

"I think he said his name was Tom Bradly of Ballycreagh," says I.

Ned took a buck in his seat, "O' my God," says he, scratching his head, almost tearing lumps of hair out. "The bloody scoundrel, I was wondering why he didn't turn up for the wedding. I spent half me life in a frenzy over Jack's bad faith and all the time it was me own half brother who created this whole damnable mess. What can I do now?" says he to nobody in particular, "sure aren't they all dead now." He blessed himself and I could hear him muttering a little prayer before he got up to leave.

After Mass the next morning I strolled up to Queensberry graveyard to lay a wreath. I stopped on my way to inspect what remained of Jack's old ruins and overgrown plot.

I could well afford to build a new house and workshop up here with the money Jack left me. I retraced my footsteps through the lych-gate and over to the corner to where Jack's grave was. I stood the wreath against the headstone where Jack's name would be inscribed beneath that of his parents, brothers and sisters.

I stood for a moment in silent prayer for the repose of his soul as I gazed at the brown frosty clay under which Jack lay. I came away from the grave with gladness in my heart that I had done my civic duty for this old man.

Outside the lych-gate I stopped and pondered to myself what if I hadn't divulged Jack's secret. Ned would never have known as to why Jack sneaked off in the middle of the night and left Sara Mooney, the prettiest girl in all Avoca, high and dry. Yes, he would have carried his anger to his grave.

I'm glad now for what I did, for Ned forgave Tom and Jack and made his peace with his God before he died.

The Rising

A Tribute to the men of Kilquiggan and its environs who fought against the Black and Tans in 1920 and were imprisoned in the Curragh Camp, County Kildare for their stance.

When the boys of our County were taken
The people fell into despair.
They were placed in a lorry and landed
At a camp on the Plains of Kildare.

It was there they were kept in confinement
And the people lamented their loss.
We knew they were kindly befriended
By their fondness for Eireann's sweet cross.

And the money it went there in handfuls
While the English were held in distain,
But soon we will have independence
'Neath the beautiful flag of Sinn Fein.

The cross we will take on our shoulders,
The flag we will steadily unfold.
It's an emblem dear to old Ireland,
Its colours are green, white and gold.

Then harra boys, harra for old Ireland
That has always been true to the Cause,
But has fallen to cruel persecution
By enactments and cruel English laws.

The Mission

The parishioners glanced at one another in their pews and gave a great sigh of relief as the Canon took his breviary from the ledge of the pulpit and swung around to go down the three steps to the chancel floor and back to the High Altar after delivering one of his hell-raising sermons. Summer or winter his sermons were never less than half an hour.

They shook and shuffled and shuddered in their seats with the cold. They daren't cough or move a limb while he was preaching. To do so would bring the wrath of the Canon on their heads. He would berate them for their lack of levity and respect for the word of God.

'Not long now,' they were saying to themselves in their own minds, 'and we'll be out of this icebox.' It was a biting cold May morning, rain and sleet and a splattering of snow was being whipped along by a strong gale as the parishioners had made their way to early Mass. Some came in their pony and traps but the majority were walking, some as much as four miles and fasting from midnight in order to receive Holy Communion.

The Canon stalled in his tracks and turned to face the parishioners again. The people swallowed hard on their gulp and shuddered again, sending a prickle of apprehension down their spines. It wasn't the first time they thought to themselves that he had done this, keeping them another ten minutes, lecturing the parents on their lack of parental control over their offspring.

"My dear brethren," says he, "I forgot to bring to your attention that the Mission will start in this parish in four weeks time, and since everyone will be in a prayerful mood and in the state of grace, I've decided to hold the forty Hours of Adoration at the same time also, when as you all know the Bishop will pay his annual visit."

To say that it came as a bombshell would be an understatement to the congregation present on that cold May morning.

As Twig the local wag put it, "That man loves to cheer people up when the weather is bad, doesn't he?"

After Mass a cohort of men gathered under the palm tree outside the chapel door, others congregated in the horse stable, the rest shuffled their way to the shelter of the graveyard wall opposite the chapel gate. Although they were shivering and shaking with the cold while they lit their pipes, they were determined to vent their anger about the pros and cons of the forthcoming event.

Momentarily they had forgotten about the biting cold as they argued the merits and demerits of holding a Mission so soon and it only three years since the last one.

"Anyway," says one, "don't we have the forty Hours every year? Don't you think that would do?"

But the Canon had spoken and there was no going back. It would be a brave man that would challenge him on any decision he makes.

"Sure," says another, "wasn't the Canon worse than any Missioner ever was, haranguing Sunday after Sunday about the evils of sin of the flesh. Those courting couples he threatened to name and shame off the Altar for their beastly behaviour behind hedgerows and cocks of hay in the summer evenings, and after house dances in the winter time."

"These kips and dens of depravity are the devil's lair,

and I'll stamp them out," he would yell at the top of his lungs as he pummelled the pulpit viciously with his fist, and scanned the audience with a steely gaze.

As soon as the Mission was announced a big cleanup took place, first around the chapel. The church was decorated with flowers at every window. All the vestments were washed, starched and ironed. Cottages near the chapel were painted, gardens weeded, tottering paling nailed up, rickety gates mended, hedges clipped and streamers hung from every vantage point leading to the chapel. The whole place gave the impression of good order.

Back at their houses an equally big cleanup was under way. No woman would like to see her house, just like the chapel, other than spotless, less the Missioner should call unexpected as would often happen if he was in the area.

The dwelling house would be whitewashed inside and out, cobwebs and other unsightly objects would be removed, even the chimney stack would get a coat of white wash. All the good clothes that had been out of use over the winter were taken out and hung on the line to blow the musty smell out of them. Farm implements or anything unsightly would be removed to the haggard or back field and the front yard swept, gate pillars would be straightened up and loose stones would be built back into place, doors and gates around the yard would be mended and painted.

The first visible signs of the forthcoming event began with the arrival of the dealers who erected their stalls at the graveyard wall opposite the chapel gate. They were full of every conceivable religious object. Holy pictures lined the wall at the back, crucifixes and other objects lined the shelves at the sides, all kinds of medals were pinned to black cloth boards, rosary beads and scapulars were hanging in the dozens at every vantage point around the entrance window. People coming to the Mission made sure to stop and peer inside, eyeing out some religious object they hoped to buy for the closing night's blessing.

A couple of days before the Mission was due to start, two Missioners would arrive in a pony and trap at the parish priest's house, usually brought there by the verger from where the last Mission was held, because the Missioners were too poor to have their own mode of transport. One Missioner was usually young, the other ancient, but both had great strong voices. Their stentorian voices would put the fear of God in those miscreants who might foolishly think they weren't in need of salvation.

The opening night's sermon was temperate and good-humoured. Father Oliver Stone, the younger Missioner who stood six foot tall, of slim build and heavily bearded, set out the programme for the week.

"Remember," says Fr. Oliver, "seven o'clock Mass every morning, followed by a short sermon. In the evening the Rosary followed by a sermon and benediction. On Wednesday, all the invalids will be attended. All the refractors and truants will be routed out of their dens and hauled down to Confession."

The parishioners sensed, by the younger man's body language and stentorian voice (belting out Hell's fire and damnation), that the week was going to be a lively and animated one.

Father James McIntyre, the older man, was more serene and easy going and nearly always kept his voice at an even keel. There was a trait of the dramatics about him. He'd ascend the pulpit with a friendly smile on his face, take out his pocket watch and chain and place it on the ledge of the pulpit in front of him. He'd draw out a large handkerchief and clean his glasses and then make an ostentatious gesture with the fluttering cloth before blowing his nose, so loud that you'd think it was a foghorn. Then without warning he'd begin to speak.

"It is easier for a camel to pass through the eye of a needle than a rich man to enter the Kingdom of Heaven."

Then, with a wide sweep of his hand, he'd bless himself.

"In the name of the Father and of the Son and the Holy Ghost, Amen."

A funny story appropriate for the occasion would be thrown in to grip the audience's attention before indulging them in the more serious aspects of the sermon.

By Tuesday night Father Oliver was in full flow. The Sixth and Ninth Commandments were on top of his list. You could hear a pin drop when he laid bare the sinful acts of these Commandments. He would prance and pummel the pulpit with his fist. He'd then lean out over the ledge, wagging his finger. I'm sure it was at nobody in particular, but to some people in the front of the church it sent a prickle of apprehension up and down their spines, lest anyone would think it was him he was pointing at. He would criticise severely all those young courting couples for their evil intent and other breakers of the Law of God.

Twig Murphy who was sniggering behind his hand commented in a low voice to his cronies in the back seat of the chapel, "If that man ain't checked soon he'll smash up that ould pulpit. Then,'" says he, "what will the Canon do?"

"Those boys," says the preacher, "who deliberately inveigle young girls behind ditches and cocks of hay, where the welcoming darkness tempts probing hands to do the devil's work. These dens of depravity are the devil's haven and should be avoided at all cost. They are a recipe for disaster."

There was froth coming out of his mouth and the veins in his neck stood out like twisted cords of rope, all from the dent of driving home his message.

"So I call on all mothers here tonight and fathers too to warn your daughters to be ever vigilant and not let your daughters be lured by these young men into such dens of depravity where neither their minds nor wills can refrain from such beastly behaviour."

"I remember one night," says Twig, "the young Missioner was giving a sermon on the evils of sin. Well be gob, he was belting hell's fire and damnation. I came to the conclusion that there wasn't one person in the chapel would get near the Gates of Heaven, let alone inside."

"I call on each and every one of you here tonight," says Fr. Oliver, "to make your Confession as if it were your last, for my dear brethren you do not know the day nor the hour when you could be called from this life. Spend plenty of time examining your consciences, pray earnestly to God and his Blessed Mother to make a good Confession," says he, raising his voice an octave and pummelling the ledge with his fist, "and on mature reflection do not forget some serious sin you had intended to confess the first time but you forgot, which necessitated you to return to Confession a second time. This is a very grave matter indeed," says he as he leant out over the pulpit ledge, wagging his finger fiercely.

Now Matt Dowling's a big, hefty man though quiet and retiring. He set out for Confession on that Tuesday afternoon. He liked to go early in the week when there would be nobody in the chapel. In order to pluck up courage his first port of call was to Mossey Whelan's Pub where he lowered several half glasses of whiskey. He chatted desultory with the barman as he drank his drink. The barman was glad of the company for seldom or ever did anyone drop into his pub in the daytime except maybe a commercial traveller.

"Must be a special mission you're on today," says Mossey, knowing full well where he was going when he was all dressed up.

"I'm going to Confession," says Matty, "I hope there'll be nobody there, only the Missioner."

The barman, who was on his knees stacking bottles on the lower shelf under the counter, jerked up his head with a start. He was going to say that it must be something very serious when you want the chapel cleared, but stayed his thoughts.

"What I mean is," says Matty, "I'm a bit hard on the hearing."

Mossey glanced at him with his eyecorner, "There'll be no bother hearing that man," says he, "you'd think sometimes he was going to bring down the belfry with his bellowing."

He smirked to himself. If Twig gets to know Matty's gone up to the chapel he might follow him and listen in on his Confession. Then for months afterwards he would regale his cronies, in Matty's vernacular, in every pub and toss school in the parish where there's be mirth and laughter at Twig's hilarious account of the occasion.

"Is that Matty I see going up the street all dressed up?" says Twig to Mossey as he stepped into his pub for a quick drink. "He must be going to Confession," says he.

"He was in here only a few minutes ago," says the barman, "getting a few small ones to settle his nerves before he went."

"I bet you anything he'll forget something and he'll have to go back again. It nearly always happens."

'Well,' says the barman to himself, 'if he does, I'll slip up after him on the pretence of going to Confession. I can kneel in the little alcove between the Confession Box and the Baptismal Font. They'll never know I'm there. Anyway I'll be back long before him for he usually spends an hour or more in the chapel afterwards.'

There was a temporary pause in their conversation

while they chewed on their thoughts. It was Mossey who broke the silence.

"On Monday did you see Pa Reilly going up towards the chapel? He must have been going to Confession."

Twig nodded his head in acknowledgement of the fact, drew on his pipe, "I was up there at the very spot, at the Baptismal Font, preparing to go to Confession and who comes in but only the bould Pa. He glanced around the chapel and, seeing no one queuing outside Fr. Oliver's Box, he slipped into the seat just in front of where I was sitting. He was so preoccupied with his own thoughts that he didn't even see me. I was going to challenge him about jumping the queue but thought the better of it lest I get an ear full and the whole church listening. After a short pause for prayer he stepped into the Confession Box. Well, he was no sooner in the Box when he stormed out again. Immediately the sniggering and tittering and winking among the penitents at the other side began. They knew something exciting was going to take place and they at least would be in the chapel to hear it. After a short pause for prayer in one of the pews in the body of the chapel Pa moved across to join the other penitents at Fr. James' Box."

Twig, who was next to enter Fr. Oliver's Box, got cold feet as it were and followed Pa, not so much to go to Confession but to listen to Pa's outcome with the young Missioner.

Twig swallowed the last of his drink and left his glass down on the counter.

"I must rush," says he, "I'll tell yis all about it here tonight after the Mission."

Mossey knew only too well why Twig wanted to delay the telling of his story. It was because Twig loved a large audience and Mossey's Bar was the place where he could deliver his narrative with dramatic effect.

Matty was all smiles when he returned to the pub sometime later. 'I'll have only a few,' says he to himself, 'then I'll be off, don't want to be late for the Missions tonight.'

'There's one happy man,' says Mossey, 'the slate clean til the next Mission.'

Matty's smile said it all. With little talk between him and the barman, Matty had plenty of time to mull over his Confession and the minute misdemeanour he was quizzed on. He thanked God he had examined his conscience properly.

'I'd hate,' says he to himself, 'to be a young boy or girl facing that man. I think not only would he take scallops off you in the Confessional, but he would take delight in naming and shaming you off the Altar. I'd say he'd be every bit as bad as the Canon ever was, traipsing the roads with his blackthorn stick on a Sunday night in search of courting couples.'

"Sunday night," he repeated out loud, sitting up with a start.

Mossey, who was stacking bottles on the lower shelves, jerked up his head with a start when he heard the sudden movement.

"Something the matter, Matty?" says he.

"Oh no," says Matty, "I must have left me hat in the chapel."

Mossey knew the real reason as to why Matty had to return to the chapel but he would not be so bold as to embarrass his old friend. Everyone knew that Matty would forget his head only it's tied to him. To see him return to Confession was no surprise. In order to cover up his forgetfulness he'd make the excuse that he'd forgot his hat.

His return to the Pub the second time was a subdued one. Mossey could easily presage by his demeanour and the way Matty slouched up the floor and slithered into a seat at the counter that Fr. Oliver had given him a severe reprimand. He took a deep laboured breath and hung his head, then let the air out of his lungs like an old man with all the world's troubles on his shoulder.

"Givess a large whiskey," says he, leaning his head on his hands, his elbows on the counter. 'The Bishop no less,' he mumbled soundless to himself. His elbows seemed to slip away from him and his head came up with a jerk just as Mossey clanked the whiskey down on the counter before him.

The barman felt sorry for this paragon of virtue who never in his life uttered a wrong word about anybody but was visibly shaken by Fr. Oliver yelping at him through the Confessional grid. 'Every other priest and Missioner,' says he to himself, 'even the Canon overlooked his lapse of memory. They put it down to his nervousness.'

"What you have done," says the Missioner, "is even more serious than the sin of missing Mass itself."

He filled his lungs and screeched through the grid, "You declared before God and me, the anointed one of God in this Confessional, that you had nothing more to confess, and now," says he, his eyes wild with anger, "you have come back, back to confess another sin, a MORTAL sin at that!"

His eyes pierced savagely into the penitent visage through the grid. "Do you know, my good man," says he, "you are standing on the brink of hell."

Matty swallowed hard on his gulp at this harrowing prospect and he only trying to rectify a simple mistake. He took a deep laboured breath as he gave a quick glance at his surroundings.

"Be gob, Father," says he, "isn't it a quare place to put a Confession Box."

The Missioner glanced at him quite miffed, "Anything else you might have forgot?" says he curtly.

"No Father," says Matty timidly.

Matty was hoping that there was nobody loitering in the chapel, nobody that is, that would carry back to the Pub Matty's public reprimand and humiliation by the Missioner, where they would regale their friends for manys a night afterward.

"Do you not know," says Fr. Oliver, "that you have committed a sacrilege?" looking at him through the grid with a steely gaze.

Matty looked vacuous at him, not knowing what he meant. To himself he thought, 'just give me whatever penance you think is appropriate for this heinous crime,' says he to himself, 'and let me go before the people start coming in for evening devotions.'

The Missioner cut across his thoughts.

"I cannot give you Absolution," says he rather curtly, "you'll have to go to the Bishop. This is a very grave matter indeed."

Matty was so taken aback that he almost slipped off the kneeler, and only for his bulk and the smallness of the cubicle he would have toppled over.

His mouth opened and closed rapidly, like a goldfish, before he was able to crank up his vocal cords.

"I'll go near no Bishop," says he.

He couldn't believe his ears at what he had just said to the Missioner, but he was glad at this moment that Mr. Power had come to his rescue and loosened his vocal cords.

"If you don't give me Absolution," says he, "I'll never set foot in this chapel again."

Fr. Oliver jerked back from the grid when he heard the determination in his voice. He began shifting and shuffling in his seat and tearing at his hair.

'If I deny this man Absolution,' says he to himself, 'and he died, suddenly he would be condemned to hell for all eternity and I would be responsible.' No, he couldn't do that.

This man was earnestly trying to rectify a simple mistake.

"For your penance say two Rosaries and do the Stations of the Cross five times. Now make a good act of contrition, O my God …"

Later that same evening Matty arrived for the Devotion. He made his way to the front pews as was his wont, whether it was for Mass or Mission, on account of his hearing. Settling his bulk in the seat he began to doze off. It was the stentorian voice of Fr. Oliver that shook him back to the present. But occasionally, from the effects of all the alcohol he had consumed, he would slip in and out of a slumber as the cadence of the preacher's voice changed. Then, as the strong voice boomed out about examining your conscience, Matty jerked up with a start and peered at the preacher who was leaning out over the edge of the pulpit and wagging his finger as he scanned the congregation with a steely gaze.

"I cannot emphasise half enough," says Fr. Oliver, "the importance of examining your own conscience thoroughly before going to Confession and not," says he, pummelling the ledge, "having to go a second time."

Matty, certain he was alluding to him, cranked up his vocal cords and spluttered out, "I knew you were bursting to tell!"

Fr. James sat as if in reverie in the Confession Box, occasionally raising his eyebrows off his deep set blue eyes and peered through the aperture in the curtain in front of him. The late afternoon sunlight was streaming down through the stained glass window, sending a kaleidoscope of colour onto the mellow pews. Motes of dust wafted lazily in the afternoon sunlight. Two multicoloured butterflies flitted about over the empty pews while a bee droned busily, sipping nectar from freshly placed flowers on the High Altar.

He leaned back in the Confession Box and gave a great suspiration of pleasure, knowing that there would be few if any for Confession at this hour of the afternoon. He clasped his hands around his generous stomach and lay back. He closed his eyes and began breathing quietly. After a short while his head sank forward onto his chest like a rag doll and he began to snore.

On this day Nell Shortall, or Nell the Raven as she was called on account of the dirt of her, decided to go to Confession. How she knew the Mission was on no one knows for she lived in a remote part of the parish at the foot of Barnasculla Hill which stretches back into the distant mountain. She seldom or never left her farm, not even to go to Mass on Sunday. She didn't take kindly to any neighbours calling. She was very suspicious of their intentions, so they wouldn't dare encroach on her solitude, for her curt dismissal of any company would soon freeze them out.

She was a tall, cadaverous looking woman with long black hair that fell in plentitude around her shoulders. She seldom or ever washed it except for the natural dowsing it got when she'd be out in a rainstorm. It looked shiny from the combination of grease and soot. There was a strong pungent smell of smoke and sweat off her. Her hands and face were as black as the hob of hell. The only towel she ever used was her bag apron and this only left smudge marks on her face.

Setting out for Kilquale Church, she took the mass path where she was sure of meeting no one. The path traversed several townlands and numerous farms on the four mile journey. At last she arrived at the lych-gate at the side of the chapel yard. Entering the porch, she dipped her finger into the water font and blessed herself without touching her forehead or shoulders. Pushing the big mahogany door open, she entered the church. She bowed her head instead of genuflecting and slipped into a seat at the back of the chapel to examine her conscience.

The thud of the big door closing caused Fr. James to jump in his seat. He gulped hard in his throat, smacked his lips closed and shifted in his seat. Leaning his elbow on the ledge under the grid, he hugged the side of his face with his cupped hand and quietly resumed his breathing.

Nell tiptoed as quietly as she could up the side aisle to the Confession Box. She opened the penitent door and entered.

Blessing herself without words, she knelt on the kneeler. Having settled herself she gave a cough, then clacked her boot off the floor to make her presence known.

The snoring quickly ceased and after a short pause the slide was drawn. When her eyes had adjusted to the semi-gloom of the interior, she could see the big fat ear cupped between thumb and forefinger. She could also see his Roman nose and his dark bushy eyebrows that shielded his bright, blue eyes. As he made the sign of the cross, the light from the church coming through the aperture of the curtains was lost and found on the priest's hands. He then framed his ear against the grid mesh.

"Yes, my child," says he.

"Bless me Father for I have sinned," says Nell, "it's three years since my last Confession."

The pungent smell seeping through the mesh made his nose twitch and his eyelids flicker. He jerked in his seat and pulled the curtains in front of him to fan the stifling air. As he did so a sliver of his conscience snatched at the blue eyes of the penitent peering out of an ebony form at the other side of the mesh. Instantly his head jerked back, his eyebrows shot up. For a minute he thought he was back among the natives on the bank of the Congo River but the voice he heard was definitely not an African voice. But who? ..., ... Were his eyes deceiving him? He jerked in his seat and at the same time he removed his hand from his ear. His eyes swivelled around and looked straight into Nell's coal black face, except for the smudge marks she made when wiping her face with the bag apron.

Dumbstruck he jerked back like a cat that had got a fright.

"Who are you?" he demanded, "or what's the meaning of this, or where did you come from?"

All in the one breath, "I'm Nell Shortall from Barnasculla, Father. I've come to make my peace with God."

Momentarily the Missioner was lost for words.

"What ... what ... has you in that state or is there no water up in your country?" says he curtly.

After fanning the curtains to quell the acrid aroma, he returned to his former position.

"Tell me your sins," says he.

"I was hungry and I stole potatoes from a neighbour. Father, I put a curse on Molly Slater that she'd never have a family because she stole me man Ned Kelly and the day set for the wedding."

"And did she?" he asked.

"Did she what Father?"

The Priest exhaled loudly, "Did she have a family?"

"No, Father."

"Go on."

"I put frog spawn into Charley Walsh's spring well so as he'd have bad luck."

"I haven't been to Mass for a long time, Father, not since the last Mission, in fact."

"And why not?" he enquired.

"Well, Father, there was this gang of rapscallions used to hide in the laurels outside there in the chapel yard.

They were forever jeering and calling me names."

"And what names were they calling you, my child?"

"The Raven, Father."

For an instant the Priest's eye corner glanced towards the penitent's box and back again. 'I wouldn't wonder,' he says to himself.

"Blast them, Father. I couldn't stand it any longer so I gave up going all together. I ate meat on Good Friday. I defamed me neighbour's character by saying he'd steal the sight out of your eye for a halfpenny. I broke the Sixth Commandment by enticing Ned Kelly into the hayloft where we made love. It was only then that he consented to marry me. Then that Molly Slatter came along and inveigled him away."

She stopped and closed her eyes to savour the enjoyment of the haybarn when the Missioner cut across her thoughts.

"Anything else my child?"

Nell momentarily had forgotten where she was and almost slipped off the kneeler at the voice. She stammered and stuttered several times before she could answer, "no … no … no, Father."

Fr. James sat up stiffly. "These are heinous offences against the commandments of God and of his church. Are you sorry for all your sins?"

"Yes, Father," says Nell.

"For your penance say one Rosary kneeling down in front of the statue of the sacred heart Jesus Christ our Saviour, every night for a month."

"I haven't got one, Father."

The Priest opened his eyes wide and glared at the penitent. "You mean to tell me," says he rubbing his chin, "that you don't agree with having a holy statue in the house?"

"Oh no, Father, what I mean is I can't afford one."

"Ohoo," says he, "well, I can tell you there's a lovely statue below in one of the stalls at the gate. There's a few little blemishes on it, nothing serious may I add. You'll get it cheap."

"I won't buy it, Father," says she.

"And why not?" says he looking at her sternly.

"Well, Father, the last Mission I spent a whole week haggling with the stall man, before he eventually agreed to sell me one of those cracked Jesus Christ's, and do you know what, Father, on me way home that night after getting it blessed an all, I smashed the shagging thing crossing over Bill Keogh's stile. Bad luck to him."

The Missioner raised his eyes to Heaven and let out a martyred sigh, "Say your rosary somewhere, anywhere," says he, "now say a good act of contrition, O' my God …"

It was at evening devotions that Twig whispered to his cronies in the back seat of the chapel about Pa and the two confessions. "I'll tell yis all about it in Mosseys after the Mission."

A huge crowd had gathered in the pub, anxiously awaiting Twig's arrival, for word had spread from mouth to eager mouth after devotions and they could hardly wait to hear the full details.

"Well, be gob," says Jack Neill when he heard about it, "a little banter wouldn't go amiss after all the tongue banging we got from that Missioner for the last week, belting out hell's fire and damnation and sins of the flesh. I could safely say," says he, "there's hardly a dacent sin to be told between the lot of us. What wrong did we ever do to anybody?"

All within earshot nodded their heads in agreement, and some repeated the sentence lovingly lest it be lost in transit.

"There's hardly a dacent sin between us all."

They were sucking on their drinks when Twig entered the bar. He marched up to the counter with an air of importance and perched himself on a high stool. He liked to dramatise his narratives with a mixture of wit and rare expressions in the vernacular to his captive audience. He lowered a copious dollop of Porter, wiped the foam from his lips with the back of his index finger and gave a great guffaw at the amusement of it all.

The cohort left down their drinks on the counter and clustered around him, some rubbing sympathetic tongues against toothless gums, while others were smiling so broadly through their toothless gums that you could have slotted a slice of toast into it. They all set their bulbous eyes on him, anxiously waiting on him to reveal in his own inimitable way this latest bit of fodder.

"I was on me knees beside the Baptismal Font, examining me conscience or doing the best I could. It's not easy to remember everything after three years."

The cohort within earshot nodded their heads in agreement as they sucked on their pipes.

"Well, as I was kneeling there, who comes in but the bold Pa looking very austere. He was so preoccupied with his thoughts that he never even saw me."

Twig took another swallow from the half filled glass and smacked his lips. He uncrossed his legs and re-crossed them the other way, pausing as though for dramatic effect. The brightness in his eyes almost disappeared between the sudden narrow eyelids as he peered around the bar for their reaction. Happy that his story was going down well, he continued.

"Well," says Twig, "after a short stop for prayer in the seat in front of me, that's the one beside the penitents box, yis all know the one,"

"I suppose," says someone, "he was putting the finishing touches to his Confession before he entered the

Box."

They all sniggered in unison.

"Anyway," says Twig, "he entered the Box and knelt down, and when the slide was drawn he started, " 'Bless me Father for I have sinned. It's four months since my last good Confession' "

He had no sooner started telling his Confession when Father Oliver cuts across him. "Are you a married man?" says he.

"I am, Father," says Pa.

"How many times have you blaggarded your wife since?"

So dumbstruck was Pa at this pernicious insinuation that he jerked back from the grid and gulped hard in his throat, his Adams apple bumped up to his chin several times as he glared at the young Missioner. To himself, 'it's no wonder these other penitents won't come near you.'

Then, without even bothering to bless himself, Pa sprang to his feet as if bitten by a mad dog and stormed out of the Confessional, leaving Fr. Oliver dumbstruck and glaring after him through the grid, his mouth half open.

Mumbling to himself, Pa went and knelt down in one of the pews, cupped his face in his hand and began to pray earnestly for guidance.

'Who,' says he to himself, 'gave him the right to pry into my private and personal affairs with my wife without justification? No one,' he answered to himself, 'in all my sixty years attending Missions has a man of the cloth insulted me in such a manner. What he needs, ' says he, 'is a good chucking.'

With a toss of his head to confirm the fact, Pa left his seat and marched over to the other side of the chapel to join the queue where Fr. James was hearing Confession. Although highly embarrassed, Pa held a staid, muscular face as if nothing had happened.

"And you followed him?" someone interrupted.

"I did to be sure," says Twig, pausing to take a dollop of Porter, then clearing his throat with a loud rattle before clucking a brown mouthful of spittle into the sawdust at his feet. The cohort shifted their positions from foot to foot, their bright piggy eyes searching on Twig to elaborate.

"Well," says he, "when his turn came, he entered the Confession Box and knelt down. When the slide was drawn, he blessed himself. Then, for no known reason, Pa's voice in the penitent box went all silent. Well, be jakers," says Twig, "I thought he had fainted or something, it was so quiet in there. For a minute I was going to open the door and take a peep, but the old Missioner, knowing the ways of nervous penitents from the years of experience in the Confessional, broke the silence."

"Speaking genially and kindly, he says, 'How long is it since your last Confession, my child?' "

All within earshot of Twig gave a jaw-drop snigger at the thought of Pa, this six foot two inch slackly built man being called a child.

"Only a minute, Father," came the reply.

Fr. James jerked in his seat and stroked his chin. He glared at Pa with his eyecorner, "What do you mean, it's only a few minutes?" says the old Missioner. He couldn't believe his ears.

"Well, Father, I was over there with that other fella and it's a row he's looking for."

The cohort opened their mouths and laughed heartily.

"And did he really storm out of Fr. Oliver's Box?" asked Mossey the barman who was enjoying Twig heartily.

"He sure did," says he.

They waited in silence for Twig to continue.

"When Pa told Fr. James, as he had already told Fr. Oliver, that it was four months since his last Confession, the old Missioner demanded to know, before he could give Absolution to Pa, that no such immoral act had taken place."

"Well, be jakers," says Twig, "Pa took a buck in the Confession Box and I thought for a minute, by his capers in there, that he was going to go through the grid and throttle him". Twig could sense Pa was about to explode. "Not you as well," blared Pa through the grid. "That's twice in one hour I have been accused of this heinous offence."

So offended was Pa with both men of the cloth prying into his private and personal affairs without justification that he burst into a violent rage and stormed out of the Confession Box again, almost taking the door with him when he went.

With a fierce face and long legs he tore down the aisle and out of the church, mumbling to himself. He turned at the church gate, raised his clenched fist at the chapel and with fierce rancour in his voice, "That's the last time I will ever go to Confession to a Missioner."

"And that's the God's honest truth," says Twig, raising his empty glass to Mossey, indicating to him that he was in need of a refill. "This story telling is thirsty work."

The Spalpeen

The old woman trudged from the lower field and up the long boreen towards the house with a bucket of spring water from the well. Her shoulders were slouched from years of hauling heavy loads. She left the bucket down on the ground from time to time to rest and wipe the sweat from her brow with the tail of her apron. Her innate modesty wouldn't allow her to discard any of her ankle length dresses, even in the hottest day of summer.

The farm was situated up on the side of Kilderry Hill, a remote part of the district that stretches back into the distant mountain. It is a beautiful place in summer when the plateau is verdant green, and where cattle and sheep happily graze. On the higher ridges purple heather and dense thickets give refuge to the varied and abundant wildlife up there too, for more years than the old woman cared to remember. She slaved on the hillside summer after summer, to save the turf for winter's burning. In winter it was an artic zone where snow and hale and biting winds whipped across its bare eminence. Her seventy years of hard work were taking its toll.

Moll let down the bucket once more and straightened up her drooped body that made her seem small and sad. Craning her neck she peered in over the hedge into the adjoining field where her husband was down on hands and knees thinning turnips.

She gave a wearisome sigh. 'What's all this slaving for',

she snarled to herself, 'and not a chick nor child to leave it to.' She felt the heaviness in her heart at the thought, but she assuaged herself somewhat by the fact that it was through no fault on their part that they weren't blessed with a family. It just happened that way.

She knew from a lifetime of living under the same roof as Lar that to voice her opinion on such a sensitive matter as adoption would hurt his ego greatly, and was sure to incur the wrath of his tongue. He was a cantankerous man at the best of times and his strong belief was that a woman should concern herself only with the running of the house and seeing to her husband's every need. The man made all the important decisions like the buying and selling of all livestock and farm produce. He even did the weekly shopping in the local village. The woman seldom or ever ventured outside the gate except to go to Mass on Sunday and Holy Days of Obligations.

A special treat afforded her was a trip to the market at Christmas time to sell her turkeys and chicken fowl. This money was hers to spend as she chose. She usually indulged herself in some clothes for herself, loose material for mending the working clothes, wool to knit and repair socks. She would often treat a neighbouring woman of the same ilk to a little alcoholic beverage to solidify their friendship. She often wondered what it would be like to have a boy around the place to help her with the myriad of chores she was obliged to do every day ever since she got married and that was over forty years ago.

Of late she was feeling the strain. She was especially feeling the loneliness in the long winter nights, sitting beside the open fire sewing or knitting, and himself, that's if he wasn't out rambling in some neighbour's house, would be sitting on his sugan chair in the inglenook opposite with his back to the wall, smoking his pipe and staring into the fire.

From long experience together it would often enable them to interpret the course of thought in each other's mind without a word being spoken. A shuffle of the shoulders indicated that the house had gone cold and the fire needed replenishing. A long look at the clock indicated that it was time for supper. The folding away of her knitting or sewing indicated it was time for bed. She often wished to hear the patter of little feet around the house or a neighbour calling to break the melancholy.

"I'll better be making tracks," says she, snatching up the handle of the bucket. "Lar will be in shortly for his tea, you know the way he gets, all fussed up if his tea isn't on the table when he walks in the door." Being the sensitive woman that she was she could easily presage his mood any day by his gait, but today she knew he was in one of his better moods. The sun was streaming down mercilessly from an azure blue sky as she trudged across the yard towards the house with the heavy bucket. She gave a long deep sigh as she approached the kitchen door, relieved to be getting in out of the raging sun.

As she put her foot on the threshold, at the same time grasping the doorjamb to help her up the step, a sliver of her consciousness snatched at some moving object up the mountain, compelling her to leave the bucket down and take a step backward. Turning, she clasped the jamb of the door at shoulder height with her hand. She strained her neck like a hen looking out of a coop. Then she saw it clearly, a figure of a man coming down the mountain towards the house. He was whistling a lively tune in his own inimitable way, a tune she recognised from her girlhood days at the crossroad dances. It gave her a feeling of nostalgia. Across his shoulder was an ash stick with something hanging from it like a pendant but she could not be sure for it was hidden behind his back.

When he drew level with her she stepped down off the

step to greet him, still holding on to the doorjamb for support. From a distance she thought he was much older but close up she could see he was only a boy, although big for his age, with a kind of idle bulk that suggests a boy that doesn't realise his own strength.

"Hello, boy," says she, her toothless wrinkled face gnarled and sucked in rosy like a brown paper bag, hair knotted into a bun at the nape of her neck. "What brings you this way?" says she.

"Morrow, ma'am," he cried jovially as he raised the stick off his back, whirled it around and let the rabbits slid off the stick on to the ground at his feet.

"Buy a rabbit, ma'am?" says he, "only caught them an hour ago, dead fresh they are."

The old woman looked at the rabbits, then at the boy. To herself, 'You are a godsend, we haven't had a scrap of meat for a week now.'

Out loud, "How much?" she enquired as she took up the rabbits to examine them.

"Four Pence, ma'am," says he.

She turned and entered the kitchen, rabbits in hand. "Come in," says she, "and sit down. You look as if you could do with something to eat."

"I wouldn't say no, ma'am," says he, rather shyly, ambling in after her and sitting at the end of the table nearest the door.

"What is your name, son?" says she as she busied herself preparing the tea.

"Tom, ma'am, Tom Gillard, ma'am," says he.

"Where did you come from, Tom?" says she, looking at him with her eyecorner, wiping bubbles of sweat from his brow with the back of his hand.

"And where might you be going to in that sweltering heat and no cap on, you could get sunstroke."

No other words passed between them until they were

having their tea. Then he related his story.

"My parents," says he, "worked for Colonel Diggel. My father was a handyman, my mother worked as a seamstress for the lady of the Manor. We lived in a rented cottage owned by the Estate. A Mr. Hampenstall was installed as his agent when the Colonel was recalled to England to stand for Parliament. My parents, like others of the same ilk, were staunch supporters of the Land Act and Home Rule. Mr. Hempenstall, being a Northerner, was fiercely against Home Rule with the result that he evicted all those who supported the measure. We lost our house and jobs on the Estate as did everyone who had been in favour of the measure and were replaced by those who were loyal to the Crown.

"My parents sold all their belongings and bought a horse and wagon and set off in search of work. Not to be exposed to the trials and tribulations and vicissitudes of life on the road, they took me to Carriganty for the hiring fair. There's a man by the name of Dinny Hyland of Coolbeg," he raised his eyes and looked out through the lattice window up towards the mountain to gesture the direction, "you probably know him. He promised me parents that he would look after me until they come back, but this morning," says he, "as I was going out to check some snares I had set, he called me aside and informed me he couldn't afford to keep me any longer, his wife died only this last week." The old woman nodded her head in acknowledgement of the fact, but wasn't listening.

She was in a reverie staring out through the window.

'Wouldn't it be nice,' says she to herself, 'to have someone like him around the place to help me with the myriad of chores I have to do every day, and I'm sure Lar could do with a helping hand around the farm. I will suggest it to him when he comes in,' her lips flexed their corners into the beginning of a smile at the thought.

Tom raised his voice an octave, "You know Dinny Hyland?" his voice pierced into her inner brain, that shook her out of her reverie, "O' yes, yes," says she, "he lives just over the ridge," she gestured with a nod of her head up towards the mountain.

She looked at this poor creature with heartfelt sadness, a sadness that only a mother could comprehend. She formed the opinion that he had some small deficiency of a mental nature and this was borne out when she handed him a Six Penny piece for the rabbits.

"I have no small change son, have you any?"

Tom searched in the lining of his coat and produced a Three Penny piece. "There's your change, ma'am."

A pang of sadness tugged at her heartstrings for this poor unfortunate who was alone in the world and mentally deficient. It would be a real act of charity, she thought, to give him a home, even if it was only until his parents returned. He could finish his schooling in his old school and be among his friends. She prayed with all her might that Lar would yield to her suggestion without much rancour.

After thanking her profusely for the meal and her hospitality, he got up to leave. Picking up his stick he ambled towards the open door, "I'll better be going," says he. Then after a little hesitation on the doorstep he turned and looked at the old woman with eyes that seemed to say, 'maybe …you'll give me a home, I'm a good worker.'

Her eyes began to mist up at the thought of such a young boy being thrown out of a home and nowhere to go. If I could only find some work for him to do until Lar comes in. She was sure that, when she related his tale of woe to Lar, he would surely yield to her request.

Suddenly her eyes flicked from him to the dresser.

"Wait a minute," says she, fetching the white enamel bucket off the dresser. "Go down to the well for a bucket of water for me, son."

She came to the door and pointed to the gate at the bottom of the yard, "Go out that gate," says she, "and down the mass path. There at the bottom corner of the field you'll see the well, you can't miss it."

Tom took the bucket and set off, blithely hopping from foot to foot in a tipup fashion across the yard.

"A nice boy," she thought. "It would be a real act of charity to give him a home."

She was pondering over these things when Lar stepped in the door.

She immediately ran to make the tea. 'It's now or never,' says she, praying hard under her breath, that Lar would yield to her request.

"A boy came by here a short while ago," says she, "looking for work." She daren't mention that it was a home he was more in need of and that he had still two years to go to finish his schooling. She was cutting slices of brown bread so didn't raise her eyes to him.

"He's employed over at Dinny Hylands of Coolbeg for the past two years."

There was no comment from Lar, he just kept on buttering his bread nonchalant to her chatter.

"He's one of those spalpeen boys he hired in Carriganty hiring fair."

"A lot of use he'd be," says Lar in his grumpy, raucous voice as he wolfed down the thick slices of well-buttered bread.

She ignored his comment. Then, to her surprise, she found herself expressing her opinion without fear of a tongue bashing from her husband. She took a deep breath and, on a roll now, she couldn't seem to stop until it was all said.

"Dinny Hyland has terminated his contract, the poor creatuir."

She looked at her husband with searching eyes.

"If there's nobody willing to take him he'll have to go back to the Orphanage in Ballinaglass until his parents return, that's if they ever will, and he's not finished all his schooling yet."

She gave a plangent sigh to emphasise her tiredness of years of hard work.

"I'm not able to haul them heavy buckets of water from the well anymore, them fattening pigs will knock me down one of these days when I go in to feed them, and that roan cow is like a mule for kicking. There's a million and one jobs a young lad like him could do around here and I'm sure you could do with some help in the fields."

'O' we have to school him as well,' he was about to say as he glanced at her from under his slouch hat but stayed his thoughts. The mouthful of bread he was chewing almost choked him at the thought of anyone invading his home to discommode him in his sunset years of life. He knew she was right but he found it hard to swallow his pride and admit it.

He slurped down the last of the tea to clear his throat. He peered at his wife for an embarrassing long time before he spoke.

"Do as you please," says he, getting up from the table.

At that moment Tom arrived in with the bucket of water.

"This is the boy I was telling you about, Tom Gillard is his name, this is my husband, Tom," says she.

"Hello Mr. Maguire," says Tom jovially, "glad to meet you," holding out his hand to Lar.

But Lar didn't reciprocate. He just peered at the lad from under his slouch hat. "Are you now," says he in his usual gruff manner, "time will tell."

His wife stood at the edge of the table, her face red with embarrassment at her husband's curt manner towards the boy and it only their first meeting.

"There's no mister in this house," says he, "Lar is the name."

And so it went. Tom bid farewell to the Hyland's, returned with his harbersack, was ensconced in the Maguires and became their ward.

Over the coming weeks before he returned to school, Tom acquainted himself with the myriad of chores, under the watchful eye of his new stepmother. She was kind and patient and gave him every encouragement. She even promised him, unbeknown to her husband, that if he proved himself, one day he might become the owner of the farm. Tom was so elated at the thought that the poor lad used to swagger around the yard with such an air of importance that one would think he owned the place and not Lar. Regularly he'd invite his school pals from the village up to play without asking Lar's permission.

Being a bit deficient upstairs, it left him prone to forgetfulness and it brought him regularly into conflict with Lar, who, I might say, wasn't quite as patient as his wife.

He chided her for allowing that 'leatherm', a moniker he used for 'imbecile', to play on her generosity and kindness.

"I find him a great help," says she as she replenished the fire with sticks and turf for the dinner.

Lar leered at her. "Help, help," he snarled sourly as he pranced around the kitchen floor, "He's more of a hindrance than a help. That 'leatherm'," says he gnashing his teeth, "will put us in the poor house before long."

"Look at the other evening, I asked him to stable the horses and give them oats and hay," ...

"And didn't he do it?" says she, cutting across him.

"O' he did it all right," says he, "he left the tackings on them all night and they couldn't lie down, and then," says he staring at her severely, "you sent him out to kill the old house cock for the Sunday dinner and what happened? He goes and kills the young cock that I paid good money for in the market only last week. 'That'll stop him from fighting,' says he as he tossed the cock on to the kitchen table."

Well, Lar had been livid! He looked at the bird in abject horror.

"You bloody looking 'leatherm', have you got no eyes in your head? That's the young cocker you've killed."

Moll looked at Tom, her mouth agape. She was going to upbraid him but stayed her tongue until Lar had gone out.

The holidays over, Tom returned to his old school in Kilquale. The journey was much shorter now than when he was living at the Hylands. He felt so proud in himself as he walked down the mass path to the village. First he had lived with a large family at the Hylands and shared a bed with two others and their clothes and an assortment of cutlery. Now he was ensconced in Maguires, had his own room and bed to himself, a dressing table, a mirror and a fireplace where he could sit and do his exercises without interruption.

When Tom reached Nestors Corner at the edge of the village, the first morning, he began to march like a soldier on parade, his head held high, his chest sticking out and his arms swinging to the rhythm of his feet. It would do your heart good to hear the grating sound of Tom's hobnail boots on the granite hard road as he made his way along the street to school that morning. The noise he made caused curtains to twitch and tongues to wag.

'Would you ever look at the get out of your manyeen,' he could almost hear them say.

He delayed his entry into the school on purpose so as to let the other pupils take up their seats. Then he marched in off the street and up the side aisle, ostensibly without breaking his stride. He was hoping to impress the old Schoolmaster, Mr. Grey, with the new outfit he had on, a red shirt, kharky trousers, knee length socks and hobnail boots that Lar had bought for him.

He stopped dead in his tracks. At the top of the school he saw a dwarf of a man standing on the dais at the old Master's desk. He was wearing a grey suit, a black tie and shirt, his black wavy hair was neatly combed back from his forehead.

Tom stared at the little man with bulbous eyes. At the same time his mouth dropped open, his tongue lolled out with fright. He opened and closed his mouth several times like a goldfish trying to say something but no audible sound would come out. He was dumbstruck. He pranced from foot to foot in confusion. He closed his mouth and swallowed hard on his gulp.

He turned around and scanned the classroom to see if all his old buddies were there. Satisfied they were, he came to the conclusion that it must be a new pupil introducing himself before Mr.Grey arrived. All the boys in Tom's class had their hands covering their mouths to suppress the sniggering and tittering at Tom's stance.

The new Schoolmaster hopped off the dais and stood facing Tom. Tom looked down his long nose at the little man who was scarcely up to his shoulder. He was about to say, 'you can't be the teacher' when the Master cut across his thoughts and said, "And who might you be," taking Tom by surprise.

Tom made an effort to talk, "Ta … Ta … Tom, sir," says he.

"Tom who?" enquired the Master.

"Tom Gillard, sir." Tom always addressed his elders with courtesy, it had been inculcated into him by his parents.

"Take your seat, Tom," says he.

The Master returned to his dais and addressed the whole school.

"I'm Mr. Murphy, the new Schoolmaster. I'm taking over from Mr. Grey. You may call me Master."

Over the coming weeks the Master used all his craft and skill to keep order and discipline on his wards. The junior boys and girls were a studious bunch and well-mannered but he couldn't say the same for the senior boys and girls. They were an unruly lot for sure if given a chance.

This cockalorum of a man would march up and down the classroom, rod in hand, slapping each desk as he passed, hoping to instil the fear of God in his pupils.

Tom, the tallest of the bunch, sat in the centre of the desk, his cronies on either side of him. It would remind you of a hen with a clutch of chickens. They eyed the Master with contempt.

"I'll do no exercise for that little midget," Tighe Collins whispered to his cronies.

The Master, reading his thoughts, boomed out, "what did you say, Collins?"

"Nothing."

"Nothing, what?" says the Master.

"Nothing, sir."

"And you, Lynch, what are you muttering about?"

"Nothing, sir."

They began to chew on their lips in ire for having to address this bantam cock as 'sir'.

Every evening he gave them plenty of homework to do so as to test their knowledge as well as their obedience. If on the next day it wasn't done he would dole out two lashes of the cane on each hand and make them repeat that exercise again along with some extra homework as a penance for their disobedience.

At lunch time a few days later they were sitting around the ball alley, feeling sorry for themselves, some with hands under their oxters to ease the pain of the cane lashes, others sucking bruised fingers, when Tighe Collins made a wild suggestion, momentarily causing them to forget their agony and pain and move closer to listen to Tighe's plan.

"Now," says he, "from now on we'll do no more homework for that … that … upstart."

They all looked from one to the other in a kind of puzzled shock, then back to Tighe.

"What will we do?" interjected Jem Roche in a half whisper.

"He'll murder us all," says Tony Nolan.

"No he won't," says Tighe with a roguish glint in his eye. "I think that little squirt is afraid of us."

"Now, this is what we'll do," and they all huddled closer to Tighe lest any of the younger boys or girls might hear his plan. "First," says he, "we must elect a leader."

They all glanced from one to the other, then down at the ground lest they might be the one Tighe would nominate. When they returned their gaze to Tighe he was looking at Tom. They all became animated for they knew what was in Tighe's mind.

"Tom will be our leader," says Tighe. "All agree …" and all hands shot up.

Tom, always anxious to please his pals in order to be one of the gang and not to be treated as a pariah which he always dreaded, accepted with alacrity.

"You'll be our hero after this, Tom," they said, as each one came forward and pummelled him on the back and winked at one another behind his back.

Being a bit mentally slow, Tom didn't realise the consequences. If the plan failed he was much more afraid of his cronies who had threatened to murder him going home from school if he didn't do their bidding.

Next morning, just before the Master arrived the cabal conducted a hurried meeting in the ball alley to verify that no homework was done. Satisfied that everyone had complied with Tighe and his brother Eamon's plan, they turned to Tom and warned him of the consequences if he didn't do their bidding.

After the morning prayers were said and the role call complete the Master looked down sternly on his wards from the dais. He could easily presage that they were up to no good for he had spotted them scampering in from the ball alley as he came around Nestors Corner at the end of the street. He knew these truants and their ilk only too well. Wasn't it scoundrels just like these that lost him his job in a school in Co. Clare! The parents had chided him, saying he wasn't stern enough or capable of stamping his authority. 'If you spare the rod you'll spoil the child,' was his father's war cry. Even the local people were beginning to have doubts about his ability to control these big lads. 'How could you expect them big, bony lads to have respect for a teacher a foot smaller than his pupils,' was the general whine around the village.

From his dais the aster gnashed his teeth in ire and breathed a few unholy expletives to himself as he leered at these mischievous rapscallions of hell, sniggering and tittering instead of doing their lessons.

He swallowed hard on his gulp. I'll show them who's in command in this school before this day is out. Whoever hasn't his exercise done I'll take him out in front of the class for all to see and lambaste him on the nether regions until he pleads for mercy. He assured himself that the example he'd make of him would act as a deterrent to all those other scoundrels who are hell-bent on making trouble.

Watching his iron jaw and his vexed look that morning, the words of the poem, The Village

Schoolmaster by Oliver Goldsmith came flooding back to the master:

A man severe he was and stern to view
I knew him well and every truant knew
Full well that boding trembling learned to trace
The day's disaster on his morning face.

He took the cane from his desk and tested it's flexibility before stepping down off the dais and, ostensibly, marched down the classroom to where the senior boys desks were and brought himself up to his full height, which was only a little over five feet. He leered along the row of boys seated doing their lessons. At least that's the impression they gave. Nobody dared make eye contact with the Master lest he be the first one to be called upon to hand up his homework.

The Master clattered the desk with the cane and called for attention.

"Boys," says he, "pass along your Irish homework til I correct it."

The other boys, being more astute than Tom, began searching in their school bags for the said copybook. Tom remained sitting, nibbling the end of his pencil and winking at one of the junior girls up front who had turned around to see what was happening, and gave no heed to the Master.

The Master bit his lower lip in ire at Tom's non-compliance to his bidding. "Where is your homework?" the Master said fiercely.

Tom gave him a quick glance with his eyecorner and returned his gaze to his copybook and began scribbling on it, ignoring the teacher's bidding.

The Master gnashed his teeth and sucked in a breath so hard that you could hear it rattle noisily against the back of his throat as he peered at Tom. He's defying my authority, he breathed to himself, and I will not stand for it.

If he was to continue teaching in this school and be respected as principal it was imperative that he stamp his authority once and for all. He knew Tom could be very stubborn if unduly harassed and was as strong as a horse for he had seen him one day at lunchtime outside Pa Long's forge, lifting a donkey foal off the ground for a bet. But he also knew he was a malleable chap and with a little encouragement was quite capable of making satisfactory progress. Although Tom was a little slow, these rascals here in front of him were a sly and cowardly lot who were using this imbecile to test his mettle and authority.

The Master pummelled the desk fiercely with the cane.

"Tom Gillard," says he sternly, "get out your Exercise Book at once and bring it out to me."

Tom Nolan, the boy on the end of the seat nearest the Master shuddered in his seat with fright lest the Master come down on his head with the cane. The other boys kept their heads low as they searched inside their bags for their Exercise Books. They'd draw one out of their bag and read the subject on the cover, then return it to it's place before extracting another only to discover it too was the wrong copybook. All the while they were glancing at the Master with their eyecorner. This was a well-known delaying tactic with boys that hadn't their exercise done.

Tom glanced at his cronies on either side of him for moral support, but all their heads were held low, busily searching for their Irish copybooks, or at least that's the impression they gave.

The threat the other boys made against Tom earlier that morning was still vivid in his mind. It would be better, he thought to himself, to stand up to the teacher than to be murdered going home from school by these roughins and, worse still, to be then treated as a pariah for the rest of his life.

His mind flashed back to the time he was in the Orphanage in Ballinaglass. Niall O'Sullivan, a big, bony lad just like him was elected to challenge Brother Ignatius, a small man but with a huge temper who had little sympathy for his wards or how or where he struck them. When Niall refused to do their bidding, Jack Quinlan and his cohorts gave him a severe beating. They even used to steal some of his dinner with the result the poor lad almost died of starvations and worse. He was treated as a pariah ever after until the day he was adopted by a family in Avoca.

The Master threw off his coat and rolled up his sleeves above the elbows. He flexed his arm muscles for all to see. The veins in his neck stood out like twisted ropes and bubbles of sweat began to ooze from his forehead and down his face that seemed to be as hard as leather. He pulled his lips tightly against his teeth and gave Tom a penetrating look.

"For the last time, Tom Gillard, I'm warning you, bring out your homework."

His cronies were still fiddling with their copybooks in their bags, anxiously awaiting developments.

Tom began to turn the pages of his copybook as if looking for his homework. Every page he turned the Master could see was blank.

'He's playing games with me,' the Master said to himself.

At that moment his father's voice pierced into his inner brain. He too had been a teacher in his day. 'Be assertive son,' said he, 'do not be afraid to confront these rapscallions, put the fear of God in them from the very first day, otherwise,' the old man shook his head and stroked his chin, 'you'd be as well to hand in your notice and resign.' That was all right for his father to talk for he was a big man and a champion boxer in his day.

Seeing the Master preparatory to giving Tom a good thrashing, the other boys began shivering with fear. Their faces were ashen, knowing full well the consequences if Tom didn't stand up to the Master. One of them even wet his trousers, but he daren't ask for permission to go to the lavatory. At this time, they would rather suffer the discomfort and humiliation than to ask.

Tighe, who was sitting beside Tom, broke out in a cold sweat with fear. He cursed himself under his breath for opening his big mouth for he knew that if Tom didn't stand up to the Master and call his bluff they were all in for a severe thrashing and he and not Tom would come off the worst if it was found out that it was Tighe and not Tom who instigated this whole sordid affair.

Tom again looked down at the empty pages, then at his cronies at either side of him. They were eyeing him and the Master at the same time, their copybooks still half in and half out of their bags.

Tom looked at the teacher sullenly. He opened his mouth to speak but no audible sound would come out. Fearful that Tom was going to betray them, Tighe gave Tom a severe kick in the shin and a prod of the 'N' pen into his backside as a reminder of the consequences.

Tom took a jump in his seat as if stung by a bee and began writhing and wriggling and gnashing his teeth in pain. He reached down and began massaging his buttocks as he stomped from foot to foot.

"What's the matter with you, you amadan," the Master screeched, come out here at once," says he, not knowing the real reason for Tom's wriggling and stomping of feet, "or I'll …"

"… or you'll what?" says Tom, his round nostrils

flared, making his nose even flatter and his upper lip curled back into an ugly sneer.

The Master turned purple with rage as he punished his lips severely with his teeth. His Adams apple bumped up and down several times as he stomped from foot to foot.

'I'll teach him a lesson he'll never forget before this day is out, I'll give him his just deserts that will put the fear of God in the rest of these other scoundrels.' He breathed a silent prayer, 'Lord please don't let me fail my first big test.'

The junior boys and girls up front were huddled together like caged animals, sobbing and crying.

The Master reached in along the desk, past Tony Nolan and Jem Roach, to grip Tom by the lapel of his coat to haul him out.

Tighe, being more alert to the Master's intentions than Tom, gave Tom another dig of the 'N' pen in the buttocks to alert him of the Master's movements. Tom jerked up off his seat in agony. As he jumped, he spotted with his eyecorner the claws of a hand reaching for him. Automatically and before he had realised it, Tom had his fists up as a defence, and the words were out of his mouth before he realised what he was saying:

"If you don't stand back," says Tom, "I'll run me fist down your neck."

The Master sprang back off the desk like a frightened cat and fell up against the wall panelling at the side wall, and teetered on his heels in shock. His whole visage had turned slate gray. He gave Tom a quick but penetrating look. Then he lazily gathered up his coat off the ground in abject humiliation and made his way back to his desk, a broken man.

He opened the desk and extracted a sheet of official writing paper. He dipped his 'N' pen in the ink bottle and began to write to the Department of Education:

To Whom It May Concern:

I, Dennis Murphy, wish to tender ...

With the diocesan examination only weeks away the parish priest was on the horns of a dilemma as to who he'd get to fill the vacancy until the new teacher was appointed. Young Father O'Mahony offered his services. With so much repetition to be gone over and new parables to be learned before the big day, Father O'Mahony couldn't give any special attention to the more backward pupils and Tom was one of them.

On the day of the exam all the boys in their Sunday best were marched out and stood up against the school wall to await the arrival of the examiner, as was the practice at the time. The girls were examined inside in the schoolroom.

After standing with their backs to the wall for two hours and no sign of the examiner's arrival, tempers began to fray, for it was well past their lunch break. As well, none of them had brought any lunch for they were told that they could have the rest of the day off once the examiner was gone.

The sudden coming of the examiner around Nestors Corner at the end of the street and his sincere apologies for the delay did little to assuage the sullenness of the boys for they were all famished with hunger. Some of them even had no breakfast that morning and would only get potatoes and buttermilk for their dinner when they'd go home.

Tom, the biggest and tallest of the lot, was first in line to be examined.

"Where do I start?" asked the examiner to the curate.

He was still rubbing the sweat off his brow after the tough cycle up the hill to the village.

Father O'Mahony pointed over to where Tom was standing, and, without further adieu, the examiner marched over and stood in front of Tom, who looked nervous and agitated lest he fail his question and be made a laughing stock by his friends.

The examiner, Father O'Boyle, looked at Tom sternly and asked: "How many Gods were there?"

Tom was taken aback by the suddenness of the question. He opened and closed his mouth several times like a gold fish but no audible sound came out.

"Come boy," says the examiner, giving him a clip around the earlobe, "I haven't got all day."

With the suddenness and severity of the clip, Tom's head jerked backwards and bounced off the school wall. He began massaging his head. A great anger welled up in him.

'Who does he think he is, coming here, throwing his weight around, That midget of a Murphy tried that but I soon showed him …'

Out loud, Tom spoke with ire in his voice, "If there was a whole field full of them now I wouldn't tell yeh."

So vexed was Tom at being made a laughing stock of in front of his classmates by the examiner that, on the way home from school, he stopped at Benns Bridge and looked down the valley, then at his schoolbag. Then, with an almighty whirl of the bag, he sent it flying through the air and down the ravine. He leaned over the parapet of the Bridge and watched the last vestige of his schooling years come to rest in the branches of a big oak tree.

"There's one thing," says he, clenching his fist and pointing it in the direction of the schoolbag. "there'll be white black birds … or is it black white birds … out before I set foot in that school again."

As the years rolled by Tom grew into a robust young man. He was able to do all the manual work around the farm, although under supervision of course. Lar, knowing the ways of a strong headed and argumentative young lad, such as Tom, gave him his head and the impression that he would soon be boss. This was in order to lighten his own workload, that it was he and not Lar who was running the farm but his mental ability didn't match his physical strength. That didn't stop Tom however from dreaming about his future plans.

Tom's love of handball or a game of pitch and toss brought him to the village most evenings after work. Nothing seemed to have changed since his schooling days, most of his bosom friends like Tighe and Jem Collins, Tom Nolan and Jer Roach were still around and working for local farmers. The continuous bragging and boasting about his daily work and his future plans for the farm began to irritate Tom's friends, who were only cottage dwellers with a small garden plot.

Tighe Collins as usual was in the fore with his plan to raise Tom's hackles. His cronies looked at him enquiringly.

"Jim Bolger is the man," says he with a roguish smile.

"We'll tell Tom that Jim was up at Lar Maguire's, looking for his job."

Now as everyone knew, Jim Bolger was a ne'er-do-well all his life, as were his brothers. All were huge men with big feet. In order to avoid paying a few shillings for a new pair of clogs Jim assured everyone he could make as good a pair as any clogmaker.

For a whole week, in the confines of his own kitchen, he tapped and paired all day making and shaping his clog soles. Satisfied with his handiwork he tacked on the uppers and the job was completed. To look at these clogs on Jim you'd think you were looking at two sail boats only much more crudely made. The soles were four inches thick and one clog was about two sizes bigger than the other.

The first airing Jim gave the boots was to the shop to buy his quart of milk, which was opposite the ball alley. The first man he encountered after stepping outside his own door was Dinny Kane, the cobbler and next door neighbour, who was standing with his shoulder against the jamb of his door, looking over the street at the lads playing a game of handball.

Without addressing his neighbour Jim cocked up one clog, hoping for a favourable comment. "What do you think of home produced?"

Dinny gave a quick glance at the crudely made clogs, then up at Jim.

This was unlike he was before, for they had been about the same height. "Get down off that tree," says Dinny, "before you break your neck." And, then to add insult to injury, he espied a sliver of bark on the side of the clog. "You could have knocked the birds off first before you got up on them." So offended was Jim that he swung around and without further adieu, marched on over the street for his milk.

Tighe was the first to espy Jim coming towards them. He gave Tom a dig in the ribs. "Now is your chance to show him who is boss at Lar Maguires. I bet," says he, " you are afraid to challenge him."

"I betcha I'm not," says Tom, "I'm afraid of no Jim Bolger."

As it was the public road, the handballers always showed courtesy to the passerby, usually stalled in their playing to let that person pass before resuming their game again. Well, Jim had just passed when Tighe whispered to Tom, "Now is your chance."

Without a second thought Tom took a trig and landed on Jim's back, yelling into his ear, "you're not going to take me job off me, Jim Bolger, I'll kill yeh if you do."

Momentarily startled, Jim staggered under the impact but quickly regained his self-control. He shook Tom off his back like a dog shaking water off its coat.

Swinging around, he gave Tom an unmerciful kick with his small clog.

Poor Tom gave an almighty yelp and ran across the street to the school steps, writhing and wriggling and massaging his buttocks.

"I'm going to tell Lar Maguire on you, Jim Bolger."

Jim looked down at his clogs and, seeing that it was only the small clog he had used, he announced, "Come back here, young Gillard for the big one."

As the years passed and there was no sign of Lar relinquishing the reins of power, Tom became more and more argumentative. It wasn't helped any by the Collins brothers, Tighe and Eamon, and their taunts and sneers about Tom being only a slave for the Maguires, and that Tom would never own the place. All this riled Tom greatly.

Moll, who always had a great rapport with Tom became very concerned and increasingly frightened at Tom's determined attitude to refuse to do any yard work. "It's out in the fields I should be," he snapped at her, "doing a real man's work."

It was only when Tom challenged Lar to a fist fight after he reprimanded him about staying out late at night that the alarm bells began to ring in Lar's head. He began to understand that if something wasn't done and soon this leatherm was liable to kill the two of them and he, Lar, wasn't robust enough to defend himself if Tom were to attack.

That evening at tea Lar informed Tom that he was going to fulfil his promise and leave him the place. He would go to Tinahely in the morning and inform his solicitor of his intentions.

Well, Tom was over the moon at this great news. He would be a real farmer in his own right. The Collins brothers wouldn't be able to taunt him as they had done heretofore about being only a slave to the Maguires.

But little did Tom know that it was to the authorities Lar was going, to have him committed before some serious harm would befall him or his wife at the hands of this leatherm.

It wasn't until the authorities arrived in Lar's yard that Tom was informed of their future plans, that the place was going to be sold and he was going to the county home to be cared for.

Well, Tom refused point blank. He danced around the yard in a paroxysm of rage, cursing and swearing at Lar and what he would do to him if he got near him – and just after promising him the place!

Seeing he was outnumbered Tom ran to his bedroom and locked himself in. After many hours of coaxing and cajoling, Lars and the authorities eventually had to smash the door down and manhandle him into the wagon. As you might guess, it wasn't peasantries that Tom was wishing to Lar as he was led away to a new life in the Wicklow County Home.

The Village School

This is a Tribute both to the pupils who attended Kilquiggan Old National School in South West Wicklow, and also to the teachers who taught there from when it opened in 1837 until it closed in 1962. Most are now dead although a few still live.

The school is gone, the church is down, only the vestry stands there still.
The pupils that once graced those walls are scattered far and wide.
The brightest sparks did make their mark on every walk of life,
From following God to schoolteachers and an Attorney-General.

The shop is gone, the pub is closed and the forge has ceased to be.
Tradesmen that once plied their trade are just a memory.
The pupils came from near and far to learn their ABCs,
In a two room school that adjoined the street and opposite the emporium.

The Masters, they were kind if severe on wards who were unruly,
Or tried to shirk their duty in the class.
The Mistresses to them were even kinder still,
To tiny tots and those have-nots who had walked for miles and miles.

We walked the dirt roads and boreens each morning of the week.
From the first of May til October day we trudged in our bare feet.
The emporium was our port of call each lunchtime to buy
A pennert of bread that was as dry as lead and not even a smear of jam.
The village pump was our teapot and it's there we'd congregate
To douse its crust then wolf it down before playing a game of ball.

The law would come to check the rolls and the truants to reproach.
Those boys that left to go to school but instead mitched into the bogs.
So we bid farewell to those schooling years as we set off on our path of life
And leave behind those frugal days when times were hard and full of strife.

Some journeyed far over land and sea with high hopes
 they'd achieve their goal with dignity.
Some strived so hard with scant success while others had
 the Midas touch.
They did us proud where aye'r they went and kept the
 faith until the end.
Some stayed at home to till the land and care for their
 elders as was their wont.

So, stay awhile and pray for our dead,
Whose wisdom and courage has stood us in good stead.
I'd like to thank our parents and our teachers, one and all,
For the prudence they inculcated in us about vicissitudes
 beyond the pale.

Terry, the Village Urchin

Mother Veronica put down the telegram, cupped her face in her hands, her elbows on the desk, and gave a great sigh. It was a sigh of foreboding for this poor unfortunate boy whom she thought might be condemned to the Orphanage for the rest of his life if an understanding foster parent wasn't found and soon.

Twice he had been fostered out. She raised up her two fingers to emphasise the fact, and twice he had been returned.

Previous foster parents all had the same story to tell about him: "A troublesome boy", they said, "difficult to handle, a bit of a schemer, up to all sorts of mischief." Then Terry put the blame on other members of the family. The simple truth is, he's a bad influence on the whole family.

But little did they know that children like Terry, who are constantly starved of love and affection often rebel in a perverse cry for attention. They would shrink into themselves at any chastisement or fear of being laughed or jeered at. It was their firm belief that no one liked them or understood them. But Veronica did.

Veronica was renowned for her skill in handling difficult children when they'd throw tantrums. That's why Terry was sent to her in Drumrath Orphanage from the Nursing Home in Ballinaglass.

Veronica would take them in her arms and lavish all

the love and praise, kisses and cuddles she could muster on them until she had them calmed down and their confidence restored. She would always give them a slice of her special current cake to soften the blow as it were. Then she would fondle and tickle them before sending them off laughing to join the other boys. She forbade any physical abuse or public humiliation, even to the most difficult of boys, but the other members of staff weren't so tolerant when Veronica wasn't around.

Veronica was beside herself with rage at Terry's return once again to the Home. All the hard work and patience she had put into making him a worthwhile, biddable and well mannered child any family could be proud of had let her down once again. Or more importantly he had let himself down. But in the midst of all the drama she had to smile as she recalled the time he was fostered out to Mrs. Deane of Crossabeg.

John Deane, the eldest, was only ten years old at the time and a year younger than Terry. He loved to help with the myriad of chores around the farmyard after school when his father was away with his big bay horse and cart, working for the County Council.

After school John would set about the chores. Terry would traipse along behind him reluctantly and only because the Mother insisted, warning him of the consequences if he didn't. "Buck up now me boy'o and do your part," says she. "I'm keeping me eye on you," but Terry would just slouch along behind and show little interest. He would rather have a comic book and hide away in some quiet corner to read it.

John would traverse the yard, ostentatiously with an air of importance, as he explained to his ward the order in which the chores were to be done. There was turf to be got in for the night and kipeens to start the fire for his father's breakfast in the morning. The cows were to be brought in for milking, geese and ducks brought in from the clover field and housed, hens had to be fed and eggs collected. Sometimes they might play a game of ball if it was still bright. Otherwise they would go in and do their homework. Then, when their father came home from work they'd all have dinner together.

The real trouble started on Saturday when Mrs. Deane went up to make Terry's bed and tidy the room. She discovered that Terry had wet the bed. She was not too perturbed about the incident on account of him being only a few nights in the house and in a strange bed, but when John heard about it he made a big scene out of it.

When they were out in the haggard and away from the Mother's scope of hearing he would tease and taunt his ward. He would call him a baby and a pissabed. Terry promised himself that one day he'd get his own back on John, 'Mister Perfect' as he called him. Well, sooner than expected Terry got his opportunity.

They were all at dinner this Saturday. Terry sensed that the whole family were making fun of him by the way they were making wild eyes and grinning at him behind his back. In his vexation he had to sing dumb, otherwise he would give Mister Perfect more fodder for his taunts and jibes, and maybe even tell it to his friends in school.

When dinner was over Mrs. Deane gathered up all the scraps from the dinner table and put them in a bucket for John to give to the pigs. Terry, who had been silent all through dinner set his own revenge scheme in motion. He could not do it in the evenings because John would be present or the Mother watching him.

Without excusing himself he dashed from the house and crossed the yard to the hay barn where he'd watch John going to feed the pigs.

'He's an abstruse child, no doubt,' declared Mrs. Deane, "he wouldn't even wait for his tea and sweet cake after the dinner," as was their wont after dinner every Saturday. She shook her shoulders at his strange behaviour but stayed her thoughts.

"John," says the Mother, "when you're finished your tea throw that bucket of scraps into the fattening pigs and for God's sake don't let them out. You know what happened the last time they broke out."

John knew only too well for it was him that got the scalding over it. One of the pigs was so badly gored that the Vet had to be called in to treat him.

Terry had ensconced himself on top of the hay in the hay barn, his favourite place to while away the time in peace and quiet as he read his comics. He also could avoid doing the myriad of chores he was obliged to do as part of his training. It was a good place to covertly observe the going's on around the yard.

When John had returned to the kitchen with the empty bucket Terry sneaked down and opened the piggery gate, then raced back up to his place on the hay to watch.

Well, for hours there was bedlam and mayhem around the yard. Pigs gored the necks off each other, which sent them into a frenzy to kill once they got a taste of blood. In their pursuit of one another they sent hens clucking and squawking in half-feathered flight around the yard.

Mr. and Mrs. Deane stormed out of the house when they heard the commotion and for hours they tried to separate and rehouse the pigs.

"Why did you do that?" asked Veronica of Terry, "don't you know mixing strange pigs is dangerous, they'll kill one another when they get the taste of blood."

Then there was Mrs. O'Hara of Coolishal, she nearly had a seizure when she caught him one day lighting a fire near the hay barn.

"You little scoundrel," says she, "do you want to burn us out of 'house and home'?"

She was so enraged that she tacked the pony under the trap there and then and hauled him back to the Orphanage without prior warning. She stormed into the foyer of the Orphanage and demanded to see Mother Veronica at once. There were sparks coming out of her eyes like sparks from a Catherine Wheel, with ire. She was dragging Terry along by the scruff of the neck lest he get away.

When Veronica appeared in the foyer she flung Terry with such force that he nearly knocked Veronica down,

"Take him," she says with real rancour in her voice, "if I have him another minute under my roof, that's if there's a roof left, I'll go mad," her face was chalk white with rage.

"Come now, Mrs. O'Hara," says Veronica, "and sit down by the fire and let's talk about it," putting her hand on Mrs. O'Hara's arm to solace her distress.

Veronica gave a flick of her head and eyes to the maid to fetch a pot of tea. While the two women were getting settled the maid returned almost immediately with the tray and put it on the little table, which she eased over to the fire in front of the two women.

Veronica poured out two cups of tea, handing one to Mrs. O'Hara. She took a sip of her own before she spoke.

"Now tell me, Mrs. O'Hara, what crime has this poor unfortunate committed this time? He does try his best you know." It was Veronica's way of calming down a potential explosive situation.

Mrs. O'Hara gave her a furtive glance but didn't comment.

After taking a few sips of well-sugared tea and Veronica's special current cake, Mrs. O'Hara relaxed in her chair, at least that's the impression she gave.

Veronica got up and began replenishing the fire with sods of turf from the old tea chest at the side of the fire, without making eye contact with Mrs. O'Hara.

She began to talk to nobody in particular as she stacked the sods of turf like soldiers around the half burned embers, but it was intended for Mrs. O'Hara.

"Children like Terry," says Veronica, "who have been briskly chastised, then starved for love and affection will rebel in a perverse cry for attention. The way I see it," continues she, "is that these children need all the love and attention one can affordably give them, and more at times, to make them feel special like."

She looked at Mrs. O'Hara with her eyecorner and saw that she was contentedly gazing into the fire, munching a piece of cake.

Confident that she had won her over, Veronica brought up Terry's name again. "Sure," says she, "he's not all bad the poor creature."

Mrs. O'Hara jumped in the chair at the mention of Terry's name. "Haaaa ... ", she screeched, her eyes ablaze with anger piercing Veronica's face, at the same time plonking down the cup and saucer on the tray with such ferocity that the tea spattered all over the tray.

Veronica jumped in her chair as if stung by a bee at this sudden outburst, spilling her own tea all over her habit. She tried to show undue concern at this mishap.

"Bad," Mrs. O'Hara repeated, clenching her fists. "Never in me life have I had the likes of him and I have had at least a dozen boys from your Orphanage."

Veronica nodded knowingly for she knew it to be true.

"The other day when I went out to bring in the washing off the line in the haggard I almost had a heart attack, what did I see but that imp," she leaned her head in the direction Terry had disappeared, "had taken me best sheets off the line and had the two dogs pulling tug-o-war with them, and he egging them on and laughing at the good of it, well," says she, gathering breath in her generous bosom to screech out in ire when she looked over at Veronica.

Veronica had her hands on her lap, dry-washing them and, looking sympathetically embarrassed, only gave an audible sigh and turned to her tea and took another sip.

"I wouldn't mind," says Mrs. O'Hara, "only Canon Moarley is coming on holiday next week. Now me good sheets are destroyed. Never again will I take any of these children. I'm gone too old for all this hassle."

They both sat in companionable silence for some time, chewing on their thoughts before Mrs. O'Hara broke the silence and got up to leave.

Ever since Terry's return to the Orphanage Veronica had bombarded the Heavens with prayers and supplications. She even asked Fr. O'Brien to offer a Mass for her intention that some kind person would come and take him before she herself left for the Missions in Africa. She knew it wasn't possible at all times in the Orphanage to give special attention to all these boys for there were too many to be looked after. Then, there were staff changes all the time as well.

Not long afterwards Veronica's prayers were answered.

The name was Sara Mannion of Kilquale, or 'Ma' as she was affectionately known in the parish for her generosity towards the less well off. Although she had no family of her own, her house was never empty of foster children or neighbours' children. Since the last of her foster children had flown the nest she was anxious to have another child in the house to keep her company during the long winter nights now that her husband was dead.

So, Terry was parcelled off to his new home with a stern warning to behave himself, otherwise he would be back in the Orphanage for good.

Veronica filled in Ma on Terry Newsome's background and how he came to be in the Orphanage.

Drawing Ma closer Veronica spoke in a whisper less any of the staff might be lurking outside the office door and overhear her.

"Terry," says she, "is the son of Angela Kilgallan, the schoolmaster's daughter from over in Glenmore."

"O' my God," says she, dumbstruck that such a thing could happen to the upper echelons of society.

"Don't be so surprised, Mrs. Mannion," says Veronica, "it happens to the rich and educated as well as to the poor and ignorant."

"But how … ," says Ma, "he hasn't got the same surname as the mother?"

"Simple," says Veronica, "when she was in the Home in Dublin, awaiting the arrival of the baby, the priest tried to coerce the father of the child, Joe Newsome, into marrying her. They even had his name put on the Birth Certificate. And the family even gave a large donation to the Home to secure this, but Joe refused point blank and immediately skipped off to England."

"And the girl?" Ma asked.

"She was disowned by her parents. They had put it about that Angela had gone to Dublin to train as a schoolteacher, a logical explanation at the time. After the baby was born it was taken from the mother and she was sent as a domestic servant to a big house somewhere in the English Midlands, never to darken the parent's door again."

Terry settled in quickly into his new abode where Ma lavished all her love and praise on him. But she did this to all her wards and they all reciprocated to her loving kindness. But she knew from what Veronica had told her that Terry would be her biggest test to date.

Terry had his own room, a big step from his time in the Orphanage where there were twenty beds in a room and often three boys in a bed. As he lay stretched out on his bed, his hands under his head, gazing up at the ceiling, Veronica's warning flashed across his brain. Her words were so vivid that he thought she was out in the kitchen, talking to Ma. But he knew that this was not possible for Veronica had already left for the Missions in Africa.

'Now, behave yourself Terry, this is your last chance, otherwise you'll be back in the Orphanage for good,' and he shuddered at the thought. He closed his eyes and promised Veronica in his own mind that he would be extra good.

Well, Terry settled quickly and made excellent progress at school. He came First in his class in every subject, although he never seemed to study. The other boys were all envious of the newcomer. The teacher said that he would go far if only he'd settle down and not be so giddy.

But Terry's giddiness was the result of boredom. He was so bright that the boys in the senior class used to get him to do their homework for them. Some wanted maths done, others Irish and others geography. Terry always demanded a payment of some kind, whether it be a bar of toffee or an apple. Others that he knew their parents were well off he demanded a halfpenny from them for this work.

After awhile Terry lapsed into his old ways. One day he brought a frog into the school in his pocket. Then, during a quiet period when all the junior class in front of him were doing their written work, and Miss Twomey was correcting the weekend homework quietly at her desk, Terry let the frog loose on the floor. Soon it was jumping it's way among the legs of the junior pupils and up towards the teacher's desk.

It was first discovered by Jenny Burke, hopping in and out among the cluster of bare legs and making for the teacher. Jenny let out an almighty screech and jumped up on the form seat, yelling and screeching. The other pupils immediately jumped up in panic although they didn't know what Jenny had seen or why she was in such a panic. As soon as they saw the frog they all joined in the frenzy.

"A frog, Miss," Jenny screeched in a falsetto wail of panic.

Immediately there was pandemonium throughout the school. All the children jumped up on the form seats they were sitting on, while others made a dash for the door.

Poor Miss Twomey jumped off her seat as if stung by a bee, almost falling off the dais in the process. When she saw the offending creature fixing its orbs on her and hopping towards her desk she, too, jerked back and let out a wail.

"Everyone out," ordered the teacher, "immediately."

On hearing the commotion coming from downstairs the Master came running to investigate.

Miss Twomey was so distraught that she couldn't answer the Master, only point to where the frog was sitting under the easel.

Terry was the first to speak, "It's a frog, sir, over there under the blackboard. Will I catch it and throw him out?"

The Master nodded. "Now who might have brought that creature into this school?" says he, giving Terry a suspicious look.

Terry, looking all innocent as he passed the Master with the frog in his hand, let it out into the graveyard, smiling wryly as he did so.

On another occasion he brought a cockroach to school in a matchbox. When Miss Twomey went to the Master's room to discuss some school business, Terry slipped up to the teacher's desk, pretending to be looking for chalk in the desk drawer but instead he opened the match box and dropped the cockroach into the teacher's lunch box. Then he tip-toed back to his seat.

"Don't see any," says he to his friend beside him.

Terry, knowing full well what was going to happen, suggested to his friends that they have their lunch on the tombstone in the graveyard nearest Miss Twomey's window.

"We'll sit on this tombstone," he says to his friends, wanting to be close by to come to her rescue. They were all sitting in silent companionship, wolfing down their meagre lunches, some with only dried crusts of bread dowsed with water from the pump, after which they'd scamper off to play a game of ball.

Terry, only nibbling at his lunch, was anxiously awaiting developments in the schoolroom. He kept his eyecorner fixed on the window and his ears cocked for any unusual noise. He was musing in his own mind about the lovely sweet cake the teacher had in her lunch box and how he was going to savour every scrap of it. A great gnawing developed in the pit of his stomach and his mouth began to water at the thought. He was always partial to sweet things and he wasn't concerned whether a cockroach had been crawling all over it or not.

Just at that moment a terrible wail came from Miss Twomey's room. As she went to get her lunch from the drawer she almost died with fright when she saw a black, ugly creature crawling all over her lunch. She let out another terrible wail. Terry ran for the window and was the first to reach it. He looked in and there she was, tettering on her heels and struggling to balance herself on the dais, her face was chalk gray.

"What's the matter, Miss?" says Terry, as he drew himself up to peer in.

"There's a terrible black creature in my lunch box, get the Master quick Terry please," says she.

"I'll take it out, Miss," says he.

He ordered his classmates to go to the ball alley where he said he'd join them in a few minutes. Then he ran around the corner through the porch and into the schoolroom.

Miss Twomey was half crouched in the corner across from her desk, her open hand up against her face as if to ward off an eminent attack. Terry, as brave as you like, fished out the cockroach into his matchbox, the very same creature that he had put there earlier, but the teacher didn't know of course. She could only give a furtive glance with her eyecorner as Terry got down off the dais, leaving the lunch box behind but knowing full well that the teacher wouldn't eat that lunch after the cockroach had crawled all over it.

"Come back," says she, "and take that lunch box and dump it down the graveyard."

"Yes, Miss," says Terry as he went at a lively clip with the box under his arm down the graveyard to his den under the palm tree to savour this sumptuous ham sandwich, sweet cake and a bar of toffee to top it off.

That evening, as the pupils were leaving, the teacher called Terry back. Well, his heart almost stopped. His face became ashen, his stomach began to churn, his knees shook so much that they nearly crumpled under him. He approached the teacher's desk, very timid and full of foreboding. Had she discovered the truth about the cockroach and informed the Master? And he, on impulse, might expel him from the school. Mother Veronica's words pierced into his inner brain.

"Don't be afraid," says she, "I won't eat you."

Terry moved towards the desk with great trepidation. He gulped hard in his throat, then dragged the sleeve of his coat across his mouth and nose to clean it.

When he saw her open her purse and take out a Halfpenny and hand it to him he gave a great sigh of relief.

"Now, that's for yourself, " says she, "for what you did for me today. I must say you are a brave lad."

Emboldened by these escapades and his desire for more, Terry began resorting to more daredevil schemes in order to feed his craving for sweets and cigarettes.

On arriving at the ball alley one evening, famished for a smoke and only a Halfpenny in his pocket which wasn't enough to buy five Woodbines, he needed Three Halfpenny's, so he challenged his friends if they would like to play a game of handball, knowing full well that he could easily beat them. But his hopes were dashed for old Tom Toole, whose home was across the road from the schoolyard, had died during the night and was lying in state in his kitchen bed. Tom lived alone and he used the kitchen for all his needs. Anyway the other rooms weren't very presentable looking, no more than the kitchen was but that's where his bed was and that's where he wanted to be Waked.

Sitting on the school wall that adjoins the street, dangling their legs they were wondering what to do now that they couldn't play ball. They couldn't play ball or have any noise or altercation on the street which would be most disrespectful. They were conversing among themselves as to what to do, go for a walk in the wood or go home, when Patsy Roach suggested that they should go over to the Wake room and pay their respects. All agreed.

Standing up after saying a prayer for Tom they began to converse among themselves as there was no one in the Wake house.

"What's the Two Halfpennies doing on his eyes" they all seemed to ask at the same time, "sure isn't he dead," says one, "he can't see anyway."

Terry, being the more precocious one, gave Tony Nolan a dig in the ribs, "Don't be such a gomila," a slang word for a fool, "do you not know that he must have died with his eyes opened and they can't keep them closed now that he's dead so they put Two Halfpennies on his eyes as a mark of respect like."

Instantly Terry's mind went into overdrive on seeing the two Halfpennies on Tom's eyes and how he was going to snatch them without anyone seeing him.

"We'd better go," says Terry, "before Mrs. Boyle comes in and catches us tittering at the corpse."

They went sauntering back along the street to the ball alley when Terry announced he had left his cap behind in the Wake room. "I'll have to go back for it," says he, "Ma will be wondering where it's gone."

As Terry turned to go back to the Wake house he advised his friends to go home. "I'll see yis all tomorrow evening," says he.

Terry got his cap and also the Two Halfpennies off the dead man's eyes. He now had Three Halfpennies to buy his cigarettes and he wouldn't have to share them with his friends. 'I don't think,' says he to himself, 'he'll be needing any money where he is going. I have never yet heard of anybody buying their way into Heaven.'

Every year when the junior boys moved into the senior school the Master called for volunteer's to fill the vacancies of the Mass Servers who had left the school the year before.

Terry was the first to offer his services. He saw it as an opportunity to make some real money. He had seen Pat Toughy, the outgoing Mass Server flashing lots of money around in the shops, money he got for serving Mass at house stations, from visiting priests, during the summer and for weddings.

Terry mastered Latin with little difficulty, and in record time he was then tutored by the outgoing Head Altar Boy as to how he should conduct himself on the altar at all times, head bent and hands firmly clasped.

The first big task for the trainee server was to present the water and wine to the priest. Next came the ringing of the bell. This had to be done at the precise time when the priest exclaimed the *Sanctus, Sanctus, Sanctus.*

The final and equally important task was to act as Acolyte at Benediction. He had to be able to raise the dome cover off the base of the thurible in order for the priest to put incense on the lighted charcoal in its base. Then he had to replace the dome cover by releasing the long chain, which brought the two parts together, where it was all secured with the holding ring. He then had to swing the thurible to and fro to keep the charcoal glowing. Its smoke sent a rich aroma around the church. This was regarded as the top job of the profession.

The parish priest was so impressed with Terry that he told the school Master that he might send him to the seminary in Maynooth. The Master gave him a furtive glance but stayed his thoughts.

As autumn turned to winter and the days became shorter and the nights and mornings much colder, the old verger, Corneleus O'Reilly, a tall, cadaverous old man, could be seen shuffling along the gravel path in the early mornings from his room over the stables in the presbytery courtyard to the chapel close by. His felt hat sat at a precarious angle, his long black coat swung loosely around his emaciated frame, his head thrust forward from his humped shoulders. His bronchial cough was raucous and severe in the cold morning air. Nobody was surprised when they heard he was struck down with bronchial flu and would be out for a month.

The Parish Priest was at the horns of a dilemma. Who could he get to replace this pedantic old man, time was of the essence. The Parish Priest went around all morning scratching his head in deep thought trying to think who might be suitable to fill the verger's post until he returns, than a thought struck him.

'Maybe,' says he to himself, 'Terry Newsome might

do the job, he's a quick learner. I will go down now and ask the Master to give him time off to prepare the chapel for Mass every morning.'

The Master had no qualms about giving him time off. 'Anyway,' thought he, "he's way ahead academically to the other boys. Maybe a few weeks practice as a verger might forward his ambitions for Maynooth … but I doubt it,' he concluded.

Although released from his duties as a verger the old man couldn't be kept away from the church. After just a few weeks he could be seen shuffling along the path from the courtyard to the chapel, giving furtive glances in all directions less someone might see him. This serene and saintly old man missed the tranquillity of the church and the daily ritual of praying and mediating before the tabernacle. He could often be seen in the back seat of the chapel, quietly praying, head bowed but at the same time fully alert, watching Terry's movements.

It was around this time that the Parish Priest became extremely concerned about the altar wine disappearing. He was sure he didn't waste it or take it to the other church for Sunday Mass. He shook his head but, without pointing a finger of suspicion at anyone, the Parish Priest was of the opinion that maybe, just maybe Corneleus might be helping himself to a little alcohol beverage to restore his flagging health. 'No way would he begrudge him a little stimulant from the vestry but why didn't he ask me,' thought the Parish Priest, scratching his head.

More puzzling than ever to the Parish Priest was when the old verger was fully fit and back at his duties the altar wine was still disappearing and in greater quantities than before. How was he going to explain to the Parish Committee about the extra expense spent on altar wine over the last few months.

There was only one way, he thought, to solve this

mystery and that was to confront Corneleus. He regretted having to do this to his oldest and most trusted friend but he had to get to the bottom of it. He couldn't be seen to condone pilfering from whatever quarter it came from.

Well, Corneleus went ballistic when he was challenged about it. Never in the Parish Priest's time in the parish did he see a man in such a frenzy of outrage.

"Never in me whole life," says he, his raucous voice almost choking him, "has a drop of alcohol passed my lips from here or from anywhere else and I don't intend starting now and certainly not with the altar wine." His eyes were ablaze with anger as he stared at the Parish Priest severely.

The Parish Priest teetered on his heels at the verger's outburst. Having regained his composure he moved quickly to rectify the terrible damage he had caused to the old man's impeccable character. He apologised profusely for the terrible error he had made in thinking of such a thing.

"I have spent the last fifty years in this church in Glenmore," says he, "and without a blemish on me character and to be accused of such a misdemeanour without adequate proof in my view is unforgivable."

He threatened to resign there and then.

After many hours of coaxing and cajoling and apologising profusely for his stupid error, Corneleus agreed to stay on, but, ... who took the wine?

The Parish Priest scratched his head as he left the vestry in puzzlement. There are only two of us who have a key.

Back at his post Corneleus worked hard erecting the crib and to have everything spick and span for the Christmas Feast. Then, the day before Christmas Eve, he was sitting in the back seat of the chapel as was his wont when he needed a rest and few moments of silent meditation. He was crouched forward, his head resting on his bony hands, which in turn were resting on the ledge of the seat in front of him. To anyone who didn't know him they would say he was asleep.

He was shook out of his reverie by the creaking of a door opening in the vestry. He cocked his head and furrowed his brow.

'I never left that door unlocked,' says he to himself, 'I never do and Fr. O'Brien is away on retreat and won't be back until tomorrow. I must investigate,' thought he. Taking up his walking stick he shuffled as silently as possible up to the vestry door that leads into the vestry.

He stretched his neck like a hen and peered into the nave of the room. He didn't see anyone but he could sense that there was some ghostly figure in the inner sanctum of the vestry.

The bristles stood on the back of his neck, a pang of angst and foreboding struck him hard but he couldn't turn back. He drew in a deep laboured breath to crank up his vocal cords, "Who's there?" the raucous voice boomed out.

With fright Terry almost let the bottle fall from his grasp. Not for one second did he think the verger would be in the church at such a late hour.

Corneleus stepped further into the nave of the vestry and yelled again, "Come out, you rapscallion of Hell." He raised his walking stick with a battle flourish, ready to defend himself should this intruder make a charge for him.

With no way of escape Terry sauntered out of the inner sanctum of the vestry to face the verger, bottle still in his hand.

The verger looked at him severely. "A hem," says he, clearing his throat, "so we have a drunkard as well as a thief in our midst."

Terry stood in the doorway, shifting from foot to foot, vacuously looking at the verger.

"How did you get in here?" asked the verger, suddenly taking Terry off guard, "I'm the only one with a key to this place."

"I made a duplicate," says Terry, taking the key out of his pocket.

"O' great," says the verger reflectively, "so we have a genius as well as a thief in our midst. I wonder what will Fr. O'Brien say when he hears this."

Terry began to cry, "Please don't tell on me, mister, please don't, I'll never do it again."

"You certainly won't," bellowed the verger, "you scoundrel, hand me that key and get out of here. You have got me into enough trouble with Father as it is, nearly lost me job I did."

The verger snapped the key from him, "Get out before I break your back with this stick."

Although livid with this rapscallion's behaviour the good verger held his peace until the festive season was over so as not to upset the Parish Priest, who was at the best of times most cantankerous.

"The first thing in the morning," says the Parish Priest, his eyes ablaze with anger, "I'll tackle the bay horse and haul that rapscallion over to the Bishop."

On bended knees Terry pleaded with the Parish Priest to give him another chance but all his pleading fell on deaf ears. "I thought highly of you," says he, "trusted you and gave you every chance. How wrong I was."

On the Bishop's advice Terry was returned to the Orphanage where he was kept under house arrest until he was sixteen years old. Then he was shipped off to join the army.

Waiting for the Call

It was a September evening, I do remember it well. It was the first week of the school year after the summer holidays. As was the custom with me since I first started school, I'd call into Martin to see if he needed some errand from the village. Since his house was adjacent to ours and the first house in the lane just off the Rock Road it was the first port of call I made every evening on my way home from school.

Although Martin was an old pensioner and I just a young lad, at the time we became very close. I suppose our closeness developed from long periods of togetherness during my summer holidays. We would go for long walks up the mountain and he would identify every wild flower and shrub for me. He had a rich store of worldly wisdom and a myriad of fine stories of which I was to be the beneficiary. It was always me he called upon to collect his messages from the shop and his pension from the post office.

It made my sisters jealous because they were left to do the menial work around the house and farmyard after school and before our evening meal. Mary reluctantly looked after the poultry and collected the eggs, bedded the fowl house and closed the fowl house before dark for fear the fox might take them.

Collette, my older sister, fed the pigs that kept up a squealing racket once they heard the sound of galvanise buckets rattling, while I was gallivanting, as they called it, around the village on my bicycle and getting paid for it.

Martin was always so kind and generous to me and my sisters. I suppose that's one of the reasons why we loved him so much.

A strange turn of events occurred that evening when I went in with his messages. He was sitting on his sugan chair beside the fire, pipe clasped between his two scrawny hands, his elbows resting on his knees. He was crouched forward, his head bent low, staring into the dying embers of the turf fire.

He was motionless and silent, which was out of character with the jolly old man I had come to know and love. I froze in my boots. I was awestruck. I was about to dash out of the house to tell mother that something dreadful had happened to Martin. Then as luck would have it, he began to shuffle his feet. I was so glad too that I hadn't dashed out and alarmed mother. I gave a sharp cough, hoping it would snap him out of his reverie. He gave a sudden jerk of his head and straightened up. It was only then that he became aware of my presence in the kitchen.

"Is there something the matter, Uncle Martin?" I ventured.

He wasn't really an uncle of ours at all but an elderly relative from my father's side of the family, a cousin once or twice removed, but since my father had no brothers or uncle, we adopted Martin as our uncle. He was treated as one of the family. I think he really liked the title.

I was almost ready to cry with fear and apprehension for this kindly old retired saddler we had become so attached to. After a short pause he looked at me. He had a woebegone look about him, the tears were trickling down his sallow cheeks like lonely drops of rain. Wiping them with the back of his scrawny hand, he blurted out in a broken voice, "Matty Ross died last night," says he, "my oldest and dearest friend has passed away."

Martin had told me many a story about the Ross brothers and their sporting achievements. He would talk about them so fondly that I felt as if I knew them.

"Sure," says I, going over to him and putting my arm around his shoulder to unction him like a grown-up would do, "sure, wasn't he an old man of ninety or more?" says I, "Hadn't he had a great lease of life? Wasn't it to be expected?"

He gave me a furtive glance and after due consideration he spoke solemnly, "I suppose you're right, son," says he, "he's only gone a few days before me anyway."

From that day onwards Martin seemed to lose his zest for life. It was as if he was next on the list, just waiting for the call.

I remember as a young lad sitting in the warm glow of the turf fire, listening to him and Swank Hayden reminiscing about their sporting days and what they had achieved, but not in any boastful way may I add. Their conversation always reverted back to the Ross brothers who were their idols when they were young.

"What became of them?" I enquired.

"Matty became a schoolteacher over in Carrivanty and Sean became a Christian Brother in Waterford."

Having an insatiable appetite for information I prompted further, "They must have been great sportsmen," says I, "when a plaque was erected to them in the village."

Swank, who had been silently smoking his pipe up to now chimed in, "They were two of the greatest sportsmen," says he, "the Parish of Glenmore has ever known. Their achievements in track and field events and other fields of physical endeavour brought honour and fame to themselves, and heaped glory on the village. They were revered by all who knew them. Their collection of cups and medals were a sight to behold."

"Were ye as good?" I ventured, thinking about all the cups and medals that adorned Martin's mahogany glass case in the little parlour.

"Maybe we were," says Swank rather hesitantly, but being the modest men that they were they always added, "sure weren't the Rosses passed their best when we came along?"

But the array of cups and medals that lined the mahogany glass case in the little parlour was a testimony to their achievements. Many's a time I took them out to clean and polish while Martin sat in the ingle with his back against the wall smoking his pipe. He would recall the venue and the event where he won each cup or medal. I knew by the way his lips flexed their corners into the beginning of a smile that he was proud of his achievements and even more proud when I told him that I'd like to be a sportsman like him. The thought of another McCrea representing the parish seemed to give him a new lease of life. Grunting, he rose stiffly from his chair and shuffled over to the window, looking out over the valley and beyond to the village of Kilquale where all those years ago he played handball against the school wall. He reminisced in his own mind about the games him and Swank played there, and all the friends he made at sporting venues all over the country as a young lad. He returned to his chair.

"Now," says he gravely, putting out his hand to ruffle my hair, "if you need any tips, don't hesitate."

Next morning on my way to school, Martin was sitting outside his front door all dressed up.

"Where are you going, Uncle Martin?" says I.

"Swank and meself are going to the Wake," he answered in a bronchial voice.

I pondered to myself a moment about the long journey these two old men were about to undertake, twenty miles of rough terrain. They couldn't possibly be able to walk that far.

"How are you going to get there?" says I.

"Your father is giving us the mule and trap."

"He won't be able to go that far," says I, "he's too old."

He looked at me sternly as if to say you don't know it all yet me boy.

"He will, laddie," says he, "and back too. They are the most honest and reliable animals God put on this earth."

If Martin and Swank's departure from home that morning was quiet, their return was even more quiet, for when father looked out the next morning from his bedroom window into the farmyard, to his astonishment there was the old mule still harnessed and under the trap outside his stable door, nonchalant and resting on three legs as if he was in his own stable.

"My God!" wailed father, "something must have happened to Martin. The mule and trap is in the yard and still under the trap."

Mother jumped up with a start. Father dragged on his clothes real quick and went to investigate Martin's whereabouts.

He was relieved when he discovered Martin at home and safe. He said he had been a little too intoxicated to unharness the mule and apologised profusely for his lapse of consideration for the dumb animal.

He refused to talk about his previous day's outing. Even mother, who had a knack of extracting news from most people, failed. He gave her a dismissive wave of his hand as much to say I don't want to talk about it.

As a senior boy in the national school I tried to emulate Martin, although I knew in my heart that I'd never be able to accumulate the same array of cups and medals as him. But as Martin often said, "it's not the winning that's important, it's the taking part."

On the day I bid farewell to my old school for the last time Martin called me in for a chat. I supposed it was to congratulate me on my academic achievements as well as on my sporting success although he didn't say it out loud.

"Son," says he, "I have made my Will and as promised I have left those yokes in the glass case for you." He looked at me solemnly, "There will be no need for them where I'm going."

I thanked him profusely for his kindness and promised to cherish them all the days of my life. He became very melancholy. A tear slid down his bony face, for he knew it was the last vestige of his sporting life.

I took out a bottle of whiskey from under my coat that father had given me and poured a copious measure for him, to assuage his grief. 'If you want an old man to talk about himself,' says father, 'always indulge him in a little of his favourite beverage, it works every time.'

A broad smile lit up Martin's emaciated sallow face.

"You're a man after me own heart," says he, taking a hefty slug of the precious stimulant while leaning back in his chair to savour the richness and taste. He raised his glass to indicate what he meant.

"There's plenty more where that came from," says I.

It was an opportunity to celebrate many things, especially my departure to college. When a few dollops of the precious alcohol reached its destination Martin nodded appreciatively and with a twinkle in his eye he again uttered, "you're a man a me own heart."

Then, as if inspiration was activated by the precious stimulant, he settled back in his favourite chair in front of the alpenglowing embers of the turf fire. Martin lit his pipe and prodded it into easy operation. As the pipe smoke coiled upwards through the black rafters to hide in the smutty thatch, he launched into one of his many narratives that had been eddying around in that ancient head of his, now loosened by the many measures of fine whiskey.

This was my cue to delve into the episode of the Wake they went to over in Carriganty and its aftermath.

We talked and laughed awhile about nothing of any great importance before I put the question to him. He looked at me askance. I was puzzled at the fixed glare he kept on me for it was curiously strange. He turned from me and began staring into the middle of the fire as if his thoughts were somewhere else. He drew heavily on his pipe and after a stony silence, he looked at me amiably.

"Well, now," says he as he uncrossed his legs and re-crossed them the other way, "it was a strange day. Come to think of it, it was an even stranger night. Maybe it's because we were two drunken men so you might think this story is only a canard ... to me, well ...".

Martin looked into the fire again and drew on his pipe. He was probably thinking, 'who would believe two old drunken men anyway?':

"We left that day, Swank and meself, in the mule and trap. It was a glorious day for travelling. We were in great spirits. The autumn sun was high in the sky and there was little or no wind. The thrushes and blackbirds were in full voice as were the robins and goldfinches that were warbling and chirruping as they scuttled from tree bough to tree bough in the hedgerows along the roadway in front of us, as if directing us like a star that directed the three wise men to Bethlehem.

"We ran out of chat after awhile so we sat in silence smoking our pipes as we admired the scenery of the countryside. The meandering Dereen River flowed serenely to meet its sister river, disturbed only by the trout leaping up to catch the hovering flies. The keen eye of the otter watched us from yonder bank, alert to our presence and was ready to dive back in should any danger arise. The hills and plains were verdant green where cattle and sheep lazed about in the autumn sun. The hares and rabbits were as lissom as the reeds that danced and swayed on the river bank.

"As we drew near Carrigantly village we could hear strange music being played. It seemed to be coming from the direction of the schoolhouse."

" Well, be the living sinner," says Swank. This was one of his favourite sayings. "She is sending him off in style."

"We tied the mule in the yard and gave him hay that I had brought, certain in the knowledge that it was going to be a long day. As we approached the hall door a cohort of men were carousing outside, drinking Porter and humming the chorus of a rebel song, while another lad was strumming a tune on his fiddle.

"We took off our hats and entered the Wake room. We knelt down and said a prayer for our old friend Matty. There was a cluster of women in the far corner of the room, keening and sobbing, heads bent as if grief stricken on this lamentable occasion.

"Having prayed awhile for the repose of his soul, Swank whispered to me, 'He must have been a very popular man during his lifetime over here. Look at the way they are crying. There won't be a tear left for the funeral.'

" Do you not know," says I, "these women are getting paid for all this keening."

" WHAT!" screeched Swank in a loud whisper, "getting paid?"

" Keep your voice down," says I, whispering back, "it's the tradition around here."

" Well, be the living sinner," says Swank, "that bates all." Rising from his knees, the cacophony of caoinings stopped abruptly and the women began to stare at us.

"Mary Kate was soon on the scene to investigate the sudden quietness. She was paying these women for their services and she intended getting her money's worth. She was about to berate them for their irreverence to the dead man, but she soon mellowed when she saw us. She became very emotional as we sympathised with her on her great loss.

" Come to the parlour," says she, "and have something to eat. Ye must be starving after the long journey."

"As she was about to leave the room she turned and glared at the silent women and wagged her finger at them as much as to say, 'get on with it, that's what I'm paying you for'.

"After the meal we sat in the warm glow of the turf fire and smoked our pipes as we chatted with Mary Kate. We reminisced about our youth and the fun we had as young lads around Kilquale, the sporting tournaments we took part in. We couldn't but notice how pleased Mary Kate was when we heaped praise and glory on her husband and her brother-in-law Sean. Our glasses were never empty and time slipped by easily.

"After hours of chatting and reminiscing, drinking large whiskeys washed down with bottles of Porter, we were over-intoxicated. We asked Mary Kate to be excused for it was time we made for home.

" You know the terrain we have to travel?" says I.

"She nodded in acknowledgement, for she and Matty had travelled this same route on numerous occasions when they were young and courting.

" We don't want to be holding you up," says Swank, "I see a lot of people arriving to pay their last respects."

" They were here in their hundreds last night," says she, "where they came from I don't really know. I suppose," says she, "past pupils."

" It just goes to show," says I, "the affection and

esteem in which he was held by all who knew him."

" I'll see you to your car," says she.

"With old age and arthritis and the excess alcohol, it took us sometime to get into the perpendicular. We waddled out, holding on to backs of chairs and doorjambs for support until we got to the yard. We slouched from side to side like two old men with their feet in parallel ditches. She chatted desultory with us as we made our way to our transport, which was the mule and trap. She thanked us profusely for coming but said she was disappointed that we weren't staying over night. She became very emotional. As she detached herself from our embrace for the last time, tears were trickling down her face like lonely drops of rain.

"But when she saw our mode of transport her maudlin feeling soon vanished. She jerked back a pace, covered her mouth with her hand and gulped hard in her throat.

" Oh my God," says she in apprehension as she pointed at the mule. She became very agitated and begged us to stay over night.

" There's nothing wrong with our mode of transport," says I, "I can assure you he's the most faithful and reliable animal in the world. He has never let us down yet."

" My father," says she, "had the most harrowing experience one night coming home from Jim McMahon's Wake with his mule. I'll tell you, he never got over it."

"All this had an almightily unsettling effect on the mule for some strange reason or another. As he moved she put her arm on my shoulder, 'For the last time as old friends I beseech you not to go. Wait until daylight. Sure, what's the hurry on yis?'

"But we weren't going to be put off by such superstition.

"When we hit the high road, the old mule began to trot real earnest. It would do your heart good to see the dancing legs of the mule and the bright sparks of the iron-shod hooves on the granite hard road as he click-clacked home at a lively clip.

"The sun was already low behind Carrignoe Mountain to the west, silhouetting it in a dark black outline. Masses of black clouds were thundering in from the east and beginning to envelope an otherwise clear sky. An icy nip had crept into the air.

"As we went we sang song after song while Swank took copious dollops of whiskey from the bottle Mary Kate had given us. He lifted the bottle high in the air about his head,

" No man is getting a better send off," says he.

" Here, here to that," says Martin, "and no man deserves it better."

"The cacophony of harsh sounds crept deep into the valley on the night air and soon every dog and fox were answering, and every rooster within earshot crowed in salutation. It wasn't long til we were tired of our singing so we sat in silence with our thoughts.

"Soon the rhythm of the click-clacking of the iron-shod hooves on the granite hard road proved soporific to Swank and me. Our heads sank forward on our chests and we began snoring. The old mule trotted along on an even pace, not in the least bit perturbed at his master's snoring. He was quite capable of negotiating his own way home without any guide. He had done so on numerous occasions before in all weathers and at all hours, both day and night.

"Then without portent or warning, we were shook, not alone out of our reverie but almost out of the trap by the sudden thud of the shafts on the road. We found ourselves half in and half out of the trap and hanging on for dear life. It would remind you of two roosters over-balancing on their perch. It took quite awhile for these two old doddering men to get their legs disentangled from one another and try to gain purchase on the rim of the trap to return it to the perpendicular. Then with some fierce grunting and growling, pushing and shoving and a litany of unholy expletives I eventually extracted myself from the trap and stood on the road.

" Give me that carbide lamp," says I, "til I examine the scene."

"I walked around the trap.

"The blasted mule has lain down," says I.

" What's the matter with him?" says Swank.

" Bates me," says Martin, thinking about Mary Kate's warning before we left.

"The old mule was trembling uncontrollably. There was froth coming from his mouth. He was covered in a lather of sweat. He was scraping the road with his hooves as if in agony. There were sparks coming out of his eyes in terror as he flung his head to and fro. Was he about to die? We could not tell.

"An eerie silence came over the place as I set forth with my lamp in search of some identifiable landmark or object.

"If I'm not mistaken," says Swank, "we are in some village or other."

" I'll go over here," says I, "and examine this object."

"Raising the lamp aloft to eye level, I proceeded gingerly along the road. In the faint glow of the guttering light, I could discern in the distance a prodigious object. As I came closer I discovered that I was in front of a stucco building but where I didn't know.

"On closer examination I saw a plaque on the wall which read, *Kilquale National School, 1837.*

"So elated at knowing where I was, I let a bark out of me. 'It's Kilquale we're in, there's the plaque on the wall! Well, that bates Banaher,' says I to nobody in particular, 'we're almost home and the blasted mule has to go and lie down.'

" Come back here," says Swank, "and don't be shouting at this ungodly time of night and let the dead rest."

"On the way back to the trap Martin looked into the graveyard and, in the faint glow of the guttering light, he saw a cohort of men going around in a circle, heads bent in great concentration.

"Martin, being a man of little fear, called out, 'Can I help yis?'

"There was no answer. He raised his voice an octave, 'The Lord have mercy on yis all, can I be of help?'

"A tall bearded man detached himself from the group and came forward and rested his elbows on the graveyard wall.

"We are selecting a team to represent Kilquale in the Taltain Games in Dublin," says he, "and we have lost the ball."

"Not to worry," says Martin, taking one out of his pocket, "I played with it almost seventy years ago."

" You see, sir," says the big man again, "we are short of a good man to make a foursome."

"Well," says Martin, drawing himself up to his full six foot, "if it's a good handballer you're looking for, then look no further than yours truly."

"When they selected four players, I included, the years fell away and my mind lapsed back into earlier times as a young man with a mop of brown curly hair, a muscular athletic frame. I remembered being on the team that represented Kilquale in the Taitain Games in Dublin in 1900 and now ... and now, I had a chance of being selected again. I was determined to give a good account of meself and show the opponents that I was as good a handballer as they were.

"Excuse me," says I, "how are we going to see? It's altogether too dark."

"A familiar voice came from the graveyard wall, 'Take my cap,' says the man, 'and then you'll see.'

"When I put the cap on, instantly the whole village lit up as if by magic. I could see all me old friends from the handballing days sitting on the graveyard wall and at every vantage point, with flags and banners.

"I tossed off the coat and waistcoat and took up my place.

"As soon as the game got under way, the old mule stood up and relaxed on three legs nonchalant as if he was at home in his own stable.

"The game was as good as I ever played. The advantage alternated from one team to the other. The cheering and shouting could be heard miles away when I displayed some of me skills at butting the ball. In the end, the opposition won 21 to 19.

" We'll play another," says I, who was never one to give in easily.

"The second game was a real cracker. It was more closely fought than the first one, never more than an ace between them at any one time. I was stripped to the waist and there were beads of sweat pouring out of my ruddy forehead. The excitement was fierce. Flags and banners were flying by men and boys at every vantage point for the new man who, in the opinion of the selectors, had proved himself the perfect choice.

"We won the game in great fashion.

" We'll play another, says Martin. I was just beginning to get into the stride.

"The big bearded man spoke, 'You have proved yourself an automatic choice for our team,' as he escorted me back to the trap.

"Come at once," says Swank, "before he lies down

again."

"Martin took off his cap and flung it back to the man on the wall.

"Instantly the whole village was plunged into darkness again. There was nobody to be seen or a sound to be heard.

"The big bearded man put a ghostly hand on Martin's shoulder and whispered into his ear.

"Martin climbed into the trap in great distress. His face was chalk white and he had a woebegone look on him. We sat in silence as the old mule set off at an easy pace.

"After a stony silence, Swank picked up the courage to question him.

"What in the name of God," says he, "happened to you at all tonight? You look as if you've seen a ghost."

"After a long silence Martin looked at Swank gravely and shook his head. With a bronchial voice, says he, 'Do you want the good news or the bad news first? Well, the good news is, there's a handball alley in Heaven.'

"And the bad news?" Swank cut across me.

"The bad news is," says he with a heavy heart, "there's a game on next Sunday and I have been chosen as one of the players on the team!"

The Road Overseer

When Bart Reilly was forced to retire as Road Overseer for the District of Shinrone, soundings went out as to who might be the best candidate to fill the post.

The job of Road Overseer was prestigious throughout the county and carried a great many responsibilities. It dealt with a large number of workers for it was the main source of employment for all men in the county area. As well, the Overseer job involved knowledge of a variety of work skills, as stone cutting in the quarry, turf cutting in the bog, and horse and cart work which pulled, carried and transported the stones and turf throughout the county and for the road maintenance jobs.

Several capable men, including Mickey Joe Courish, applied for the job. When interviews were complete it was Mickey Joe who was the successful candidate. This decision was made by the County Engineer, Ned Griffin, who found him to be a most reliable worker and excellent timekeeper in doing his own days work. These attributes secured the post for Mickey Joe and all the workers wished him well in his new post

Since he was a local man, everyone was sure Mickey Joe would treat them as favourably as did the retired Overseer. But Mickey Joe was determined not to fall into the same trap as his predecessor by being too lenient with his subordinates. Old Bart had overlooked bad timekeeping by some of the men, and that eventually got him the sack.

This great hulk of a man took his position very seriously. Mickey Joe would rise before six every morning, winter and summer. He would set off on his big Raleigh bike to his first port of call, usually the quarry, to check that everyone was on time. Not even Dick Carey the timekeeper was exempt from this rule.

Starting time was eight o'clock and no deviation was tolerated. If a man was just a few minutes late Mickey Joe would order Dick to 'quarter him'. That meant that late arrivals had to stand out for two hours before they were allowed to start work. All these men had travelled long distances every morning and were solely dependent on every hour they could get to feed their wives and loved ones. Two hours lost was a great loss to their meagre wages.

If they offered to work on into the evening after finishing time to make up for the lost time Mickey Joe wouldn't allow such a practice, and neither would he compensate any work they would do during those two hours, even if they worked just to keep themselves warm.

Mickey Joe showed no mercy. He would rebut any plea for leniency, even from Dick Carey, on their behalf. For the slightest offence he would retaliate and dismiss a man.

Another cruel method of punishment he had was to never let a man work in his own locality. He usually sent them to the furthest end from their home so that every day these men had to travel long distances to their work, whether it was to the quarry or to breaking stones or for general labouring work.

Before leaving the quarry on his morning rounds Mickey Joe would oversee the blasting of the rock with gelignite. First, holes were bored into the rock with a hammer and cold chisel. Then the sticks of gelignite were placed in the rock, wired up to each other and covered over with clay to prevent shattered rock from spreading over a wide area where it might injure someone. This job was done by Ben Power who was an expert in the field of dynamite. When Ben thought it was safe to return after the blast he would signal to Dick Carey that all was clear. The timekeeper immediately ordered the men to return and mount the rock head. They then began to prise out the large, shattered boulders with crowbars and toss them down to the quarry floor. There the sledgehammer men set about reducing the boulders to a more manageable size before they were carted away by the carters, in one ton loads, to designated points around the area. There the pieces were further reduced to small stones and chips suitable for road making. These cartmen received only an extra shilling a day for the hire of their horse and cart.

Several men, mostly small farmers who had a horse and cart and a little time on their hands, applied for and got a stretch of byroad to repair and maintain on a contract basis. This was work done at an agreed price and for a set period of time, usually one year. Naturally, so long as the repair work was done to the satisfaction of Ned Griffin, the Engineer, he didn't care how many hours were spent at the work, as long as the road was kept in good repair and the water tables running free for that period of time. These lucky few men were independent of Mickey Joe.

Other men employed at stone breaking at the side of the road were also working on contract. Their hands were rough and calloused from handling these rough stones. With all that sitting on rough, broken stones while pounding all day, their bottoms were scratched and bruised so they would bring a small bag of straw to use as a cushion.

Then there was another hazard that went with the job,

the likelihood of a stone breaker crushing his finger or thumb if a heavy hammer accidentally slipped off the stone a man was holding and reducing to chips.

Mickey Joe knew from experience that these men were quite capable of breaking more stones than their allotted amount of three loads for any one day. Since the payment for three broken stone loads was equal in value to the day worker's pay there was little incentive for the breakers to earn extra money unless Mickey Joe sent them an extra load. They regularly pleaded with him to do that, to send just one extra load to boost their weekly wage but this seldom if ever happened.

Certain men Mickey Joe would favour with the extra load if a man had done some work for him, like ploughing his plot, sowing his potatoes or carting home his turf for him. Otherwise he'd do his utmost to thwart their ability to earn extra money.

If a farmer was a horse and cart man seeking work Mickey Joe would take delight in putting him on at his busiest time of the year. For a farmer, that was when he was putting in his own spring crop. This put a terrible burden on both man and horse to cope with both jobs. When the crops were sown his employment was sure to terminate til maybe harvest time.

If the weather was inclement the stone breakers on contract would set about their work with gusto so as to finish as quickly as possible and head off home. This practice was to Mickey Joe's great annoyance. If he found out or if Ned the Engineer happened to come by and the contracting men weren't on their job until the official finishing time, it would show Mickey Joe up in a bad light and was sure to get him a severe reprimand. So to avoid this embarrassing situation he'd call in during the afternoon just to check on them to make sure they were still at their post even though they had their work complete.

These crafty men had their own way of fooling Mickey Joe. They'd leave a big stone or two unbroken so, when he arrived, the men were busy working but as soon as Mickey Joe was gone and the workers were reasonably certain he wouldn't return they would toss the big stones in over the ditch so as to leave no trace. Upon returning the next morning they'd retrieve those stones and add them to their next heap for breaking.

To show his authority over his subordinates Mickey Joe would sometimes arrive in a frenzy to examine the work, having heard that the men had left early the day before.

He'd hop off his bike and throw it against the ditch with angry energy. He'd gnash his teeth as he marched over to the stone breakers who were slaving away at their work, and lash out with his boot at the heap of stones viciously.

"Hutch me, man," he'd exclaim, this being his favourite saying, "them stones wouldn't pass through a cart wheel with the spokes out. Yis will get no payment until yis go through all them stones again and put them right."

Some of the men like Dave Price or Christy Deacy cared little about Mickey Joe's bullying tactics. Whenever they had their allotted work done they headed for home to look after their own small farm holdings and the few stock they managed to have. Mickey Joe would never comment in these particular cases because, as example, it was Christy who used to partner Mickey Joe's niece Big Tess at the waltzing competition in the village hall. Big Tess was smitten by Christy and Christy played his part in this deception. He played up to Big Tess in order to get all the work he could handle from Mickey Joe, for he wanted to buy a little farm that adjoined that of Mickey Joe's. But

Christy had little interest in Big Tess other than to get work.

Whenever stones were needed urgently for road repair, Christy was the man Mickey Joe sent for. He could break twice as many stones in a day as any other man. Mickey Joe was forever singing his praises for one day he was certain that Christy would marry Big Tess, his niece. And if and when he did Mickey Joe would recommend him for the post of Road Overseer when himself retires.

Being under pressure from his solicitor to come up with the money to buy the farm he had chosen, Christy approached Mickey Joe for extra work. He told him that he was buying Sam Jenning's farm that adjoined Mickey Joe's land just next door. Mickey Joe was only too willing to oblige for he was thinking in his own mind that he was doing Christy a favour as well as for his niece Big Tess whom he would be marrying soon.

Over the coming weeks Christy worked all the hours possible at stone breaking. It took two cartmen to keep him supplied with stones. Nobody could believe, not even Mickey Joe, the number of loads Christy had broken in such a short length of time.

With enough money to buy the farm Christy retired from the road, unbeknownst to Tess or Mickey Joe, and married his childhood sweetheart, Kitty O'Shea.

When Mickey Joe heard about the wedding he was livid. So much so that he severed all connections with Christy.

Mickey Joe still hadn't heard about all the unbroken stones hidden at the bottom of the heaps on the roadside which Christy had left.

It wasn't until two weeks later that Christy's shabby work came to light. County Engineer Ned Griffin, seeing all the stones ready for road repair, ordered Mickey Joe to have these stones carted over to Grannery Road which was in bad need of repair. "I'll be there myself in the morning to oversee the work," says Ned.

The following morning the cart men and their helpers set about loading the stones into their carts. Mickey Joe was close by, chatting with Pat Breen, the road repair timekeeper. He gave one swift, embracing glance at these men struggling to pierce the heap of stones with their shovels. They were jumping on the shovel step, trying to enter the heap so as to extract a shovelful before tossing them into the cart. It was all to no avail.

Seeing the carrying on Mickey Joe stormed over to chastise them. His first words were viciously underlined, "What the fuck are yis playing at," he barked, "are ye not able to load a few blasted small stones into the cart. If ye don't want to do it yis can go home."

Jimmy Maguire almost threw the shovel at him with ire. "You do it then if you are such a great man," he barked.

Well, Mickey Joe grabbed the shovel with determination and in his own mind was thinking he was going to show them how it was done.

He put the nose of the shovel against the heap and jumped on its step to drive it, as he intended, right up to the step head, thinking it would be easy, then he could really berate them. Well, the shovel bounced off a big stone in the heap, which was lying just under the small stones and chips with the impact of the shovel bouncing off the big stone. Mickey Joe was jerked back with such force that he almost lost his balance, and staggered around the road.

"Who in the name of Jasus," says he, "broke these stones, I'll sack the man that did it."

"Christy Deacy," they chorused in unison, glad of the opportunity to rile Mickey Joe about his white-haired friend who had had an unlimited amount of work just because he danced with Big Tess.

He gulped mouthfuls of rage as he danced around the road with the shovel still in his hand, banging it off the stones at the way that he had been duped. But Christy was gone and these stones would have to be paid for a second time to be broken. Mickey Joe's face was distorted in ire. Sparks came out of his eyes, with rage and he after telling Ned Griffin that he'd have all the stones at the designated point by ten o'clock first thing that morning. His mind flashed back to Christy Deacy, thinking his intentions were honourable and that one day he would marry his niece. Mickey Joe was full of rage.

If an unfavourable story was related to him about a workman, whether it was true or false, he acted without due consideration or thought. If he didn't sack the man in question he'd send him to the furthest end of the district, cleaning water tables or trimming ditches on his own. Oftentimes these unfavourable stories were trumped up by the timekeeper who might have a private grievance against the man or his wife or assortment of loved ones, or if he felt his own position was being undermined. Mickey Joe, however, acted without any forethought as to their validity no matter where it came from.

On most Sundays at Mass Mickey Joe or his brother sat in the back seat of the chapel, watching for any misdemeanour from his employees or their wives or loved ones. If they should look at his niece lasciviously or sniggered at her walking up the chapel, he could almost hear them say, "Will you look at yer one with her big arse and Clydesdales legs and mini skirt. Wouldn't it turn your stomach to look at her, especially in the house of God, the brazen hussy."

But everyone kept a serious face lest they bring down the wrath of Mickey Joe on their men folk the next day.

In the summer time the Council cut turf in Mount

Garry Bog, where it was saved. Then it was carted away to the railway station to be transported to Dublin for winter fuel for the people of the inner city.

Men were placed in groups of four or five on each turf bank around the bog. They would share the workload between them. Some would 'skin the bank'. That was to take off the top few inches of dried up peat. This was dumped into the hole from where last year's turf was cut out of. Then the slane man, when he had the slane sharpened, set about cutting the turf. This implement was like a spade but it had a wing attached to one side. This made it possible, when driven into the turf bank, to cut and shape the turf at the same time.

Turf was cut usually one foot long and four inches square. These pieces of sod were tossed up onto the bank for another man to load on to the barrow with a two-prong fork. Some groups of men were more crafty than others for they would catch the turf in transit with their hands as the slane man tossed it up, and then place it on the barrow. This way it made the work easier.

Twenty five turf per barrow was the usual load. If too many sods were placed on the barrow the barrow man would complain, as the terrain was often rough and the ground unsteady. It made wheeling difficult, even for the fittest of men, for often times the turf had to be barrowed as much as fifty yards from the turf bank. They all worked in harmony, taking turns every hour.

When the barrow man dumped the turf another man was out there to spread them out side by side to dry. After about ten days the sods were stood up into footings which took four sods, standing up well-angled like a pyramid. One sod was placed on the top. This sod prevented the rain from entering the top of the sods. It also steadied the footing and allowed air to blow in and out through them. All this stacking encouraged the sods to dry quicker.

A week or so later when the sods were drier they were made into bigger heaps. They were now protected from all rain.

Since it wasn't safe to bring big heavy horses up close to the turf banks a bog donkey or mules were used to sleigh the turf up to drier ground near the road to be stored in a large clamp. Later it was carried away to the railway station by the cart men with their big Clydesdale horses.

Dick Carey, being the sole timekeeper on the bog, had many groups of men under his command during the peak of turf cutting season.

There were as many as ten groups at times, scattered around this huge bog on different turf banks. Checking on the first group as they were about to start work, Dick would answer any queries they might have. Then he would set off to the next group and do the same thing. Glancing around the bog he might see a group away in the distance, loitering. Immediately he'd set off in that direction at a lively clip to chastise the culprit before Mickey Joe arrived and saw them. If that happened Dick would be sure to get a right telling-off for not doing his job as it should be done.

As Dick was about to leave one group, he would glance around the bog again to see if there were others loitering anywhere else, and there was sure to be especially if it was a Monday morning,

On a Monday the younger men, having been out all night dancing, would be glad of a moment or two's rest. Spying these culprits, Dick would set off, muttering unholy expletives to himself while keeping his eyes steadfast on the culprit so when he'd get there he'd give him a severe reprimand. But in his determination to keep his eyes on the rouges he would forget about the turf holes and down he'd go. By the time he had extricated himself and refocused his eyes on the culprits they were again all working diligently. He was confronted with the same problem at every turf bank for they watched Dick's every move and the direction he was heading. Knowing that he was sure to founder along the way they would switch places and confuse him. They all pleaded innocent that none of their gang was loitering.

On one particular Monday morning Dick was late arriving. Being in such a hurry to get there before Mickey Joe arrived, he hadn't had time to eat his breakfast. He grabbed his lunch bag that he thought his sister had left ready from the night before. Hurriedly he put his head through the loop and swung the bag on to his back. Grabbing his bike from the scullery he rushed out the gate to the road, running several strides alongside the bike. He took a trig and landed on the saddle without first putting his foot on the peddle. Controlling the bike he pressed savagely on the peddles as he cycled up the hills and down dales.

"I wouldn't mind so much," says Dick, "only Mickey Joe was coming to arrange for the turf to be transported to the railway station."

By the time he arrived in the bog Dick was exhausted and in a lather of sweat. He just flung the bike against the other parked bikes and dropped his lunch bag on the ground beside it.

He gave a great sigh of relief as he wiped the sweat off his brow. He had made it in time but only just for in the distance he could see Mickey Joe thundering down the roadway.

Seeing all his wards at their post, but few of them working, Dick set off immediately to give the first group a severe reprimand. But when he got there they were all working as usual. To show his authority he'd gave them all a general tongue banging nevertheless.

Before leaving the turf bank Dick would scratch his head, wag his finger at them and exclaim, "Be the tarlen a man, yie will get us all sacked."

All morning he was up and down the bog after each group. He must have done ten miles at least that morning, trudging over tuffocks of grass and foundering in turf holes. He was wet to the knees.

By the time lunch break was called, Dick was a tired and worried man. Nothing had gone right for him and, to add to his woes, he hadn't yet had any breakfast. He flopped down on the ground beside all the other men who had assembled at the top of the bog to have their lunch and gave a martyred sigh. He was looking forward to some well buttered home made brown bread inside him. He almost tore open the bag to get at his lunch, he was so ravenous. Well his heart sank in his boots when he saw what he had. It was a school bag full of books that belonged to his daughter.

"Be the tarlen a man," says he, "look what I've got here."

His wards when they saw Dick's lunch began to snigger and laugh behind their hands at his dilemma but nobody was over-flushed to the extent they could afford to share their lunch with him, so he had to settle for a mug of tea.

And to add further to his woes Mickey Joe informed him that Ned Griffin the Engineer was coming to inspect the work progress on the bog and to remove any group that was not pulling their weight. This, Mickey Joe knew, would torment Dick greatly.

All afternoon the boys began to play real tricks on Dick. Some would leave the bog and go to the nearest hiding place to answer the call of nature. They would spend a half an hour or more there just to annoy him. When finishing time eventually came Dick Carey was a tired and forlorn looking man leaving the bog that evening, and he had still to cycle four miles home.

When the turf cutting was complete it was holiday time. Two weeks were allowed, and then the crews returned to their normal work, whether it was on the road or in the quarry.

Mickey Joe applied the same strict adherence to the rule of discipline at home as he did at work, even more so at times. If an animal or even the fowl didn't obey his orders they were liable to be severely beaten or even shot.

As the years passed Mickey Joe became more fond of the drink. In the evenings he would tackle up his pony and trap and repair to the pub. There he would indulge himself in several half whiskeys followed by many bottles of Porter.

His old pony Neddy was left outside the pub door. Mickey Joe never tied him, and the pony never moved, not even when a local man coming to the pub might try and coax him out on to the road and order him to go home. The old pony wouldn't move for he knew the voice was strange, but when his master got into the trap he knew the voice right away,

"Off home now, Neddy,".

The old pony was not in any great hurry to move but Mickey Joe would then raise his voice an octave.

"Off home now, I won't tell you the third time."

The wise old pony could easily tell by his master's voice that if he didn't move quickly he was in for a severe beating, so immediately he'd set forth before the third order was given.

It was one of those evenings that Mickey Joe met Mary Kate O'Brien from Ahade. She was home on holidays from England and had called in to say hello to her school friend, Matty Neary, the publican. Matty introduced Mary Kate to Mickey Joe, with the result they became firm friends.

Mickey Joe became smitten with her charm and garrulity. He wasn't a great man for the talk, especially where women were concerned. Every evening he was off to the pub on the pretence that he wanted a drink, saying he was very thirsty, but everyone knew his reason for going. Even the road men could see a change in him. He had become more sociable and placid with his wards of late.

Then one evening while they were having a quiet drink Mary Kate informed him that she was going back to England in a couple of days.

Well, Mickey Joe got into a right pucker. He was thinking that this might be the last chance of ever meeting another woman and settling down, but he didn't know how he could even go about proposing to a girl. What would he say to her? His upbringing had left him a stranger to the female artifice and the art of courtship.

So he called to his old friend Twig Murphy late one night for advice, hoping no one would see him or where he was going. It would be very embarrassing for him if it was found out that he had to call on the local wag for advice on such a private and delicate matter.

He offered Twig a Pound note for his advice, on condition that he keep his business a secret. Twig readily agreed, but deep down Twig had no intention of keeping such a secret to himself. He couldn't wait to get to the pub the following night to relate this great news.

As the evening began Mickey Joe set out his case as best he could to Twig, as they sat around the dying embers of the open fire. Mary Kate was going back to England and he had only another day to settle matters between them. He had an inkling by the way she was talking that if she could get any kind of work locally she would like to stay in Ireland. Twig showed great sympathy and understanding to his old friend by yeahing and yesing and nodding his head at every thing Mickey Joe said.

"Now," said Twig, "there are a few ways to make an impression on a woman when proposing and you want to be very subtle, for women are a funny kind of individual."

Mickey Joe listened attentively to Twig's every word and syllable. He was sure he had everything clear in his head.

"Mary Kate will fall into your arms when she sees the great effort you are making to woo her."

Well Mickey Joe went home that night a happy man, sure in the knowledge that he had everything clear in his mind as Twig had told to him.

On their last night together Mickey Joe got very inebriated. He wanted this woman very badly but he kept putting off the vital question as long as possible. He was happy to just sit with her in the snug and listen to her light-hearted garrulity, as she chatted desultorily with him.

It was only when Mary Kate finished her own drink and got up to leave that it struck him that if he didn't do something quick he was going to lose this woman forever. He staggered to his feet and took the proffered hand in his two.

"You don't have to go yet," he spluttered. He was trying to delay this dreadful ordeal he had to undertake as long as possible. He had rehearsed many times in his own mind everything Twig had told him. He was sure he had everything clear in his mind. He began spluttering and coughing and humming and hawing.

"I want to ask you a very personal question," says he, swaying back and forth with half closed eyes, "Do you understand?"

She nodded her head in acknowledgement.

"Would you like to hang your washing on my clothes line?"

"What?" says she, looking at him for a long minute

with searching eyes.

"How would you like to be buried with my people?"

She took a sudden jerk away and peered at him steadfast for a long minute. "Is this," says she, "a promise to kill me or a proposal of marriage?"

Mickey Joe got all flustered, "Oh no, no, no, yes, yes, yes, it's a pro, prop, proposal of marriage, you're right that's what I was trying to say."

To herself, 'well, that's the funniest way I've ever heard of anyone proposing to a woman.'

In his own mind Mickey Joe was livid at the way Twig had set him up and if he could lay his hands on him this minute he'd kill him.

Mary Kate pretended to be taken aback by the suddenness of it all, and all the time in her own devious way she had been leading him on to this very moment. But Mickey Joe was so smitten with her that he couldn't see it.

She promised she would let him know the following evening.

Mickey Joe lived in torture for the next twenty-four hours, not knowing whether she'd accept or reject his proposal.

Later, when the diaspora had dispersed and the pub was quiet Matty and Mary Kate were having a quiet drink. She enquired from him of Mickey Joe's suitability as a husband. Matty gave her his blessing but warned her of his fierce temper and his strict adherence to his bidding. " When he gets into one of his tantrums, and I'm very sure he will, give him a wide birth," he said.

Mary Kate weighed up the pro's and con's of her own situation. 'I have no home and not likely ever to have one and my looks would never endear me to many men,' she thought. She decided to accept the proposal. 'At least I'll have some security in me old age.'

Then, the next evening after she had accepted his proposal, Mickey Joe invited Mary Kate to his home, which she readily accepted. 'I'd like to see his behaviour in his own home,' she said to herself.

Well, she hadn't long to wait.

While they were engrossed in an intimate conversation around the fire and the kettle was coming to boil, Molly the hen, seeing the kitchen door half open, left her companions in the yard and sauntered up toward the open door and hopped up on the step.

On hearing the murmur of voices at the fire, she craned her neck and scanned the kitchen from the end of the table. Not happy with the view, she took another few steps past the end of the table. She stood on one leg, listening to the strange voice inside. Slowly she closed the claws of her foot into a fist as she considered whether to chance going any further, thinking about her father's lucky escape a few days earlier in the kitchen. Mickey Joe flung the poker so hard at him that it almost severed his head off as he fled out the door.

But her curiosity was greater than her father's warning. She sauntered up the floor towards the fire. When she got close she cocked her head to one side as she viewed this stranger.

Seeing that it was a woman by the fire Molly gave out an almighty shreek, "de-gaugha, de-gaugh-ga," she went on, as if warning Mary Kate of impending danger from that unpredictable lunatic.

Mickey Joe looked at Molly, then at Mary Kate as much as to say, 'we can't have a quiet conversation without someone interrupting us.'

"g'out a that," he ordered, banging the tongs on the hearthstone.

Molly took no notice of his bidding, she just kept sauntering around the kitchen, picking up crumbs off the floor as she went.

"g'out," he ordered, "I won't tell you again."

Molly jerked up her head at the sudden thud of the tongs on the floor and glanced at Mickey Joe. 'He wouldn't be so vindictive,' the hen seemed to think, 'especially with a visitor in the house.' But Molly had badly underestimated Mickey Joe's vehement reaction when she wouldn't do his bidding.

Mary Kate sensed by his body language that Mickey Joe was going to take stern action, but what she didn't know. She sat crouched in the corner, her mind full of foreboding as Mickey Joe jumped up from the fire as if a bee had stung him, snatched his gun off the dresser and shot the hen in the doorway.

"Now", says he, "you'll do what you're told in the future."

Mary Kate was flabbergasted at such drastic action with a dumb bird. She looked in awe at this hulk of a man and her mind was in a turmoil. 'If he'd do that to a dumb bird,' she thought to herself, 'what might he do to her if she refused his bidding.'

There was a cauldron of unsavoury thoughts swimming through her head as she sat crouched in the corner of the ingle, her hand guarding her face as if warding off another gun blast. She soon slowly dropped her guard and was shook back to the present when a stentorian voice boomed out,

"You'll cook that chicken for dinner tomorrow evening, won't you?"

Mary Kate's heart still fluttering from the shock, just nodded her head in agreement.

The wedding was a very quiet and simple affair. Mickey Joe wouldn't hear of any extravagance. He went to Shinrone and ordered a pony and trap and a bridesmaid. The driver and the lady were to be the witnesses at the wedding. They were to collect Mickey Joe and Mary Kate at his house on their way to the wedding.

To make things convenient for this special day Dick Carey promised that he would bring Mickey Joe's pony and trap up and leave it at Matty's pub so the newlyweds would not have to walk home after the wedding. To be doubly sure, Dick tied the pony to the gate pillar outside the pub for fear the pony might decide to return home without his master.

After the wedding the four went to Matty's pub for a meal. It was a very simple meal of bacon and cabbage. They had a celebratory drink after it, with the bridesmaid and best man, before Mickey Joe dispensed of their services and sent them home. Mary Kate and him had another drink before leaving. He was going to make the best of this day for he couldn't envisage himself taking another day off work for a very long time.

Leaving the pub they were both quite merry now. He opened the door of the trap for his new wife to enter. She was very impressed by his manly act. 'It wasn't going to be so bad after all,' she thought to herself.

He sat in beside her and took hold of the reins.

"Off home Neddy," he ordered.

The old pony never moved.

"Off home, Neddy. I won't tell you a third time."

The pony tossed his head in the air, rather agitated.

'This is strange,' he said to himself.

"Neddy, I've warned you for the last time. Now move it."

Mickey Joe gave a side glance at his new wife, as much as to say, 'he'll do what I tell him.'

Still no move.

Mickey Joe stormed out of the cart in a mad rage. He was going to show his wife and all and sundry that everyone does his bidding, even the pony. He took out his gun and began loading it.

Mary Kate, sensing the outcome, also jumped out of the cart and, within seconds, she was standing between Mickey Joe and the pony.

"You'll have to shoot me first," she challenged.

He was in a blind rage by now. "He'll do what I say or he'll get his comeuppance."

Mary Kate was shaking like an aspen leaf as she stood before the gun and him. She didn't care what he said or did to her. It was one thing to shoot a hen but another to shoot the pony. She was looking forward to doing the weekly shopping with him.

"You bloody looking bedlamite," she screeched, "can't you see Neddy is tied. How could he move?"

"Who the blasted hell tied him," he bellowed.

When they reached the house after their long trek home Mickey Joe insisted on carrying her in across the threshold. The incident with the pony was forgotten.

He stood her up on the kitchen floor and gave her a big hug.

"Welcome to Cranmore, love, I hope you'll be happy here."

Mary Kate reciprocated with her own amorous embrace.

They relaxed by the fire with another celebratory drink before Mary Kate got up to make tea. The meal over and dishes washed and put away it was mid-afternoon by then.

He looked at his wife, "Up the stairs, Mrs. Courish," says he.

"We can't go to bed at this hour of the day, love," says she, "wait til later, sure there's no hurry."

"On up them stairs, Mary Kate, I won't tell you a third time."

Mary Kate, sensing the unpredictability of this

crackpot flew up the stairs, not waiting for the third command. The incidents with Molly and Neddy flashed through her mind and she wasn't going to be the next victim.

After twenty-five years of an unhappy marriage and three children, two boys away and working, Mary Kate made up her mind that as soon as their youngest daughter was married off she would leave him.

She had discussed this many times with an old friend, Joe Deane, from the village. These trysts she looked forward to, especially when Mickey Joe was at work.

Often on a Sunday afternoon Mickey Joe and Mary Kate would go visiting friends over in Ballycrea, in their pony and trap.

Doreen, their youngest daughter was left at home to mind the house. She would make herself busy doing embroidery or knitting socks. Mickey Joe had forbidden her from seeing Jack Hanbery, a local lad who, in his estimation, was quite unsuitable for Doreen. He was a bit of a fly-by-night and, as well, was of a different religious persuasion. A bad combination Mickey Joe thought.

But Doreen was smitten with Jack and he with her and no amount of threats from Mickey Joe were going to keep them apart.

When the parents had departed on their visit, Doreen would go to the avenue gate, stand on one of its bars and wave a white handkerchief to indicate to Jack that the coast was clear. Although Jack was a quarter of a mile away at his own home he could easily see the white flag for it was the signal he had been waiting for all afternoon. He didn't dare venture over when Mickey Joe was there. Jack always gave him a wide birth. When he saw the flag Jack set out post haste to spend a couple of leisurely hours in Doreen's company without interruption.

Late one Sunday afternoon they were sitting on the

couch in the kitchen in an amorous embrace when they heard the clip-clop of the pony coming into the yard. With the back door locked and the key missing Jack had no way of escaping. Thinking fast he crept under the couch in the kitchen and Doreen sat on it with knitting on her knee.

"Yis didn't stay long," says she casually.

"Oh, the pony lost a shoe," says Mickey Joe, "and I thought it better to return home for fear he might go lame."

After an hour of chit-chat they retired to bed.

"I'd better set this mouse trap first," ways he, "and see if I can catch that blasted mouse."

With the trap set Mickey Joe pushed it under the couch almost against Jack's nose. 'It'll be out of everyone's way in there,' says he to himself.

Well, Jack was shuddering with apprehension. The slightest move and the trap would snap shut and his nose in it. After an hour of uneasy wait, and sure that all was quiet in the house, he wriggled out from under the couch and slipped out the hall door and away home.

A few Sunday nights later a dance was held at Mickey Joe's. All the young eligible men were invited in the hope that Doreen would select one of them for a husband.

Jack wasn't invited but that didn't stop him from sneaking over to have a peek at the dancers. He crept into the scullery at the back of the house and peered in through the keyhole in the door that lead from the scullery into the kitchen. A Half Set was in full swing. He could hardly see the dancers with the dust rising from the concrete floor.

'Very soon they'll be needing fresh air, after this set is over,' he says to himself, so Jack decided to play his own trick on Mickey Joe and embarrass him in front of his specially invited guests.

Looking around the scullery in the half-light for

somewhere to anchor the rope, he could not see anything that was convenient. He stood momentarily admiring the lovely antique dresser that was standing against the back wall. It was stacked to capacity with cups, saucers and plates of the finest china, all ready for the guests' meal, and bottles of the finest whiskey lined the lower shelves. He was envious of such style and grandeur. 'The rich have everything,' he thought to himself.

Then a thought struck him. Why not use the dresser as an anchor. He snatched the rope off the gibet that held the pony's bridle and tied the rope around the dresser. He hooked the other end of the rope to the latch on the inner door and pulled the rope taut.

He crept out of the scullery, out the back yard and climbed up the yew tree to await developments.

The Half Set finished, the dancers, coughing and spluttering and choking for fresh air, headed for the back door to get out in the open. They tugged and tugged at the door, but no go.

They informed Mickey Joe, who marched over with determination and gave the door a mighty tug. He couldn't shift it. A sudden rage came over him. He placed his foot against the base of the wall to gain purchase, caught the door in a vice-like grip and gave a mighty heave.

"I'll open it," says he, "even if it has to kill me,"

He gave another might tug. The door only gave slightly at first. Another mighty heave and the door crashed fully open against the wall. As it did it brought the dresser with it, crashing to the floor. All the expensive china was in a thousand pieces on the floor and the whiskey was running out the back door.

Mickey Joe grabbed the slashhook and burst out the back door and circulated the yew tree like a man possessed. He was gouging chunks out of the tree with vexation.

"If I could only lay me hands on that scoundrel who did it I'd chop him into mulch."

Doreen was not impressed by the young suitors that had come to the dance that night. When her father refused to give she and Jack his blessing she eloped with Jack to Dublin and got married.

Mary Kate was now free to pursue her own goal as soon as the dust settled and Mickey Joe came to terms with Doreen's elopement.

She too would leave.

Sitting in Patrick Jones the solicitor's office, she outlined what she thought were grounds for a separation. She mentioned the mental torture she had had to endure over the last twenty-five years which was unbearable. Since their daughter eloped Mickey Joe was never out of the pub. She was more lonely now than she had ever been, even in London all those years ago.

"I'll not stay another minute with him," says she, "I'll go mad if I do." She looked at the solicitor with pleading eyes. "There must be some way that I can separate without losing my dignity."

Solicitor Jones listened to her tentatively, he then rubbed his chin.

"Now, Mrs. Courish," says he, "just because you dislike your husband is no grounds for separating." He thought to himself, 'somebody must be putting these daft ideas in her head.'

"Do you understand that when a woman marries, she immediately becomes the property of her husband? There is no such thing as separation in the Catholic Church."

"There has to be some way out, I need my share of the estate or cash," says she, "I want to go live with ..."

She stopped short and took out her handkerchief and blew her nose to cover up the gaff she had made, but Solicitor Jones wasn't one to be hoodwinked. He had heard of her liaison with Joe Deane.

"Now, Mrs. Courish, I'll make a few proposals and you can confirm or deny them. Has he ever physically abused you?"

She looked at him blankly.

"What I'm trying to say is, did he ever strike you?"

"No, my son would kill him if he did."

"Did he ever abuse your children when they were young?"

"No, not that I can remember."

"Did he ever leave you short of money?"

She knitted her brow in thought. "No, he always gave me sufficient money for the housekeeping."

The solicitor was beginning to run out of questions. 'Well at least ones I could indict her husband on', he thought. He rubbed his chin, 'I'll have to think of something or this woman will walk out of here and I'll get nothing for my time.' Then a thought struck him.

"Was this man ever unfaithful to you?"

She jerked in her seat with excitement. "Yes, I think we have him there," says she.

The solicitor looked at her with a wry smile of satisfaction on his face. His time wouldn't be in vain after all.

"Well, Mrs. Courish, let's hear it."

"I know for certain he's not the father of our last girl."

The old solicitor stared at her. Then he snarled,

"Get out of my office," he advised, "and don't come back," as he held out a hand for his fee.

Ned's Romance

Ned stood at the side of the grave as the grave diggers patted down the last of the brown earth on his mother's grave. He was numb, confused and bewildered at the suddenness of it all.

'Imagine,' thought he, 'it was only last week she was swaggering around the farmyard full of life, feeding the pigs and fowl and milking the cows. You'd think she was going to live forever, but then destiny overruled.'

He had on a few occasions approached the subject with her of getting married. Well, she nearly hit the ceiling at the thought. She turned and looked at him with a piercing glare.

"What's wrong with the way I'm looking after you," she snarled, "good, wholesome meals, clean clothes every week, a tidy house and a few shillings in your pocket every weekend. What more do you want? Get that nonsense out of your head. No interloper will ever share my hearthstone while I'm alive."

"But mother," he pleaded, "I'm nearly fifty and it's time I was getting married."

She gave him a sidelong glance, then whipped the white enamel bucket off the granite stone shelf beside the dresser and stomped out of the house to fetch a bucket of fresh water from the well, as much as to say the matter was closed.

Ned slouched across the yard after completing the

myriad of chores his mother made so light of and entered the cold and lonely kitchen.

It was almost midday and he hadn't got his breakfast yet. He looked around the kitchen at the mess it was in. No floors swept, dirty clothes and muddy boots strewn everywhere. The ash pit beside the open fire was full to capacity and overflowing with ashes onto the hearthstone. The fire was black out. The table was cluttered with dirty dishes, cutlery and potato skins. Two buckets of eggs that were supposed to have been cleaned and delivered to Morrissey's grocery shop were still in a bucket on the floor.

He looked around at the dishevelled state of the place and scratched his head. "My God," he swore as he lashed out with his boot at the heap of dirty clothes and sent them flying out the back door. "This is all mother's fault," as he growled to himself, "she was always so domineering, wouldn't let me get married when I wanted to."

He set about tidying the kitchen, only to find it was more dishevelled by the time he was finished. He gave a long, deep sigh of frustration. "I think, what this place badly needs is a woman's touch."

"When I go to the village this evening to deliver them eggs, I'll call on Barney O'Hara. I'm sure he'll be able to fix me up with a good woman. He's supposed to be good at that sort of thing." Ned knew he wouldn't have the courage to ask a girl out on his own initiative, for his upbringing had left him that way.

That night, in front of Barney's glowing fire, Ned stated his case, the way his mother had mollycoddled him and wouldn't give him his head.

Barney listened attentively to Ned as he carved tobacco for his pipe. When he had it lit and prodded into easy operation, he sat back in his chair and dry-washed his hands to dislodge the excess motes of tobacco and ash from his hands.

"So it's a wife you're looking for," says Barney as he oscillated the pipe to and fro between his lips and stared at this slackly built man in front of him.

'I suppose,' says he to himself, ' with a little bit of comfort and good, nourishing food that emaciated frame would soon fill out.'

"Well, what kind of wife would you be looking for, like, good and strong and not afraid of hard work?"

"I'd rather have a young and pretty maid, one that would keep me young, like."

Barney gave him a furtive glance. "Did you see that face of yours in the mirror lately? You're not what I might call a spring chicken anymore."

Deeply offended, Ned jumped up to leave. He had a vicious scowl on his face and angry thoughts, 'This superannuated quack is not going to insult me like that, I'd rather stay single than to suffer such ignominy.'

"Hold your horses a minute," says Barney, "you needn't be getting so hot under the collar." Barney paused a minute. "I know," says he, "where there's a good woman, she's over in Glenmore, I think. She'll suit you down to the ground in my opinion, her name is Mary Ann Murray."

When Ned heard this he forgot about Barney's insults and sat down again.

"Now," says he, "she has a good few miles on the clock, but that shouldn't worry you. I know for sure, there's a handsome dowry going with her."

Ned was elated when he heard this. He sprang from his seat as if a bee had stung him.

"Let's go over and meet her now, there's no time like the present."

The matchmaker stalled in his carving of the tobacco. The brightness in his eyes disappeared between the suddenly narrow eyelids.

"Not so fast, me buck-oo," says Barney, pointing the extended blade of his penknife at him, "first things first."

Barney knew only too well that if monetary arrangements weren't agreed beforehand for his services he could be without any benefit at all.

"I'll ramble over there tomorrow night and see how the land lies. In the meantime get yourself trimmed up a bit. Get a decent shirt and trousers, and give them boots a good clean up. First impressions are so important, and another thing," says he. "Don't forget a bottle of Francie Mannion's poteen. The old man is partial to a drop of fine liquor. It could be the difference between winning and losing her hand. And the lady I have no doubt has a sweet tooth. Bring her a box of nice paper-wrapped chocolates. Good women don't come cheap nowadays."

Ned was beginning to have second thoughts about this romantic undertaking and, not being used to handling money, he thought the expense was enormous.

The Murray house looked immaculate, homey and inviting to the cursory glance that night. The two brothers, Jim and Pat Murray, were seated on a form stool at one side of the big open fire under the arch with their backs against the wall, while the Father sat opposite. A fire of sticks and turf were glowing in the chimney.

After exchanging the usual pleasantries, they drew their chairs up to the fire and trotted out well-worn items of news as they carved their tobacco and filled pipes. When the conversation began to drag Ned thought he would liven it up by producing the bottle of poteen. He offered it to the old man who accepted it with alacrity, as Barney set out his business for which they had come.

"So you say," says the old man, "you have fifty acres of land beside the Dereen River."

"I have indeed, sir, and a hundred acres of collop rights on the mountain,"

The old man tended the spirits and the questions at the same time.

"Have you any stock, like … ?""

"O' yes sir, I have six cows and their followers, two sows and two shire horses, and a yard full of fowl and also ewes."

The old man Dinny was the first to sample the rich beverage. When the dollop reached its destination he smacked his lips and nodded appreciatively. Then gazed into the fire. He was silent and absorbed as he pondered over Ned's recent answer, then to nobody in particular says, "it's a farm worth having in the family."

The sudden realisation that they were talking about her, Mary entered the kitchen from the parlour on the pretence of replenishing the fire but in fact she wanted to scrutinise her latest suitor.

"This is my daughter, Mary," says the old man, nodding his head to Ned, who proffered his hand to this fine, buxom woman.

For a minute she kept her eyes low, knowing he was looking her over, and accepted the scrutiny as part of the necessary ordeal. It wasn't the first time she had to suffer such scrutiny but she hoped it would be the last.

In order to show his manliness Ned extracted a bag of Bullseyes from his coat pocket.. He had considered the box of sweets with the fancy wrappers to be too dear altogether for his pocket.

"Anyone care for a nice sweet?" says he, proffering the bag to Mary first.

Barney, on seeing the drab paper bag of cheap sweets, flicked his eyes to Heaven in abject disgust.

After tea the men sat over by the fire to polish off the remainder of the spirits. In the warm glow of the turf fire the old man became very intoxicated and began talking through his spittle.

Barney, sizing up the situation, lavished praise on Ned before bringing forth his own proposals, to which the old man agreed wholeheartedly. Old Dinny pummelled Ned on the back, as a sign of his blessing that Mary and Ned should start walking out together, a polite phrase used at the time for courting.

Over the coming days Mary was in a reverie of excitement awaiting her first date. 'I hope,' says she to herself, as she looked at herself in the mirror after washing and preening her hair, 'that he won't lead me on for four years like Peter did … '

Peter Dillon had real prospects. He had a nice home and only his elderly mother living with him. But his upbringing had left him a stranger to the female artifice and art of courtship.

Although of serious intent in his meeting with Mary, in his innocence, he thought that by just being in Mary's company at night in the kitchen and with the family present at all times, this was sufficient grounds to lay claim to her without an amorous word being spoken between them.

One evening, Mary's mother, alone with Peter in the kitchen, began carving up a slaughtered pig into portions to hang up in the chimney to smoke and cure. This was the wont at the time. Watching Peter with her eyecorner as she removed the ham, she gave it a smack of her open hand to show its firmness. "Won't that be an ideal feast for a wedding breakfast?" she commented.

Well, Peter was so elated to hear this remark from the mother that he thought the matter of marriage was finally settled between himself and Mary, and he wholeheartedly agreed with her.

The next day Mary, ran into the kitchen in a panic to consult with her parents about the dilemma she was in.

"Peter," she exclaimed, stopping dead in her tracks

and putting her hand to her throat. "What am I to do at all, at all, he's coming over tonight! I should have called off this tryst long ago but for awhile I hadn't the courage to tell him. Now, what to do?"

The old man just gave her a sidelong glance, then took the pipe from his mouth, and sent a spit careering through the air into the hot ashes, where it sizzled for a moment, than died out.

"Set the terriers on him," he advised. Old Dinny always called the two sons the "terriers" on account of their fighting abilities.

That same evening Peter was in high spirits as he washed and shaved and dressed himself to meet his girlfriend and future wife which he had convinced himself she was to be.

He had even broken the exciting news to his mother, who was ecstatic.

'At last,' says she to herself, 'he's getting himself a wife, and not a minute too soon,' although not daring to say that to him.

Peter set out, at a lively clip, down the avenue, his head held high. The old mother shuffled towards the kitchen window, resting her two hands on the table in front of her, looking out at Peter departing. She smiled at the antics of her son as he jogged down the avenue. She thought how animated he had become of late. Slowly she turned from the window and shuffled towards the chair beside the fire. 'Isn't it great,' she repeated reflectively, taking out her rosary beads to begin to pray.

Out on the road Peter settled into a more leisurely walk. He whistled and hummed some romantic tunes as he subconsciously made wedding plans. Yes, Peter seemed to be the happiest man in all County Wicklow that autumn evening. The birds, that seemed to be rejoicing with his happiness as they sang in the nearby trees along the road to Murray's house, gave no portent that his happiness would be short-lived.

As he swung into Murray's avenue gate, he encountered the two terriers standing like soldiers on sentry duty inside the big gates, their lips turned up in anger.

Dumbstruck and confused at the stance of the two men blocking his entry, Peter faced his two future brother-in-laws from the outside of the gate, unable to talk or comprehend what was going on. He eyeballed these two surly pugnacious rowdies for what Peter thought was an eternity, but in fact was only a few seconds.

Jim, the older of the two, was the first to speak. "You are not welcome anymore in our house,"

"Why?, why?," exclaimed Peter, dumbfounded at the change of attitude since his last visit which had been only three days ago, "but the wedding … " he stuttered, pointing towards the house.

"You've had four years," says Pat, "to propose to Mary. You got every encouragement, but you weren't a man."

Under his breath Peter cursed himself for his shyness.

"I have to see her," says he, getting all agitated and prancing from foot to foot.

"O' you will," says they, "but you are coming with us first to the barn."

It was there that they stripped him, tied him to a pillar, then painted him all over with liquid tar, and, to add insult to injury, they emptied the contents of a feather pillow all over him and set him free.

Quickly Ned and Mary's romance went well. Soon she began to look forward to his weekly visits where she wined and dined him in the privacy of their parlour. When he had left she'd begin daydreaming about being mistress of her own house and not to be a slave to her two lazy brothers' every beck and call.

As weeks stretched into months and months stretched into a few years and no sign of her vows being accomplished, Mary began to lose heart. She felt she had exhausted all her womanly wiles to prod him into proposing, but all to no avail. She knew he was a malleable man but to get him to pop the question was a different matter altogether, and the leap year was still three years away!

At forty, she had for some time now subconsciously reconciled herself to the thought that she would never marry, and each year that she had to wait was a loss, not a gain for her.

Then, one evening, as the mother was entering the front hall with a basket of turf she heard the resonance of whimpering coming from the parlour. Dropping the basket of turf she stormed into the room and there she found her daughter crouched over the fire, sobbing like a distressed child. She moved hastily to her side and put her arms around her shoulders with motherly concern,

"What's the matter, darling," says she, "you look as if you have been crying for a week."

Through the tears and sobs she eventually blurted it all out.

"I'm calling off this romance, he's never going to ask me," she sobbed uncontrollably into her mother's breast. All the while that the mother was patting her daughter on the shoulders she was cooking up her own plan.

When Dinny heard about this plan he scowled in anger, clucking spits like bate into the fire.

"Set the terriers on him and give him a good send off," he said. He gazed at the two sons sitting opposite on the form stool in the inglenook, their hands clasped behind their heads, leaning back against the wall, apparently asleep but in reality wide awake and listening.

The mother decided it was time that she took matters into her own hands. She took a deep breath and tilted her chin pugnaciously.

"Look here," says she as she ground her teeth, "there's more ways than one to make a pig squeal besides slitting his throat. I have invited John Harkins of the Redmills over on Sunday night. Mary can entertain him in the parlour, " says she, giving her husband an archy smile, "and when lover boy comes he can wait for Mary here in the kitchen. That should put a stir under him."

Dinny was in silent reflection as he drew on his pipe. He clucked a spit into the fire before he spoke. "It'll never work," says he, flicking his eyes towards his wife and shaking his head.

"Of course it will," says she, giving him another archy smile without looking up from making a cake in the bowl on the kitchen table, "it worked for me."

On hearing this old Dinny bucked in his chair, scrabbled the heel tips of his boots to and fro on the hearthstone, his mouth turned down in bitter resentment at the sly way his wife had exploited his shyness and duped him into marrying her. He yanked up and down his shoulders several times at the embarrassing situation he had found himself in front of his family, his eyes darting to and fro as if he was about to prance on a rat.

The black and white cat was sitting on the hearthstone with her back to the fire, always a sure sign that a storm was on the way.

Dinny lifted up his boot and gave it a mighty kick, "Get out of here," says he savagely.

The cat leaped about a foot off the ground with a frightened mor-rouge and wail as she fled from the scene, jumping over the half-door and away from danger.

"I should have known," says he as he flicked his eyes in the direction of his wife and growled into his moustache, clucked more spittle into the fire. Then the incident was forgotten.

Many Sunday nights passed but Ned found no Mary's welcome at the hall door as in earlier days of their courtship, so he was obliged to traipse around the house to the back door in the dark where he'd join the rest of the family in the kitchen and wait patiently until the visitor was gone.

As he would pass the parlour window his eyes were drawn to the parlour table and the light of the glass bowl kerosene lamp with the corrugated crumpled chimney top like petals of buds opening Moving closer to the window he peered in, as the curtains weren't drawn. There he saw his old friend, John Harkins, sitting in the big armchair that he himself had occupied when entertaining Mary in front of the big ornate fireplace. They were conversing very seriously Ned thought.

At first he put it down to the casual visit of a neighbour. There was nothing to fear from this old man, he assured himself. He was a confirmed bachelor. Then a pang of doubt crept into his mind as to why Mary should be entertaining him in the parlour and not in the kitchen.

After some months, Ned became very concerned. He came to the conclusion that this man was an opponent and seriously bidding for the love and affection, and, in time, marriage to his girl. 'Drastic measures will have to be taken,' he told himself, 'if he was to win over the love and affection of this girl and show her that he is really serious, that's if I'm not already too late,' says he to himself, clenching his fists.

The following Sunday night about eight o'clock, Ned marched up the avenue wheeling his bike, his jaw set in fierce determination. Suicidal thoughts were cramming his brain. He parked his bike against the wall of the cart house, which adjoins the dwelling house. He quenched his carbide lamp, dropped his cigarette on the ground and extinguished it with the heel of his boot, then yanked up his shoulders. 'It's decision time,' he says to himself.

He walked with long, firm strides towards the hall door, passing the parlour window and, just as on previous Sunday nights, the curtains weren't pulled and the big lamp was standing as usual in the centre of the big mahogany table.

He peered through the net curtains and his heart sank for there he saw his old friend, turned adversary as he believed him now to be, ensconced in the armchair in front of the glowing turf fire with an evil grin on his face and he was winking at Mary lasciviously. He raised his clenched fist at the window in anger.

'I'll never set foot in that house again,' says he to himself, ramming his fist into the palm of the other hand. The muscles of his leathery jaw twitched savagely, as much with jealously as ire.

He tiptoed back to the cart house and groped around in the dark until he located the big dray cart with iron-shod wheels. Taking a rope off the hook inside the door, he mounted the cart, stood in the nave and reached up and attached one end of the rope to the rafters above. Then, making a hangman's noose with the other end, he slipped it over his head and tightened it around his neck, preparatory to jumping to his death.

He was so distraught with jealousy that he was almost suicidal. 'If she doesn't consent to marry me this very night, she can bury me tomorrow.' How could I live with the shame of an old man stealing my girl from under me nose.

When the grandfather clock in the hall struck ten, Mary became very concerned. She got up and pranced around the room in an agitated state, her fingers chewing on the palm of her other hand. She was convinced that her mother's plan had backfired and, if so, "tomorrow morning," says she, "I'm going to join the Poor Clare nuns in Dublin."

"I'll go out and see if Ned's bike is there," says she to John, "he's not in the kitchen."

"You do that," says he "and I'll go to the kitchen and join the other folk."

Taking the storm lantern Mary ventured out into the front yard through the hall door. An eerie feeling came over her as it was very dark and quiet. Then a fox yelped close by that startled her out of her skin. She took a deep laboured breath and cautiously made her way past the parlour window. She kept one hand on the wall, as much for security as for comfort.

Then she saw, in the faint glow of the guttering light, the silvery handlebars of Ned's bike shining where it leaned against the wall of the cart house. Her heart leaped for joy in her chest. She murmured a silent prayer of thanks.

'He's here,' says she, 'he must be sitting in the cart.' It was their regular courting spot.

"Ned, love, are you there?" says she.

Ned didn't speak, only gave a throaty cackle.

Trembling, she moved a few paces through the open door into the shed.

When her eyes had adjusted to the dull light she could see the form of a man standing up in the nave of the cart. She raised the lantern aloft to shoulder height to get a better view. It was then she saw it, a car rope dangling from the rafters down to Ned's neck.

"O' my God," she wailed as she jerked back a few paces and in the process almost toppled over the shafts of the cart. "He's hung himself," and she let out another almighty wail and dropped the lantern on the ground in fright. For a second she thought she would pass out. "My

God," as she searched around in the dark for the lantern, "what am I going to do at all … ," and tears began streaming down her cheeks.

'This is all me mother's fault,' she sobs softly, 'I should never have listened to her.'

"Ned, Ned," she pleaded, "tell me you're not dead."

"Nooo," says he, "but soon will … ," came the husky reply.

"What in the name of God," says she, "are you doing up there in the cart with that rope around your neck?"

Not waiting to answer her, he demanded to know, "Is it on or off?"

"What are you talking about? What do you mean, 'is it on or off?' "

Again he demanded to know, "you marry me, if it's on I'll take this noose off me neck, if not, I'm jumping to me death here and now."

"Of course it's on, there was never any doubt about it. I thought you were never going to ask," says she.

Ned untied the rope from around his neck and got down from the cart. He looked at her sternly, "But what about your … ," he nodded towards the parlour.

Mary gave a girlish laugh and put her arms around his neck.

"Him, sure John is my Godfather. You know, his sister died a few months ago, and he was very lonely down there on his own so my mother invited him up just to get him out of himself."

A Fall from Grace

On that autumn evening, the setting sun with its pink and orange glow was silhouetting both man and bike like a moving molecule in a sharp black outline. Sergeant Kane gingerly negotiated his way along the narrow winding road from Widow Hanrahan's house in Barnaculla to the Shinrone Guard Station with a bulky load of farm produce on his bike.

He mused to himself that his faith in his fellow man hadn't wavered. Or at least that's what he assured himself. As he trudged along with his heavy load little did he know that his fate had already been sealed, not by any unkind act of his fellow man but by his own greed.

The real beginning of this unfortunate episode began when Sergeant Kane came to Shinrone to replace the old Sergeant Green who had retired. He was a six foot bulk of a man with broad shoulders and a large midriff, a rubicund complexion, black hair cropped tight under his cap and eyebrows black and bushy covering blue eyes, sharp and fierce. His Roman nose ended in a walrus moustache. He rode a large Raleigh bike with carriers over front and back wheels.

It's always a difficult time for people to adjust to the ways of a new law man. From the outset he likes to stamp his authority by strict adherence to the rule of law. His enthusiasm and ambition would be patently obvious, but more than that this man was cunning and devious. He would roam the highways and byways, making mischief.

He would round up all stray animals and impound them. You could see the evil grin on his face as he put them safely under lock and key. Then, having established their true identity, he would mount his bike and set off for the offending farmer's abode, not with the intention of summoning them for breaking the law, as he would have them believe, but to extract farm produce from them, in his own devious ways and for his own use. They were well aware of his unscrupulous methods of taking advantage of these small farm holdings and being held ransom by this rapscallion of Hell. The farmers had little redress because most of them could neither read nor write.

It is true to say that the people of Shinrone and surrounding districts were addicted to the vice of trespassing on the "Long Acre" as it was called. This was the grass margin along the side of the public road. On account of their own little bit of land being so poor, and since there was no work available for these men outside the farm, it left them totally dependant on the Long Acre for their livelihood. Therefore this grass was more precious than gold. It allowed them to keep an extra animal or two which otherwise they wouldn't be able to do. Some allowed their stock to graze on their neighbour's Long Acre. The majority of neighbouring farmers didn't mind this overlapping on one another's patch. They were more concerned in keeping a watch on the lawman lest he pounce unbeknownst on them for their own law breaking. Others, however, took revenge by taking trespassing animals to the pound or informing the Sergeant of such trespassing.

In such cases, the Sergeant would march into the farmyard on his big Raleigh bike in a pretentious show of ire. He would knock on the hall door severely. Without pomp or ceremony he would barge into the kitchen, stand in the nave of the kitchen in that intimidating stance of his and launch into a parley about the breaking of the law and its consequences. From past experience he knew that they would be on their bended knees, begging for mercy. They would do almost anything to avoid being prosecuted. This added humiliation could also be disastrous. It meant appearing in court where a hefty fine could be imposed, and probably eviction for the farmer, his wife, and assorted loved ones if they couldn't pay up.

In such dilemmas the women folk were more astute than their husbands when dealing with this law minion. She would banish her husband from the scene and deal with the matter herself in a more amicable way, less he inflame an already tense situation.

She would invite the Sergeant to the table and set before him some of her finest griddle bread that she knew he was so partial to. She would praise and cajole him for all her might. Then, half coddle, half earnest, she would offer him some farm produce, a dozen eggs or a bag of potatoes. Finally she would add a deprecating little ghost of a laugh that sounded as if, on second thought, she had said the wrong thing.

His sullenness would soon mollify on seeing her take down a basketful of fresh eggs and set about cleaning them before taking them to the shop where she would sell or barter them for household essentials such as tea, sugar, flour and meat, etc..

She would watch the Sergeant with her eyecorner at his interest in and longing for a fresh egg. She was well aware of the Sergeant's insatiable greed for alms, whether big or small. He would overlook any misdemeanour in exchange for free goods.

"Would you like a dozen of fresh eggs, Sergeant?" she would ask in as jolly a tone as she could muster. "We have plenty of them here."

Not to show undue haste in his acceptance of her bribe, he would stand and strut in the nave of the kitchen, looking down his Roman nose at her. He would push back his cap by its peak and scratch his head. He would reset his cap with his two hands, all the while leering at her for what seemed an eternity but in fact only a few seconds before cautioning her about bribing of a law officer in the course of his duties. At the same time holding out his hands in tacit consent.

He would then back out of the kitchen door, nodding his head with maximum deference as he did. Nobody would dare challenge his authority in public or it would bring down the "full force of the law" on the family, friends and loved ones.

Not every farmer was intimidated by this rapscallion and not every animal was prepared to surrender its freedom to the long arm of the law.

One such animal was owned by Barney McKeown of Ballycrean.

Barney always called his mule "Heron" on account of his long neck. Well, Heron was well known in the locality for his roughing. He could open any gate into a neighbour's field and take his fill of fresh grass, or sneak into a barn and gorge himself on some of the choicest food, then scuttle off unnoticed. He was the bane of every farmer in the locality. As Barney would often caution, "He understands every word you say, look at the way he cocks his ears."

On one of his errands, in order to replenish his larder, the Sergeant encountered Heron grazing on the roadside, nonchalant to passers-by. The Sergeant rubbed his hands in glee at his good fortune. He had been waiting a long time for this opportunity to trap this scamp's animal. He visualised in his own mind his replenished larder with the goods he would extract from Barney as a bribe for not taking him to court.

Leaning his bicycle against the hedge, he approached the mule gingerly with his lanyard at the ready to halter him. Then he would have his evidence to confront this perpetual lawbreaker.

Little did he know that not alone was the mule clever, he also detested men in uniform. Before the Sergeant knew it, the mule swung around with his head and snapped at the Sergeant's arm, tearing off the sleeve of his uniform and inserting a deep gash with his teeth in his forearm. Then he swung around again and lashed out with his hind legs, just missing the lawman's head. He did a heels-up act a number of times while emitting an ear-splitting backfire of disapproval. Then off with him down the road home at a lively clip.

From the sudden impact the Sergeant momentarily teetered on his heels before toppling into a dyke that was full to overflowing after the recent storm.

But the tough lawman wasn't going to be defeated. He soon regained his self control, extricated himself from the furze and briers and nettles and stood on the road, glaring at his torn uniform and the ugly gash on his forearm that was pumping thick blood. He gnashed his teeth in ire and agony, but, not one to be hindered by either man or beast in the execution of his duties, he took it with the stoicism of a Red Indian. He put out a few unholy expletives on Barney and his mule and what he was going to do with him.

Barney was a distance away and observed the way the mule passed at such high speed down the yard, his head held low, his ears tucked in tightly against his neck, shaking his head, that something was amiss. His demeanour was uncanny. The old mule never passed his master without first begging for a carrot as was his wont. That was how Barney trained him to come when he was called. But not today. Barney scratched his head as his eyes followed the mule as he disappeared around the gable end of the barn into the haggard.

'There must be something serious the matter,' says Barney to himself as he stood in the turf shed door.

Well, he hadn't long to wait for in cycled the Sergeant at high speed. He brought his bike to a sudden stop in front of Barney and jumped off it.

"Look," he invited, "what that wicked mule has done," pointing to the missing sleeve of his uniform and the nasty gash on his arm that was still pumping blood.

"What mule?" enquired Barney innocently, as he stood at the turf shed door. He stretched out his right arm, placed it against the doorjamb, and leaned on it in an attitude of relaxation.

"Your mule!" bellowed the lawman, holding his injured arm and drawing a grotesque face in agony.

"I'm taking that dangerous animal in to the pound this very minute."

'That's if you can find him,' says Barney to himself.

Out loud, "I know nothing about a wicked mule," says Barney derisively.

"Be careful," says the lawman, "or I'll have you arrested for obstruction of the law."

Barney disclaimed any knowledge of such animal and challenged the Sergeant to produce this so-called savage.

The Sergeant knew from previous encounters with Barney that he would be well advised to proceed with caution. If he imposed a fine without the requisite evidence under his thumb, this cunning rascal could have him stripped for his aberrant behaviour in administration of the law. 'There's got to be another way to trap this ruser', he thought to himself, 'now that his first evidence was missing.'

He didn't intend leaving without first pursuing all

known avenues to trap his prey. He stood with his back to Barney, reconnoitring the farmyard while pondering his next move. He could not be seen to be defeated and then have to walk away shamefaced.

Then, the oldest trick in the lawman's armoury, struck him.

"Have you any dogs?" enquired the lawman.

"Two," answered Barney after a little hesitation.

The lawman smiled slyly through the pain and agony. 'My journey wouldn't be in vain after all,' he assured himself.

If he's like all the other farmers in the locality he surely hasn't taken out a dog license. If he had I'd known about it in the barracks.

He could see in his mind's eye Barney pleading for leniency and hear him say, 'I'll give you all the potatoes you can carry home, and anytime you are passing the house there will be a bag left outside the kitchen door for you,' and then, winking at him in a conspiratorial fashion, saying,' I'm sure, Sergeant, it is possible to overlook this trivial offence.' But he would at first do as he'd always done before accepting alms. He would caution him about the seriousness of bribing a law officer in the course of his duties.

The lawman was shook out of his reverie when Barney, with a derisive grin on his face, tipped him on the shoulder.

"Are you feeling alright, Sarge? You don't look too good."

The lawman gritted his teeth and swung around to face Barney.

To himself, 'I'll not let you know how I feel. I have come here on a specific mission and I'm going to see it through to the bitter end.'

Now that my first evidence has run to ground I'll have

to fall back on the oldest trick in the lawman's armoury, the dog licence. He stared at the farmer McKeown severely from under his bushy eyebrows.

"No," answered Barney, "don't need any."

The lawman was taken aback by his arrogance. He inhaled large gulps of rage as he pranced from foot to foot. The law was being challenged, he thought to himself, and his authority was being undermined by this scoundrel. If he was to save face and gain the initiative he would have to act quickly and decisively. He drew himself to his full six foot and eyeballed Barney

"You mean to tell me you have two dogs and you don't need licence!" bellowed the lawman.

Barney nodded his head tacitly.

"Oh, you seem to know more about the law than I do," still in a high pitched voice, hoping to intimidate Barney. But Barney wasn't a man to be intimidated by such boisterous aggression. He kept his cool.

"What colour are these dogs?" the Sergeant asked fiercely, his fiery red face grotesque from the pain and agony of his mangled arm.

"A blue and a green," says Barney more derisively than ever.

"A ... blue and a green," repeated the Sergeant in a falsetto tone, his argot became fierce and rapid and his drooping moustache fanned out over his pursed lips. He stared at the farmer askance. Was this joker really testing his knowledge of dog breeds or his patience or just having a joke at his expense?

He could not tell, but one thing he assured himself was that this rapscallion of the Devil would not be allowed to flout the law and get away with it.

'Whoever heard of a green dog?' he snarled to himself. "Let me see these dogs," demanded the Sergeant curtly.

"Certainly, sir, follow me."

Barney deliberately took the Sergeant through the scullery where he had bags of potatoes and turnips ready for delivery to Hosey's Grocers Shop.

The Sergeant flexed the corners of his mouth into that evil grin of his. He pondered in his own mind as to how he was going to transport such a heavy load along the narrow dirt road to the village. He was jerked back to the present when a voice rang out from the kitchen.

"In here, Sarge."

The Sergeant entered the small, modest kitchen, his bulky frame almost blotting out the light from the small lattice window. He stood in the nave of the room, facing the open fire.

"Where are these dogs?" he says fiercely.

"You are looking at them," says Barney, pointing to the mantle piece over the fire where the two delft dogs sat.

The Sergeant glared at the two dogs, then at Barney.

His face fell in shame and humiliation. He turned and with an abject snarl he sallied out of the house, his pride badly dented.

The village was quiet as the Sergeant walked up the main street leading his big Raleigh bike. It was the afternoon of the carnival fair in Avoca. He left the village behind him and sauntered up the winding dirt road through Kilcroney. The sky was cloudless and only the gaudy voices of gulls and jackdaws and the bleating of lambs relieved the melancholy.

His head was tilted. He was in deep thought. He had a serious decision to make. Each house he passed he could see with his eyecorner the twitching of curtains of the Peeping Toms behind the lattice windows. The children were scampering off to the fields to check on their stock, for fear they might have strayed onto the public road.

He continued his uphill climb, occasionally stopping to rub the sweat from his brow. Further on he came to

Ballard Cross, the highest road junction before the summit of the hill. There he turned right, mounted his bike and cycled eastward along the level road until he came to the derelict mineshaft. He dismounted and left his bike lying against the hedge. He decided to take a long rest in the cool of the big oak tree. There was no incumbency on him to rush back for it was his half-day and he could spend it as he wished.

He sat on a boulder at the base of the tree. In the peace and quiet of the afternoon he began the ritual of lighting his pipe. These were the moments he yearned for, away from his busy life and the knowledge that no one in the village knew where he was or could reach him.

Vague sounds of the countryside came to him on the sweet smelling air. The distant songbird, the soft murmur of a breeze in the tall meadows, the creaking of a branch over his head and the rattling of leaves in the tree. This was heaven to him.

In slow, deliberate stages he took out a pipe and gripped it between his teeth. Then he rummaged in his waistcoat pocket and extracted a lump of tobacco, roughened by earlier cutting. After examining it from every angle he carved off a few well-chosen slides, not too much, not too little, just enough to fill his pipe. Then he placed it in the cupped palm of his left hand. With the heel of his right hand he kneaded the tobacco lovingly, all the while looking straight ahead down the large expanse of the valley towards the village.

Automatically he was reconnoitring the highways and byways for any misdemeanour. 'Once a lawman, always a lawman,' he thought.

With the tobacco teased to his liking he raked it into the bowl of the pipe with his index finger, then pressed it down firmly but gently. He set a lighted match to it and drew on the pipe strenuously until a red glow appeared on the top of the bowl and began to expand. Again he pressed the red mass down and put a lighted match to it again and gave one more strenuous pull. Satisfied that it was lighting to his satisfaction he clamped the lid down on it. The ritual complete, he dry-washed his hands in order to dislodge any motes of tobacco from them.

Leaning back against the trunk of the tree, he drew on his pipe with long, gentle draws. He watched the smoke coil upwards into the tree bough and gave another curious glance around the countryside. 'I could stay here forever,' he mused to himself as he stretched out his long legs to make himself more comfortable. With the heat of the afternoon and the peace and quiet of his surroundings he was soon lost in reverie.

His mind went back, back to the days of his youth in Clonmanny in Co. Sligo where he was born and reared. He remembered going to school, him and his two sisters in their bare feet. The girls wore floral dresses and him in a petticoat, which was the common garb worn by boys at the time.

What always reminded him of home more than anything else was turf smoke. He smiled nostalgically to himself. He remembered as a boy going to Lackeen Bog with his father to cut and save the turf. As if it was yesterday, he imagined in his own mind that he could still hear the squelch and slap of the black sod as his father cut and tossed the peat onto the bank. Then he drew it home with the donkey and cart and stacked it in a beehive clamp at the gable end of the house.

He enjoyed cutting the hay with the scythe in the rock field. To encourage it to dry faster he turned it with forks made from a forked branch of a swallow tree.

He could see himself and his two sisters running through the meadow that was shoulder high, looking for corncrakes' nests and hearing his father screeching and shouting, "be the chopsticks-of-war, if I catch yous husseys I'll kill the lot of yous for trampling the meadow!"

He looked forward to the frocken picking the last Sunday in July on Callery Hill. Early in the morning his father would harness the donkey and put him under the cart. Then he installed the buckets and cans for the frocken picking in the nave, and as well not forgetting the picnic baskets laden with mother's homemade goodies tucked in and around. He would return in the late evening, tired but happy.

Later on, we would pick blackberries around the hedgerows on the farm and along the roadside. These were sold to buy schoolbooks and clothes for the winter.

All these things floated back into the Sergeant's mind as he sat stolidly by the big oak tree. ' How proud,' he thought 'his parents were the day he passed his exams for the police force, and proud of the day at his passing out parade in Dublin. How proud,' he thought, ' they would be today if they were alive to see him Sergeant and principal law officer in the Bailiwick of Shinrone.'

In his subconscious he could hear his parents droning on about their offspring's future, late at night as they sat around an open fire, and when he was in bed and supposed to be asleep. They never discussed anything important when we children were present.

"There's nothing for them here," he'd say to his wife, "only hardship. That Seamus lad is sure too astute to be tied to these few miserable acres of windswept mountain and barren ground. That lad will go far. Mark you my words,"

Molly, his wife, nodded her head tacitly.

The Sergeant twitched his walrus moustache in acknowledgement of his parents' foresight and their unselfish toil year in, year out on those few miserable acres so as the children could have a better education and life away from the land in some well paid job. Yes, he knew they would be proud of him today.

He was extolled by his senior officers for his efficiency in dealing with the filchers in the Bailiwick of Shinrone, altercations in the village and truancy in the schools. He was satisfied in his own mind that his way of dealing with lawbreakers was the more sensible way than summonsing them to court where a hefty find could be imposed. Yes, with his way everyone was a winner. The culprits would get off with a gentle caution and he himself would get all the goods he needed free gratis. In time he thought his popularity would burgeon but instead it diminished. Soon he found himself being treated like a pariah. The once friendly and loquacious people who had befriended him and often invited him into their homes for tea as he trudged the country roads were now behind closed doors and curtained windows as he passed. The indignation of being treated in such a fashion by the peasants whose lawbreaking he often overlooked was more than he could tolerate.

He opened his eyes and scanned the rich green valley below for some inducement to solace his confused brain, but could find little. He cupped his face in his hands and prayed with all his might for some enlightenment to his dilemma.

Then, from the recesses of his brain he could see Molly Hanrahan, beckoning him. Molly was the widow's daughter from Ballycrean whom he had been courting for some time. She was a fine girl, he thought, and a great worker, but more than that she had a good farm and a beautiful house. He knew he could make a success of farming. Wasn't he brought up on a small farm himself?" He cogitated for a long minute on these matters. He knew the widow was in favour of his company keeping with her daughter, so much so that she sometimes left a bag of potatoes outside her kitchen door for him. This seemed to him as much an incentive as an approval.

He was shook back to the present by the braying of a donkey in the nearby field. He straightened up, lit his pipe and pondered why he came up here in the first place. Then, as if by some stroke of the supernatural, it all became so vivid.

He could see his whole future laid out before him. Yes, he would retire from the force as soon as was practical and marry Molly Hanrahan. His mind definitely made up, he mounted his bike and set off to ask the widow for her daughter's hand in marriage.

By the time he reached the widow's house, the sun was already falling low and yellowing over Slevemoon. The afternoon was beginning to cool.

'A cup of tea would be most welcome', he thought to himself but to his disappointment there was no reply to his knock. 'They must be gone to the carnival fair in Avoca,' he says to himself. 'I think,' says he, 'Molly mentioned it the other day when we were talking.'

But his disappointment was assuaged somewhat by the generous amount of potatoes and turnips that were outside the widow's door in readiness for him. Was it telepathy or just a woman's intuition? He didn't know but he thought she was being overgenerous this day. Not one to refuse alms in large or small amounts, he loaded all his cargo on the bike and set off to the barracks.

Barney McKeown was not one for festivities. While many of his neighbours that morning were packing up and leaving for the day at the Avoca fair, Barney worked at home preparing his farm produce for delivery to Hosey's Grocers Shop as was his wont every week.

Last evening he had loaned his mule Heron to his neighbour, Pete McHenry, to take his piglets to the show and sale in Avoca. How could he refuse his old friend and neighbour after Pete told him the sad story about his horse had gone lame and he had already entered his pedigree piglets in the show and was hoping to win the Devlin Cup for the third year in a row?

This put Barney in a right pucker. How was he going to get his goods to Hosey's on time? He cursed himself for his stupidity and lack of forethought. But what was done was done, he says. He took off his cap and scratched his head. It gave him more scope for thought.

'Do you know?' says he to no one in particular, 'I'll slip over at first light of day in the morning and ask Mrs. Hanrahan. I heard her say that she was going to Avoca for the day. She is a good neighbour. We often do little turns for each. She won't refuse me.'

At first light this morning Barney found himself at the widow's kitchen doorway, cap in hand and looking rather agitated. He bowed as he addressed the two women.

"Ma'am, Molly, I've come to ask a great favour."

"Certainly, Barney," the widow assured him, "just leave them outside the back door and we'll take them with us when we are going."

Barney thanked her profusely before leaving to fetch the goods and bring them back. He would have to pack them in the wheelbarrow and make a trip or even two back and forth to the house, a slow laborious job.

'I'll have a cup of tea now,' he thought, 'before I start the long haul.'

Later that afternoon Barney was standing in Hosey's Shop, exchanging pleasantries with other customers. While awaiting his turn at the counter to collect his money, buy his weekly groceries, then join his friends for a drink, Mike let go direct to him.

"Where are those goods you promised to deliver to me?" he snapped, "the one busy day of the year and you had to let me down!"

Barney looked hard at him, dumbfounded, and swallowed hard on his gulp. He was so embarrassed he could hardly talk, only stare with his mouth open. He wasn't sure as to whether Mike was joking or in earnest, he was noted for his play-acting.

"Them potatoes didn't arrive," he said curtly without taking his eyes off the scales where he was weighing out two ounces of tea for Mrs. Daly.

Barney turned the colour of beetroot with embarrassment as he stomped from foot to foot. To be upbraided in front of a shop full of customers was most humiliating and it not his fault.

Without a reply Barney stormed out of the shop. There were sparks of vengeance in his eyes. His plan for a quiet evening drinking with his friends was badly disrupted. He grabbed his bike, didn't wait to put his foot on the pedal but ran three or four paces with the bike to gather speed, then, taking a spring, he landed on the saddle. Having controlled the bike he leaned hard on the pedals up the Ballycrean Hill to the widow's house, mumbling unholy expletives on her for letting him down.

Arriving at the widow's breathless and in a lather of sweat, there were no potatoes to be seen outside the door where he left them. He took off his cap and scratched his head.

'Well, that bates all,' says he to himself. 'It can't be possible that the widow brought the potatoes to Avoca with her. 'No ... ,' he shook his head, 'she'd never do that,' he assured himself.

She was a reliable woman. 'She would never let him down, but where are the potatoes gone to?' he asked himself. He cautioned himself against jumping to conclusions. He would have to wait until the widow returned to get the true facts, but at the back of his mind he had the niggling feeling the Sergeant was the culprit.

Pete McHerny, a quiet and taciturn farmer from Barnaculla, won first prize that day with his litter of piglets. The Devlin Cup was now his to keep, having won it three years in a row. All the farmers came to his cart to inspect his prize animals, and when they were put for sale farmer after farmer tried to out bid each other in the hope of securing them as foundation stock for themselves. But their hopes were soon dashed when who should arrive only Colonel Diggle of Laken Estate who outbid all comers and bought the piglets.

Molloy's Public House was where the cup was presented to Pete. He called for drinks for the house. Several rounds were served up. Then a great hunger came over Pete, so he invited Jack O'Hara and Tim Delaney, two solid farmers and bosom friends, to accompany him to Conroy's eating house where a hearty meal of bacon and cabbage was lowered, followed by a copious serving of trifle washed down with several cups of well sugared tea.

"That'll make a sound base for more drink," says Jack O'Hara.

Pete nodded tacitly.

They returned to Molloy's where the real drinking began and after a couple of hours the party was a merry one. From all sides Pete was being pummelled and patted by well-wishers. The bums and inebriated despots jostled with each other to shake his hand, knowing full well a free drink was in the offering.

Pete, not being used to the excesses of drink, became very intoxicated. His shyness disappeared. He became more vocal and, with a little encouragement from the receptive crowd, launched into one of Tom Moore's famous melodies, "*The Meeting of the Waters.*" He received a rapturous applause from the bums and hangers-on who called for more and more.

Jack and Timmy were well aware of Pete's generous

nature when he went on a spree. They were very solicitous about his befuddled state and the way these bousie wastrels, who cared little about his achievements and less about his money, were milling around him like a swarm of bees around their queen for the sole purpose of having a good time at his expense.

To shorten the road Pete bought himself a bottle of whiskey. Jack and Timmy led the way and he waddled out on to the street, which was now empty except for two stall women preparing to leave for home.

Jack helped Pete into the nave of the cart while Timmy untied the mule and set him on the road home.

Earlier Pete had plied Heron, the mule, with a sufficiency of oats and hay so he was in a right fettle. He was anxious to get on the road home, away from the hustle and bustle of the fair. When the mule hit the high road he began to trot in real earnest. It would do your heart good to see the dancing legs of the mule and the bright sparks from the iron shod hooves on the granite hard road as he sallied on at a lively clip. Pete took a copious dollop from the bottle and began to sing some of his favourite ditties, but the click, clack of the hooves on the road proved soporific to Pete and he was soon fast asleep. Heron wasn't perturbed when his minder fell asleep. He was quite capable of negotiating his own way home. He had done it many times before with Barney.

By the time he reached Shinrone, daylight was giving away to darkness. Coming around the courthouse corner Pete was not just shook out of his torpor but also out of the cart. He lay prostrate on the road among a pile of potatoes and turnips that seemed to be doing a war dance around him. As the atmosphere of a nightmare cannot be shaken off for some minutes after waking, so this monstrous poltergeist held for awhile its ambiance of dread.

Pete had never before encountered a lawman. He never expected to meet the Sergeant on this night above all nights for it was known that he spent his half-day on the farm with his girlfriend and her mother.

Every time Pete tried to stand up his legs were whipped from under him by the rolling potatoes and he was soon down again. Finally he got to the perpendicular and, with great effort, freed the Sergeant from under his mangled bike. The Sergeant struggled out on to the road, writhing and wriggling, his puckered face flushed in the wan light.

"What is the meaning of this?" croaked the lawman, "no light on your cart, travelling at the wrong side of the road, and in charge of an animal and cart while drunk."

Well, Pete was trembling like an aspen leaf. Never in his life had he met such a belligerent character or such boisterous language. But sedate Pete thought it best to admit liability and avoid any further scene that might alert the whole village. He apologised profusely for his lapse of concentration and promised to repair his bike and replace all his goods.

The Sergeant calmed down somewhat on hearing that he would be at no loss.

"I apologise again, Sarge," says Pete contritely, "Heron must have mistook the bend on the road in the dark."

"WHO?" screeched the lawman, his voice reaching a crescendo.

"Heron," says Pete suavely.

"That bloody, cross-eyed, cross-bred mule tried to kill me before!"

When Heron heard the familiar boisterous voice, he lowered his ears and stripped his teeth and, with a quick toss of his head, reached out to snap at the Sergeant.

The lawman jerked back suddenly a pace or two. He stared at Pete.

"Get that dangerous animal out of here at once," says he, "or I'll have you arrested for the deliberate obstruction of a law officer in the course of his duties."

'Some duty,' declared Pete to himself, 'with six bags of potatoes on your bike. God only knows what unfortunate has suffered that loss in order to appease you.'

Out loud, Pete pleaded with the lawman not to press charges, explaining the reason for him being delayed and again repeated his promise to make good any damage caused.

But he wouldn't listen. He took out his notebook and jotted down in a terse fashion all the details.

They all knew locally that it wasn't Pete that the Sergeant had a grudge against, but Barney. The opportunity had presented itself, and the lawman now had firm evidence to have the mule put away for good.

"You'll be hearing from me in due course, Mr. McHenry."

Early the following morning after the accident the Sergeant arrived at Molly Hanrahan, his girlfriend's house, with his arm in a sling. Well, Molly nearly died when she saw his grotesque face and torn uniform.

"What in God's holy name have you been doing to yourself, or what happened at all?" she pleaded, sitting him down in the warm glow of the turf fire.

She made him a cup of strong, well-sugared tea and he related the whole story of him calling to her house the day before and getting no answer, of how he saw the potatoes outside the door and assumed they were for him.

"I loaded them all up on me bike and set out for the barracks. It was almost dark when I reached the outskirts of the village. Negotiating the turn around the courthouse corner, I was under enormous pressure trying to keep the bike on the road. And then, for some unknown reason, I lost control and crashed into Pete McHenry. He was driving Barney McKeown's mule and cart. He was flustered, drunk, on the wrong side of the road, and no light. I ended up on the dyke, the potatoes and bike on top of me. That's the result," pointing to his hands and face and torn jacket.

"O' my God," says Molly when she heard about the potatoes. "You're in real trouble, says she, "them potatoes you took belonged to Barney McKeown. They were left here by Barney for us to deliver to Mike Hosey in the village on our way to Avoca. When we told Barney our side of the story, and the reason we had to leave sooner than expected, he was real vexed and laid the blame on you. For he saw you on the road yesterday evening. He vouched to see you behind bars if not stripped. He was going to make an official complaint to Dublin about stealing his potatoes and also about the way you have been coercing people, poor people at that, into handing over goods as an amerce fine, so as not to be taken to court."

When Barney discovered his potatoes were stolen he was beside himself with rage. He vowed to have this scoundrel apprehended and charged. It wasn't the first time it had happened to him. He decided not to report the matter to the Sergeant on account of the bad blood that had arisen between them. No, he would take his case to a higher court as it were. In his own mind he had a sneaky feeling who the culprit might be, so he kept his council to himself.

He wrote to the superintendent of the force in Dublin, a long time friend of the family. He outlined his case and his reason for bypassing Sergeant Kane.

Within the week two detectives arrived in Shinrone, their suitcases tied firmly on their bikes. They had come to stay as long as was necessary to crack the case.

The detectives weren't helped by the fact that the

Sergeant had taken sick leave and it wasn't known when he'd be back. Only Molly Hanrahan knew of his whereabouts and she wouldn't divulge anything when questioned.

After ten days of enquiries and many statements taken, the detectives were about to scale down their enquiries and return to Dublin when a break came.

They were acting on the throw-away word of a boy in the village school about Pete McHenry having an accident with Barney McKeown's mule.

Since the accident, Pete had become a recluse. Not even the detectives could get an answer to their knock on the previous visit but this time they were determined to make contact with Pete in order to eliminate him from their enquiries.

As Pete looked through the aperture in the curtains in his kitchen window and saw the two detectives outside his door an eerie feeling of apprehension encompassed him. Were his worst fears about to be realised?"

The Sergeant, he thought, had sent the two law officers to apprehend him. No doubt they would charge him with the maiming of a law officer in the course of his duties, of being in charge of a wicked mule, and without the requisite light on his cart. In his mind's eye he could see himself being handcuffed and led away by the two law officers to serve a month in jail for his crime.

He was shook back to the present by a severe knocking on the door and a lawman bellowing, "Open up, police! We know you are in there."

Well, Pete was petrified!

He shuddered in the nave of the kitchen, his face had turned a pure pallor of marble. He looked around the kitchen. There was no escape, not even a back door. He was doomed.

He timidly went to the door and opened it the

smallest of apertures and peered out. A shaft of light glowed on his sallow face. He was expecting the lawmen to rush him and overpower and handcuff him. But the big man with the soft voice spoke first.

"Mr. McHenry, could we have a quiet word with you?"

Pete immediately became quite relaxed. He was amazed at his ability to talk to the strangers without stammering or stuttering.

He outlined his itinerary for the day in question: how he had borrowed Barney McKeown's mule to take his piglets to the show and sale in Avoca. And winning first prize for them! A celebration ensued which delayed his return home. As he rounded the courthouse corner he met Sergeant Kane coming in the opposite direction. He was transporting an enormous amount of potatoes and turnips.

"To my mind it rendered him incapable of controlling his machine. He held me responsible for the accident and vouched to see me in court. He would also see that the mule would be sold to the factory or put down."

"I pleaded with him to drop the charges, saying that I would repair the bike and replace his goods, but he wouldn't listen."

"Mr. McHenry," the lawman spoke again as he stood up to leave, "we will be calling on you to testify in court, but I can assure you that you have nothing to worry about. This man's activities have been under scrutiny for some time. We have had a lot of complaints lately about his unethical behaviour which is unbecoming for an officer of the law."

It had got to the Sergeant's ears that it was known that he was convalescing in Bray and that two detectives were in hot pursuit of him and an arrest would be made soon.

In order to avoid any ugly scenes, which he knew his return would create, he would retire from the force and advise Molly to sell the farm and move with him to Sligo, and with her mother as well if she wished.

But the case came to court before he could put his plans into action.

He was summoned to appear before the Magistrate in Shinrone at the next sitting, to answer charges relating to amerce fines without the requisite authority and the purloining of Barney McKeown's potatoes from outside Mrs. Hanrahan's door.

He pleaded innocent to the charges of imposing fines, saying that the people in question offered the goods to him.

"And I suppose," says the Magistrate, looking at the Sergeant from over his horn-rim glasses, "you are going to tell me that the potatoes you purloined from outside Mrs. Hanrahan's door were a present for you also?"

"Yes, your Honour, I had firmly believed that to be so."

The Magistrate gave a sullen glance at the Sergeant, a glance that would suggest that he was none too impressed with this so-called upholder of the law. A rapscallion of Hell would be more fitting a name for him and he was going to make an example of him. Justice must be seen to be done even among the law's minions.

"Mr. Kane, Sergeant," says the Magistrate as he began his summing up, "your behaviour is unbecoming for a minion of the law, and it leaves me with no option but to dismiss you from the force forthwith. And as for the repair of your bike, it shall be borne by you and you alone."

Then he struck the gavel on the desk and declared the matter closed.

The solid farmers that came to give Pete moral support, and the peasants that were standing around at every vantage point at the back of the hall turned to one another and began to converse in whispers.

The Sergeant could almost hear their tongues wag.

'That rapscallion of Hell has got his just deserts at last and rightly so,' he could almost hear them say.

The now ex-Sergeant stepped down from the witness stand with a mighty heavy heart. His face was slate gray. He was so weak that he teetered on his heels. He held on to the side of the witness box while he composed himself. He gave a cursory glance down the courtroom. All's he could see was sneering faces staring back at him, and he still had to walk the gauntlet all the way to the street. He shook his shoulders and, without looking right or left, he walked the gauntlet all the way as if nothing had happened.

Espying his Molly with her pony and trap he raced forward to join her midst the gibes and taunts of the cabal who were determined to see him out of the village and out of their lives forever.

Pete the Farmer

My name is Pete McHenry, I'm a man that is well known.
I live in Barnaculla in a place I call my own.
I raise cattle on my farm and swine around the yard
But the beginning of my misfortune was to meet with
    Kane the Guard.

On the fourth day of October I was coming from the fair.
Coming round the courthouse corner I was taken unawares.
The road it was so narrow for my jennet and my cart
When I happened to meet with Kane the Guard and he
    hadn't room to pass,
He pulled the brakes too quickly and was thrown into the
    dike.
He smashed the brakes and handlebars and buckled up the
    bike.

When he recovered consciousness he demanded my name.
I gave him lots of impudence and he gave me the same.
I apologised profusely when I saw him spouting blood.
You inebriated amadan he blared at me right mad
As he took out his pen and paper and jotted down the
    facts.
A summons you'll receive from me within the next two
    weeks
And I advise you to be more civil when you go before the
    judge.

From far and near the crowd did come to the courthouse in Shinrone
To hear the lawman rebuke Pete's testimony.
Your Honour upon this book I do swear that
The goods that I was carting home were a gift from my girlfriend.
But the lawman he is lying shouted Pete from the dock.
Those goods that he had purloined were for Hosey's grocers shop.

The Magistrate leered austerely at the sergeant in the dock.
His antipathy and his ire he dare not show.
Your avarice and your amerce is unbecoming for a minion of the law
And for this I do remove your stripes and duties as a Guard.
As for the bill for bike repair it will be borne by you alone
Then he smacked the gavel on the bench to declare the matter closed.

The sergeant closed his eyes and sighed a mighty sigh.
The boys and girls in court that day at him began to gibe.
You were a proper scoundrel he could almost hear them say
And the sentence that was passed on you we're all so mighty glad.

The ex-sergeant shook his shoulders and jerked his head on high.
Then walked the gauntlet of prying eyes until he got outside.
He espied his lovely Molly with her pony and her trap
And sallied forth to join her with the cabal in hot pursuit.

I think I will get married and give up repairing bikes.
I'll propose to my dear Molly and take her for my wife.
When she sells her house and farm I'll take her far away
To my little house in Sligo near the Isle of Inisfree.

A Reprieve for Old Dan

Harry lay in bed in a trance, feeling the worst from his previous day's drinking. He wasn't a drinking man as such but yesterday was a special day for him, the selling of the old Clydesdale and the purchasing of a younger animal. He prided himself on his ability to recognise a kind, reliable animal. Sure, wasn't he a judge at the local shows for forty years or more?

His head was throbbing. He turned and twisted many times in quest of a more comfortable spot on the pillow to ease the pain.

He was oblivious to his sister's presence in the room. The chasm of ill feeling between them after all her years in America hadn't abated one iota.

"Get up, you fly-by-night!" she harangued, "I told you it would happen. You just wouldn't listen."

Harry jerked in the bed. For a moment he thought he was still at the fair and the voice he heard was that of Dealer Devlin, warning him to be careful or the horse might trample on him. He opened one eye a sliver and squinted around the room. He couldn't see his sister very clearly but he recognised her hat that sat high on her head like a tea cosy.

"Oh, it's you," he mumbled. He scrambled out of bed, snorting and snuffling with tiredness and sat on the edge.

The ray of sun coming through the aperture in the

curtains was more than he could tolerate. He squinted around the dimly lit room, hoping to discern some familiar object like a painting or picture. He didn't know where he was. He couldn't remember anything that had happened the previous day. Was he in trouble with the law? Did he loose his brother on the way home or had the horse disappeared from the stable? Anything was possible, he thought. He opened his eyes again only to find the room swirling about him. His head was vibrating from the continuous haranguing. He cupped his face in his hands, his elbows on his knees, and sort of cuddled it.

"What's the matter with you at all at this ungodly hour of the morning," he protested, "or can a man not have one morning off in peace?"

What's the matter?" she chided him, raising her voice several octaves above normal. "Get out into the yard and see for yourself," says she storming out of the room, slamming the door behind her.

The sound of the slamming door made Harry shudder and moan with pain. He squeezed his head more tightly to ease the throbbing.

The whole wrangle started some thirty-five years earlier when the matchmaker, which was the tradition at the time among the aristocracy, failed to produce a suitable partner for his sister Mags, or Margaret Og as the mother liked to call her. Mags was enraged at this abject trading on her behalf yet behind her back. She felt she was being treated no better than a heifer on the farm, or a battery hen trade-off to the highest bidder for mating. Her happiness was only secondary. She knew she wasn't pretty and neither was she getting any younger, but this horse-trading for her body was more than she was prepared to tolerate. She intended to break the mould and show them that it was possible for even a plain Jane like herself to woo a man of her choice without the aid of these quacks. She was going to face the challenge with the stoicism of a Red Indian. She had nothing to lose, only her pride, and it was already badly dented by this horse-trading.

She met and fell in love with Jack Henry, a labouring man, who lived outside the village of Kilcommon, about five miles away.

When word got back to her parents of her impending marriage all hell broke loose. The Father, who was an old man at the time, took to bed. The shame and shock was too much for him and he was never seen out again. The Mother, who was boss when serious decisions were to be made, took the matter into her own hands and set about putting an end to this 'outrageous episode', as she called it.

She jerked her chin dictatorially and pranced around the kitchen. When she spoke, she spoke with the authority of a hanging judge. She was so distraught that spittle oozed from the corners of her mouth and sparks from her eyes like the sparks from a blacksmith's anvil.

Margaret Og, as her mother liked to call her, had badly underestimated the Mother's venomous reaction when the rendezvous was discovered.

"Get that nonsense out of your head!" she bellowed. "No proletarian will ever set foot in this place while I'm alive, and neither will I allow the rabble class to invade my home. You'll go to your uncle in America," she pronounced, banging her fist on the table.

Reluctantly Mags went to America. To do otherwise would have driven the Mother into a fierce frenzy with dire consequences for Mags. She was now back and was also equal partners in the farm for the parents had died intestate. Although they had promised the farm to Harry, destiny had overruled. Mags intended making life difficult for Harry for informing on her and so depriving her of her independence and a married life with John Henry.

"What's this I hear?" says she, "you selling the old

Clydesdale and buying a younger animal?" she demanded to know in her belligerent tone. There was a vicious scowl on her face as she pranced around the kitchen preparing evening tea, "or have I no say anymore?"

Harry displayed his usual politeness to her provocations.

"The horse," says he evenly, "is unable for the heavy work anymore. We need a younger animal."

"Who's going to buy him?" says she, "you're half blind." She was staring him hard from the opposite side of the table.

"I am," he retorted. "I have been buying and selling horses for the last forty years. Wasn't I on the judging panel at the county show for years?" Harry tried to press home his advantage, "My abilities in that field are well known."

Mags was taken aback by his assertiveness but she wouldn't let go. She gave a petulant toss of her head and a great guffaw. "What about that horse," says she, "you bought for Parkie Moran of Cooladine. He became broken-winded and had to be sold to the factory. Yes and the pony you bought for Jenny Slater. It developed a frog foot."

Harry sensed that to continue such a line of argument with Mags was futile so he sung dumb, but Mags was in full flow and nobody was going to stop her having her say.

"Buy a tractor," says she, "and get someone to drive it, you're going to kill that brother of yours and him with a bad leg."

Deep down Harry knew she was right. The winds of change were coming, but the horses had served him well. They were part of the way things were done for as long as he could remember and change always held fear for Harry, but he wasn't going to give in to Mags' domineering attitude. He would rather sell out first. A farm without a horse was unthinkable as far as Harry was concerned.

The morning broke bright and clear over Rathmullen as Harry and his brother Tom set out for Ballycrean fair. The sky to the east became awash with cardinal red from the fiery rising sun over Sugarloaf Mountain. There was a nip in the air. As they went along the light got better and soon they were able to appreciate some of the sights and sounds of the countryside. He recited a rhyme to himself that he once learned at school as a boy:

A red sky at night is a sailor's delight, a red sky in the morning is a shepherd's warning.

Then Harry murmured a short prayer to himself, imploring the Good Lord to direct him in his task ahead.

As he approached the outskirts of the town, human voices and the lowing of cattle came to his ear. His heart missed a beat for he loved the hustle and bustle of the fair. But his spirits were soon dashed when a red haired woman stepped down from a caravan with a stack of galvanised buckets hanging from the crook of her arm.

"Good morning, sir," she greeted him, "a lovely day for the fair," and then in the same breath, "would you like to buy a bucket, sir? I've nice, cheap ones here."

Harry sat bolt upright in the cart, a strange feeling came over him. He gulped hard in his throat. Was it an omen or just an old man's foolish thought? He checked himself for his foolishness, but he couldn't stop his mind flashing back to what the old people used to say, that it was unlucky, even believed to be disastrous, to meet a red haired woman first thing in the morning when going to the fair. Having reflected on it for a long moment as he stroked his moustache, he shrugged his shoulders to dismiss it as just one of those old wife's piseogues that was put about to frighten people. He looked at his brother sitting on the slat of the cart, dangling his legs to and fro, oblivious to Harry's anxiety and apprehension.

The horse broke into an abrupt trot. Harry stood up in the body of the cart, grunting with exertion as he did so, and held the driving reins firmly in his hands to balance himself, the pipe gigging between his teeth. He slowed him up to a lively walk as the streets became closely packed with animals, horses and carts and human beings. A group of interested spectators were eagerly watching a buyer or seller offering advice and helping energetically to clinch a bargain.

Harry greeted all his friends and neighbours with a nod of his head as he made his way to the town centre where he would take his usual stand beside the village pump. He had eyed out a few fine horses that would suit his requirements as he made his way along the street. No problem choosing a good animal from that lot, he assured himself, but his first task was to sell the old Clydesdale.

Harry had no problem finding a buyer. Ned Kane, an old friend and dealer, was only too happy to buy Harry's horse. He had been looking for such an animal for a riding school in Avoca. The deal complete and the horse handed over, Harry and Tom decided they'd have a meal before any other business be transacted. So they retired to McCoy's Hotel where they would be assured of a good meal and a hearty welcome.

It was while in there that he met all his old friends and ancient colleagues from the equine world. There they talked and drank and reminisced of times passed. Drink flowed freely between them and time slipped easily by. Harry was so engrossed in his reminiscing that he forgot all about the purchasing of another horse til he was reminded by his brother, Tom. He gave Tom a dismissive wave of his hand. "Ned Kane says he is looking out for a horse for me. He'll probably be in shortly."

Back in the square the Dealer Kane's accomplices and their associates were hard at work on Harry's horse, away from the limelight, in O'Grady's yard. They were giving him a makeover. A short tail and mane, shortened fringe, clipped his fetlocks and washed his hoofs. They gave him a good grooming before obliterating the star on his forehead with black polish. He certainly looked ten years younger.

The November evening was beginning to close in fast. The market square was almost deserted bar a few stalls where women were gathering up their wares after the day. There was only one group of horses tethered together awaiting their master's return to take them to their new destination. The Dealer Devlin, Ned Kane's accomplice, came into the hotel to inform Harry that Ned left on the four o'clock train with a load of horses. The stationmaster wouldn't let the young horses travel unattended.

" He sends his sincere apologies."

"The bloody scoundrel," Harry snorted and swore. "I should have never trusted him." He took out his pocket watch and looked at it, "Oh my God," says he, "look at the time. What am I going to do now? I've no horse going home." He got into a terrible pucker. What was he going to do with the cart and tackling? And then Mags' advice seared into his brain.

"Calm down," says Devlin, putting his hand on Harry's shoulder. "I have a nice horse outside that will suit you to the ground. Ned Kane recommended him."

Harry was rather reluctant to deal with Devlin. He had heard of his many shady deals over the years but nothing could be proved. Harry was now on the horns of a dilemma. To return home without a horse would be yielding to Mags' bidding and that was out of the question as far as Harry was concerned. But his overstay in the hotel had left him with little choice but to deal with Devlin.

Grunting with exertion Harry got to his feet with the

help of his brother. He waddled out through the hall and vestibule to the street after Dealer Devlin. His eyes ablaze, his feet moving in opposite directions away from him, his rear end protruding in an effort to keep his balance, he looked around the square. Where it had been a hive of activity earlier in the day it was now empty save for one bunch of horses tethered head to head a short distance away from the footpath.

His heart sank in his boots when he thought that here he was going to deal with the very man he had spent all his life politely avoiding having any truck with.

"Where is he?" hiccupped Harry as he staggered and swayed as if he was top heavy.

The Dealer stepped forward and untied the Clydesdale from the bunch and brought him forward to be examined. In doing so, he stood the horse a few paces away from the footpath.

'If he's going to examine him,' Devlin says to himself, 'he'll have to get down off the footpath,' and the dealer was pretty sure that at that moment Harry wasn't capable of moving too far without a helping hand, and, being the man he was, he'd be too proud to ask.

The bums and hangers-on were lavish in their praise for Harry and his renowned capabilities in judging a good horse but these same bums knew little about the finer qualities of a good horse and cared less as long as it yielded a free drink.

"Come from one of the best farms in Ireland," declared the Dealer Devlin, "always kindly treated and well fed. Look at his shiny coat. Also his nicely trimmed mane and tail and tidy fetlocks. There's not a better ten year old horse in this fair today than him. He'll be good for the next ten or twelve years. I know you'll look after him. You won't be sorry if you buy him, sir."

Harry gave him a furtive glance. To himself, 'I don't

know about that.'

Harry reached out to grab hold of the horse's bridle in order to examine his teeth. Forgetting the step on to the road he lost his balance and toppled into the water channel beside the footpath, then rolled out onto the road between the horse's two front legs.

"Merciful God," declared the Dealer, "he'll be trampled on. Woo, boy," says the Dealer, speaking kindly into the horse's ear, at the same time patting him on the neck. But he needn't have worried for the old horse knew his master's voice even in his drunken stupor, and stood stock still.

After much puffing and grunting, snorting and swearing, Harry eventually scrambled to his feet with the aid of the horse's forelegs. When he got to the perpendicular and regained his balance, he mumbled to himself through his whiskers.

"He's quiet enough anyway. Give me a look at his teeth," says Harry. When the Dealer parted the horse's lips for Harry to examine them properly, "I don't think he's too young," says he.

But the Dealer knew his job. He was a cunning rascal who had already made his pile that day and Harry was the next victim.

"Look at them," he invited, "a fine ten year old."

"I can't see anything," says Harry, "bring his head here."

The Dealer allowed the horse to snap his head away. "He's tired of people," says he, "looking in his mouth all day. Take my word for it, sir, I wouldn't cod a friend for all the money in the world."

Harry mumbled into his whiskers at this rapscallion but stayed in his thoughts.

"Trot him up and down the street til I see him," says Harry.

The Dealer's accomplice stepped forward to parade the horse while the Dealer stayed close to Harry to distract him by giving him a running commentary on the fine qualities of this Clydesdale. George set off up the street at a lively clip, sparks were flying from the stony road as the big animal was paced up and down in bursts and held in short grip by the flying handler. Only that orange, sweaty complexion betrayed the strain.

From the footpath sideline the bums and despos shouted encouragement, but little did Harry know that the Dealer had given the Clydesdale a copious dollop of his special coax-el-orum to enhance his performance. A prod of a stick would send him into a frenzy.

Setting off a second time up the street the handler goaded the horse severely in the ribs with his stick. Old Dan gave a quick swish of his tail and kicked up his hind legs as he danced away from the handler, emitting an ear splitting backfire.

The bums and despos craned their necks to look.

"A sign of a healthy horse," they chorused together.

Old Dan became nervous and edgy and began snorting and prancing as he tried to escape from his handler. Never in his whole life had the old horse been treated in such a fashion.

All the while Harry's brother Tom was sitting on the edge of the water trough, apparently taking little interest but in reality was wide awake, looking at the shenanigans of the Dealer and his cohorts and their zealousness to clinch a deal. For they knew Harry was in a real dilemma and they were going to take advantage of it.

Harry now had a cart and tackling and no horse.

Mags' warning seared through his brain. He gave a deep sigh of anguish as he enquired from his brother his opinion.

"He's a fine horse," says Tom, "much livelier than Old

Dan. The only difference I could see is, he has got no star on his forehead."

"That's no disadvantage," says Harry beckoning over the Dealer with a dubious and heavy heart to clinch the deal.

Daylight was giving away to dusk as Harry and Tom set off for home. The new horse quickened his step as he hit the open road.

"He seems to know his way," remarked Harry, but thought nothing further of it.

They sang to their heart's delight at the fruitful day they had. From time to time Harry would uncork the whiskey bottle and partake a wholesome slug from the rich beverage, then hold the bottle in the air in salutation.

"I'll show our Mags that I'm as good a judge of horses as ever I was."

The two men must have fallen asleep for when they woke they were in their own yard. The horse was standing outside his stable door nonchalant, with the two men fast asleep in the cart. When Harry woke up, he was dumbfounded as to how the horse could find his way to their yard and he never there before. Harry couldn't remember guiding him to his home.

After being aroused from sleep by Mags Harry arrived in the yard next morning to where she was standing on the midden with hands on hips. The new horse had his head over the half door of his stable and gave a welcoming whinny to his master, hoping he would soon be released to the freedom of the paddock and peace and quiet of the farm.

Harry saw the harness strewn around the yard so thought this was what all the hullabaloo was about. He listened to her outburst with secret impatience. His head was throbbing, his legs were weak, he longed for that mug of coffee that Mags refused to make for him. No, she had to see things through to her satisfaction first

"I'm not talking about the harness," she raised her voice several octaves, "it's the horse I'm talking about."

"I can see nothing wrong with the horse," says Harry, "he's the same horse I bought in Ballycrean yesterday."

Harry looked at Tom for some hint as to what was wrong when Mags cut across him, "You told me the horse had no star on his forehead. How come he has one now?"

Harry looked at the horse in abject amazement. His worst fears were realised. He hung his head in shame as he walked back to the house. He cursed Dealer Devlin from under his breath. He was right in his early thinking but it was too late.

As he entered the kitchen he turned to Tom, "I think, lad," says he, "our next purchase will be that tractor."

The Culchies

Danno's excitement had been suppressed all day long as he toiled in his father's bicycle repair shop in Kilberry. He was bursting to tell someone but it would have to wait.

He was tempted to tell his parents at dinnertime of his good luck at the card game last night but they abhor such practices. As they often said, the only way to earn an honest living was to work for it.

And neither could he divulge it to any customer that called to the shop for they were sure to bring it up in conversation with his father, then he'd have an earful.

That evening after tea he mounted his bike and cycled to the village at a lively clip to give Seamus Doyle, his bosom friend, the good news. His elation was so high it was almost at fever pitch. His heart was thumping hard in his chest, and he was rubbing sweat from his brow. He was thankful for the cool evening breeze that was eddying around his face. The journey seemed to be much shorter than he had ever envisaged it before. Certainly not when he was going this same road to school.

Dismounting his bike outside Nora's Pub and Grocer Shop he laid his bike against the gable end of the pub in gay abandon. Lifting one foot he rested it on the crank of the bike and removed one trouser clip. Then he repeated the procedure with the other foot. He stood momentarily to adjust his tie, then removed his trilby hat and combed his hair back with his fingers. He replaced the hat at an audacious angle before pushing open the pub door and swaggering up to the bar counter.

I could easily tell the minute I saw him coming through the door, with that air of importance, that there was something on his mind.

"Hey Laddie," says he. He always called me that since our childhood days playing together when I was holidaying at Aunt Nora's.

He gave a jerk of his head to summon me over to serve him.

"Give me a Baby Power and a bottle of Porter," says he, "and bring it over to the table in the corner," and leaned his head in the direction of the table. "I want to have a word witch-ya."

When I had finished secondary school I got a job in Neary's Wholesale Merchants in Dundale. With plenty of free time on me hands at weekends I used to cycle out to Aunt Nora's to help her in the Pub and to have a bit of crack with Danno and his friends. I felt I owed Aunt Nora that much after all the kindness and hospitality she had showed us children while holidaying there. But the more sceptical observer is sure to say that there was method in my madness and they could be forgiven for thinking otherwise for I was hoping that maybe, just maybe, one day she would favour me to take over the business rather than some other member of my family. And also there was Nancy Corcoran, that comely and lissom blond that I was keen on. She was the daughter of Matty Corcoran, the Manager of Nora's Pub and Grocer Shop and I knew she liked me.

With a lull in the serving I slipped over to Danno's table and sat on the edge of a chair opposite, holding a soiled glass in one hand lest I give any inkling that it was no more than just a friendly word with a customer.

Danno sampled the spirits, then took a copious dollop

of Porter from the glass before dragging the back of his hand across his mouth as he swallowed hard in the throat before talking.

"Laddie," says he, "I had a great bit of luck at the card game in Gregorie's at Glenmore last night. They were holding a game of cards to raise funds to buy a football field in Ardtae, and do you know what?" says he, "I won first prize."

When he didn't elaborate any further I had to ask.

"O," says he, "I won two tickets to the All Ireland on the 24th September next, it's between Cavan and Kerry, you and I are going to go to that match," says he.

"To Dublin," says I, all excited and shocked at the same time.

"Yae," says he, "come hale or high water, I'll go for I promised myself that whenever Cavan was in the Final I will be there to witness that special occasion."

I looked at him enquiringly as I gulped down a mouthful of air, "But how are we going to get there?" says I, thinking that only one bus went to Dublin on Sunday's and its stop was five miles away.

He leaned forward in his chair, his feral eyes darting around the bar lest anybody was within earshot, then back to me. "Ask Nora for the car," says he in a half whisper. He then leaned back and crossed his legs, raising his glass, he winked at me in a conspirator fashion.

"What ... ," I almost screeched out loud, "she'll never agree." I was thinking of the way she looked after that car. It was the only car in the locality at the time and she felt so proud of it when she went out driving. I gave a quick glance over to where Nora was having an amicable chat with a local customer, then turned back to Danno. "Who'll drive it?" says I in a low whisper.

"I'll drive it," says he, giving me a roguish smile.

"What'll happen if it breaks down," says I, thinking about the last time he went about fixing it for her.

I spotted a customer at the next table with me eyecorner, raising his empty glass, indicating he wanted another drink.

"I got to leave," then, turning forward towards Danno and resting one hand on the table for support, stared at him hard, "she'll never agree to it," says I.

Danno took another dollop of porter and rubbed his mouth. "Laddie," says he, "did you ever hear the old adage, 'nothing ventured, nothing gained'?"

Later that night, with a lull in the serving, Nora and I were standing with our backs to the till, facing the customers. We were talking about nothing consequential, at the same time giving a cursory glance now and then around the bar lest some customer wanted service with the wave of their empty glass. I seized the opportunity to put the question to her.

She gave me a quick but penetrating look.

"You can't drive," says she, "what'll happen if it breaks down?"

"I'll bring Danno with me," says I, whispering in a low voice lest I draw the attention of the men in front of us at the bar counter, "he knows quite a bit about cars."

"Are you serious?" she retorted in the same low voice, "Look, the last time I asked him to fix it, he removed almost every working part before he discovered the battery was flat."

'And whose fault was that,' thought I in me own mind.

Momentarily I was lost for words and lest our conversation come to an abrupt end and she walk away to serve another customer, I had to think fast.

"But," says I, "he was kind enough to teach you to drive," and, to himself, 'when everyone else was even afraid to sit in the car beside you when you were learning,' and out loud, "and he didn't charge you anything."

"That's true," says she, nodding her head.

After pondering over my request for what seemed a very long time she agreed.

Immediately a surge of delight welled up inside me and I winked over at Danno, who acknowledged my success with a broad smile and wave of his glass.

For the next week the only topic of conversation in the Pub at night was the big match and Danno's luck at winning the two tickets. The night before the match Danno came into the Pub to make the final arrangements and to join me and a few of our friends to celebrate our adventure.

"I gave that car the once over," says he as proud as you like, "and just to be on the safe side I brought an extra tube, me toolbox and a container of water as a back up."

Next morning after early Mass I packed plenty of sandwiches Nora had made for us into the shopping bag along with a flask of tea, milk and two mugs and placed them safely in the boot of the car, for Mick Wheatly told us that Dublin as well as Croke Park can be a mighty hungry place.

We were about to move off when Nora appeared at the door of the car. The after-Mass shoppers, mostly women, going in and coming out of Nora's shop tarried in the Square outside the shop to exchange greetings with one another, and to wish us luck and a safe journey. But more importantly they wanted to watch Nora. They knew she hadn't done us a favour without a payback. On the other hand we were determined that no matter what the request, it wasn't going to spoil our day.

"I want you to take these eggs to a friend of mine in Fingal," says she, "Molly Maguire is her name," she looked at us with all innocence.

I was about to ask, 'why can't we buy her eggs in Dublin ... or send her the money and let her buy them herself,' when she cut across me thoughts.

"These are no ordinary eggs," says she, "these eggs are Rhode Island Reds for hatching."

When I saw them I had to agree they looked lovely, all uniform size, neatly placed in a honeycomb plat tray, all two and a half dozen of them.

"Now be extra careful with them, and on the peril of your life don't let them get broken. I'm warning yis. Put them on the back seat, they should be alright there."

She stepped back and closed the door and waved her hand at us, "Good luck to yis in Dublin and bring back all the news."

We set off at a steady pace. There was no need to rush for we had given ourselves plenty of time for the journey. Danno gave me a sidelong glance, for he could sense I was worried lest we get a break down or lose our way or even break Nora's eggs.

Danno put his hand on my knee to assure, "Seamus, me ould friend," says he, "all roads lead to Dublin sooner or later, only some may be a bit longer than others."

Satisfied that everything was going to be alright, I relaxed in me seat and was soon able to appreciate the sights of the countryside.

We crossed the Liffey at midday and finally reached Mountjoy Square without a hitch. Parking wasn't a problem in those days: we drove down a quiet street just off the North Circular Road and parked the car. Nora's sandwiches were delicious and we washed them down with well-sugared tea. Having finished, we relaxed for a few minutes and smoked a cigarette.

We were about to move off when a large, buxom woman dashed out from one of the redbrick houses with a broom in her hand. I thought she was going to waylay us for parking in front of her door. Her shrieking was piteous.

She grabbed Danno's arm, partly overbalancing him. Momentarily he was dumbstruck. He didn't know whether to run or to stay. When he regained his self-control and steadied himself, he glared at the frenzied woman.

"What's the matter, Ma'am?" says Danno, "has your husband beat you or something?"

"No," she snapped, "she's going to have a baby!"

"That's great altogether," says Danno, "and on All Ireland Day at that, do wish her the best of luck from Seamus and me."

"Aaa mister," says she, "would you be so kind and take her to the hospital. I hate to impose on you but it is an emergency. You'll be there in a few minutes, there's plenty of time before the match starts."

"Well, now, me good woman," says Danno, "we know nothing about such matters, and anyway," says he, "we don't know the way."

But the big woman wouldn't take 'no' for an answer.

"Virginia!" she bellowed into the big hallway, "these kind gentlemen will take you to the hospital."

With no way out Danno opened the car door. This being only a two-door car, you had to tilt the front seat forward to allow the passenger into the back seat.

Then, this prodigious young girl waddled out onto the street.

"This is Virginia," says she, "we call her Virgin for short."

Danno threw a look at this huge teenager who was about to give birth, and says to himself, 'not anymore you won't, ma'am.'

After much puffing and grunting and some pushing from the mother, Virgin flopped into the back seat behind the driver.

"In beside her, young fella," says the mother to me, pointing to the back seat. I was about to protest but thought the better of it.

"I'll sit in the front seat," says she, "and give directions. Go up that street and turn right into Gardiner Street," says she, "then we turn left into Dorset Street, it's straight ahead from there."

Everything was fine until we hit Dorset Street.

"Merciful God," says the big woman, "look, the road is blocked, there's two fire brigades."

Before I had time to protest to tell her this was a bad idea from the start, Virginia moaned in the back, "Hurry up, Mammy," she says, "I feel faint."

"Turn up that street," she yelled, "and we can go down O'Connell Street, across the Liffey and up Dame Street."

Passing the Castle we hit an almighty pothole, the young girl moaned in the back.

"Hold her hand, young fella," says she, "you'll never learn younger."

I jerked in my seat, a shiver ran up and down my back and my Adams apple bumped up and down several times at the thought. Reluctantly I pushed out my hand to the girl, then drew it back a few times before I could pick up the courage to clasp the hand she had proffered.

Danno was going a lively clip to the Coombe, not thinking as to how he was going to find his way back through the labyrinth of roads, but Danno was always cool in crisis.

"Not far now, love," says she, "I can see the hospital."

'Thank God for that,' says I to myself.

Then the big woman began singing our praises, "I knew yis were gentlemen the minute I saw yis outside in the car. I'll pray for yis every day."

Then Virginia bucked in the back seat and gave a might wail, "OOO Mammy," says she, "I think me waters have broken, I'm soaking wet."

"O darling," says the mother, "hold on, we'll be there in a few minutes."

With the panicking of the two women Danno took his eyes off the road to glance around at what was taking place, when the car hit a huge pothole and burst a tyre. He managed to control the car and guide it to the side of the road.

"Yis may all get out," says Danno, "I won't be able to jack up the car with yis all in it."

"Haa," yelled the mother, staring wild eyed at Danno, "you can't expect that poor girl in that condition to get out and walk,"

"She'll have to," says Danno, "because it will take us an hour to mend this tyre."

Well, I never heard of anyone in all my life to change their attitude towards us without warning!

The woman erupted into a litany of blasphemous barrages, I never thought that it was possible for a woman to manufacture such outrageous curses. She condemned us to Hell and back, "I never yet saw a culchie with dacent transport," says she.

Foaming mad she hauled herself out of the car with the help of the car door. I thought she was going to pull it off the hinges with the weight of her. She was still mouthing unholy expletives as she looked up and down the road.

Then, as luck would have it, we heard an ambulance siren coming up the road.

The woman dashed out on to the middle of the road so swift that it belied her size. She raised up her two hands and flagged it down. Agitated, she related her tale of woe to the driver and nurse. They immediately got out of the ambulance and arrived at the car door just as the pregnant girl was puffing and scuffling her way backwards out of the car.

"O' my God," says the nurse when she saw the girl's nether regions horribly soiled, "you must be going to have triplets."

Being ignorant of such facts and inquisitive at the same time, we couldn't help but see the yellow larva streaming down the girl's legs as she was led over to the ambulance. "Something dreadful must have happened to you, love," says the nurse, "no afterbirth could look like that."

Everything was under control as far as we were concerned. I returned to the car to get the car jack. It was then that I saw it ... the whole crate of Nora's special eggs were in mush on the back seat.

"O' holy Jasus, Danno," says I, "that was the eggs that were stuck to the girl's bottom."

Danno looked at the mess on the back seat and rubbed his brow.

"I hope," says he, pointing to the tray, "that she'll have better luck than them little fellows."

"What are we going to tell me Aunty?" says I.

Danno and I were about the same age but I regarded him as the clever one. Whenever a problem arose it was he that I always looked to for a solution and to his credit he wasn't found wanting on this occasion either.

"We'll buy her two and a half dozen of eggs in some shop, sure she'll never know."

The matter settled, Danno looked at his watch, "We'll better get cracking," says he, "that match is on in half an hour."

We fixed the wheel in double quick time and were ready to be off when we discovered we didn't know our way back to Croke Park.

We espied a man up the road wearing what looked like the Cavan colours. "We'll ask him," says I.

"Go down that road there," says he, "and take the first turn on the left, then the next on the right, then you're almost there, you'll probably hear the crowd roaring and shouting."

We were happy to have made it in time. We parked our car and set off at a lively clip, happy in the knowledge that we had done our civic duty to the pregnant girl.

The cheers were at fever pitch as they sped toward the turnstiles.

Danno stopped suddenly. "O' me God," says he, searching his pocket, "I've lost the blasted tickets." He let out a few unholy expletives. "I put them in my pocket last night ... ," showing the empty pocket to Seamus. He searched the other pockets thoroughly but no luck.

"What are we going to do now," says Seamus, scratching his head.

They were thinking about the money they had spent on petrol and now the two and half dozen eggs for Molly Maguire.

"Well, I'm not going home without seeing the Match," says Denno. He was thinking about the laughing stock they would be if it was found out at home about him losing the tickets, after all the fuss and all the preparations that went into the venture.

"I'll pay," says Denno, as he took a One Pound note from his pocket and gave it to the turnstile man. They went through the turnstile and up long concrete steps to the very top of the open stand where there was only standing room.

"This must be the Canal end," says Danno. "I often heard George Carter talking about Standing Room Only on this stand.

Being a bit late we were deprived of a good view. The

men in front of us were tall and we rather small. We were constantly leaping up on our tippy-toes to get a good view over the shoulders of the men in front of us trying to see the match.

"Do you recognise any of the players?" says I.

"I think I see big John Joe Reilly."

Then a huge roar went up. The big man in front of us, knowing that we couldn't see the players spoke over his shoulder, "It's a goal for the Blues."

We took it that it was a goal for Cavan, not knowing that this was the way they cheered on their teams, by the colours and not by the County.

"Can you see Mick Higgins?" says I.

"No," says Danno, "but I think I can see Peter Donohoe, the Full Forward, look … look … , I think that's him that's going to take that free." The next minute the ball was in the net, the big man turned his head around to us, "it's another for the Blues."

"Can you see Paddy Barn Brosnon?" says I, "he's the man that can take the ball out of the sky, so Michael O'Hehir always says."

Then another mighty roar went up.

"What was that?" says Danno.

"It's a goal for the Hoops."

"Do you know what?" says Danno, "I'll never come here again. I'm most disappointed. If we were at home listening to this match on the wireless we'd hear Peter Donohoe or Mick Higgins of Cavan sending balls over the bar from every angle and Paddy Bawn Brosnon soloing forty yards with the ball on his toe and sending it over the bar or into the net. That's the first time I ever heard an All Ireland played and not a point scored by either team."

Then a mighty roar went up as the final whistle sounded

We were confused about the score. How could we go

home and not know the final score, what would they say in Nora's. So we asked the big man the final score.

"Three goals to two,"

"So Cavan won," says I.

The big man stood and threw a look at us, "I was thinking," says he, "yis were culchies. Not only were yis at the wrong match but yis were in the wrong park. This is Tolka Park and this was St. Finbars playing Bohemians in the Cup Final!"

Glossary

A

alpenglow = reddish glow; often in sky before sunrise and after sunset
alana = my lovely little girl
amaden = a fool
amerce fine = to punish by a discretionary fine
amour proper = self-respect
angst (mouth of) = dread and fear
avenue = dirt road off main road leading to a house

B

Baby Power = mini bottle of Power's Irish whiskey
bailiwick = sheriff's jurisdiction
ball alley = rectangular building with high walls used for batting a handball
banshee = supernatural being, woman of the fairies who gives warnings by her wails of an approaching death
barrow = wheelbarrow
bates out = metaphor for beats out
bedlamite = lunatic
beirer = wooden stand or frame used for carrying a coffin
Black & Tans = English armed force sent to Ireland in 1920, so called by the colour of their uniform
black out = adversary

bladdering = annoying chatter
blaggard = conjugal rights without cooperation
blow-in = interloper
bog = soggy marshland; area of land where turf is extracted
bonhams = young piglets, just born
boreen = narrow pathway often on a hillside
bousie = lout, ill-tempered person
Bovril = hot beef broth drink
Bullseyes = un-wrapped sweets

C

canat = roughin, gangster
caoin = (also keen) to lament loudly
Catherine Wheel = fireworks which rotate as it burns; also: outrageous person
cawing = cry of a crow
ceili = an Irish dance with two or four couples; type of half set dancing
charwoman = woman hired to do odd jobs of household work
chin wag = to gossip
cincture = girdle or belt
clanger = a mistake
coax-el-orum = enhancing drug, potion
cockalorum = boastful, self-important person
cockerel = male fowl
cod (verb) = to deceive someone
coign = advantageous position
collop rights = grazing rights
coping stones = stones that surround a grave
corncrake = a migratory bird
cosy = (see: tea cosy)
Courtown Harbour = an inlet with deep water; (n) in county Wexford.

craic = having fun
creatuir = poor unfortunate creature
crock = dilapidated bicycle
Croke Park = Gaelic football grounds in Dublin
culchie = country person, not a city person
curmudgeon = churlish, miser
Curragh = famous racetrack in Co. Kildare

D

delft = ceramic glazed kitchenware as cups, saucers, etc.
despos = perpetual drunkard
dollop = mouthful of spirits
dottle = half smoked tobacco in the bottom of a pipe

E

eyecorner = to encompass a scene without turning your head

F

fairy fort = mythical dwelling place of the fairies
farrow = to produce young piglets
firkin = wooden utensil for carrying butter to the shops
followers (of cows) = their young
form seat = long piece of timber w/legs at each end, no back
form stool = piece of timber w/legs at each end, no back, no arms
frocken = wild berries
fulmination = to explode

G

garsun = a boy
gelignite = dynamite

gibet = projecting arm attached to a wall for holding items
gig = light two-wheeled one horse carriage
gigging = up and down movement
glass wreaths = flowers enclosed in glass, left on a grave
gleisoil paddocks = unproductive small, enclosed fields (see paddocks)
gnash = to grind
gomila = fool
greesach = hot ashes
greisoil = unproductive land
Guard = present day 'Garda', Ireland police force

H

haggard = small piece of enclosed ground where hay or straw is stored
Half Set = swing and dance by 2 couples together at an Irish dance
hansom = light 2-wheeled covered carriage with driver's seat elevated behind
harbersack = back pack
harra = hurray; an expression of total approval
hussey = ill-behaved girl

I

ingle = fireplace, fireside
inglenook = corner seat beside fire
ingleside = beside the fire
IRB = Irish Republican Brotherhood, secret organisation founded in 1858 to overthrow British rule in Ireland

J

jennet = mule, small female horse, a Spanish ass
joint top = a cone shaped top, a play thing

K

keeners = professional mourners; paid for loud, mournful crying at Wakes
kharky trousers = khaki pants, stout tweed worn by soldiers
kipeens = small pieces of timber to light a fire
kips = immoral houses

L

lane = short driveway
latchiko = useless character
leatherm = imbecile, idiot
Long Acre = grass margin along side of public roads
louse-banks = houses that are infested with fleas
lych-gate = a roofed gate that leads to a church yard

M

magistrate = Justice of Peace
malla vougue = to strangle
manyeen = young man coming to manhood; teenager
mass path = path used as a short cut by Mass goers
maw = a mouth, gullet, opening
midden = heap of farmyard manure stored in the farmyard
Mission = religious service conducted by a Missioner
Missioner = preacher of the Gospel
mitched = to skive, to evade ones duty
mor-rouge = a meow sound, cat cry
Mr. Power = mini bottle of Powers whiskey
mule = a hybrid donkey

N

nave = the centre of a room
N pen = writing pen used in early 1900s that came after

quill pen

O

on the hoof = farmer buys livestock, kills it, then sells it on into the market
over the odds = over the going rate
oxters = armpits

P

paddock = small, enclosed field used for pasturing, exercising farm animals
pennert = a penny's worth of money
philtre = a potion
piseogues = superstitions
plangent = a lamenting sigh, woeful expression
Porter = beer
poteen = illicit alcohol brew
potholing = exploring underground passages
publican = keeper of a public house; a pub
puck goat = male goat
pulper = a machine for reducing material to pulp

Q

quare = metaphor for queer

R

raking = to go with speed
rapscallion = a thief, a scamp
Red Indian = race of people in American West; stoicism; indifferent to pleasure or pain
rick = stack of hay or straw
roughin = person who loves to inflict punishment, cruel person

roughing = to trespass; sneak into others' property
ruser = wily subterfuge, trickster

S

scamp = a rascal, tricky fellow
Sanctus, Sanctus, Sanctus = Communion part of Mass
scuttle = large basket for turf
settle bed = couch type bed with high back used as a seat in the daytime and opened out at night as a bed, used in farm house kitchens in early 1900s
shindy = an uproar
shire (horse) = a large strong horse
shiuler = busybody, gossip
skivvy = female servant doing rough work
slacing = to toss off, shake something off
slacked = to toss off
slane = spade with wing attachment
slane man = man who cuts turf with a slane
slagging = to abuse someone
slashhook = type of sickle but with a long handle
sleigh = flat wooden or iron-base skid tied to a mule that slides over ground
slibhin = a devious, sly person
snug = small enclosed area in pub house, place to have private conversations
spalpeen = casual hired worker; for short period of time, usually teenagers
stiles = stone steps set into a wall or fence
straw rick = a stack or heap
strutly = straightened upright
stoup = vessel for holding Holy Water
sugan = 12" diameter, three-legged stool, no arms or back
superannuated = old person
superannuated shiuler = old busybody

T

tarlen = spontaneous outburst, usually anger, or anxious, approval
tea = light meal with tea later in the day
tea cosy = padded cloth, cone-shaped covering to keep a teapot warm
tipup = up and down movement
thurible = vessel for burning incense in church
tick = a straw mattress
Tolka Park = a football grounds in Dublin
toss school = a game where 2 pennies are tossed up in the air
townlands = division of land of various sizes
trap = type of cart, either open or covered
trespass = to enter unlawfully upon another person's land
trig = a hop, step and jump
trilby hat = a wide brim hat
tuffocks = clumps or whins of growing grass
tuggery = rough play

U
V

valeman = native of the vale or valley of Avoca of county Wicklow
verger = a caretaker at a church
viscid = semi fluid, sticky-like buttermilk

W

wake = to keep watch or vigil over a corpse
walking out together = courting
wards = employees
whins = tufts of growing grass
wont = usual practice

Woodbines = cigarettes, in pack of 5 cigarettes

X
Y
yis = plural for 'you'

Z

Printed in Poland
by Amazon Fulfillment
Poland Sp. z o.o., Wrocław